SKANDAR
AND THE
PHANTOM
RIDER

BOOKS BY A.F. STEADMAN

Skandar and the Unicorn Thief
Skandar and the Phantom Rider

SKANDAR
AND THE
PHANTOM
RIDER

A.F. STEADMAN

SIMON & SCHUSTER

First published in Great Britain in 2023 by Simon & Schuster UK Ltd

1 3 5 7 9 10 8 6 4 2

Simon & Schuster UK Ltd
1st Floor, 222 Gray's Inn Road
London
WC1X 8HB

www.simonandschuster.co.uk
www.simonandschuster.com.au
www.simonandschuster.co.in

Simon & Schuster Australia, Sydney
Simon & Schuster India, New Delhi

A CIP catalogue record for this book is available from the British Library.

HB ISBN 978-1-3985-0291-8
ANZ HB 978-1-3985-2107-0
eBook ISBN 978-1-3985-0293-2
eAudio ISBN 978-1-3985-0294-9

Typeset in the UK by Sorrel Packham

Printed and Bound in the UK using 100% Renewable Electricity
at CPI Group (UK) Ltd

MIX
Paper | Supporting
responsible forestry
FSC
www.fsc.org
FSC® C171272

For Popa
– who taught me that
you can always change boats

THE ISLAND

WILDERNESS

FIRE ZONE

THE ARENA AND CHAOS COMPOUND

THE SILVER STRONGHOLD

THE SECRET SWAPPERS' TREEHOUSE

THE EYRIE

FOURPOINT

AIR ZONE

CONTENTS

PROLOGUE

Two unicorns crossed a battle-scarred plain on a moonless night.

The first unicorn galloped across the Wilderness, urged on by a masked rider. The second unicorn walked in time with its rider's rotting heart. It was a slow beat, a steady beat, the rhythm of a heart accustomed to chaos.

The masked rider reached the meeting point first, the flames in his eyes the only light in the endless darkness. He watched the Weaver approach; the thump, thump of her unicorn's decaying hooves beat on the dust like a funeral drum.

The rider's eyes flickered with fear as the Weaver's immortal creature circled him. He was always afraid of her. And it made him feel alive.

The Weaver sensed that she instilled terror in him. She would always be feared. And it made her feel nothing.

'It is time to begin.'

The Weaver's voice wasn't quite human, the words decomposing like her unicorn's wings.

The flaming-eyed spy inclined his head and rode back towards Fourpoint.

The Weaver watched him go, a choked breath of wind catching her black shroud. She did not think about the defeat she had suffered, or the son who had betrayed her. She thought only of the future.

For if she couldn't win the game – she was going to change it.

THE KNOCK
AT THE DOOR

On the eve of the summer solstice, Kenna Smith sat on the beach and watched the sun sink into the sea. As the lights of Margate sparkled to life behind her, she took Skandar's letter out of her pocket, stared at the envelope and then put it away again – unopened. She'd had it for three days. She wanted to read it. She really did. She missed her brother so much that sometimes when she was half asleep, she'd take a breath to whisper to him in the dark. Something silly. Something scared. Something secret. And then she'd remember that his bed was empty. That it had been empty for almost a year. Instead, he slept in a treehouse on the Island, and in the daytime he learned elemental magic with his very own unicorn.

That was the problem with the letters. They reminded Kenna that she was never going to have a unicorn. Two years ago, she'd failed the Hatchery exam that determined whether she was destined to become a rider. That meant she was never going to bond with a unicorn, and she was never going to live on the

Island. And ever since Kenna had visited Skandar a few weeks ago and met his unicorn, Scoundrel's Luck, she was finding it much harder to read her brother's letters.

She couldn't stop thinking about the way Skandar and Scoundrel had mirrored each other's movements like they were carved from the same soul. The way the muscles in the black unicorn's neck had rippled, sparks flying off his wings like flecks of stardust. The fierce love in Skandar's eyes when he'd looked at Scoundrel. A bond that went deeper than brother and sister. A bond that could make magic.

Kenna brushed sand off her feet and put her school shoes back on. Her friends had been here earlier – her new ones who didn't care about unicorns. When she'd returned from watching Skandar's Training Trial, she'd become so fed up with everyone asking about the Island that she'd venomously announced that it was a worse version of the Mainland and that unicorns were just scary horses with ugly wings. Most people hadn't liked hearing that, but the anti-unicorn crowd had treated her like their queen.

At break they'd huddled around Kenna and laughed as she told them how the riders were forced to dress in battered old jackets and live up trees. And Kenna had felt a glimmer of hope that she might belong here on the Mainland, after all. That she could do this. She'd even refused to watch the Chaos Cup this year with her dad. She'd pretended not to see the hurt on his face when she'd left him by the TV to watch the world-famous unicorn race on his own. Kenna had stopped herself thinking about how disappointed her mum would have been in her, and instead she'd wandered the deserted town centre with her new friends.

That day Kenna had missed Nina Kazama becoming Commodore of Chaos – the first Mainlander in history to win the Chaos Cup. She'd acted like she wasn't bothered. But when she'd shut herself away in her bedroom, she'd watched hundreds of clips of Nina and her unicorn, Lightning's Mistake, passing under the finishing arch. And she'd realised she didn't really belong with her new friends; that she was only pretending.

Arriving home, Kenna punched in the code for the main door of Sunset Heights and thought about the treehouses she'd glimpsed on the Island. She couldn't help wishing that she lived with Skandar and his friends in the Eyrie and that she had a unicorn like Scoundrel's Luck in the stables below. The truth of it, even after two whole years, was that Kenna still wanted a unicorn more than anything else in the world.

'Kenna?'

'Hi, Dad,' she called as she let herself into Flat 207.

He was already dressed for his night shift at the petrol station. She was relieved – some days she had to talk him into going to work, and some days there was no persuading him. But today was an easier day – the kind Kenna reported to Skandar in her letters, not one of the tougher ones she kept to herself.

They stepped round each other in the hallway – a familiar dance. She snagged her jacket on the hook behind his head, as he dropped his keys into the front pocket of his shirt.

'Did you check the post?' Dad asked.

What he was really asking was whether there'd been a letter from Skandar.

'Yeah, I checked it. Nothing,' Kenna lied.

'Ah well. Won't be long, I expect.' Dad kissed her on the top of the head. 'Night, sweetheart. See you in the morning.'

Skandar's letter burned in her pocket as she retreated to her bedroom. Kenna knew she should have shared it with Dad, but she couldn't face it – not tonight. It was the eve of the summer solstice. Thirteen-year-olds across the country had taken their Hatchery exams today, all hoping to hear five knocks on the door at midnight – to be summoned to become unicorn riders. Kenna was sure that if she'd told Dad about the letter all he would want to do was talk about Skandar being called to the Island this time last year.

In fact, all Dad ever wanted to talk about was Skandar and Scoundrel's Luck. It made Kenna feel like anything she did – getting a high mark in a Maths test, making a new friend, crying herself to sleep – wasn't even worth mentioning. Though she had to admit she loved seeing Dad happy – for most of her childhood he'd barely smiled. So Kenna was trapped between her own feelings and his.

But she was keeping something else from Dad besides her unhappiness. Kenna was convinced that there had been more to Skandar's unusual journey to the Island than he was letting on. She'd combed through every book in the library, every website, every forum for evidence that some children were so talented they weren't required to take the Hatchery exam.

There was nothing. Every child who turned thirteen before the summer solstice was required to take the Hatchery exam. It was in the Treaty. It was the law. Though, apparently, that hadn't applied to Skandar. Kenna was ashamed of the unkind thoughts that filled her head. How she had always been stronger, faster, cleverer. She'd helped raise Skandar; she would have known if he was exceptional. And – although she loved him very much – he wasn't. He'd always needed her. And that had to mean Skandar was hiding something.

It was late now. Kenna wriggled under her duvet, placing

Skandar's letter carefully on her bedside table. She'd read it tomorrow. Maybe. She stared up at the ceiling, willing herself not to wait for midnight. It would be the third midnight she'd been left without a knock on the door and a call to the Island. She tried not to imagine her own unicorn, the way she had on the summer solstice her whole life: its colour, its wings, its elemental allegiance.

Knock. Knock.

Kenna sat bolt upright. Had Dad forgotten his keys? But, no, she'd seen him drop them in his pocket.

Knock. Knock.

She wasn't dreaming. She was definitely awake.

Kenna tiptoed to the front door and hesitated. She'd answer the door if there was another knock. Otherwise she'd be sensible. She'd go back to bed.

KNOCK.

Heart pounding, Kenna threw open the door of Flat 207 and found herself facing a pale man dressed all in black. The man's green eyes flicked to the left and right of her, and then settled unnervingly on her face. His cheekbones looked dangerously sharp in the corridor light; a strange flash of silver came from his tongue as he opened his mouth to speak.

'Dorian Manning.' He held out a thin hand.

Kenna didn't take it.

'President of the Hatchery and head of the Silver Circle.' He cleared his throat importantly and scrunched up his nose like he expected her to say something – it made him look like a sewer rat.

'Okay . . .' Kenna's heart beat wildly at his mention of the Hatchery, but she managed to keep her voice level as she tucked a strand of brown hair behind her ear. 'And what are you doing here?'

'I've come to make you a deal,' he said pompously.

Kenna started to shut the door. This man was clearly some kind of unicorn eccentric. It was just a coincidence that he'd knocked in the first minutes of the summer solstice. The disappointment settled on top of all the others Kenna had suffered, and it hardened her heart a fraction more.

But the door wouldn't close. Dorian Manning had blocked it with the toe of his shiny black boot.

'Aren't you interested in finding your destined unicorn, Kenna Smith?'

CHAPTER ONE

A BLOODY PICNIC

Skandar Smith watched his black unicorn, Scoundrel's Luck, lick blood off his teeth. It was a beautiful day for a picnic. The August sky was bluer than water magic and the sun's warmth kept the chill of autumn firmly in the future.

'Where have all the sandwiches gone?' Mitchell Henderson asked, his brown glasses halfway down his nose. He shuffled on his knees, searching methodically through a wicker basket.

'I ate them – obviously,' Bobby Bruna said, not bothering to open her eyes.

'They were supposed to be for everyone!' Mitchell cried. 'I specifically divided them equally between us . . .'

Bobby propped herself up on her elbow. 'I thought this was a picnic. Isn't eating sandwiches exactly what you're supposed to do?'

'Here you go, Mitchell.' Flo Shekoni crawled across the blanket they were sitting on. 'You can have one of mine – I already took them out of the bag.' Arguments were Flo's least favourite thing, so it was unsurprising that she was willing to trade a sandwich to keep the peace.

'Did Bobby make this one?' Mitchell nibbled suspiciously on the edge of the triangle Flo had given him.

Flo laughed. 'I don't know, but I'm not having it back now! Give it to Red if you don't want it.'

Skandar lay against Scoundrel's flank, the feathery tip of the unicorn's folded wing tickling his neck. It was the most relaxed Skandar had felt since he'd arrived on the Island over a year ago. And he was happy; how couldn't he be? Skandar finally belonged. He was bonded to a unicorn. He had *friends* – Bobby, Flo and Mitchell – who wanted to go on picnics with him. The four of them made a quartet, which meant they shared a treehouse in the rider training school known as the Eyrie. They had all made it through the Training Trial at the end of their first year as Hatchlings and were about to start their classes as Nestlings.

Skandar's heart beat faster as he remembered the day of the Training Trial, and Scoundrel rumbled deeply, trying to reassure him. After barely making it through the race, Skandar and his friends had come face to face with a deadly enemy – the Weaver – and fought to stop her wild unicorn army attacking the Mainland.

Skandar had tried not to think about the Weaver since – or the horrifying discovery that she was his *mum*. He tried not to relive her riding towards him and Scoundrel on her wild rotting unicorn. He also tried not to think about how he hadn't told his older sister, Kenna, that their mum was alive. He rummaged in his pocket to check for the letter she'd sent just before the summer solstice. He didn't take it out. He just ran his thumb along its edge – as though that could bring her closer to him, could make him feel better about what he was hiding from her.

'Can you believe training starts again in a few weeks?' Flo said nervously as she watched her unicorn, Silver Blade, drinking from the river a few metres ahead of them.

'I wish we could start tomorrow,' Bobby said. The feathers of her mutation fluttered along her arms with excitement.

'You just want to start battering people with elemental weapons,' Mitchell groaned.

Bobby grinned dangerously. 'Of *course* I do. It's jousting! As Mainlanders say, I'm going to have more fun than a flea at a funfair.'

Skandar chuckled at Bobby's made-up expression. She winked at him.

'I'd rather stay here.' Mitchell lay back and closed his eyes. 'It's simpler.'

Skandar certainly agreed with that. When he'd first arrived on the Island, Skandar had believed there were only four elements: fire, water, earth and air. But after Scoundrel had hatched, it had become clear that they were allied to an illegal fifth element – the spirit element – just like the Weaver. With a lot of help from his quartet, Skandar had managed to pretend he was a water wielder for most of his first year. The truth had come out eventually, though, and now that everyone – other than Kenna and Dad – knew he was allied to the so-called *death element*, whispers followed him along every swinging bridge and up every ladder. It was going to be a long time before the Eyrie trusted a spirit wielder.

'We get saddles before we start training,' Flo pointed out.

Skandar sighed. '*You* get saddles. I'm not sure any saddler is going to choose me.'

'You keep saying that.' Flo frowned. 'But Jamie was okay with you being a spirit wielder. If your blacksmith is fine with it, why wouldn't a saddler be?'

'Jamie knows me. It's different.'

'And he's nice,' Mitchell added. 'He said my hair was cool.' The flaming strands of his hair burned brighter, as though showing off the mutation.

'Talking of the Saddle Ceremony.' Bobby was fully upright now. 'I heard a rumour that Shekoni Saddles doesn't choose a rider every year. They're so famous that they only ever present saddles to riders they're certain will make it to the Chaos Cup.' Bobby had gone misty-eyed with longing. 'Flo, you are *literally* a Shekoni. *Surely* you know something?'

Flo shook her head, the silver in her black Afro catching the sunlight. 'Dad won't tell me anything. He said it wouldn't be fair, and I think he's right.'

'Fair, shmair. You're such an earth wielder,' Bobby grumbled, as she got up to brush mud off Falcon's grey leg. The unicorn peered down at her rider to ensure she removed it all. 'What's the point of having a saddler's daughter as a friend if she won't spill any secrets?'

It wasn't just Bobby who'd been badgering Flo for saddler information over the past few weeks. And because Flo didn't like disappointing her fellow riders, she'd taken to hiding in the treehouse to avoid them. Skandar couldn't blame the Nestlings for their interest. Securing a good saddler was key to a rider's success, so everyone was keen to know whether Shekoni Saddles would be at the ceremony. Olu Shekoni was the best saddler on the Island, but he was also saddler to the new Commodore of Chaos, Nina Kazama. Skandar still couldn't believe a Mainlander like him had won the Chaos Cup or that she was Commodore now – the most important person on the whole Island.

Scoundrel stood up – knocking Skandar playfully with his wing – and went with Falcon to join Red and Blade by the river. They began to play a game that looked like *which unicorn can kill the most fish*. Skandar wasn't even sure unicorns ate fish, but Scoundrel and Red were having great fun snapping them out of the water with their sharp teeth. Scoundrel even managed to skewer one on the end of his black horn. After a few rounds, however, Falcon sneakily froze a section of the river with an elemental blast, and Red and Scoundrel both bashed their jaws on the hard ice. Blade snorted imperiously, seemingly disapproving of their foolishness, and watched the fish swimming safely beneath the glassy surface with stormy eyes.

Skandar was glad they'd chosen the water zone for the picnic. Although they had flown less than thirty-minutes from the Eyrie, the terrain was completely different. Rivers and their tributaries ran like blue veins across the flat plane, lush grass growing along their bends. On their way they'd flown over bowing willows where the zone's residents built their treehouses, and spotted the occasional fishing boat creaking under aerial bridges criss-crossing the canals below.

In the centre of the zone Mitchell had pointed out the famous floating market, where traders from all over the Island set up stalls on the water. Some customers balanced on wooden lily pads to inspect their goods, while others rowed their purchases downstream. Near river bends, water overspilled into lakes where Islanders could swim in the clear water and thirsty animals could stop to drink – when they weren't being snacked on by hungry unicorns. The zone even had a different kind of smell—

Skandar gagged.

'Did you eat one of Bobby's sandwiches?' Mitchell asked sympathetically. 'I told her nobody likes jam, cheese and Marmite as a filling, but she never listens to anyone, let alone—'

'Can you smell that?' Skandar asked urgently.

The unicorns started shrieking loudly down by the water. Scoundrel skittered backwards up the bank, flapping his black wings in alarm. Scoundrel's fear spiralled with Skandar's own along their bond. *Not here*, he thought. *Surely not here.*

Flo grasped his arm. 'Skar, what's wrong?'

There was a gust of wind. Flo's eyes widened in horror and then Skandar knew he wasn't imagining the danger. She could smell it too: the rancid smell of decomposing skin, of festering wounds, of death. And there was only one creature it could belong to.

'We need to get out of here. If the smell is that strong, it must be close!' Skandar jogged towards Scoundrel, intending to fly him away before danger arrived.

On the riverbank, the unicorn's neck was wet with sweat. He was shrieking down at something in the water, his eyes rolling from black to red to black again. Skandar looked down too. The others moved to stand beside him.

Blood roared in Skandar's ears. Distantly, he heard Flo's scream, Mitchell's curse, Bobby's gasp.

There was a wild unicorn in the water.

And it was dead.

Skandar's mind jammed. It couldn't possibly be real.

'I don't understand,' Mitchell croaked. It wasn't something he'd usually admit to.

The wild unicorn's immortal blood swirled and churned in

the flowing water. The smooth rocks and nearby reeds were coated in it, flies already buzzing around a great wound in the unicorn's chest. Skandar thought the body must have been washed downstream by the current before coming, finally, to rest in this bend of the river.

'Is it definitely dead?' Flo whispered.

Mitchell crossed his arms. 'Well, I'm not going to check.'

Skandar and Bobby jumped off the low bank and waded into the water. The smell of decay was so overpowering that tears sprang to Skandar's eyes. Scoundrel squeaked worriedly above him, sounding as young as when he'd just hatched. Skandar tried to send reassurance to Scoundrel through their bond, even though every nerve in his body was on high alert: ready to sprint up the bank at any sign of movement from the wild unicorn. Bobby's mouth was a sharp line of determination as she knelt close to the chestnut unicorn's transparent horn.

She shook her head and Skandar bent down next to her, his trousers now soaked with bloody water. One of the wild unicorn's red eyes was visible on the side of its head, unseeing. Skandar stretched out a hand and gently closed the wrinkled eyelid. Something about the thick eyelashes – so like his own unicorn's – made Skandar impossibly sad. A rumble of approval came from Scoundrel on the bank.

'I think this is a young one,' Bobby murmured. 'It's not as gross as some of the other wild unicorns we saw in the Wilderness.'

'Skandar!' Mitchell's voice rang out over the gentle lapping of the river. 'We have to get you out of here! Spirit wielder? Wild unicorn? You can't be seen anywhere near this.'

Skandar blinked up at him and Red on the bank. 'Spirit wielders can't kill wild unicorns.'

'*Nothing* can kill wild unicorns. They're supposed to be immortal *and* invincible. And yet here we are.' Mitchell ran an agitated hand through his flaming hair.

'Come on, Skar. Let's go.' Flo was already scrambling on to Blade's silver back. 'I can think of a few people who'd love to blame this on you.'

Dorian Manning's face flashed into Skandar's mind. At the end of last year, the head of the Silver Circle had been completely against a spirit wielder returning to the Eyrie.

Once Skandar was safely astride Scoundrel, he took one last look at the wild unicorn's body in the river below, fear creeping up his spine. Wild unicorns didn't die. They were supposed to live for ever; they were supposed to be indestructible. But if they could be killed – if there was some way . . . What dark power had taken the life of an immortal that was supposed to live – and die – for ever?

Mum? Skandar tried to fight the most obvious answer. The idea that she had already regained enough strength to kill an immortal creature was truly horrifying. He wanted to believe she wasn't responsible, that it would take someone *more* powerful, *more* evil, to commit this impossible murder.

But Skandar couldn't think of anyone worse than the Weaver.

CHAPTER TWO

TRUESONG TROUBLE

Within days, the Eyrie was abuzz with the mystery of the wild unicorn's death. The body had been found by a patrolling sentinel mere hours after Skandar's quartet had left the water zone. The instructors had encouraged the young riders not to jump to conclusions about who might be responsible and to wait for the results of Commodore Kazama's investigations. But rumours about the Weaver were rife, especially as – except for the new Hatchlings – all riders were still on their summer break from training. They had nothing to distract them from the wild unicorn or the Weaver, and Skandar noticed the whispers around him getting louder too.

Everyone knew Skandar had faced the Weaver at the end of his Hatchling year, though most weren't aware of the details. But since the wild unicorn murder, he had overheard conversations in the dining treehouse – the Trough – about whether Skandar might know anything and whether being allied to the spirit element meant he knew what the Weaver was up to. Being the only spirit wielder in the Eyrie was always going to be difficult, but Skandar hadn't counted on an unexplained wild unicorn death. And it didn't seem to matter at all that the spirit element could only kill *bonded* unicorns, not wild ones.

'Ignore them,' Flo had urged Skandar a few days after they'd found the dead unicorn. 'They'll forget about it soon enough.'

'I wouldn't count on that,' Mitchell said.

Flo gave him an exasperated look.

'What?' Mitchell pushed his glasses back up his nose. 'You have to admit it's intriguing! How *do* you kill an unkillable monster?'

'It's not *intriguing*; it's horrible! And it's against Island law for riders to hunt wild unicorns – they're as much a part of the Island as riders are. They've been here longer! Even though they're not – well – not very nice.'

Bobby snorted. 'Only you would describe a wild unicorn as "not very nice", Flo.' She turned to Skandar, tipping back in her chair precariously. 'Why is your mum always so dramatic with doing things *nobody* has done before?' Bobby counted on her fingers: 'Stealing the most powerful unicorn from the Chaos Cup, building a wild unicorn army, now killing a—'

Mitchell grabbed Bobby's chair and pushed it forward so the legs were safely back on solid platform. 'We don't have any proof the Weaver is behind this. Not yet anyway.'

'Who else would it be?' Skandar said miserably.

The four friends sat in silence for a moment. Then Flo started talking about how worried she was about her first Silver Circle meeting. Her unicorn, Blade, didn't just look impressive – with his coat that shone like molten silver – he *was* impressive. Silvers were special on the Island; they were the rarest and most naturally powerful unicorns, and with that came great responsibility . . . and danger. Now Flo had made it through the Training Trial and into Nestling year, Blade was getting even stronger, and it was time for her to start going to meetings with the other silver riders – the Silver Circle – to learn their history and, most importantly, to develop techniques to control her unicorn's magic.

'I just don't want to let them down. I'm the first silver rider in years! What if I get everything wrong? What if I'm useless at learning to control Blade? What if they don't like me?'

'Don't be ridiculous, Flo,' Bobby scoffed. 'Everybody likes you. You're the nicest person on the planet – it's completely exhausting.'

'Really?' Flo said, her voice small.

'Really,' Bobby, Skandar and Mitchell said together.

'You honestly think it's going to be okay? Me training with the silvers?'

Skandar knew this question was mostly for him. Silvers and spirit wielders had a long history of rivalry – mainly because silvers were the only bonded unicorns too powerful for spirit wielders, like Skandar, to kill.

He tried to smile reassuringly at Flo. 'You'll be great.'

'Perhaps don't mention Skandar too much, though,' Mitchell advised.

As Flo continued to tell them what she was expecting from her first Silver Circle meeting, Skandar couldn't help but feel grateful that she'd moved the conversation away from the Weaver.

———

The end of August arrived. The night before the Saddle Ceremony, Skandar, Bobby and Mitchell were in the treehouse –

mostly stressing out. Mitchell was sitting on the red beanbag next to the bookcase, flicking aggressively through an enormous book called *The Complete Saddle Guide* and blurting out random facts like he thought there might be a test: 'It's the Eyrie that pays for the saddles . . . Did you know the saddlers went on strike in 1982?' Bobby was murmuring tactics to herself for the race they'd fly in front of the saddlers the next morning, while making one of her cheese, jam and Marmite emergency sandwiches. And Skandar was sitting by the unlit stove, worrying about the Weaver *and* the Saddle Ceremony, while rereading the last letter he'd had from Kenna – the one she'd sent just before the summer solstice:

Hey Skar,

Thanks for asking about me, but honestly there's not much to tell. I'm fine. School is fine. Friends are fine. Dad is fine. Money is fine – thanks to Dad's job and your rider money. You said in your last letter that you hope I'm happy, but I think you know the truth really. I can't stop thinking about riding Scoundrel. I'm sad about not being destined for a unicorn, Skar. I think I always will be. I'm sad that we don't get to see each other any more – I miss you so much and once a year doesn't really cut it, you know? And I'm sad because when we were younger we never used to have any secrets from each other. I know you must be keeping things from me now. I'm sure you have your reasons but . . . Anyway, I guess I'll just have to wait to feel happy again someday. I'll be okay, but it's taking longer than I expected. How's the Eyrie? How's Scoundrel?

Love you,

Kenn x

Skandar had been rereading Kenna's honest words for weeks and they still made his stomach hurt. She was sad. So sad that she wasn't even pretending to be okay, like she had when they were growing up. It was as though she'd run out of energy to put on a brave face. And she could somehow tell he was keeping things from her. When Kenna had come to the Island in June, she'd said to him: *there must be secrets; there must be more.* He'd wanted so badly to tell her about the spirit element, about his suspicions that *she* might be spirit-allied too, and been unfairly barred from the Hatchery door because of it. To tell her their mum was alive. But . . . he hadn't. He'd worried he'd just make things worse for her; now he was wondering whether he'd done the wrong thing. He'd replied to her devastating letter immediately, asking more questions about how she was feeling, but Kenna hadn't sent him a response for nearly two months now. It always took a few weeks for letters to get through the Rider Liaison Office, but this – this was the longest it had ever been.

CRASH!

Flo practically fell through the treehouse door, grinning from ear to ear. She half placed, half dropped four large buckets on the floor.

'Surprise!'

Bobby squinted over at the buckets. 'Surprise . . . you've brought us a thousand gallons of milk?'

Mitchell looked up from his book. 'Florence, we have a very important day tomorrow.'

Flo marched over and flipped the book shut. Mitchell looked more offended than if she'd punched him.

'Listen,' Flo said, looking round at them all. 'It's been a stressful time, what with the dead unicorn and the Saddle Ceremony tomorrow. I thought we should do something fun tonight.' She pointed at the buckets. 'I've been planning it for ages,' she added, sounding more unsure.

'Great idea,' Skandar said, moving towards her.

Bobby put down her sandwich. Mitchell slid his book back on to the shelf and all four of them stared into the buckets. Inside was gloopy liquid, each bucket holding a different elemental colour: red, yellow, green or blue.

'Is that paint?' Bobby asked.

Flo nodded enthusiastically. 'It's not *just* paint. My mum made it for me, and since she's a unicorn healer she put elemental herbs in it so it has some magical characteristics and I checked with the instructors and they said it wasn't against the rules so I was thinking we could maybe paint the inside of the treehouse?' Flo spoke so quickly, it took Skandar a minute to understand what she'd said.

Bobby was quicker. 'Paint it any way we want?'

'Yeah!' Flo said breathlessly. 'I thought we could take a wall each and use our own elemental paint.'

'I love it,' Bobby said, her tone surprised.

Flo handed her the yellow paint for air. Now Skandar looked closer, it appeared to be sparking with electricity.

'Fascinating.' Mitchell picked up the red bucket. The paint was bubbling like molten lava and smoking slightly.

Bobby claimed the wall opposite the door; Mitchell took the one behind the stove.

'Skar,' Flo said, handing him the blue bucket. 'I'm really sorry I couldn't get you any spirit paint. Mum wasn't sure how to make it, and also I thought it probably wouldn't be allowed so—'

'Don't worry.' Skandar tried to sound upbeat. 'A white wall would be boring anyway.'

Flo looked relieved. 'Do you want to paint the wall behind the bookshelf?'

Skandar smiled. 'Sure.'

Although he loved drawing, Skandar had never painted a wall before – they hadn't been allowed to decorate their flat in Sunset Heights. Nervously, he dipped the brush in the blue elemental gloop. It splashed like water and smelled a little salty too – and that gave Skandar an idea. He began to paint the sea in undulating waves. The colour sparkled blue like the sun on water, and some strokes even came out with glistening sapphire fish scales. When Skandar leaned in he could hear the crash of waves on a distant shore, as if he was holding a shell to his ear.

Standing back to admire the finished result, Skandar realised with a jolt that he'd painted the view from Margate beach. He and Kenna had spent hours on that curve of sand, wishing for a different future. Wishing for unicorns. He really missed her. But looking at the painted sea view, he could almost pretend she was beside him.

The others had finished too. Bobby's yellow wall was a sparking fizz of unapologetic element spirals, sharp lightning bolts and wild tornado gusts. There was movement everywhere, and standing next to it Skandar could almost feel the wind whipping through his hair. Mitchell's wall was far more carefully done. He'd covered the wall with intricate painted flames, the red paint crackling and smoking, imitating the real blaze in the wood-burner below it. And Flo's wall at the front of the treehouse was a jungle of intertwined green plants – trees and flowers growing over and under each other – and the elemental paint smelled like fresh earth, the texture rough and lined like leaves.

The quartet dragged the four beanbags into the middle of the treehouse and sat to admire their handiwork. 'This was a *really* good idea.' Skandar sighed, a silly grin on his face.

'Yeah.' Mitchell yawned. 'It's completely distracted me from—'

'So, saddles.' Bobby turned to Flo. 'You *must* know if Shekoni Saddles are going to be presenting now. The ceremony is tomorrow!'

'I don't know anything,' Flo said grumpily. 'All I know is that if Dad *does* present, he won't be picking me – that certainly wouldn't be fair. And we're supposed to be relaxing, remember?'

'Roberta,' Mitchell said, 'even if Shekoni Saddles do come, there's no guarantee Flo's dad is going to choose you.'

Bobby looked affronted. 'Yes, he will! I won the Training Trial!'

Skandar's mouth twitched as he caught Mitchell's eye. 'So humble, isn't she?'

'If there's a Shekoni saddle to be had, it's got my name on it. I'm an air wielder and a Mainlander, like Nina, and I'm going to win the race at the ceremony because I'm the best.' Bobby straightened the grey feathers round her wrist. 'It makes perfect sense.'

'The size of your ego is truly astounding.' Mitchell's amazement was genuine.

'Thanks!' Bobby got up and walked towards Skandar's blue wall. He followed her, feeling oddly protective of it. 'What are you—'

Bobby pulled a piece of white chalk from her pocket. She snapped it and gave half to Skandar. She scanned the cresting waves, then stopped to draw something where the white froth should have been. Skandar was annoyed, until he realised what she was doing.

Bobby had drawn four interlocking white circles: the spirit element symbol.

'Well, you're not really a water wielder, are you?' She winked at him.

Skandar's heart swelled as he took his own chalk and drew another symbol where the foam of a wave should have been. Mitchell and Flo came over, and Bobby handed them chalk and soon the waves looked frothy with white spirit symbols.

When they were done, Skandar took a deep breath. 'Thank you – for, you know, being my quartet and—'

'Okay, that's quite enough of the mushy stuff,' Bobby announced, picking up her paintbrush.

'What are you doing?' Mitchell asked. 'We've finished our walls, haven't—'

She flicked yellow paint right in his face. 'That's for calling me "Roberta" earlier!'

'Right, that's it!' Mitchell snatched up his own brush and splashed fire paint at her.

'Stop! Stop!' Flo said, but she was half laughing. Skandar grinned and grabbed his own bucket, flicking blue paint at Flo.

'Hey!' She retaliated with green, and soon they were all trying to duck the flying paint drops, chasing round the central trunk of the treehouse.

Within ten minutes the four of them *and* the tree trunk were covered with a mixture of elemental splashes. Skandar could feel the fizzing of the air paint, smell the freshness of the earth, hear the crackling of the fire, taste the salt of the water. They collapsed on to the beanbags in fits of giggles, admiring their splattered skin and staring up at the trunk.

Finally Flo asked, 'Do you think we should wash it off?'

Skandar stood up and quickly dotted white chalk between the other colours on the trunk. 'Nah,' he said, smiling. 'I think we should keep it.'

On the morning of the Saddle Ceremony, the Eyrie's forest was bathed in bright morning light, the smell of pine strong and fresh. The warren of suspended bridges swung gently; the rider treehouses nestled peacefully in the leafy canopy. Shafts of sunshine hit the armoured trees and the whole training school shimmered so beautifully that Skandar should have been in high spirits. But instead he left breakfast early for Scoundrel's stable, unable to bear the buzzing conversations in the Trough.

He usually enjoyed eating at the tables perched on platforms nestled in the trees, especially given the generous supply of his favourite food – mayonnaise. But today the conversations about the Weaver had bothered him more than ever. Was she responsible for the wild unicorn murder? How had she done it? Why had she done it? What was she going to do next?

What was she going to do next? This haunted Skandar more than anything.

But today he couldn't think about any of that. He needed to concentrate on the race in front of the saddlers, rather than worry about his mum killing wild unicorns. The race was the last chance the riders and unicorns had to impress the saddlers before they made their final decision.

Skandar yelped. Scoundrel had just shocked him with the air element because he'd stopped mid-brush. 'Was that necessary?' Skandar raised his eyebrows at the unicorn, arm still stinging.

Scoundrel bared his teeth at Skandar in an impression of a goofy smile. Most people would have run a mile from a bloodthirsty unicorn's teeth, but Skandar could tell the difference between Scoundrel's *I'm going to bite you* expression and his *I'm messing around to cheer you up* expression.

Joy reverberated along the bond between their two hearts like laughter. The rider–unicorn bond was what distinguished Scoundrel from the wild unicorn that had washed up in the river. It joined their lives together – a bonded unicorn could not survive their rider's death. And it linked them emotionally too: as the relationship became stronger, their feelings were able to move through the bond. Scoundrel always knew when Skandar was sad, and he tried his absolute best to make him feel better.

'Do you want a saddle, or are you going to hide in here all day?' Bobby and Falcon's Wrath stuck their heads over Scoundrel's stable door.

'Hide in here all day,' Skandar mumbled, fiddling with his yellow jacket sleeve, which now had a second pair of wings sewn on to show he was a Nestling. He was full of nerves and excitement. This would be the first-ever race where he could openly use his own element.

'Come on, spirit boy,' Bobby urged.

As they headed side by side towards the Nestling plateau, Skandar noticed that Falcon's grey mane was plaited into a line of tiny round bunches, just visible along her armoured neck.

'Bobby, what—'

'Don't even go there. I've been up since six styling those.' Bobby was probably the last person you'd expect to be up early making her bloodthirsty unicorn look pretty, but Falcon really cared about her appearance – so much so that she fought more ferociously when she felt beautiful. As Bobby liked to say: pampering wins prizes.

Jamie – the blacksmith who made Scoundrel's armour – rushed up to Skandar as soon as he arrived on the plateau. He didn't stop talking the entire time as they followed Bobby into the melee of unicorns, riders and spectators.

'Okay, so what you have to remember is the reason you're all racing today is for the saddlers who are undecided.'

Skandar frowned down at Jamie through the eyeholes of his helmet. 'Undecided?'

'Yes, yes,' Jamie said impatiently. 'Some saddlers will have made up their minds at the Training Trial about which rider they want, but others will have a shortlist of three, sometimes more. They'll have made multiple saddles in preparation. Some riders get presented with more than one saddle and they have to choose which they prefer. It can get quite competitive.'

'I'm not sure I'm going to have that problem,' Skandar muttered, as they got further into the training ground. The saddlers chatted and called to each other as they unloaded boxes and set up pointed tent frames, before draping them in colourful tarpaulins that flapped in the breeze. The tent colours – from raspberry pink to deep indigo – matched the individual sashes across the saddlers' chests, their names emblazoned in bright letters:HENNING-DOVE, MARTINA, REEVE, NIMROE, TAITING, BHADRESHA, GOMEZ, HOLDER . . . Many of the saddlers stopped to stare as Scoundrel passed, whispering behind their hands.

Jamie ignored this and continued giving Skandar advice. 'A Shekoni saddle would obviously be the best, but with the whole spirit wielder thing I think they might not be a runner. I've always admired Martina saddles. Ooh, a Reeve might be nice, or a Bhadresha—'

'Jamie, I—'

'Although there was a big scandal about their leather being flammable, so maybe one to avoid if you're a fire wielder, but you're not so—'

'JAMIE!' Skandar half shouted.

The blacksmith stopped and looked up at him on Scoundrel's back.

'What happens if no saddler picks me?'

'That's not going to happen. I don't think that's *ever* happened.'

'But say it does . . . ?'

'I don't think anything would *happen* exactly,' Jamie mused. 'It would make things a lot harder for you, I suppose. You would stick out – although you do already with the whole *skeleton* mutation and *unicorn with a spirit blaze on his head* thing.'

'Thanks,' Skandar said sarcastically.

'But, Skandar, you'll be learning to joust this year. Which basically means you're trying to knock riders off their unicorns with elemental weapons. A saddle would *really* help you stay on. Without one, I'm not sure you'd make it through the tournament at the end of the year.'

'What tourn—' Skandar tried to ask, but Jamie ploughed on.

'And even if you did manage to make it through, a saddler is a rider's ally in the world beyond the Eyrie. They have connections with healers, unicorn-food suppliers, sponsors – some of the best saddlers even sit on the committee that oversees the Chaos Cup Qualifiers.'

'So basically you're saying that I *need* a saddler to choose us.'

Jamie's expression was serious. 'I know you're worried about your reputation, Skandar, but saddlers are competitive. They care about their riders being the best, more than they care whether you've helped kill an immortal monster.'

'Tell me that's not what people are saying!'

Jamie held up a hand to silence him; Scoundrel sniffed it, smoke curling round his nostrils. 'None of that matters if you can be the best today, do you see? You're a fast flier, and now you can use the spirit element you might even be in with a chance of winning the race and then . . .' Jamie raised an eyebrow.

'Then a saddler might want me anyway, even if I'm a spirit wielder.'

'Exact— Hey! Watch it!' Around thirty people barged past Jamie towards a wooden platform to the left of the starting bar. Unlike the riders – who were wearing jackets in air-season yellow – this group were all dressed in different colours. Scoundrel snorted sparks, watching them form a semicircle on top of it, as though about to perform. The platform stood atop a nest of green vines that grew up and over to create a flowery canopy. A man and a woman waved in Jamie's direction. He scowled.

'Who are they?' Skandar asked.

'My parents,' Jamie said uncomfortably. Jamie and his parents hadn't exactly been on the best terms since he'd decided to become a blacksmith, rather than a bard like the rest of his family. They still tried to convince him to become a singer any chance they got.

'Are the bards about to start?' Mitchell asked from Red's back; Flo and Blade and Bobby and Falcon were on either side of them.

'Yes,' muttered Jamie.

'Is it true they compose a new song for the Saddle Ceremony every year?' Flo asked enthusiastically.

'Yes,' Jamie said again, sounding like he wanted the ground to swallow him.

Bobby wasn't interested in the bards at all. She had her eyes fixed on the saddlers' tents.

'I don't think Dad's coming,' Flo said in Bobby's direction, her voice barely audible over the excitement of people and unicorns alike, as Nestlings, saddlers, instructors and spectators all gathered in front of the stage. 'I can't see his orange tent anywhere.'

'Maybe he's just late,' Bobby snapped.

'If Shekoni Saddles aren't here then the best saddler is probably—'

Mitchell was cut off by an explosion of song from the bards. The wall of sound washed over the gathered crowd, and even the unicorns fell quiet, listening to the interlocking melodies. The notes swooped, dived and rose again, weaving in and out of each other playfully. It was the most beautiful music Skandar had ever heard. Somehow the rise and fall of the notes captured perfectly the way he felt when he and Scoundrel flew together – the thrill and the joy and the pure fun of it. The bards swayed, leaning into their harmonies, their faces transfixed with the same bliss mirrored on every face in the crowd. The notes started to climb to a crescendo, to the highest of heights when—

The music jolted.

Something was happening on stage. Notes popped and disappeared like burst balloons. Only a few bards were still singing; the others had turned, distracted by an elderly man who was being helped to the front of the stage. Skandar's eyes widened as steam billowed from the man's ears, flaming patterns fizzed above his head, the air either side of his arms sparked with lightning, the stage shook under his feet.

'What's happening?' Bobby and Skandar whispered in unison.

'Truesong.' Jamie's eyes were fixed on the old bard.

'Really? *Really?*' Flo sounded delighted. 'I've never heard one before!'

'But what *is* a truesong?' Skandar hissed.

'Shhhh!' People on either side of Skandar's group shushed them.

All the bards had stopped singing now. The crowd held its breath in the silence, watching the old man bent double at the very edge of the stage. And then with the elements dancing around him, the bard straightened and began to sing:

'This Island belongs to the immortals;
So it's been since the hatching of time.
The immortals belong to this Island,
So I warn of a terrible crime:

Take the life of one dying for ever,
And the Island shall have its revenge.
Spill the blood of the elements' ally,
And all five shall be used to avenge.

There is only one hope for us mortals,
To atone for an immortal's death:
Win the fight for the First Rider's last gift,
Taking form at the Queen's final breath.

Only then will the thunderbolts silence,
Only then will the earthquakes be stilled.
Only then will the floodwaters shallow,
And the flames of the wildfires be chilled.

Yet another force grows on this Island:
True successor of spirit's dark friend.
And the storm it will bring when it rises
Will see all we know brought to an end.

This Island belongs to the immortals;
So it's been since the Eyrie's first chime.
The immortals belong to this Island,
So leave them to live for all time.'

The bard finished singing, took a shuddering breath and collapsed, exhausted. There was a smattering of applause, but most people were murmuring to each other in worried tones. Others had scribbled down the words of the song and were showing their friends.

'Revenge?' said someone nearby. 'How can the Island get *revenge*?'

'*Only one hope*, he said. But the First Rider's long gone, isn't he?'

'Did you hear the part about wildfires? Earthquakes?'

'Did he sing something about the spirit element?'

'Why is everyone looking at Skandar instead of the old guy who just made fireworks dance around his head?' Bobby demanded.

'What *are* truesongs?' Skandar asked again, although this time he was worried about the answer.

Mitchell sniffed. 'Flaming unicorn dung is what truesongs are.'

'Mitchell, don't be rude,' Flo said quietly. She turned to Skandar. 'Bards sing all the time, but only one song in their whole lives will be their truesong.'

'I don't get it,' Bobby announced.

Jamie answered this time. He sounded worried. 'The words of a bard's truesong tell us things about the past, present or future that are true – completely true.'

'Debatable,' Mitchell murmured.

Bobby wrinkled her nose. 'Like singing fortune tellers?'

'Unsurprising that there are people who believe this nonsense on the Mainland too, I suppose,' said Mitchell. Jamie looked up at him sharply, and Mitchell's hair flared guiltily in response.

Skandar swallowed as he felt the eyes of the crowd on him. They clearly believed the song, but what had it said? He could only remember snatches. Out loud, Skandar asked, 'It said something about spirit, didn't it? About revenge?'

'You can't think about that right now,' Jamie answered quickly, although Skandar didn't miss him exchanging a concerned glance with Flo. 'You need to get to the starting bar for the race.' Bobby and Falcon had already begun to head towards the other Nestlings.

'Islanders take truesongs far too seriously,' Mitchell scoffed.

But Skandar was beginning to panic, and caught up with Falcon. 'Bobby, did you hear the song? I don't understand—'

'Skandar, it's not the best time. I've got a race to win.' Falcon spat hailstones at Scoundrel, who sneezed in retaliation.

'Please.'

Skandar saw Bobby roll her eyes through the holes in her helmet. 'I didn't actually *understand* a word of it, but it definitely said how killing wild unicorns is a bad idea yada yada, then revenge is coming somehow doo-bee-doo, something about a First Rider's gift cha-cha-cha, and something to do with spirit's dark friend.'

'*Spirit's dark friend*? What does that mean?'

'Skandar, the bar!' Bobby shouted suddenly, as Scoundrel approached the metal bar that would rise for the start of the race. Skandar swerved into the smoky, sparking mass of unicorns blasting any element they felt like and barging for good positions. All the Nestlings were here, not just those from Skandar's Hatchling training group. Scoundrel's mane froze over and then melted in his excitement, drenching Skandar's hands and knees.

He spotted Alastair riding Dusk Seeker up and down the line of unicorns. He was talking to a couple of riders Skandar didn't know very well – Naomi and Divya – and pointing over at Skandar.

Don't think about the song. Don't think about the wild unicorn. Don't think about the Weaver. Just race, Skandar told himself. Blade and Red slotted in either side of Falcon and Scoundrel at the bar. Red's rust-coloured armour scraped against Scoundrel's black chainmail. The air was so full of swirling elemental debris from the young unicorns that Red's flaming fart of greeting was completely lost in the tangy mixture of magic.

'What's Alastair up to?' Mitchell shouted. Skandar wasn't surprised Mitchell had noticed – he'd been bullied by Alastair and his friends before he'd even arrived at the Eyrie.

Skandar shrugged, convinced it would be nothing good.

Instructor O'Sullivan rode her unicorn, Celestial Seabird, along the starting bar with Instructor Saylor on North-Breeze Nightmare. Skandar heard Instructor O'Sullivan muttering to the air instructor. 'Honestly, this ceremony gets more and more elaborate every year. And now a truesong?'

'I think it's rather lovely.' Instructor Saylor smiled warmly at the Nestlings, her honey curls wafting in the breeze. 'It reminds me of getting my own saddle.'

'That truesong didn't sound "very lovely" to me. It sounded like a warning.' Instructor O'Sullivan's swirling whirlpool eyes landed on Skandar, who'd been eavesdropping. She dodged a fire blast from Sarika's unicorn, Equator's Conundrum and rode Seabird towards him. 'You look worried,' she snapped. 'Explain.'

'Erm, no. I'm fine,' Skandar lied.

'Where's your spirit pin?' she asked, her tone as pointed as her spiky grey hair. Skandar's hand went to the pocket of his jacket. He drew out the gold pin with its four entwined circles, and held it up for Instructor O'Sullivan to see.

'I don't know whether I should wear it today,' Skandar murmured, thinking about the muttering of the saddlers.

'Nonsense,' Instructor O'Sullivan barked. 'I might have allowed you to be an honorary water wielder, but you're a spirit wielder in here.' She touched her hand over her heart. Her bond. 'Show the saddlers you're proud of your element.'

Scoundrel screeched and the morning sunlight caught the bright white blaze that ran down the centre of his black head.

Instructor O'Sullivan grinned at the unicorn. 'Show them you're not ashamed. Scoundrel's Luck certainly isn't. How about pulling that sleeve up, too? Your mutation really is something.' She raised one eyebrow, waiting.

Skandar didn't dare argue with Instructor O'Sullivan. So he pushed up the sleeve of his yellow jacket, exposing the translucent white skin of his spirit mutation. The tendons and bones shone through his arm like a skeleton in the sunshine, from the inside of his elbow all the way down to his wrist.

Skandar couldn't work out whether the instructor's words had made him feel better or worse, as he watched her gallop Seabird out of the starting bar's way.

'On my third whistle, the bar will rise,' she called.

Meiyi and Rose-Briar's Darling barged Gabriel and Queen's Price sideways a few unicorns down. Then Briar's fire blast forced Niamh and Snow Swimmer, as well as Zac and Yesterday's Ghost, out of the line so that Kobi and Ice Prince and Alastair and Dusk Seeker could take their places. Skandar couldn't help but notice that the fourth member of the Threat Quartet was missing. Amber and Whirlwind Thief were further down the line of unicorns.

'Should be an easy race for you, spirit wielder!' Meiyi shouted.

Alastair and Kobi laughed loudly, and Skandar tried to ignore them.

First whistle. Scoundrel sliced his shining black horn from side to side, his eyes rolling from red to black then red again. The atmosphere along the starting bar was charged with energy, unicorn muscles bunched, horns sparking.

Second whistle. Skandar plunged his hands into Scoundrel's black mane, ready for take-off. He couldn't stop thinking about what Instructor O'Sullivan had just said:

Show the saddlers you're proud of your element.

Third whistle.

Show them you're not ashamed.

CHAPTER THREE

THE SADDLE CEREMONY

The bar creaked and banged as it shot upwards for the start of the race. As if he knew this was his chance to show the saddlers just how fast he could go, Scoundrel took off in under two strides, his wing joints exploding outwards in front of Skandar's knees. The grass of the plateau jerked out of view, the crisp wind making his eyes water. They were first in the air. They were in the lead.

A flash. A bang. A scream.

Skandar looked over his shoulder to see Mabel and Seaborne Lament crash-landing below. Then, through the sky-battle smoke, a chestnut unicorn advanced on Scoundrel, the crackle of a star mutation on a rider's forehead.

Amber and Whirlwind Thief were coming for them – just like at the Training Trial. But Skandar wasn't going to lose this time.

Skandar summoned the spirit element along the bond and into his right palm – the palm scarred with the wound Scoundrel's horn had given him in the Hatchery over a year ago.

Spirit magic filled his hand, and it glowed white as Thief barged Scoundrel's right shoulder. Amber's yellow bond shone brightly between her and Thief's hearts – a sight only a spirit wielder like Skandar could see. Then her palm glowed blue for a water attack, and she blocked Scoundrel's path forward.

The black and chestnut unicorns faced each other in mid-air, as other battles raged behind them around the Eyrie's hill. Thief reared up, pawing the sky with sparking hooves, teeth bared just like her rider. Scoundrel screeched at his opponent, black wingtips lighting up white as they pumped at his sides.

Show them you're not ashamed.

The aroma of cinnamon and vinegar filled Skandar's nostrils – the way the spirit element always smelled to him – but he forced the air element into the bond alongside spirit until his palm glowed yellow. At the same time Amber's water attack streamed from her palm like a crashing fountain and Thief blasted liquid from her horn. Gallons of water frothed and swirled towards Skandar through the sky with enough force to knock him clean off Scoundrel's bare back.

Show them.

As the water crashed towards them, and the air element filled their bond, Scoundrel began to change the way only a spirit unicorn could.

First his mane, then his tail, started to crackle with electricity until they were alive with lightning, the black colour draining away like ink. Then the unicorn's stomach, hindquarters and neck became pure magic until Scoundrel was sizzling with raw energy. It was like riding an electrical storm, the spirit element allowing Scoundrel to *become* the air element itself. The black unicorn screeched in triumph, and it was impossible to tell where his jaw ended and the lightning began.

Skandar had been so afraid the first time Scoundrel's whole body had turned to fire that he hadn't tried any attacks. But now he was allowed to wield the spirit element – and he wanted to fight. He wanted to win. So he sent a lightning bolt from his palm right into Amber's stream of water. Almost simultaneously, Scoundrel's whole body pulsed and electrical charges exploded from the unicorn's sparking frame, colliding with the water coming from Amber's palm and Thief's horn.

'Well done, boy!' Skandar cried.

Amber screamed and Thief roared as the electric current shocked both rider and unicorn. But instead of fighting back, Amber and Thief soared down towards the ground.

'Coward!' Skandar called after her.

But then he noticed the others.

One by one, Nestlings were dropping out of the sky. Out of the race altogether. Scoundrel was slowly returning to his usual black colour, but Skandar barely noticed as he watched Kobi abandon his sky battle against Flo mid-ice blast, Blade screeching in confusion as Ice Prince landed. Sarika and Mitchell had been fighting a furious fire battle, the sky smouldering between them, but suddenly Equator's Conundrum dropped away. Skandar spotted Niamh and Snow Swimmer swerving from Bobby and Falcon, joining the rest of her quartet – Farooq and Toxic Thyme, Art and Furious Inferno, Benji and Cursed Whisper – on the ground.

Now, ahead of Skandar, the sky was completely clear. Of smoke, of elemental debris, of unicorns. Of everyone, apart from the three riders that made up Skandar's quartet.

Scoundrel joined Blade, Falcon and Red as they flew towards

the finishing line, leaving the other Nestlings on the plateau below.

'What's going on?' Bobby shouted over the unicorns' beating wings. 'Why aren't they racing?' Falcon screeched along with her rider's anger as they descended towards the saddlers.

'They'll all be disqualified,' Mitchell said, ash streaked across his face. 'If a rider lands before the finish, it's automatic disqualification.'

As the quartet touched down and crossed the finish together, there was a shocked silence. No applause from the saddlers. No congratulations from the instructors, who were just staring at the rest of the Nestlings dotted along the course.

The silence didn't last long, though. As the other riders trotted towards the finishing line and the saddlers' tents, the four instructors started yelling at the wielders of their own elements, demanding to know why they'd abandoned such an important race. The saddlers also raised their voices in frustration, complaining that their last chance to make up their minds about the Nestlings had been ruined.

'It's embarrassing is what it is!' Instructor Anderson was telling Meiyi, the flames around his ears flaring. 'What kind of a stunt were you all pulling? The saddlers are here to watch you race, not drop from the sky! I've half a mind to declare you all nomads and throw you out of the Eyrie immediately.'

Meiyi glanced over at Skandar and answered loudly. 'None of us felt comfortable racing once we saw Skandar use his element. Especially after what the truesong said: *spirit's dark friend*? I mean, it couldn't be any clearer – Skandar *is* a spirit wielder.'

Skandar couldn't believe what he was hearing. So this had been planned? He remembered Meiyi's taunt at the beginning of the race, Alastair going up and down the line of riders. Had they convinced the other Nestlings he was dangerous? He felt all his shame flooding back. The shame that came with trying – and failing – to fit in.

Skandar was blushing and fighting back tears as Kobi said, 'We don't know what Skandar's capable of. What if *he* killed that wild unicorn, Instructor O'Sullivan? What if he's not against the Weaver, like he said, but teaming up with her? What if that's the revenge the truesong was talking about? What if he sets his sights on Nestling unicorns next?'

Flo jumped to Skandar's defence. 'Skandar is not killing the wild unicorns!' she cried, just as Mitchell shouted, 'That is *not* a justifiable interpretation of the truesong.'

'I'm very disappointed in you,' Instructor O'Sullivan spat at Kobi, turning away. She blew her whistle for quiet several times.

'There's no time to race again.' Instructor O'Sullivan sounded flustered. 'I'm sure most of the saddlers had already chosen their riders before today, so . . . I suppose, I suppose we have to get on with the ceremony now. Line up in front of the tents, please!' She blew her whistle again for good measure, as though that could make things less awkward. Many of the Nestlings were still muttering, though Skandar couldn't hear what they were saying as they had left huge gaps on either side of his quartet. He tried to take a deep, steadying breath.

Bobby, on the other hand, was not taking any deep, steadying breaths. 'I can't believe this!' she cried, as she dismounted and pulled Falcon into line. 'Not seeing us race properly might affect the saddlers' choices.'

'You won the Training Trial last year, Bobby,' Mitchell spluttered, his temper frayed too. 'I think you'll be fine.'

'Shekoni Saddles isn't here, though!' Bobby raged on. 'And they're the ones I want. I want to have the same saddle as Commodore Kazama!'

'There are plenty of other great saddlers here,' Flo said reassuringly.

'I'm sorry, Bobby. It's all my fault,' Skandar murmured.

'Don't be stupid,' she snapped at him. 'It's not your fault you're a spirit wielder. Not your fault some old bard decided to sing a prophecy right before the race. Not your fault that you're a magnet for trouble every—' Bobby was distracted from her rant, as the saddlers rolled up the fronts of their tents with a flourish to reveal their precious designs.

All the saddles had the same basic shape – two leather flaps to sit either side of a unicorn's spine, a seat that curved at the back to support the rider and a high pommel at the front to hold on to – but each saddle had its own personality. Some were bulky and made a statement with heavy chains in elemental colours adorning their edges, while others were elegant and simple, with stitching rather than metalwork for decoration. The Nestlings stared hungrily at the creations sitting proudly on their display stands, wondering which saddler would choose them. A few were still casting terrified glances at Skandar. Were they genuinely afraid of him? Surely they wouldn't have risked dropping out of such an important race if they weren't? Or had they been pressured by Alastair, Kobi and Meiyi?

There was a noticeable drop in the level of noise as the saddlers lifted their designs and flooded towards the line of Nestlings. Scoundrel didn't like this at all. He tried to back away, as though he was under attack, and he wasn't the only unicorn who was spooked. A white-faced Romily dived sideways as Midnight

Star's black mane ignited, and two saddlers had to duck as water blasts came their way. Skandar didn't blame the unicorns. The saddlers were practically running towards them, shoving each other out of the way.

In a few short minutes, however, many of the riders and unicorns had already been paired up with a saddler. Flo had been the first to be chosen by Martina Saddles – the head saddler was sobbing as they celebrated together in her bright blue tent. She would make every saddle the silver unicorn would ever need, and share in his success.

But not one saddler approached the spirit wielder. Skandar's heart sank: would he be the only rider left without a saddle?

To make things worse, *two* saddlers had approached Mitchell – Nimroe and Taiting – and he was trying to choose between them. It was obvious to Skandar that Mitchell liked the Nimroe saddle best. He kept running his hand along the ash-coloured leather and fiddling with the little gold flames studded around the leather flaps. For some reason, though, he kept returning to the Taiting saddler. It was rare for Mitchell to be indecisive, especially when it came to something he'd researched.

'Just pick the Nimroe – you obviously like that one best,' Skandar told his fire wielder friend impatiently. *And let the other one present a saddle to me*, he thought.

'It's not that simple,' Mitchell murmured. 'I'm not supposed to go with a Nimroe saddle; my father—' He stopped himself. 'Anyway, Taitings are really good too. Some would say better; my family have been riding in them for generations.'

'You know best.' Ever since Mitchell had made it through the Training Trial, Ira Henderson had been writing stern letters to his son about the importance of training hard and befriending the *right* people. Skandar assumed that he, a spirit wielder, was *not* the right people, so he decided to leave Mitchell to it. He didn't want to make things worse.

Mitchell looked longingly at the Nimroe saddle. 'I'll go with the Taiting.'

The Taiting saddler beamed. 'Just like Ira. Your dad will be so proud. He was telling me only last week that after your performance in the Training Trial, he has high hopes of you becoming Commodore one day.' Her yellow sash dropped from her shoulder as she pumped Mitchell's hand enthusiastically.

Mitchell didn't meet Skandar's eye as he left the line.

Amber Fairfax and Whirlwind Thief were the only other pair left now. Amber hadn't placed very well in the Training Trial after Mitchell had battled her, but Skandar couldn't help thinking something else was going on. Perhaps it was the fact that her spirit wielder father, Simon Fairfax, had been caught helping the Weaver last year.

But then, inevitably, Amber was chosen by the disgruntled Nimroe saddler. After all, unlike Skandar, Amber was only *related* to a spirit wielder – not training as one.

Now all the other riders and unicorns were celebrating in the colourful tents, cheers erupting and corks popping as the saddlers opened bottles of fizzing liquid that matched the colours of their tarpaulins. But still no saddlers approached Scoundrel, even those who hadn't been able to secure a unicorn at all. Disappointment tugged at Skandar's chest and shame coloured his cheeks. What had he expected anyway, after his fellow Nestlings had dropped out of the sky rather than race him? After the truesong had reminded everyone about the danger of the spirit element? What saddler would want to be associated with a rider like that?

Skandar was about to ask Instructor O'Sullivan if he could return to the Eyrie, when two figures crashed through the gate to the plateau. Skandar squinted at the orange-clad strangers, trying to make them out. Until he realised they weren't strangers at all.

Shekoni Saddles had arrived.

Olu Shekoni – Flo's dad – and Ebb – her twin brother – put up their orange tent calmly, as though everyone on the training ground wasn't staring at them. Ebb cracked open the only wooden box they'd brought with them, and the sound felt deafening in the stunned silence. Olu lifted out the saddle with one muscled arm, and marched straight towards the only remaining unicorn.

Scoundrel roared as Olu approached, but he only laughed – low and deep. Skandar wasn't paying attention to his unicorn. The saddle in Olu's dark brown arms was the most beautiful he'd seen that morning. The leather shone so brightly black it could have been marble.

'Sorry we're late; we were delayed back at the workshop,' Olu explained.

Skandar was struck, as he had been when he'd met Flo's dad after the Training Trial, by the warmth of his smile.

Olu Shekoni placed the saddle just behind Scoundrel's wing joints so it followed the curve of the unicorn's spine. It fitted perfectly.

Skandar swallowed. 'Mr Shekoni, you don't have to choose us just because we're the only ones left.'

Olu and Ebb burst out laughing at the same time. Skandar didn't understand.

'Skandar,' Olu managed to wheeze between his chuckles, 'my team has been working on this saddle for weeks. It was made especially for Scoundrel's Luck. For you. After I heard how you saved New-Age Frost from the Weaver, well, I knew I wanted you to be a Shekoni Saddles rider.'

'If you don't believe him,' Ebb piped up, 'take a look at the stitching.' Flo's twin was grinning so broadly that there were deep dimples in his cheeks.

Heart hammering, Skandar leaned close to the saddle, inhaling the leather's scent. Then he saw it. All five elemental symbols had been stitched into the black seat in bright spirit-wielder white.

'So? What do you think?' Ebb asked, fiddling with one of his tight black curls.

'I think that even if I'd had the pick of every saddle today, I'd have chosen this one. No competition.' Skandar could hardly believe it. Shekoni made saddles for the Commodore! Jamie was going to be so excited.

As Skandar and Scoundrel made their way past the deep purple tarpaulin of the Henning-Dove tent, Bobby appeared in its doorway. She didn't say congratulations; she didn't even make a joke. Her brown eyes were fixed on the saddle balanced on Scoundrel's back, refusing to meet Skandar's gaze when he waved. Was she angry with him?

At the Shekoni Saddles tent, Skandar tried to forget about the expression on Bobby's face. He gulped down an orange drink.

'Are you going to tell him why we were late, Dad?' Ebb looked fit to burst with the secret.

Olu raised his eyebrows. 'Well, I wasn't going to worry him with it, but you've not given me much choice now, have you?'

Ebb cringed.

'What happened?' Skandar asked quickly.

Mr Shekoni sat down heavily on the saddle box, a frown knitting into his forehead. 'We were in the workshop this morning, putting the finishing touches to your saddle, when I heard banging. I thought it was from one of the shops across the way. Ebb and I, we just ignored it. Then it happened again. I went to look outside, but I couldn't get out. I went to the back door – it wouldn't budge and all the windows were dark.'

'I don't under—'

'Someone had boarded the workshop doors and windows shut – put massive slabs of pine across them – so me and Ebb were locked in.'

Skandar's mouth fell open. 'How did you get out?'

Ebb answered. 'Luckily Bronwyn from Battle Bargains saw what was happening. She was incredible, wasn't she, Dad?'

'She's got some muscles, that woman, I'll tell you that much. Pulled one of the boards straight off a window and then smashed the glass with her broom handle. We packed up your saddle and rushed straight here.'

'But who would want to trap you in your workshop?'

Olu shrugged. 'The Saddle Ceremony has certainly become more and more competitive over the years, but I've never experienced foul play before. We saddlers are friends, and I can't think of anyone who'd do that to me; I've known them all for decades. But then I thought about *who* I was intending to present my saddle to this year . . .'

'Oh,' Skandar breathed.

'I'm not certain,' Olu rushed on. 'I didn't tell anyone who I had in mind – not even Florence – though a reporter from the *Hatchery Herald* practically bribed me to tell him. But someone with an eye for detail might have been able to guess from the dark-coloured leather, or my measurements and plans.'

'And you have no idea who it might have been?'

'I could guess at someone – someone who has made no secret of the fact they don't want a spirit wielder on the Island, let alone training at the—'

'President Manning!' Ebb interrupted, clearly trying to be helpful.

Olu gave his son an exasperated look. 'Maybe. But the trouble is, Skandar, you're not exactly the most popular rider on the Island right now. It's not just Dorian who's unhappy.' Olu sighed, as though he was sorry for what he was about to say. 'You're the first spirit wielder in training in over a decade,' he said gently. 'Then there's that wild unicorn being killed. Killed! When we all thought it was impossible. And now people are gossiping about a truesong. I didn't hear it, but I expect it had nothing at all to do with you. But once the spirit element is involved people hear what they want to hear. Some would rather blame you than accept the possibility that the Weaver is making trouble again. Especially if they want you out of the Eyrie.'

'People are really saying I killed the wild unicorn, even though I *stopped* the Weaver last year?' Skandar's heart sank. He remembered the line in the truesong about the Island taking revenge. If that really happened, would he be blamed for that too?

Olu spread his hands. 'It's just rumours. But it isn't helping your friendly spirit wielder image.'

Skandar sighed. Wild unicorns and spirit wielders. Always linked. Always feared.

'Don't worry,' Olu said kindly. 'You've got the backing of Shekoni Saddles now. People will come round.'

But Skandar wasn't so sure.

'Forking thunderstorms,' Mitchell murmured, as he read the *Hatchery Herald* in the Trough the next morning. 'This isn't good.'

'What isn't good?' Skandar looked up from his favourite breakfast of sausages swimming in mayonnaise. He didn't think he could take more bad news.

Mitchell hesitated, his eyes flicking to Skandar and back down to the newsprint. Skandar grabbed it from him, and Flo scooted her chair across the leafy dining platform to read too. Bobby had been quiet since Skandar had been presented with the Shekoni saddle, but she took eating very seriously so it was hard to tell if she was concentrating on that or still annoyed with him. Skandar began to read:

TRUESONG TERROR!
WILL THE ISLAND REALLY SEEK REVENGE?

Yesterday a truesong was sung by a bard named Mark Berriman at the annual Nestling Saddle Ceremony. Read the song on Page 5. It appeared to be a warning about the recent killing of a wild unicorn and, according to Dorian Manning – president of the Hatchery and head of the Silver Circle – it also held clues about the culprit. Manning confirmed the Weaver is still a suspect but indicated that the truesong has resulted in new leads being investigated. Commodore Kazama declined to comment directly but reminded our reporter that truesongs are often metaphorical . . .

'*New leads being investigated*?' Skandar said, worry leaking into his voice. 'Do you think that means . . . me?'

Skandar took his friends' silence as a yes. He groaned.

Mitchell sighed. 'The trouble is, even though *I* think truesongs are nonsense, most Islanders don't.'

Skandar flipped over to the printed song. After shooing a squirrel away from her plate, even Bobby stood to read over Flo's shoulder.

'*Take the life of one dying for ever,*' Skandar said. 'That must be about killing a wild unicorn.'

'Yes, and then it says, *And all five shall be used to avenge.*' Flo peered down at the page. 'So the Island is going to use the elements to get revenge for the wild unicorn's death?'

'How could it do that?' Skandar wondered. 'Does it mean riders will use the elements? Hunt down the killer?'

'It doesn't *sound* like riders would do it. There's that verse about floodwaters. Could the Island flood itself? We'd have to fly people to safety!' Flo sounded scared.

Mitchell cleared his throat. 'This is my point about truesongs – it's all flowery nonsense. The Island is a piece of land. It doesn't have a sense of right and wrong, a sense of justice!' He was almost laughing.

Flo ignored him. '*Spirit's dark friend* – surely that has to be the Weaver?' She glanced nervously at Skandar.

Mitchell couldn't help but dive back in. 'If that's true, then according to the song there's this *other force* to worry about as well.' He pointed at the verse. 'It says *successor of spirit's dark friend.*'

'I really hate riddles,' Bobby grumbled. 'Why make life *more* complicated?'

Reading the words again, something horrible occurred to

Skandar. *True successor of spirit's dark friend.* If spirit's dark friend was the Weaver . . . then maybe the truesong really *was* talking about him. He was the Weaver's son – a secret only known to him, his quartet and his aunt, Agatha Everhart. True, the Weaver had revealed it to her soldiers, but Mitchell's dad had told him – disappointedly – that the new inmates could hardly remember anything from when they had been falsely bonded to wild unicorns. A new fear hit Skandar. If anyone found out, surely they would *assume* Skandar was the Weaver's successor? And another fear. Maybe he was? But no. No. He wasn't a force of darkness. He would never be like her. She'd asked him to join her, and *he'd said no.* To distract himself, Skandar reread the part of the truesong about hope.

> *There is only one hope for us mortals,*
> *To atone for an immortal's death:*
> *Win the fight for the First Rider's last gift,*
> *Taking form at the Queen's final breath.*

'It says *the First Rider's last gift* can help fix things,' he ventured. 'What kind of gift would that be, do you think? And how does something form at a *Queen's final breath*? Did the Island have queens?'

'The Island supposedly had a Wild Unicorn Queen, I think. Before the riders even arrived.' Flo frowned down at the paper on the dining table.

'And the gift?'

'There are old stories about the First Rider leaving something behind for the Island when he died,' Mitchell said dismissively.

'But what?' Skandar persisted. 'Has anyone found it? Has

anyone – what was it? – managed to *win the fight* for it before?'

Bobby made a loud scoffing noise.

'What?' Skandar asked, distracted.

'Oh, nothing.' She ripped a handful of leaves from a nearby branch.

'Seriously, what?'

'It's just kind of exhausting how you're already trying to be the hero. You're already thinking about fighting for some gift you heard about two seconds ago.'

'I'm not *trying to be the hero*. I'm a Mainlander. I'm interested!'

Bobby shrugged. 'If you say so.'

Skandar wanted to defend himself, but she was probably still annoyed about the Shekoni saddle. He decided to drop it.

Flo's eyes flicked between them nervously. She hated conflict. 'I don't think Skandar would be able to fight for it anyway – even if he *did* want to. Nobody has ever found the First Rider's gift.'

Mitchell snatched the *Hatchery Herald* away, making them all jump. 'Nobody has ever found it because there's no evidence it exists. Nobody even knows *what* the gift is supposed to be. It's a myth, a legend, a fairy tale.'

But Skandar wasn't going to be deterred that easily. After all, unicorns had been fairy tales on the Mainland until not too long ago – and now he was riding one.

He started to open his mouth, but Flo interrupted him. 'Maybe nothing will happen,' she said hopefully. 'Maybe the Weaver didn't kill the wild unicorn and it was all an accident, and none of the scarier stuff in the truesong will come true?'

'Exactly, Flo,' Mitchell said approvingly. 'It's completely irrational to believe words in a song can tell the future.'

'Do bards sing truesongs about riders?' Bobby was suddenly

more animated. 'I bet there'll be one about me when I'm famous. Maybe there is already? Like a prophecy!'

Mitchell scoffed. 'I don't think a bard would waste the one and only truesong of their whole life on *you*, Roberta.'

'I thought you didn't believe in them,' Skandar teased.

'Bobby Bruna and Falcon's Wrath shall win the Chaos Cup five years in a row,' Bobby sang in a spooky voice, wiggling her fingertips over the table.

Skandar and Flo started laughing, the earlier tension broken. Even Mitchell had to stifle a grin. 'See, Bobby gets it. We shouldn't be worrying so much.'

'I don't know what you mean.' Bobby waggled her eyebrows so they moved against her sharp fringe. 'That was my truesong. Didn't anybody write it down?'

THE GIRL WITH
THE SECRET

'There can't be a fifth element – there just can't be,' Dad said for the hundredth time.

'If the president of the Hatchery says there's a spirit element, there's a spirit element, Dad,' Kenna said stubbornly, also for the hundredth time.

It had been a couple of months since Dorian Manning's visit. Kenna and Dad were at the kitchen table of Flat 207 arguing – again.

'But why wouldn't Skandar have told us?'

Kenna wanted to know the answer to this too. Sure, her brother was a water wielder, but why hadn't he mentioned there were five elements, not four? Perhaps the spirit element was so rare that even Skandar didn't know about it? After all, she'd never seen a spirit wielder in the Chaos Cup. And Skandar wouldn't have kept it from them on purpose, surely?

'It doesn't matter,' she said aloud. 'What matters is that I'm a spirit wielder and my unicorn is still out there somewhere.

Waiting for me! President Manning just has to find it. He's already looking!'

Dad rubbed his eyes, the skin raw. 'Tell me again why you failed the Hatchery exam?'

'Because spirit wielders like me are really rare! It was all a big mistake. I should have passed! I would have opened the Hatchery door if they'd let me try it.'

Dad sighed. 'Something just feels a bit iffy about it. This man—'

'The president of the Hatchery. He's very important.'

'Right. He turns up at midnight, tells you there's been a mistake two years after you failed the exam and wants you to meet him in the middle of the sea in November?'

'He said he couldn't take me with him straight away! And yes, I have to row out to meet him.'

'*I'll* be the one rowing you out to meet him.'

Kenna's heart hammered in her chest, daring to hope. 'So you'll let me go?'

A dark shadow of uncertainty flickered across Dad's face but – finally – he nodded. Kenna squealed and threw herself into his arms.

Dad grunted at the impact but tightened his arms round her. 'This is the happiest I've seen you in two years, sweetheart. I'm not going to keep you here when it's only making you miserable. I know I'm not always the best dad, but I want you to be happy. I want you to have your dream.'

Kenna swallowed back tears of relief. The truth was, she would have gone with President Manning without Dad's blessing, but this was much, much better. 'My own unicorn, Dad! I'll get to live with Skandar in the Eyrie! Maybe we can be

Chaos riders together? Like we always wanted.'

She stopped, feeling guilty, and disentangled herself from his arms so she could see his face. He looked so tired. 'Are you sure you'll be okay on your own? What if you need help with bills or cooking or a job application or—' Kenna broke off. Now Dad had agreed to let her go she was suddenly full of panic about the reality of leaving him.

'You don't need to worry about any of that.' He tucked a stray strand of hair behind her ear.

Kenna had a lump in her throat. 'I'll miss you, Dad.'

He laughed, yet somehow the sound was sad. 'No, you won't.'

'I will! I'll write to you all the time. Me and Skandar can send you joint letters, how about that?' Kenna had a sudden image of her brother at six years old, colouring in a unicorn. Maybe he would draw her destined unicorn for her now?

Tears glistened in Dad's eyes. 'Two rider children. What are the chances? Your mum would have been so proud. I wish she was here to see it.'

'Let's visit the graveyard on Sunday,' Kenna suggested. 'We can tell her all about it?'

Concern crossed Dad's face. 'You really should write to Skandar. Let him know that you're coming. I'd feel better if—'

Kenna shook her head. 'We can't. President Manning said we have to keep this quiet. It's not usual to bring children to the Island outside the solstice. If my story gets out, every Mainlander child who failed the exam is going to think they're a spirit wielder too, aren't they? President Manning said that if that happened he might not be able to take me to the Island after all. It could ruin everything!' Kenna was so panicked she barely took a breath between sentences.

'But if we just tell Skandar . . .'

'No,' Kenna insisted. 'The letter would have to go in the Mainland post. It's too risky.'

'All right, all right.' Dad held up his hands in defeat. 'But isn't Skandar going to get suspicious if you just stop writing to him? Won't he worry?'

Kenna had already planned this out too. In her last letter to Skandar she'd told him she was really sad – and that had given her an idea. 'I don't want to lie to Skar in my letters, so I thought you could write to him instead? Tell him I'm finding it too hard to write about unicorns at the moment. That way, when I go to the Island, it won't be obvious I've left.'

'So you want me to lie to him?' Dad muttered, leaning back. 'He'll be able to tell if I'm lying!'

'And what am I supposed to be saying in these letters?' Dad was losing his patience.

'Just that I'm fine but I need some time to come to terms with not being a rider.'

'But you *are* a rider, according to this president bloke.'

'Yes, but Skandar can't know yet,' Kenna repeated. 'I'm sure I'll see him practically as soon as I get to the Island, and then it'll be a lovely big surprise!'

Dad grunted. 'You know best, I suppose.' He still didn't look convinced.

'It's just until everything's sorted out,' Kenna insisted.

'All right, I get it. Sheesh. Your mother was exactly the same, persuasive as anything – always won an argument.' That made Kenna beam from ear to ear.

Later, Kenna lay on her bed, staring at Skandar's old poster of Aspen McGrath's unicorn, New-Age Frost. She turned to her brother's empty bed, but she didn't feel sad any more. Her heart was full to the brim with hope. She hadn't been entirely truthful with Dad. President Manning had said it might take a while to find her unicorn once she got to the Island and that it might be a few months before she could see Skandar. That's why the letters from Dad were important – she didn't want Skandar to worry.

But once she had her unicorn, she would see Skandar every day. She imagined them riding side by side, brother and sister reunited – maybe even training together? Then she let herself, just for a moment, imagine passing under the finishing arch of the arena. She imagined the cheers, the commentator announcing: 'Kenna Smith, Commodore of Chaos.'

Kenna fell asleep with a smile on her face – because now, for the first time in a very long while, anything was possible.

CHAPTER FOUR

THE UNWELCOME VISITOR

A few days after the Saddle Ceremony, the first Nestling training session arrived. Skandar had been obsessing so much about the truesong, the Weaver and the dead wild unicorn that he'd almost forgotten they would be starting jousting. And now, as he mounted a fully armoured Scoundrel to fly to the training ground, he felt the familiar first-day nerves churning in his stomach.

A shout came from behind them. 'Race you!'

A slate-grey unicorn soared into the cool September air like a bullet. Bobby, of course. Skandar grinned, his spiralling thoughts dissipating. Scoundrel roared and gave chase, wings snapping out, and taking off in three strides. Falcon's Wrath was fast – she and Bobby had won the Training Trial last year, after all – but Skandar knew Scoundrel could fly faster. They soared downwards, the slope of the Eyrie's hill rushing beneath them, Scoundrel diving after Falcon. They were almost level—

'Ground!' Bobby yelled, whether to Skandar or herself he

couldn't tell. He plummeted after her; suddenly all he could see was the green of the grass instead of the blue of the sky. Bobby managed to slow Falcon enough to land on her hooves, but Scoundrel was flying far too fast, horn pointing straight at the upcoming ground of the Nestling plateau.

'Scoooundrelll!' Skandar gritted his teeth. 'What's the plaaaan heeeerre?'

Inches from the ground, Scoundrel stretched his neck back up towards the sky, flung his rear hooves out and forced his wings through the air so strongly that they whooshed up, away from the impending collision. Skandar gasped for breath, as though they'd dived into water and were coming back up for air.

When Scoundrel landed for real, Bobby slow-clapped from Falcon's back. 'Nice acrobatics. Though you still lost, spirit boy.'

Skandar shrugged. 'You had a head start by miles. I almost caught you!'

'That's what they all say. I'll always be faster than you!'

Skandar couldn't help but notice the edge in Bobby's voice again: something more than just friendly teasing.

Meiyi landed Rose-Briar's Darling a few metres away, quickly followed by Kobi on Ice Prince and Alastair on Dusk Seeker. Amber was missing from their quartet, just like she had been at the Saddler Ceremony. Whirlwind Thief was at the other end of the plateau, Amber turning the chestnut unicorn in tight circles to calm her.

'Hey, Skandar!' Alastair shouted. 'Isn't it interesting how the Weaver seems stronger than ever since you had your little chat with her in the Wilderness?'

'We didn't have a—' Skandar attempted to say, but Meiyi interrupted him.

'Your little story about defeating Erika Everhart isn't very believable now, is it? Though of course *I* never believed you. You barely made it through the Training Trial!'

They all laughed.

'And the water wielders don't believe you either,' Kobi announced pompously, his ice-mutated lashes flashing in the sunlight as he circled Scoundrel on Prince. 'We just voted against allowing you into the water den. The Well is no place for someone like *you*.'

Skandar was so shocked that he didn't say a word as the group rode away. He knew that each element had their own underground space in the Eyrie – Skandar's quartet had managed to find the abandoned spirit den last year while investigating the Weaver. But the *official* dens were the Furnace for fire, the Well for water, the Hive for air and the Mine for earth, which were open to Nestlings and older. Although if what Kobi said was true, Skandar would be excluded this year too.

'Kobi's probably lying,' Bobby said fiercely. 'Last year Instructor O'Sullivan said you were an honorary water wielder. She *said* you'd be allowed—'

'It's fine. I'm fine,' Skandar muttered, reminding himself of Kenna's words in the last letter she'd sent him. She *still* hadn't written back. He felt even worse. 'I wouldn't belong.'

'Who'd want to go the stinking Well anyway?' Bobby was seething. 'It's probably linked to the Eyrie sewage system; it's probably cold and wet, and . . . smells of rotten fish and pondweed.'

Skandar sighed. 'It's okay, Bobby.'

Scoundrel made a small squeak of concern and a couple of feathers on his wings ignited.

Out of habit, the Nestlings lined up on the plateau. As

Scoundrel and Falcon reached Blade and Red, Skandar noticed that the nearest riders – air wielders called Ivan and Harper – moved their unicorns further along the line. Skandar decided there and then he couldn't face telling Flo and Mitchell about being barred from the Well just yet – he didn't want to see the anger on Mitchell's face, the pity on Flo's. Instead, Skandar studied the training ground. Instructor Webb and Instructor Anderson were already on the plateau with Moonlight Dust and Desert Firebird. Each instructor had a handful of wooden stakes and was hammering them one by one into the ground to make a straight line.

Finally, Instructor Anderson blew his whistle for quiet.

Flo winced from Blade's back. 'Why can't they just ask nicely?'

'Congratulations on making it to your second year of training and earning your saddles,' Instructor Anderson called out, now riding Desert Firebird. His red cloak sat neatly atop his unicorn's hindquarters. 'Nestling year is all about weapons: learning to mould and use weapons of pure elemental magic.'

There was an outbreak of feverish whispering. Bobby looked like all her Air Festivals had come at once, but Skandar felt a swoop of nerves. He knew how to summon magic along the bond and into his right hand, how the elements would explode from the wound Scoundrel's horn had given him when he'd hatched. But he had no idea how to make a weapon.

Instructor Anderson held his hand up for silence, the flames around his dark brown ears flickering in warning. 'Yes, yes, all very exciting. I'm sure you will have seen experienced riders using elemental weapons during the Chaos Cup, alongside the magic attacks and defences you used last year in the Training Trial.'

There was a murmur of agreement. Skandar certainly

remembered the incredible lightning sword Nina Kazama had used to help her race to victory in the Chaos Cup back in June.

'Weapons are more precise than shapeless magic, but they take practice and dedicated teamwork with your unicorn. We'll be working on moulding different weapons first – in all four elements, not just the one you're allied to.'

Skandar winced. Four elements – not five.

'We'll then move on to attacking and defending at a standstill around the Fire Festival, then finally we'll introduce movement. For unicorns, jousting is more about bravery than it is about their own elemental magic. They have to learn to work with you, as well as gallop right at an oncoming attack. Remember, it won't be a race that determines whether you advance to Fledgling year; it will be a jousting tournament.'

Skandar cast his mind back to the display at the previous year's Fire Festival – the two riders galloping towards each other, shining weapons in hand.

Instructor Webb took over, his white forehead wrinkled with age. 'Jousting has been a staple of Eyrie training since it was founded by the First Rider. It teaches young riders a vital lesson. Falling off is *never* an option. Fall off in the joust – you lose. Fall off mid-battle – no magic. Fall off in mid-air – you die.'

Gabriel didn't seem deterred by this solemn warning. 'When you say "jousting", do you mean what knights used to do?' the Mainlander asked excitedly, his stone hair eerily still in the wind.

'Island jousting is a little different, so I hear.' A mischievous grin crossed Instructor Anderson's face. 'Let us demonstrate.'

Whoosh! Two unicorns in full armour swooped down to the training ground.

Instructor O'Sullivan landed Celestial Seabird at one end

of the line of wooden stakes just as Instructor Saylor landed opposite – North-Breeze Nightmare snorted sparks, his plates of armour scraping against each other. Both unicorns were frothing at the mouth. The instructors held their reins in one hand and a round metal shield in the other – one studded with blue, the other yellow. Skandar had never seen the instructors in full armour, and they looked just as terrifying as any Chaos Cup rider. To mark their elemental allegiances, Instructor O'Sullivan had a painted blue droplet on her back, Instructor Saylor a yellow spiral.

Instructor Anderson blew his whistle.

The two unicorns exploded forward on either side of the stakes. They galloped at full tilt towards each other, hoofbeats shaking the ground.

Instructor O'Sullivan's palm glowed blue; Instructor Saylor's glowed yellow.

Instructor Anderson blew his whistle a second time.

A shining trident of pure white ice leaped into Instructor O'Sullivan's right hand. Instructor Saylor pulled back the fizzing string of a bow forged from lightning itself, the arrow a dangerous mass of sparks. As the unicorns passed each other, Instructor Saylor released the crackling bowstring. Instructor O'Sullivan swung her ice trident and connected with Saylor's arrow, its electricity spluttering into thin air. Instructor Saylor raised her palm and summoned another arrow to her sparking bow, as her opponent drew back her trident for a second time. But it was too late.

Instructor Saylor attempted to block the three-pronged blow with her shield, but the water wielder's trident hit its target with a sickening clang of ice on metal. Instructor Saylor's whole body rocked backwards in her saddle so that her helmet flew off, honey-coloured curls brushing Nightmare's back. Astonishingly, she stayed in the saddle – pulling herself upright again – though sweat poured down her tanned face.

'Direct hit for Instructor O'Sullivan!' Instructor Anderson held out his arm towards the side now occupied by Celestial Seabird. 'One to zero.'

After a beat of awed silence, the Nestlings exploded into noisy cheers.

The two instructors jousted for five rounds, and Skandar could hardly keep his mouth closed as he watched the spectacle. He'd seen elemental weapons before, but watching two expert riders create them up close was something else: a green-thorned mace, a sparking sabre, a magnetic lance. The ease with which the instructors moulded their magic into weapons was beautiful; it showed what the bond could really do. The riders and unicorns seemed to anticipate every move – like they were the same being. And Seabird and Nightmare showed no fear as they galloped at top speed towards each other. Skandar wondered if his bond with Scoundrel would ever be as seamless.

'Instructor O'Sullivan is definitely going to win,' Mitchell murmured. 'She's won three out of the four rounds so far.'

Instructor Anderson blew his whistle for the fifth and final round, first for the unicorns, then for the weapons. Instructor Saylor reacted much faster than she had previously, and Skandar barely had time to blink as she threw a sharp javelin – thick with interwoven strands of electricity – straight at Instructor O'Sullivan's armoured chest. The water wielder didn't even have time to lift her flaming broadsword to protect herself, the weapon extinguishing uselessly by her side as the javelin's blow forced her clean off Seabird's back.

There was a horrified silence as Instructor O'Sullivan lay in the dirt of the training ground, her white unicorn standing protectively over her – as though Seabird was worried the air wielder would attack again. But instead, Instructor Saylor dismounted and offered a hand to help her opponent to her feet.

'I'd forgotten how good you were with that javelin,' Instructor O'Sullivan grumbled, removing her slightly dented helmet.

'Me too.' Instructor Saylor grinned, and then the two women were shaking hands and laughing – though the water instructor's face was still a pasty white.

'Instructor Saylor wins!' Instructor Anderson called.

'B-but,' Mitchell spluttered, 'but how? I thought that was three points to two in Instructor O'Sullivan's favour?'

'Unseat the other rider and it's an automatic win,' Instructor Webb explained as he rode by on Moonlight Dust.

'I just *love* that!' Bobby cried and Falcon shrieked along. 'You can be losing, and then, *WHAM*, you take your opponent down on the last round and they're history.'

Skandar had never seen Bobby and Falcon so excited. Secretly, he hoped he didn't have to fight them in a joust any time soon. He suspected his friendship with Bobby wouldn't stop her trying to smash him off Scoundrel's back.

'When do we get to joust? When can we start?' Bobby asked the instructors loudly.

Instructor Saylor smiled at her, teeth glittering. 'You're not quite ready yet, sweet pea. You'll need to learn how to mould your magic into simple shapes first.'

It was a testament to how much respect Bobby had for her air instructor that she didn't bat an eyelid at being called *sweet pea*.

'And we'll start small,' Instructor O'Sullivan added, still slightly more dishevelled than usual. 'You will begin with a dagger forged from the element you wield. Daggers are the simplest weapon you can summon, and using your allied element should make things easier.'

'Let the fire, or water – or whatever you're allied to – build in your palm, until there's an unformed cloud of magic in front of you,' Instructor Anderson explained. 'Then imagine it forming into the weapon you desire. It's a slow process when you're just starting out. Use your hands to help you, as though you're moulding wet clay. But once you've mastered the technique, you'll be able to summon weapons as quick as a spark!'

The instructors held out daggers forged from their own elements for the riders to imitate. Soon the smell of the magic filled the air. Each element had a unique aroma to every rider, and – as Instructors Saylor and Anderson rode along the line of Nestlings – Skandar caught the citrus smell of the air dagger and the whiff of bonfires and burnt toast from the fire dagger.

Further down, Skandar saw Marissa and Demonic Nymph both lean forward to marvel at the shining water dagger in Instructor O'Sullivan's hand. Blue light danced across the frosted strands of her hair. Aisha, an earth wielder, gasped at the diamond dagger in Instructor's Webb's palm.

'Best training session yet.' Bobby grinned happily from Falcon's back as electricity built in her palm and she moved her hands through the crackling magic, pushing it this way and that, trying to forge a copy of the weapon in Instructor Saylor's hand with her mind.

But Skandar didn't have an example to copy. As far as he knew, none of the instructors could summon the spirit element any more. After the Training Trial last year and his agreement with Aspen McGrath, he had been promised a spirit instructor. For weeks, Instructor O'Sullivan had been assuring him that one of the newly freed spirit wielders would come to the Eyrie to teach him. But so far there'd been no sign of that happening.

'We can do this, Scoundrel,' Skandar murmured, urging the white of the spirit element to his palm. 'And if we have to do it alone, so be it.' Scoundrel flapped his wings, as though readying himself too.

The bond flooded with spirit magic, the cinnamon-sweet smell filling Skandar's nostrils. Once there was a bright white ball of glowing element floating in front of him, Skandar shut his eyes and imagined a shining dagger of pure spirit: an unforgiving sharp blade, a hilt heavy enough to weigh in his hand. Without even meaning to, his hands began to twitch – tracing the outline of a blade as though he was sketching. He opened one eye and almost lost his concentration. The weapon he'd imagined was starting to form! Handle first, then shimmering white magic blurring along the blade. Skandar tried to take hold of the dagger, but somehow he couldn't feel the hilt in his hand.

Skandar was so focused on trying to take hold of the spirit dagger that he didn't hear the screaming right away. It wasn't until Mitchell yelled at him that he looked up.

'SKANDAR! Do you want it to eat you? Get out of the way!'

Then the smell hit the back of Skandar's throat: the smell of rotting fish and mouldy bread and death.

A wild unicorn.

A bellow echoed deep in Scoundrel's chest. He bared his teeth then roared at the unicorn, blasting flames from his throat as a warning.

Skandar's ears were ringing, the fearful shouts of his fellow Nestlings a distant jumble.

The wild unicorn didn't move. Its breaths rattled the ribcage visible under its thin coat. The sound was audible even over the screaming riders – who were launching their unicorns into the sky. A wild unicorn could easily kill a Nestling rider – and with them, their bonded unicorn. The Islanders had been told the stories in their cribs. The Mainlanders had been warned. They'd all had the nightmares. They weren't taking any chances.

But Skandar stared back at the wild unicorn: at the wound festering on its shoulder, at the ghostly transparent horn, at a broken bone splintering from its gnarled knee. Its dapple-grey chest was covered in flecks of blood from a kill, almost like someone had flicked red paint into the swirls of its grey and white coat.

Wait. Dapple grey? Skandar suddenly knew why this all felt so familiar. It wasn't just that he'd faced a wild unicorn on the path to the Eyrie before – it was the *same* unicorn.

Skandar was vaguely aware of the rest of his scattered quartet refusing to leave the plateau with the other riders. Instructor O'Sullivan and Instructor Webb were shouting at them, and they – mostly Bobby – were shouting back. But Skandar, still on Scoundrel's back – was only half listening: 'What do you want?' he asked the wild unicorn.

Something grabbed his leg. Skandar saw a hand with gnarled white knuckles clutching his knee.

'She's attracted to the spirit element.' The voice came from a figure on the ground below, wispy hair escaping from a grey hood.

'She?'

'The wild unicorn – she won't leave until you stop doing that!'

The stranger's voice was suddenly harsh. Skandar realised that the white glow was still in his palm, left over from moulding the dagger. Skandar thought about stopping the spirit magic, but instead he spoke to the wild unicorn again. 'What do you want?'

Then, much more gently than she'd spoken, the hooded woman took Skandar's glowing right hand in hers and closed his fingers over his Hatchery wound.

'Enough,' she growled. 'That's enough now.'

Skandar blinked and looked up to see all four instructors firing magic after the wild unicorn as it jumped the iron gate of the Nestling plateau and disappeared.

The woman let go of Skandar's palm. A bulging leather satchel was slung across her shoulder. She threw back her grey hood, exposing a spirit mutation marking both her pale cheeks.

Skandar sucked in a breath. 'What –' his voice was shaking – 'are *you* doing here?'

Her sharp brown eyes snapped up to his, and Skandar felt waves of fear and revulsion wash over him.

Agatha Everhart really did look just like her sister.

Skandar heard muttering from his quartet – grouped on their unicorns a few metres away, having avoided being ushered back to the stables by the instructors. He wondered whether they recognised Agatha from her photo in the *Hatchery Herald* last year, whether they recognised her as the Executioner – the traitor who had killed all the spirit unicorns over a decade ago, saving their riders' lives but condemning them to solitude and grief. Skandar wondered whether they also noticed the family resemblance Agatha had to her sister, the Weaver.

'What are you doing here?' Skandar repeated, his voice hollow. The last time he'd seen Agatha, she'd been behind bars.

'Do you know each other?' Instructor O'Sullivan had trotted over on Celestial Seabird.

Skandar reacted first. 'No, Instructor. I've only heard of her. And what she did to the spirit unicorns.' He didn't have to fake his disgust.

Skandar hadn't seen Instructor O'Sullivan look this awkward before, but there was no mistaking the clearing of her throat, the not quite meeting his eye. 'Well, yes. I suppose— Yes, you would have.'

'I thought you were still in prison!' Skandar blurted at Agatha, the wild unicorn encounter completely forgotten. He hadn't realised how angry he was with her until now. She'd *known*. She'd known from the beginning that Erika was his mum. And Kenna's mum. And she hadn't said a word. She'd sent him after the Weaver and she hadn't even *warned* him.

'Skandar!' Instructor O'Sullivan barked. 'That's no way to talk to your new spirit instructor.'

'My – my what?' Skandar spluttered.

Instructor O'Sullivan ignored him. 'How have you been, Agatha?' she asked briskly.

'Incarcerated, mostly,' Agatha grunted.

Instructor O'Sullivan ran a hand through her spiky hair. 'I have to say, I wasn't expecting Skandar's spirit instructor to be you.'

'To be honest with you, Persephone,' Agatha said, 'neither was I.'

They shared a significant look. Skandar sensed his quartet edging their unicorns closer – concerned and curious.

Instructor O'Sullivan sighed. 'Well, Instructor Everhart, I suggest you go up to the Eyrie, report to the sentinels and settle into your treehouse.'

'You're letting her *live* here?' Skandar asked, horrified. *Instructor* Everhart?

'This is hardly living,' Agatha muttered murderously. 'The Eyrie is a fortress; Arctic Swansong is under guard miles from here; and I'm practically under treehouse arrest.'

Instructor O'Sullivan cleared her throat even more awkwardly. 'Skandar will meet with you soon to discuss his training programme.' The last two words were almost lost as she hurried Seabird away.

As Agatha turned to go, Skandar couldn't help himself. 'Why did you agree to do this? You must have known how difficult this would make things. How hard it would be to see you after—' His voice broke, choked by his memories of the Weaver in the Wilderness. His mum riding straight for him, murder in her eyes. Eyes that looked just like Agatha's, like Kenna's – like his.

'Listen, Skandar,' Agatha said, her expression as fierce as when she'd left him at the Mirror Cliffs. 'There wasn't anyone else for the job.'

'What do you mean?'

'Dorian Manning.' Agatha glanced sideways at Flo, who was pretending to be very interested in Blade's left ear. 'He had the Silver Circle threaten the freed spirit wielders. Told them their families would be arrested if they tried to help you. O'Sullivan knows all about it, if you don't believe me. Some of the spirit wielders tried to volunteer anyway, and they were beaten up. Most of them have now gone into hiding.'

Skandar thought about Olu and Ebb Shekoni being barricaded in their workshop before the Saddle Ceremony.

'Aspen McGrath wrote it into Island law that you were to

train in the spirit element, but the Silver Circle are trying everything they can to prevent it.'

'Then how come you—'

'The new Commodore, Nina Kazama. When she heard that none of the other spirit wielders were volunteering to be your instructor, she persuaded the Silver Circle that I was the best option. With Arctic Swansong in prison, she said I'd toe the line. Said I wouldn't teach you anything *dangerous*.' Agatha sounded revolted. 'Other than you, I'm the only spirit wielder with a unicorn left to lose.'

'But you're the Weaver's sister,' Skandar hissed. 'You're my aunt.'

Agatha glared at him. 'I'm your instructor. And my connection to the Weaver might be common knowledge now but *nobody* can find out yours, especially not Dorian Manning – he hates my sister more than anyone else does. Detests spirit wielders. And with a truesong verse about spirit's dark friend and a wild unicorn washing up dead? Wild unicorns and spirit wielders are always connected – this impossible death adds to the suspicion around us, the idea we're not like everyone else. And being outsiders makes people less bothered when we get hurt. It makes us an easy target, makes *you* the easiest target of all. Do you understand?'

'Do you think it's her?'

They both knew who Skandar was talking about.

'I don't know. I don't know why Erika would kill a wild unicorn. Or how.' Agatha turned away again. 'It's supposed to be impossible.'

But Skandar couldn't help thinking that something being impossible had never stopped Erika Everhart before.

CHAPTER FIVE

WILDFLOWER HILL

A couple of weeks after they'd begun training, Skandar, Bobby and Mitchell rode into the Island's capital, Fourpoint, to gather supplies. Mitchell wanted to order a book on jousting from Chapters of Chaos. Bobby wanted new brushes, since hers were worn out from all the pampering Falcon demanded. And Skandar was in desperate need of some new black boots. Flo, on the other hand, had gone to her first Silver Circle meeting, which Bobby was still annoyed about.

'I can't *believe* Flo's joining up with President Doddery Maggot and his shiny sidekicks.'

Skandar snorted. 'Doddery Maggot?'

'Flo hatched Blade. She doesn't have any choice about joining the Silver Circle – even if President Manning *is* spreading rumours about Skandar,' Mitchell said matter-of-factly, dismounting. They had landed at the end of Fourpoint's long shopping street where a few other unicorns had been tied to rings along a line of trees. They left Scoundrel, Falcon and Red munching on bloody meat hanging from the branches.

'Of course she has a choice!' Bobby argued as they all turned down the street together. 'She could just *not go*.'

Mitchell shook his head. 'From what I've read, if she refused to attend meetings, the Silver Circle would pull her out of the Eyrie.'

'They'd declare her a nomad?' Skandar asked, horrified.

'Not exactly.' Mitchell grimaced. 'She'd be forced to live at their base, the Silver Stronghold, instead. She'd have to train there until she was a fifth-year Predator.'

Even Bobby was shocked. 'She hasn't mentioned this to me!'

'Why? Why would she have to go to the Stronghold?' Skandar demanded.

'The Silver Circle say they have to be able to influence the training of silver unicorns. Without their guidance, apparently a young silver is too dangerous to be allowed to roam freely on the Island.'

'No way!' Skandar protested. 'That's just so Dorian Manning can control her!' He felt sickened by the idea that Flo could be wrenched from their quartet and locked up in the Silver Stronghold.

Mitchell nodded. 'That's what I thought.'

'Smells more suspicious than a fish-finger sandwich, if you ask me.' Bobby raised both her eyebrows.

'*Than a fish-finger sandwich?*' Skandar asked, sidetracked. 'Don't they just smell—'

'Fishy. Exactly.'

Mitchell sighed. 'I really don't understand Mainlanders sometimes.'

'Well, I just hope Flo's okay,' Skandar said. 'I don't trust Dorian Manning.'

'No,' Bobby said seriously. 'I don't trust Dumbo McSneakface either.'

They wandered along the shopping street for a while. Skandar tried to ignore the looks he was getting from passing Islanders – looks that ranged from disapproving to terrified. He supposed he shouldn't be surprised after using the spirit element at the Saddle Ceremony. He wondered, too, whether word had got out about him summoning a wild unicorn to the training ground. He tried to focus instead on how much he loved it here in Fourpoint, with its array of treehouses: the elemental colours jumbled up like the paint splashes on the quartet's tree trunk.

The shopfronts were at ground level with gold swinging signs and elaborate window displays dedicated to anything a unicorn or rider could wish for. Skandar had never had enough money to go shopping for himself back on the Mainland, but on the Island he was given a generous rider's allowance. He still didn't buy much – only what Scoundrel needed. Usually he saved it up – just in case – and hid it in the front pocket of his rucksack. He didn't need *things* anyway. But recently Instructor O'Sullivan had commented on the tattiness of his black boots – and you didn't argue with her.

'Look at this!' Mitchell rushed out of Chapters of Chaos with that morning's edition of the *Hatchery Herald*. He held it up so it was practically touching their noses.

'Mitchell,' Bobby growled, 'if you don't get that newspaper out of my face, so help me, I will punch right through it.'

But Skandar was already reading:

TRIPLE WILD MURDER!

Two more wild unicorns found dead, taking body count to three. President of the Silver Circle insists the Weaver cannot be acting alone . . .

'So much for Flo's theory about it being an accident,' Bobby murmured.

Now Skandar understood why so many Islanders had been staring at him. 'Come on,' he said, starting to walk. 'Let's get going – we don't want to be late.'

'You haven't bought your new boots yet!' Mitchell protested, jogging to keep up.

'I don't think that's going to happen today,' Skandar said grimly, as the sign on the door of the Brilliant Boot Company flipped from OPEN to CLOSED as he passed by.

Skandar, Mitchell and Bobby had been invited to spend that weekend in the earth zone with Flo and her family. After a long flight, Scoundrel, Red and Falcon had soared down towards a pretty square framed by treehouses on top of a hill. Skandar had never been to the earth zone before, but it was even more spectacular than Flo had described. From the air he could see flourishing green farmland that gave way to rougher moorland inhabited by goats. Further in, it was all mountains and gaping caves and standing stones. Fields of herbs grew in the shadows of spectacular rock formations, which stood like ancient guardians over the colourful fields – giant fists frozen mid-shake at the unicorns flying above. In contrast to the water zone – which was flat, with water-logged pastures, weeping willows and winding rivers – here Skandar had counted eleven hills so far, some steep and rocky, others rolling and green. As the shadow of Scoundrel's wings passed over their emerald brows, the bruised purple of snow-capped mountains loomed in the distance. Skandar was desperate to capture the scene in his sketchbook.

The eleventh and furthest hill from Fourpoint was Wildflower Hill – home to the Shekoni family – and it more than lived up to its name. A wildflower meadow blanketed the mound in every colour, from bright blue to burnt orange, filling Skandar's vision as Scoundrel descended.

'Flo's already here! Look, there's Silver Blade!' Bobby pointed as they dismounted by a grassy square.

'That smell!' Mitchell cried.

'Is it another wild unicorn?' Skandar looked around anxiously.

Mitchell pushed his glasses up his nose. 'Umm . . . I was talking about the *flowers*. The meadow, don't you think it smells nice?'

'I mean, the flowers *could* be deadly, Skandar. Why don't you stamp on some, just in case it saves the Island? I'm sure that'll impress Mr Shekoni even more,' Bobby joked, though she didn't smile.

Skandar grimaced as Bobby and Mitchell headed towards the main treehouse in the square. Embarrassed, he hung back – watching Flo's fierce silver unicorn sniff a patch of giant daisies, incinerating any that moved too quickly in the September breeze. Blade wasn't the only unicorn out in the wildflower meadow. Skandar spotted at least ten others trampling the fragrant flowers or chasing small creatures through the long grasses. One had a bandaged wing, another kept sneezing different elemental blasts, and another was so shrouded in smoke that he kept bumping into his fellow unicorns. Skandar started to wonder why they were all injured, until he remembered Flo's mum. She was a unicorn healer, and these must be her latest patients.

Skandar removed Scoundrel's saddle so he could join them. The white stitching – with all five elemental symbols – made him feel a little better after their trip to Fourpoint. At least Shekoni Saddles believed in him. Skandar could feel Scoundrel's desperation to play fizzing through the bond, especially once his best friend – Red Night's Delight – started galloping up and down the hill, fire billowing from all her hooves and turning flowers to ash. But Skandar was reluctant to leave his black unicorn. It wasn't that he thought Scoundrel would be in any danger here; it was more that he was nervous to go into the big family treehouse.

Skandar had never been invited to a friend's house for dinner before. Well, for anything, actually. On the Mainland he hadn't had any friends at all, other than his sister – and they'd lived in the same room! What if there were rules that he had no idea about? Should he have brought something? What if he made some horrible mistake and the Shekoni family never wanted him to visit again?

Scoundrel launched a bubble of reassurance into the bond, and Skandar took a deep breath, rummaging in his pocket to find the packet of Jelly Babies Kenna had sent with her last letter. There was only one sweet left. Scoundrel snatched it from Skandar's hand greedily, then nudged Skandar sideways. When his rider didn't move, the black unicorn poked his horn against the toe of Skandar's scruffy black boot.

'Oi!' Skandar jumped up and down on one leg. 'Okay, I'll go. You win!'

Pleased with himself, Scoundrel snorted sparks and blazed

across the meadow, leaving a trail of dead flowers in his wake.

Skandar climbed the steep plank that connected the grass of the square to the main entrance of the Shekoni treehouse. It reminded Skandar of a castle drawbridge, although much prettier, since flowering vines grew in intricate patterns to stop you accidentally stepping off either edge. At the top, Skandar hovered among colourful pots of strange-looking plants that smelled a little like elemental magic. From here, rope bridges painted in bright colours connected the main treehouse to all the others lining the small square. Flo had mentioned that her family housed apprentices – both saddlers and healers. Perhaps the Shekonis owned the whole square?

Feeling even more intimidated, Skandar stalled by a smoky-smelling red fern. He wished Kenna was here. She was much better than him at meeting new people. She'd smile and ask them interesting questions and tell good stories everyone wanted to listen to. Then he remembered that she hadn't written to him since the solstice. The hurt mixed with his own guilt; he just wished he could see Kenna and talk to her properly. She was right: once a year just wasn't enough—

Flo's voice drifted through the open front door. 'Dad, are you going to tell Nina?' She sounded very worried.

But a young voice answered. 'Ah, c'mon, Flo, I don't want a fuss. Don't really want my parents finding out, to be honest. They were already concerned when the whole spirit wielder thing came out. But with this too? They'll be enrolling me in a bard apprenticeship before you can say truesong!'

Was that Jamie? What was he doing here? Skandar moved closer to the floral-painted door.

'The Commodore needs to know – *and* Skandar,' Olu Shekoni

said firmly. Then, more sadly, he added, 'Though the poor boy's got enough to deal with – I ask you, the *Executioner* teaching him the spirit element?'

Someone whimpered. 'Sorry, sorry – that's going to sting. My elemental herbs are a bit strong; they're meant for unicorns, you see.' The woman speaking had to be Flo's mum.

'Are you sure they're safe for humans? Is he going to be okay? Have you ever healed a person before?' Mitchell's voice wavered between bossy and anxious.

'Yes, I'm sure; thank you, Mr Henderson. And, anyway, people are much more straightforward on account of their lack of magic and bloodlust. Although if you keep questioning me, I expect I can muster up some of the latter.'

Completely confused, Skandar pushed the door open wider and light illuminated the scene. Olu Shekoni was pacing the length of a bright yellow kitchen table. Flo, Mitchell and Bobby were sitting on a spindly white bench on one side of it while Ebb and Sara Shekoni were leaning over someone slumped in a chair. If Skandar hadn't just heard him speaking, he wasn't sure he'd have recognised his blacksmith. He had red welts and cuts all over his face and both eyes were swollen.

Skandar gasped. 'Jamie! What happened?'

'See! I told you he'd panic,' Jamie croaked through a split lip.

Olu told the story, because Sara insisted that the patient keep still while she dabbed strange-smelling ointments on to his face.

Earlier that day, Jamie had been in his forge alone, testing out the resilience of a new breastplate for Scoundrel while the other blacksmiths went out to a treehouse tavern for lunch.

'I'm just so dedicated to my work, you see,' Jamie cut in. Sara shushed him.

A man and a woman had entered the forge, hoods low. Jamie had tried to defend himself with pieces of armour, but that hadn't lasted long. He'd shouted for help, but nobody had come. The strangers had knocked him out. Half an hour later, Olu had come to ask about armour fastenings on Scoundrel's saddle – and found Jamie on the floor.

'But why?' Skandar asked, horrified.

Olu and Sara looked at each other, as though deciding how to answer.

'They told Jamie if he didn't stop making armour for the spirit wielder, they'd come back to finish the job.' Sara's voice was low and disgusted.

'Finish the job?' Mitchell asked. 'What does that—'

Jamie answered. 'Basically, if I keep being Skandar's blacksmith, they'll kill me. Dramatic, isn't it?'

The fire in Mitchell's hair flared in shock.

'Why are you so calm about this?' Skandar asked Jamie. 'What are we going to do?'

Olu stopped pacing and put a hand on Skandar's shoulder. 'The way I see it – I was right. Dorian Manning and the Silver Circle have to be behind this. He's made no secret of the fact that he doesn't want a spirit wielder training in the Eyrie. And what's the easiest way to stop you training?'

'Threatening my friends!'

'Not quite.' Olu shook his head. 'You being declared a nomad. Think about what's happened already.' He counted on his fingers. 'They tried to stop Jamie making your armour; they tried to stop you getting a saddle; Dorian Manning threatened the freed spirit wielders so no one but the Executioner would teach you; *and* he keeps talking to the *Hatchery Herald* about "new suspects" for the wild unicorn killings, about the Weaver having an accomplice. Combined with the truesong, of course people would start turning against you—'

'The Brilliant Boot Company wouldn't even open for Skandar this morning,' Bobby added.

'Don't you see?' Olu Shekoni's voice was serious. 'Of course Manning would love to arrest you for the killings, but he has no proof. Instead, they're trying to disrupt your training so you don't make it through the jousting tournament at the end of the year. Your fellow Nestlings wouldn't even *race* you last week. It's the simplest way to get you out of the Eyrie – and out of its protection – without the Commodore realising they're interfering.'

Sara looked up from Jamie's swollen face. 'Which is exactly why nobody will be giving in to these bullies.'

'I can't let you risk—'

'You're not *letting* us do anything.' Sara put down her sponge. 'So the people with the power don't like spirit wielders. What if they decide they don't like healers next? Or saddlers? Or riders with flaming hair? Nothing gives the Silver Circle the right to abuse their power. If we give in now, where will the Island end up?'

'Your mum is so awesome,' Bobby whispered loudly to Flo. 'She could take down President Dusty Meatloaf any day.'

Flo attempted a smile.

The love in Olu's eyes as he looked at Sara was the kind of fierce, unswerving love Skandar had never really seen before. He couldn't help but wonder whether Dad had looked at Erika Everhart that way once.

'Why don't you children set the table? We'll eat outside in the square.'

Skandar was handed a colourful stack of plates and followed Bobby, who had fists full of cutlery. Halfway into the treehouse-lined square she dropped a handful of forks and began searching for them in the grass. She was still bent over when Skandar passed her, and he noticed the whistle of air in her throat as she struggled for breath. A panic attack.

Flo and Mitchell had also noticed Bobby – and so had Falcon's Wrath, who careered into the square, eyes rolling from black to red as she rushed to her rider in concern. The quartet – now used to Bobby having occasional panic attacks – sprang into quiet action. Mitchell prised the remaining forks from her hands, Flo relieved Skandar of his stack of plates, and they busied themselves elsewhere. Skandar stayed. Falcon stood over both riders protectively as Skandar sat cross-legged next to Bobby and tried not to wince as she gripped his hand tight, her breaths coming in ragged gasps just like they had the first time he'd found her like this in Falcon's stable over a year ago. Skandar knew now that the panic attacks weren't necessarily brought about by anything he might notice as stressful or anxiety-inducing. He couldn't properly understand them, but he could be there for Bobby when they came.

Twenty minutes later, Bobby had recovered and it was as though the serious conversations about the Silver Circle had never happened. All of them – the Shekoni family, the quartet, seven young healer and saddler apprentices, and Jamie – sat at a large round table that was more tree than furniture. The legs were twisted roots, the chairs had branches instead of arms, the tabletop was ringed like a trunk and Skandar – who had forgotten all about feeling nervous – had accidentally dislodged a bird's nest with his knee when he'd sat down between Jamie and Flo.

'Your hair is *very* cool, though,' Jamie said to Mitchell. 'If I was a rider I'd definitely want to be a fire wielder like you.'

'That makes sense,' Mitchell replied. 'Fire and blacksmiths are sort of meant for each other.' He suddenly realised what he'd said, a blush creeping up under his brown skin. 'My dad doesn't like my hair much; he says it's too showy,' Mitchell rushed on, almost tripping over his words – which was very unlike him. 'Only one strand of his hair turned to water and I get his point about that being more sophisticated. And he already thinks that Red's too smelly and scruffy. You see, he wants me to become Commodore one day. It's his dream for me, now I'm through the Training Trial.'

'But Commodores have had all kinds of mutations!' Jamie said. 'Your hair is definitely the best I've seen. And isn't your dad a water wielder? That would explain why he doesn't get it.'

Mitchell looked even more gloomy. 'Why he doesn't get *me*.'

'Do you even *want* to be Commodore?' Jamie peered into Mitchell's face with his mismatched green and brown eyes. He looked a little threatening, with bruises blooming across his pale face.

'Who wouldn't?'

Jamie shrugged. 'That's what my parents used to say about being a bard.'

Mitchell moved his food around his plate miserably.

Jamie changed the subject. 'Did you read that new book on the evolution of armour?'

'Oh yes! Completely fascinating!' Mitchell sounded relieved they'd moved back to the safer territory of books.

Bobby's voice floated over from the opposite side of the table. 'But you *must* know who I am!'

Amran, the healer apprentice she was talking to, looked scared. 'Of course, I do. You're Bobby Bruna. You're one of Skandar Smith's best friends.'

'No! I mean, yes –' Bobby looked like she might stab him with her fork – 'but that's not what I'm famous for. I won the Training Trial! I'm the best in my year, future Commodore—'

Skandar turned to Flo, who had barely touched her food. 'How was your Silver Circle meeting?'

Flo speared a potato with her fork. 'It wasn't completely awful. The closest Silver Circle member to my age is Rex Manning; he only left the Eyrie a couple of years ago and he gave me some good tips for controlling Blade. Rex—'

'Dorian Manning's son?' Skandar spluttered.

'Don't say it like that!' Flo laughed. 'He was actually nice. He told me he used to skip training sometimes just to have a break from all that power at the end of his reins. It was reassuring to hear someone else talking like that. Understanding that riding a silver isn't always a good thing.' She shrugged. 'I suppose the meeting did make me feel a little less alone – to know there are people who really understand what it's like to have a silver. And Blade seemed to like it a lot in the Stronghold.'

It wasn't long before everyone started arguing about the wild unicorn killings.

'Well, my dads say it's definitely the Weaver. They're convinced,' said Caroline, a pink-faced, blonde-haired saddler apprentice. Ebb had told Skandar that the apprentices who lived at the Shekoni treehouse were all in their first year of training. It hadn't been that long since they'd failed to open the Hatchery door.

'My mum says the same,' Amran agreed. 'But she says the Weaver must be getting help from the freed spirit wielders.' He looked suddenly guilty. 'No offence to you, Skandar. Obviously. My mum is always a bit funny about spirit wielders.'

Sara looked very irritated with her healer apprentice. 'The dead wild unicorns have physical wounds. Mortal wounds. That suggests it's not magic killing them, and definitely *not* the spirit element.'

'But how can a wound kill a wild unicorn?' Olu shook his head. 'It feels wrong somehow – don't you think? The immortals have always been here. Killing them feels . . .'

'Evil,' Skandar said bluntly, remembering how the wild unicorns had helped him defeat the Weaver.

'And there's the warning in that truesong,' Ebb said, his forehead crinkling into a frown. 'What if there's some kind of punishment for killing the wild unicorns? What if that bard was right?'

The adults chuckled. 'I wouldn't worry too much about that.' Sara smiled at her son. 'As Commodore Kazama keeps telling everyone, the "revenge" the bard sang about was symbolic. How could it not be?'

'I think truesongs are a load of nonsense,' Mitchell scoffed. 'That's what my mother says anyway.' Mitchell's mother, Ruth Henderson, was a librarian at Fourpoint's water library. Mitchell's parents didn't live together any more, and by all accounts his mum was a lot nicer than his dad. Skandar felt sad whenever he thought about Mitchell choosing the Taiting saddle over the Nimroe because of Ira's expectations.

'Is someone jiggling their leg under the table?' Bobby asked. 'It's moving – a lot.'

Skandar looked down, but the tabletop was too blurry to focus on. His chair started to shake, then the branches overhead.

Apples plummeted to the ground, birds took off from the treetops in feathered clouds, and Skandar felt Scoundrel's fear mix with his own in the bond.

'EARTHQUAKE!' Sara and Olu shouted together. 'Get away from the trees!'

Skandar and Flo sprinted down the flower-filled hill towards their unicorns. Mitchell was slower, helping the injured Jamie to his feet first. Bobby was already on Falcon's back, pulling an apprentice up with her.

The ground was still quaking as Skandar reached Scoundrel. The unicorn wouldn't calm down, his eyes flashing from red to black to red. His head turned, black horn pointing back towards the Shekonis' treehouse. Mitchell and Jamie reached Red – who was just as scared, smoke rising off her back. Silver Blade bellowed out into the distance, Flo trying to calm him. Bobby and the apprentice dismounted when the slate-grey unicorn started screeching uncontrollably. Further up the hill, Sara desperately tried to calm the unicorn patients.

There was an almighty crash. One of the apprentice treehouses had toppled from its tree and lay in a colourful pile of splintered wood.

The earth stilled.

'Is everyone okay?' Olu called.

Sara counted her healer apprentices; Olu counted his saddler apprentices. And then they came to stand among the crushed wildflowers.

Sara pulled her daughter into a hug. 'Thank goodness we were all outside.'

'Are earthquakes common here?' Mitchell asked.

Skandar was dreading the answer.

'We do have them,' Olu said quietly. 'But we've never had one that big.'

'That bard sang something about earthquakes, remember?' Bobby said, voicing exactly what Skandar was thinking.

Flo turned to her parents. 'You don't think that's what the song meant, do you? You don't think that was the Island's revenge?'

'Two more wild unicorns were found dead this morning,' Jamie murmured.

'I think it's just a coincidence,' Mitchell said boldly.

'I thought you didn't believe in coincidences,' Skandar retorted.

'Well.' Sara gave Flo another squeeze, and then motioned for them all to follow her back up Wildflower Hill. 'Even if that *was* the Island's revenge for the wild unicorn deaths, frankly it wasn't very impressive. None of us are hurt, and we can easily rebuild a treehouse. If that's all the Island's got, then I think we can breathe a sigh of relief.'

But Skandar didn't think she sounded convinced – and he couldn't shake the fear that had gripped him since the earthquake had hit. What if the bard's song was telling the truth? What if the Island was going to take revenge for the deaths? And what if that was *exactly* what the Weaver wanted?

Since the quartet had returned from Wildflower Hill, Skandar had been scanning the *Hatchery Herald* for other disturbances that could be linked to the truesong. Mitchell had told Skandar he was being ridiculous when he pointed out a report of a river flooding in the water zone – 'It's the water zone; it always floods!' – or an out-of-control bushfire in the fire zone – 'Clue is in the name, Skandar! They have fires *all* the time.' – but Skandar couldn't help worrying. If the Weaver was killing wild unicorns, then he felt responsible. She was his mum, after all. And he needed to know what she was planning.

But one day in late September, Skandar didn't need to search for anything about the wild unicorn deaths or disturbances. The evening *Hatchery Herald* headline read:

THE IMPOSSIBLE EIGHT:
WILD UNICORN BODY COUNT NOW APPROACHING DOUBLE FIGURES.

Eight?

Skandar tried to distract himself by visiting the post trees on the way to the stables. The five trunks – one each for first-year Hatchlings, second-year Nestlings, third-year Fledglings, fourth-year Rookies and fifth-year Predators – were dotted with holes that held metal capsules, where riders' letters were stored. He removed his half-blue, half-gold capsule from the Nestling tree, expecting to be disappointed again. When he twisted off the top to find a letter inside, Skandar's heart soared. Kenna had written back! Finally! But as he ripped open the parcel – a packet of Jelly Babies for Scoundrel dropping to the forest floor – he realised it wasn't from his sister at all.

DEAR SKANDAR,

IT'S DAD. HOPE EVERYTHING'S WELL WITH YOU AND SCOUNDREL. I STILL CAN'T BELIEVE HOW BRILLIANT YOU WERE IN THE TRAINING TRIAL.

KENNA WON'T BE WRITING FOR A WHILE – SHE WAS QUITE AFFECTED BY
HER TRIP TO THE ISLAND AND IS TRYING TO LOOK AFTER HERSELF. SHE
MISSES YOU A LOT, BUT SHE THINKS NOT WRITING WILL HELP HER FORGET
ABOUT UNICORNS, JUST FOR A BIT. SO YOU'RE STUCK WITH ME INSTEAD!
HOW'S TRAINING GOING? WHICH SADDLE DID YOU GET?
    WRITE SOON,
    DAD X

Skandar felt like the ground had disappeared beneath his feet. His stomach hurt so much he thought he might be sick. Kenna wasn't going to write to him any more. He replaced the canister in a daze, blinking back tears. He hadn't realised how much he'd wanted to hear her voice – even in a letter – until it had been taken away. What if she never felt happier? What if he never heard from her again?

He kept rereading the letter as he readied Scoundrel for bed. The black unicorn wasn't impressed by this and kept attention-seeking – at one point snatching the paper with his teeth. The third time Skandar took the letter out of his pocket, Scoundrel roared and sent a blast of cold air at his rider.

'Hey! Oh, I'm sorry.' Skandar ran his hand along Scoundrel's black coat before he retrieved the letter from the straw. 'I'm sorry for ignoring you.'

The unicorn snorted a few indignant sparks, but then – fixing Skandar with a black stare – brushed his wing gently against Skandar's back. Scoundrel knew. He always knew.

The whole treehouse went to bed late that night. Mitchell, Flo and Bobby had visited their elemental dens for the first time – each wearing the jacket of their own allied element – and returned to the treehouse after dark. They came in quietly, obviously trying not to make Skandar feel even worse about being barred from the Well. His heart squeezed, so grateful for them as they started discussing training in the morning instead of the exciting night they'd all just had.

Skandar grinned. 'Aren't any of you lot going to tell me what I'm missing?'

'We thought you wouldn't want to hear about our dens,' Flo said gently, tracing a hand over a plant she'd painted on her earth wall.

'Honestly?' Skandar sighed. 'I could do with the distraction.' And he told them all about Kenna not wanting to write to him any more.

Bobby tried to be reassuring. 'I wouldn't worry; my little sister never writes to me. She's far too busy getting top marks in all her Hatchery classes. She's even more perfect than me – if you can believe that.'

'Umm, Bobby,' Flo said. 'You have never *ever* mentioned your sister before.'

'Never,' Mitchell confirmed.

Bobby shrugged. 'She's the youngest, so she always used to get *all* the attention at home. And my parents think she's such an *angel*. It was all, "Bobby, you're the oldest, you should be the sensible one", "Bobby, we expected more from you", "Bobby, why can't you behave like your little sister?" It's been quite nice having a break from all that, to be honest. At least for a couple of years – knowing her, she'll be front of the queue for the Hatchery door when her time comes.'

'Why didn't you tell us all this before, Bobby? We could have cheered you up about it,' Flo said, gently.

Bobby shrugged. 'You never asked.'

There was an awkward silence. Skandar decided to change

the subject. 'Come on, then, tell me everything about the dens. I want all the details.'

The three of them exploded with enthusiasm:

'There are tiny caves in the Mine with thousands of diamonds arranged to match the constellations! You can crawl into one all cosy, read a book and pretend you're looking at the night sky.' Flo sighed dreamily.

'And I'd obviously read about how the resident fireflies in the Furnace fly in formation, but they make any shape you want, Skandar! I think it might have been one of the coolest things I've ever seen,' Mitchell said, adjusting the gold fire pin on his T-shirt as though particularly proud of his element tonight.

Bobby's eyes were fizzing with glee like the yellow treehouse wall behind her. 'There was this floor in the Hive, and it had electrified squares, right? And sparks exploded upwards in different colours when we danced on them!'

Flo looked horrified. 'That sounds terrifying.'

Bobby shrugged. 'That's because you're an earth wielder. I don't much like the sound of those fireflies either. Ever seen one in the daytime? They're dead creepy.'

Eventually Mitchell and Skandar got into their hammocks, but it turned out neither of them could sleep – Skandar because of Dad's letter; Mitchell because of all the excitement in the Furnace. So instead they started throwing around theories about how the Weaver was killing the wild unicorns.

'If we could work out *how* the Weaver is killing the wild unicorns – or whoever it is . . .' Mitchell tailed off, looking guiltily at Skandar.

'I think it's her too,' Skandar said quietly. 'I don't mind you saying it.'

'Okay, well, maybe if we knew how it was happening it would help Commodore Kazama catch her. And that might be something *we* can find out from the elemental libraries!' Mitchell sounded very excited by this prospect. 'My research skills *are* exceptional.'

'The false bonds she made last year,' Skandar said, trying to match his friend's enthusiasm. 'She was messing with the wild unicorns then, making bonds they never should have had. I wonder if that's how she's killing them?'

'But mortal wounds!' Mitchell said, getting so animated he jumped out of his hammock. 'The wild unicorn we found was bleeding! That doesn't seem like magic, just like Flo's mum said at—'

CRASH.

Mitchell had fallen over Skandar's rucksack.

Skandar scrambled down to help him – and realised there was money all over the floor . . . *His* money.

Mitchell held up a wad of notes and looked up at Skandar curiously. 'What's all this?'

Skandar blushed scarlet. He shared almost everything with Mitchell, but this – this was his secret thing. 'It's from my rider's allowance. I'm saving up,' he said evasively, starting to stuff the notes back into the rucksack.

'No wonder you need new boots!' Mitchell said. 'Have you bought *anything* since you arrived on the Island?'

'I told you – I'm saving up.'

'What for? A golden saddle?'

Skandar bit his lip and decided to tell the truth. 'I have this idea – this dream, I suppose – that maybe one day if I made it through the Eyrie and I became a Chaos rider, maybe my dad and Kenna could move here. My sister's so unhappy on the

Mainland that she's stopped writing to me! I thought maybe they could both live on the Island. With me. One day. I don't know if it's allowed, but Kenna's technically half Islander and . . .' He tailed off, face burning.

'You're saving up for a treehouse?'

Skandar nodded.

Mitchell blinked. 'You know, I really can't believe I thought you were evil when I first met you.'

Skandar smiled weakly. 'I know it's a stupid dream. I just miss them.' He thought of Dad's letter and the floor seemed to wobble again. Nothing was right without Kenna.

Mitchell bent down to help collect up the money. 'It's not stupid, Skandar. It's family.'

That night, Skandar tossed and turned in his hammock, unable to sleep, going over the events of the past few weeks. '*Family*,' Mitchell had said. Right now his family was back on the Mainland, Kenna refusing to write to him. Agatha was family here, but it wasn't the same. Like Olu had said, he was going to be taught the spirit element by the Executioner – the rider who'd used her element to *kill* all the other spirit unicorns. He didn't trust her; he wasn't even sure whether she'd brought him to the Island last year to stop the Weaver or help her. What on earth was their first training session going to be like?

Attracting a wild unicorn to the training ground hadn't exactly helped the whispers about him. Ever since, there had been rumours that Skandar's apparent ability to summon wild unicorns was how he was helping the Weaver to kill them. And although Jamie had recovered from his injuries, Skandar still felt so guilty. *And* the water wielders had voted against allowing him into the Well. He felt like more of an outsider than ever.

Skandar was adjusting his pillow again when—

'OUCH!'

'What's going on?' Mitchell sprang out of his hammock to light the lantern.

'Something spiked me!' Skandar cried, feeling for the offending object. It clattered to the floor.

Skandar dived for it, blinking in the sudden flare of light. It was a metal feather. The long thin piece of grey metal came to a sharp point – the point that had poked Skandar. On either side there were tiny delicate pieces in lighter and darker shades, intricately woven to create a striped effect. It was one of the most beautiful objects Skandar had ever seen.

'Flaming fireballs!' Mitchell cried, rushing over and pointing enthusiastically at the object between Skandar's fingers. 'It's a *peregrine falcon* feather, Skandar!'

Mitchell was grinning, beside himself with excitement, as though expecting Skandar to know why this was a big deal.

'Oh, right!' Mitchell shook his head, his hair glowing in the low light. 'Of course – Mainlander. I forget sometimes. Did it come with a note?'

Skandar went back to his hammock and searched. As a last resort, he shook out his blanket and a small note fell to the floor:

SKANDAR SMITH & SCOUNDREL'S LUCK
9 OCTOBER 6 P.M.
SUNSET PLATFORM

'What's this all about?' Skandar said, reading the note.

Mitchell was hopping up and down. 'Skandar! It's an invitation! You got in!'

'An invitation to what? And I've never even heard of the Sunset Platform!' Skandar protested, feeling more like a Mainlander than ever.

Mitchell explained that the Sunset Platform was the highest point in the whole of the Eyrie, and he was just starting to give extremely detailed directions when Bobby burst into their bedroom in her pyjamas, looking murderous. 'Could you *be* any louder? Some of us actually want to train tomorrow! What could you possibly be—'

'Skandar got invited to join the Peregrine Society!' Mitchell's face was shining with pride.

'The what?' Bobby snapped.

Mitchell took a deep breath. 'The Peregrine Society! Named after the peregrine falcon – the fastest bird in the world. All they care about is how fast you fly. They don't even allow you to wear an elemental jacket. They're the absolute coolest group in the Eyrie. Really secretive, invitation-only, and some of the best riders EVER were members. My father was.' Mitchell's face fell, but he continued. 'They must have been watching you and noticed how fast you and Scoundrel fly. You *are* really fast,' he added, handing Skandar the metal feather.

'But I didn't even try out,' Skandar spluttered. 'How could I be in it?'

'My friend, you don't *try out* for the Grins—' Mitchell started, but Bobby spoke over him loudly.

'Because you're Skandar Smith.' Then she turned on her heel and slammed the door behind her.

CHAPTER SIX

THE PEREGRINE SOCIETY

Bobby avoided Skandar for most of the next fortnight. On the day of the Peregrine Society meeting, the Nestlings had their first real jousts against each other. Skandar thought Bobby's enthusiasm for knocking people off their unicorns would mean she forgot all about their argument, but she intentionally rode a pristine Falcon away from where Blade, Scoundrel and Red were lined up on the training ground, and stood next to Mariam and Old Starlight instead.

The air training session didn't get any better from there. The only way to describe it was a complete and absolute shambles. The armoured Nestlings were separated between four long training pistes marked out by wooden stakes. Pairs of unicorns would gallop towards each other at full speed, while their riders attempted to summon air elemental weapons and score points. By sheer luck, Skandar and Mitchell were jousting each other first. Scoundrel seemed very keen to start galloping towards his fiery best friend at the other end of the piste, and Skandar had a tough job holding him back.

First whistle. The black unicorn threw himself forward, his whole mane sparking with electricity. Skandar summoned the air element into the bond, his palm glowing yellow; Mitchell did the same at the other end, Red's hooves burning the ground as she thundered towards Scoundrel.

Second whistle. Skandar tried to stay in his saddle, hold on to his reins with his left hand, and remember how to shape a small lightning sword with his right. Okay, so it looked a bit more like a large dagger, but he'd done it! Red was only a few metres away now, mane on fire, an impressive pointed lance glowing in Mitchell's hand. Both boys drew their arms back to strike and—

Their unicorns slowed to a walk. Then . . . stopped altogether.

Scoundrel and Red stood either side of the wooden stakes, making little shrieks and squeaks as though they were having a perfectly lovely conversation. The boys' weapons fizzled out pathetically.

'Rehhhhd,' Mitchell groaned. 'We were going to win! Just because Scoundrel's your friend, doesn't mean you don't fight him! Skandar and I are good buddies, but it's perfectly logical that I would try to hit him with a weapon because that is the *whole point of what we're doing.*'

Skandar started to laugh. '*Good buddies?*' he spluttered.

'It's not funny,' Mitchell said. 'We need to practise!'

'It is *kind* of funny, though.' Skandar's eyes were watering now. Scoundrel was hissing through his teeth in rhythm and Skandar wondered whether it was his impression of his rider. The bond was full of joy; Scoundrel loved it when Skandar laughed.

'New pairs!' Instructor Saylor sang cheerfully.

'Flaming fireballs,' Mitchell swore. 'Now we'll have to wait ages for another turn.'

They moved off the piste to make room for Anoushka and Sky Pirate, who were due to joust Mateo and Hell's Diamond. Skandar glanced at Red. 'Umm . . . Mitchell? How is Red so neat and tidy?' Skandar couldn't believe he hadn't noticed before now. The unicorn's red mane was free of tangles for possibly the first time ever, and her blood-red coat gleamed. Red tended to set Mitchell's brushes on fire when he tried to groom her, so they'd come to an understanding months ago that he wouldn't even try.

Mitchell suddenly looked more cheerful. 'I know! I'm not sure what's got into her. This morning I couldn't work out why she wouldn't leave the stable, until she started shrieking when someone walked past with a comb in their hand. She wasn't satisfied until she was completely clean. I'm going to have to start asking Bobby for grooming tips.' Mitchell patted his unicorn's neck. 'I'm actually very pleased. Father did comment on how untidy Red looked at the Training Trial last year and he says if I'm to become Commodore one day we'll need to set a good example.'

'Right,' Skandar said. He wasn't exactly the biggest fan of Ira Henderson, whose main job last year had been keeping spirit wielders locked up.

'Oh, look,' Mitchell said, pointing over at another piste. 'Flo's jousting.'

More accurately, Flo was *trying* to joust. What was actually happening was that Silver Blade would rear up imperiously at one end of the stakes, start galloping and his unicorn opponent would take one look at the mighty silver and swerve off the piste completely. Gabriel and Queen's Price refused to even *start* jousting against Flo and Blade. And things weren't any less terrifying for the riders who managed to keep their unicorns in a straight line. When Flo moulded weapons, her magic was so strong that she seemed to have no control over the elemental allegiance of the weapon or, more alarmingly, its size. Skandar saw Flo mould a flaming spear so long it touched the ground, a lance with such a strong magnet at its point that riders' helmets flew off towards it and an enormous ice mace so heavy it pulled her right out of the saddle.

'I guess that's why she has to go to her Silver Circle meetings,' Skandar murmured to Mitchell as they looked on in horror.

'Watch out, Scoundrel's doing it again,' Mitchell warned suddenly.

Scoundrel's wings were glowing white – the white of the spirit element. An Islander called Ajay yelped from his unicorn Smouldering Menace and started whispering to his earth wielder friend Charlie on Hinterland Magma, who turned to Mabel on Seaborne Lament, who pointed at Scoundrel's ghostly glowing wings – all the bones and sinew now visible between his black feathers.

Skandar sighed. This had been happening a lot lately. Scoundrel seemed to be so happy to be able to use his own element freely that it didn't matter one bit if it brought Skandar trouble. If it reminded everyone that he was allied to the same element as the Weaver.

To round off the truly terrible training session, Bobby and Amber's joust had turned into more of a brawl. They too had come to a standstill, but instead of their weapons fizzling out like Mitchell's and Skandar's had, they were moulding any and every weapon they'd learned in training, from flaming sabres to granite axes.

Instructor Saylor's whole neck crackled with electricity when she eventually managed to get between them. 'Choose one element. Choose one weapon. *That* is jousting etiquette. I expected better from my air wielders.'

Falcon's Wrath wasn't listening. She took the opportunity to bite a chunk of flesh out of Whirlwind Thief's hindquarters.

Neither Bobby nor Amber looked very sorry to have broken the rules either.

That evening, Bobby was nowhere to be seen as Flo and Mitchell waved Skandar off to his first Peregrine Society meeting.

'Be careful,' Flo warned by the treehouse door. 'My mum says the Peregrine Society is really dangerous. They fly so fast that they get in tons of accidents!'

'You have to tell me everything when you get back,' Mitchell said desperately. 'I'll wait up!'

'Okay, I'll be careful.' Skandar grinned at them, but he didn't miss the doom on Flo's face as she waved goodbye.

On his way down to the wall a group of Hatchlings scattered, squawking like startled birds as Skandar crossed a swinging bridge towards them. And as he neared a pair of third-year Fledglings, they halted their conversation abruptly; the whisper of 'spirit wielder' hung in the air as he jumped to the ground to enter the east door of the wall. Skandar gritted his teeth, wishing he could prove it was the Weaver killing the wild unicorns – then at least *he* wouldn't be a suspect any more.

But Skandar wouldn't let the whispers affect his good mood. He was going to his first Peregrine Society meeting – he'd never been invited to join anything back on the Mainland! He passed the time before six o'clock hanging out with Scoundrel in his stable: brushing his ebony coat to make it gleam, polishing his hooves with oil, combing his tangled mane and straightening his sparking feathers. When Skandar opened the packet of Jelly Babies he'd received with Dad's most recent letter, the unicorn practically bit off Skandar's hand as he fished out Scoundrel's favourite red flavour.

As he watched him chomping, Skandar felt a bubble of Scoundrel's joy, followed by a whoosh of his own sadness. Although the Jelly Babies must taste the same to Scoundrel, it didn't feel right Dad sending them rather than Kenna. Skandar was desperate to write to her, to try to help somehow, but what could he say? He couldn't stop being a rider. He couldn't change Kenna failing the Hatchery exam. And after what Dad had said in the letter, Skandar was worried that hearing from him would upset Kenna even more.

The clock on the wall opposite Scoundrel's group of stables struck six. In a panic Skandar tore off his green jacket, pinned the metal peregrine feather to his black T-shirt and saddled Scoundrel up. The unicorn kicked up sparks of indignation as Skandar pulled him through to the clearing. Jumping on, Scoundrel took off over the four fault lines crossing at the Divide and soared into the open sky. They circled the green canopy, and it didn't take long for Skandar to spot the Sunset Platform. A small group of unicorns were gathered on a large metal circle with criss-crossed legs attaching it to the branches of the trees below. It was *very* high.

'Come on, boy.' Skandar pointed Scoundrel towards the platform. 'Let's go for a neat landing, okay?'

It wasn't neat – Scoundrel's landings rarely were – but at least they didn't miss the platform altogether. As Skandar dismounted he noticed that the centre of the platform had a big brass sun moulded into it. Round the edge were birds carved in rough 'M' shapes with initials under their wings.

'And that makes eight.'

The voice belonged to a boy who looked about Rookie – fourth-year – age. He had tawny brown skin and black hair that arched over his head like a cresting wave, the white tips frothy. The water wielder's unicorn snarled at Scoundrel, who hissed back. Skandar could feel his own unicorn's anxiety in the bond – *she could definitely take me down in a fight.*

'Welcome to the Peregrine Society, Skandar Smith and Amber Fairfax.'

Skandar jolted at hearing Amber's name, and, sure enough, to his left the air wielder stood proudly beside Whirlwind Thief. She refused to look in Skandar's direction, her upturned nose more prominent than ever. Bobby was going to be even more annoyed now that Amber had been invited to the society too.

'I'm Squadron Leader Rickesh, and this is Tidal Warrior.' Rickesh gestured to the enormous unicorn standing beside him. Skandar thought the unicorn's colour was called 'bay' – a dark brown coat with a black mane and tail. 'All of you have shown exceptional flying ability, and that is exactly what the Peregrine Society is about. Once you're in, you're a Grin for as long as you stay in the Eyrie. You'll notice there aren't any Preds in the society this year. Nobody in that year has ever been fast enough to be invited. That's the way it goes. We're the Eyrie's elite flying squad – we don't care how old you are or which element you're allied to. We don't even care if you're a spirit wielder.' Rickesh winked at Skandar. 'All we care about is how fast you can fly.'

Even though Amber was here, Skandar felt his chest inflate

with happiness. This was the first place in the Eyrie – outside his treehouse – where there hadn't been whispers about him being a spirit wielder. Although he'd left his jacket behind, nobody had even stared at the skeletal spirit mutation on his bare arm. Who cared about not being allowed in the water den? The other Grins were nodding at him; some smiled encouragingly. Here he and his unicorn could just be Skandar and Scoundrel, without being stared at or accused of being the Weaver's successor and killing unkillable beasts.

'The peregrine falcon is the fastest bird in the world,' Rickesh continued, his voice hushed.

'Here he goes.' A Rookie with red hair rolled her eyes.

Rickesh made a sweeping gesture with his hand. 'When a peregrine falcon dives, it can reach speeds of over three hundred kilometres per hour, making it the fastest animal on the planet. That's what we aspire to.'

Skandar recalled the dive he and Scoundrel had done before the first training session of the year, when they'd been racing Bobby and Falcon. Perhaps Rickesh, or one of the other members of the society, had seen it? Perhaps that was why they were here?

'As squadron leader, I plan our training for the year. If you have any problems, you come to me. Last year our squadron leader was Nina Kazama; you might have heard of her?' There were a few chuckles. 'Countless Commodores were Grins. Being fast wins Chaos Cups.'

The red-haired girl cleared her throat. Rickesh put a hand on her bare white shoulder. 'And this is Flight Lieutenant Primrose, my second in command.' Skandar noticed that her eyebrows were knitted from tiny flames. 'Prim might have a flowery name, but, let me tell you, she will annihilate all of you in the skies. She and Winter Wildfire hold the record for the fastest one-hundred-metre sprint ever recorded at the Eyrie. How about a quick demonstration of what we're all about?' Rickesh grinned at the flight lieutenant. 'Go for the double?'

Prim raised a flaming eyebrow. 'Triple.'

Rickesh laughed, shaking his wave-topped head. 'In your dreams.'

'In yours.' Prim winked, and jumped on to Winter Wildfire.

As soon as they were in the air, it was easy to understand why Flo had said that the Peregrine Society was dangerous. Wildfire flew up so high and fast that Skandar could hardly see the ash-grey unicorn. For a moment she was suspended above the Eyrie, her wings hanging by her sides. Then they snapped back, and Prim and Wildfire plummeted so fast towards the Eyrie wall that it seemed impossible they weren't going to hit it. They were going to crash. They were— No. The grey unicorn rolled sideways in the air over and over, Prim keeping low and clinging to Wildfire's neck. Then they were soaring back to the platform, as though the acrobatics were nothing.

'Whoa!' The other Grins were in awe. 'Triple side-roll!' 'Nice one, Prim!'

'Well, I'll be damned.' Rickesh shook his head, clearly impressed. 'This is going to be a *good* year.'

'Erm, will we be learning to do that . . . soon?' Skandar nervously asked the rider next to him, who had just taken his fingers out of his mouth from whistling his approval.

'This one's impatient to get started on the dangerous stuff, Ricki.'

Skandar gulped. He couldn't stop thinking about what would have happened if Prim had messed up the rolls. Or if she'd fallen. He supposed being a Peregrine meant trying to leave all those worries in the sky behind you.

At some unspoken signal the Peregrines started to mount their unicorns.

'Last one to the edge of the Wilderness doesn't get any marshmallows!' Prim shouted.

There was a horrified gasp from everyone except Amber and Skandar, who had no idea why this was such a big deal. Scoundrel sent a bolt of electricity along the reins to Skandar's hands to try to hurry him up, as the other unicorns took off from the Sunset Platform.

Scoundrel charged after them, his wings jolting Skandar's knees as they opened outwards. The black unicorn ran out of platform very fast, and for a moment his front hooves were dropping towards the Eyrie trees – Skandar's stomach somersaulting as he grabbed the front of his new saddle for balance. But then Scoundrel's great wings were beating faster and faster, propelling him towards the line of unicorns silhouetted against the setting sun as they raced out towards the zones.

Skandar could feel Scoundrel's desperation to catch up spiralling through the bond. He crouched lower on the unicorn's back, making them more streamlined as the wind whipped past his ears in a whistle, the speed making his eyes water.

Now they were level with the Fledglings at the rear of the group.

'I'm Patrick, though people call me "Bolt"– you know, because I'm so fast?' shouted the rider on his left. His mousy hair looked as though it had been electrocuted; the ends sparked and stood up on end. An air wielder mutation. 'And this is Hurricane Hoax.' He pointed to his black unicorn. 'That's Marcus and

Sandstorm's Orbit.' He pointed to the earth wielder boy with a buzz cut, whose unicorn was edging ahead of them. 'He's *trying* to beat me, but he's got no chance against Hoax's wingbeats per minute.' Skandar's heart soared. He'd always loved unicorn speed stats, and now he was a member of a whole group *obsessed* with how fast they could fly.

'Patrick! *Nobody* calls you "Bolt"!' Marcus yelled back. 'And you know we're faster!'

Hoax and Orbit each put on an unbelievable burst of speed and Scoundrel was left struggling to catch up again. It was going to be a while until they could win a race against *these* riders.

Now they were approaching the zones, Skandar could see Rickesh and Primrose out in front, the air zone on one side of them, the fire zone on the other. Somehow Tidal Warrior and Winter Wildfire were able to keep up their speed while carrying out elaborate stunts in the air. But just as Rickesh pulled out of a dive—

FLASH. BANG.

Lightning almost struck Warrior's left wing. Rickesh swerved, but then a tornado came for Prim, and both unicorns dived, screeching in alarm.

FLASH. BANG.

'Skandar! Fly across to the fire zone!' Patrick yelled, panic all over his freckled white face. The other Grins had turned their unicorns round already, and were racing back towards Scoundrel.

FLASH. BANG.

They were caught in the middle of the biggest electrical storm Skandar had ever seen. Forked lightning lit up the sky, then exploded three windmills in the air zone below. Scoundrel was being buffeted this way and that by impossibly strong winds, and Skandar almost slipped out of his saddle. This was no ordinary storm.

The Grins dived and swerved their unicorns like winged acrobats, trying to outfly the storm. But as soon as they were in the fire zone, Skandar realised that this was no better. Smoke billowed from trees burning on the edge of the zone, so thick Skandar could hardly see. He thought of the earthquake on Wildflower Hill, the reports of flooding and fires he'd read about in the *Hatchery Herald*, and he realised what he was seeing.

The Island's revenge. It was really happening.

Suddenly Skandar was furious. Furious with his mother. The truesong was right: killing the wild unicorns had a price. People were going to get hurt, and it was all *her* fault. He bet she didn't even care. She didn't love the Island like he did – all she had ever done was try to destroy it. Anger took hold of his heart and Scoundrel roared with him. He was going to fly to the Wilderness. He was going to find the Weaver. He was going to prove to everyone that this was her fault, not his.

'Skandar! Where are you going?' The question ended in a cough. It was Rickesh, the outline of his wave of hair just visible through the belching smoke.

Skandar kept flying Scoundrel through the fire zone.

'SKANDAR! It's too dangerous. What are you doing?' Warrior was level with Scoundrel now, echoing her rider's warning with a snarl.

Skandar ignored them, intent on reaching the Wilderness.

With a burst of speed, Warrior overtook and blocked Scoundrel.

Scoundrel reared up in protest, screeching at the top of his lungs.

Rickesh's voice was firm. 'I am your squadron leader and this is an order, Skandar. TURN BACK!'

Skandar's anger suddenly evaporated, and he began to cough up ash. 'I'm sorry,' he managed. 'I don't know—'

Rickesh's hair was frothing, his tone severe. 'Just *what* were you trying to prove, Skandar? You could have got yourself killed, or another Grin could have been killed trying to save—' He broke off at the stricken look on Skandar's face. 'Come on,' he said, the smoke still swirling round their unicorns' pulsing wings. 'Let's get you back to the platform.'

As Scoundrel followed Warrior back towards the Eyrie, Skandar felt drained. His anger had engulfed him entirely. And what had he thought he was going to do once he found the Weaver? Fight her alone?

Back on the Sunset Platform, Skandar overheard Prim say, 'Well, that was exciting.'

'Not exactly what I had in mind for my first group flight as squadron leader.' Rickesh sighed. 'The elemental destruction, Prim. It's getting worse.'

Skandar couldn't help but ask, 'Have you seen it like that before?'

Rickesh sighed again. 'I haven't, but Fen –' he pointed over to a rider with short black hair and light brown skin – 'one of the Fledglings, has. She was out flying Eternal Hoarfrost two days ago on a stamina flight and saw landslides tearing through the earth zone.' Rickesh seemed suddenly to remember Skandar's refusal to leave the zone. 'Are you feeling okay now? You seemed . . . confused out in the sky?'

'I . . .' Skandar wasn't sure what to say. 'I'm sorry. I'm fine.'

'I'm glad.' Rickesh nodded. And Skandar was relieved he didn't ask anything else.

'*Please* can we eat now?' asked Fen, the Fledgling who'd seen the landslides. Her mutation made it clear that she was a water wielder – her hands were completely frozen over, clear and glassy like an ice sculpture, with snowflakes for knuckles.

'How about . . . marshmallows? Fresh from the Mainland!' Rickesh retrieved a paper sack from his unicorn's saddlebag and held it triumphantly in the air.

Everyone cheered very loudly, the elemental destruction seemingly forgotten. Prim started setting up a fire pit. She and the other Grins began to collect up crunchy leaves and twigs that had fallen on to the platform; Prim put a hand on her unicorn and summoned flames to ignite the metal bowl of kindling.

Everyone huddled cross-legged round the fire pit to keep off the autumn chill.

'Why marshmallows?' Skandar finally plucked up the courage to ask the rider next to him. She had olive skin and a mass of dark curly hair that, up close, wasn't hair at all but writhing black ringlets of smoke that crackled like a log fire when she moved. The fire wielder looked older than him by a good couple of years.

She smiled. 'About a hundred years ago, the newest member of the Peregrine Society was dared to fly to the Mainland.'

'Dared?'

She laughed at Skandar's shock. 'Peregrines like dares, okay? You'll see. Don't worry, we don't dare each other to fly *that* far any more – the sentinels would catch us. But a century ago, this new member brought back marshmallows, to prove she'd actually made it to the Mainland. And since then – because it was such a daring flight – the Peregrines have toasted marshmallows on the Sunset Platform to welcome their newest recruits.' She handed

Skandar a pink marshmallow. 'So welcome, Skandar. I'm Adela – and that's Smoke-Eyed Saviour.' She pointed to a black unicorn standing with the others, munching on strips of meat rather than sweets. Skandar noticed that Scoundrel's Luck and Whirlwind Thief were eating side by side. Occasionally Scoundrel would toss some bloody meat into the air and Thief would snap at it with overly large bites, as though messing around. Skandar knew unicorns formed their own friendships, but he'd had no idea these two had become closer over the summer break. And he also hadn't realised that Thief was quite so . . . goofy. She seemed the complete opposite to Amber – he'd rarely even seen the air wielder smile.

He stopped watching the unicorns when Patrick sidled up to him and made a fist near Skandar's face, as though he was holding up a microphone. 'And now we're talking to the hero of the hour – or should I say villain, given what we've just seen out in the zones?'

'I'm sorry,' Marcus said, his dark brown face fixed in a grimace, embarrassed by his Fledgling friend. 'Third year in the Eyrie is pretty tough; you'll have to excuse him.'

Patrick persevered. 'Are you helping the Weaver kill the wild unicorns? Are you acting alone? Or are we all mistaken? Care to comment?'

'Patrick, stop it!' Adela said, batting his hand away from Skandar's face.

'A Nestling couldn't kill a wild unicorn,' Rickesh said from across the fire pit. 'The last person to actually *kill* a wild unicorn was the First Rider.'

'Oh, not this again,' Prim said through a mouthful of marshmallow.

'The First Rider?' Skandar asked, secretly pleased that the

squadron leader had defended him in front of everyone.

'Tell the story, Rickesh!'

'Come on, Ricki!'

Rickesh bowed his frozen hair tips to the Grins over the fire. He looked halfway between an old man and a cartoon character.

'I've been telling this story for a long time,' Rickesh said thoughtfully, his audience – including Amber – now hanging on every word. 'My parents told it to me when I was growing up, and their grandparents told it to them – you get the picture.' He winked at Skandar. 'Other riders laughed at their fascination with it. But nobody's laughing now. The Island is waking up; it's angry. You heard the truesong. You all saw the zones tonight. So this old tale of the First Rider has shifted, changed form, the way magic can break out of the moulds we try to place it in.'

The Grins made spooky howling noises, putting on a show for their eccentric squadron leader.

Rickesh held up a hand for silence. 'The First Rider was a fisherman, not much older than a Hatchling, when he washed up at the foot of the Mirror Cliffs. Half drowned, far from home and desperately hungry, the First Rider had no idea how he was going to survive.

'The washed-up fisherman wandered the Island as though something was calling to him: something more than just food or shelter. Until he found *her* – his destined unicorn. Boy and unicorn grew up together, getting stronger and braver every day. She taught him magic, and in return he protected her from the wild unicorns that dominated every corner of the Island.

'Of course, the fisherman couldn't live on the Island without human company for ever. So before long, the First Rider and his unicorn travelled far and wide to bring new humans to the

Island from every corner of the earth. No doubt he would have been a Peregrine like us if he could fly so far and fast. Many people answered the Island's call.'

'Get to the part about the Wild Unicorn Queen!' cried Prim.

Rickesh sighed. 'You have absolutely no respect for the art of storytelling.'

'Bite me.'

Rickesh laughed and continued. 'As every Islander is taught, the First Rider accomplished many noble acts. He built the Hatchery, the Eyrie, founded Fourpoint – although it was called Fivepoint then.' Rickesh raised an eyebrow in Skandar's direction, who blinked in shock. Had they really changed the name of the capital when they'd banned the spirit element?

'But his *most* astonishing act is dismissed as more myth than history: the First Rider's defeat of the queen of the wild unicorns. She was ancient. The most fearsome queen of monsters the Island had ever known. And the First Rider knew that if he did not kill her, his people – the riders – would never be able to live in peace with the wild unicorns. For a wild queen will always wage war on her enemies. So the First Rider and his unicorn faced the Wild Unicorn Queen in combat. And after weeks of battling across the Island, the First Rider found some deep reserve of strength from within the bond itself – and he killed her. The last queen of the wild unicorns.'

'But how? How did he do it?' Amber demanded, hanging on every word.

'Nobody knows.' Rickesh shrugged. 'But the story goes that once she was dead, the First Rider made a weapon from her bones. It's rumoured to have special powers. For centuries riders have searched for the First Rider's tomb in times of trouble, believing the weapon may be hidden within it. But – no luck.'

'Are you saying the gift in the bard's truesong is this weapon from your story?' Skandar breathed. 'A weapon made from the Wild Unicorn Queen's bones?'

Rickesh's eyes were twinkling. 'Perhaps. But I'm less interested in a bone weapon than I am in the question everyone is asking. *Who* is killing the wild unicorns now?'

'It's obviously the Weaver, Ricki,' Fen said. 'We've been through this a hundred times.'

Skandar shifted uncomfortably.

'Maybe,' Rickesh mused. 'But I prefer my theory.'

'What's that?' Skandar asked quickly.

'The First Rider's back.'

Prim actually laughed out loud. 'Don't be ridiculous!'

Rickesh ignored her. 'Back as a vengeful phantom, or perhaps he never died in the first place. Nobody knows where he's buried. The First Rider is the only one who has ever killed a wild unicorn, after all.'

'But why would the First Rider destroy his own island?' Adela asked. 'The truesong tells us these disasters in the zones aren't a coincidence. Three earthquakes last week, and the floating market has been abandoned for days because of flooding.'

'And the electrical storm and wildfires tonight,' Marcus added solemnly.

'Exactly.' Adela nodded at him. 'Why would the First Rider cause the Island to take revenge? Why would he want to hurt his own people? Because that's what's going to happen if these wild unicorns keep getting killed. Fires, floods, earthquakes, storms – there won't be an island left for us if that carries on.'

Prim rolled her eyes. 'A bit dramatic, Adela.'

'You forget – the Island is a big fan of drama,' Rickesh said, toasting another marshmallow over the fire. 'But if last year's anything to go by – Skandar knows that already.' He winked, before popping the sweet into his mouth.

Much later, Skandar crept into the dark treehouse, trying to be as quiet as possible.

'How was it?' Mitchell sat on a beanbag by the stove, a thick book open in his lap.

'You scared me!' Skandar whispered, although he was secretly very pleased he could share Rickesh's story right now – that way he wouldn't forget any details about the tale of the last Wild Unicorn Queen and the First Rider's weapon.

'Well?'

'It was brilliant. But listen, I found something out. About the First Rider.'

When he'd finished, Mitchell said, 'A weapon made of the Wild Unicorn Queen's bones? I don't understand how that would help. How would a weapon *atone* for the immortal deaths? Stop the Island's so-called revenge? Are riders supposed to use it to defeat the wild unicorn killer?'

'I don't know,' Skandar said. 'And it doesn't help that nobody knows where the First Rider's tomb is. Rickesh said something about the weapon being buried with him.'

'I'm not sure Rickesh has many of his facts straight, if I'm honest,' Mitchell said a little snootily. 'Didn't you say one of his other theories is that the First Rider is haunting the Island as a phantom out for revenge? I mean, I'm trying to be more open-minded, but given that I don't believe in truesongs in the first place, it's—'

'Mitchell, the stuff in the truesong really *is* coming true. Tonight the Grins were caught in this huge electrical storm *and* there were wildfires. And the *Hatchery Herald* has been reporting all sorts. I'm sorry, but I don't think you can deny it any more. You like evidence, right? Well, I saw it with my own eyes!'

Mitchell sighed. 'Even if the bard's song is accurate, I still think a legendary bone weapon that solves all your problems is a bit of a stretch. I mean, come on!' Skandar tried to interrupt but Mitchell ploughed on. 'And I don't think that the Island is *actually* taking revenge. Yes, there might be elemental disruption, and, yes, it *might* be linked to the unicorn deaths, but there has to be a more logical explanation than the Island having a tantrum.'

'But the tomb—'

'Look –' Mitchell sighed – 'let's forget about possibly fictitious gifts and long-lost tombs for now. *Stopping* the wild unicorn killings, that's far more important.'

'Well, let's do that, then!' Skandar said desperately. He was sick of doing nothing. Seeing the zones in chaos tonight had ignited a kind of fever in him. The Island was his home. He needed to do something to help. He needed to do something to stop his mum. 'We need—'

Skandar stopped. Bobby had appeared at the bottom of the treehouse trunk.

'Oh, hi, Bobby!' Skandar said. 'Do you want to hear the story that the squadron leader of the Peregrine Society told me. It's—'

'No.'

'Oh. I suppose it is pretty late. Maybe tomorrow, we—'

'No, Skandar. I don't want to hear how you want to go searching for some weapon that can save the Island. I can't—

I can't do this any more.' All the grey feathers on Bobby's arms were standing up, from her wrists to her shoulders.

'Do what? What do you mean?'

'Do you know what other riders say when they meet me?'

Skandar and Mitchell stayed silent.

'Do you remember what that apprentice said at Wildflower Hill?'

'No,' Skandar answered honestly.

Bobby shook her head. 'Of course you don't. He said: *You're Bobby Bruna. You're one of Skandar Smith's best friends.*'

Skandar was completely confused. 'So? Both of those things are true.'

'Argh, Skandar! It isn't about them being true. I *won* the Training Trial. I was the *best* rider in Hatchling year and the first thing people think about when they see me is YOU!'

Skandar was getting annoyed now. 'Most of them are only thinking about me because they believe I'm murdering wild unicorns!'

'It doesn't matter; don't you understand? It doesn't matter whether you're loved or hated, saving the day or destroying the Island. Because of who you are: the only spirit wielder in training, the Weaver's son, the one who defeated her—'

'We *all* defeated the Weaver!'

Bobby was already shaking her head. 'We helped *you*. But I don't want to be your sidekick, Skandar. I want to be the hero of my own story, of my own life – not existing on the edge of yours, waiting to help you save the day. That isn't who I am. It isn't what I need. I can't be me *and* be friends with you.'

It would have hurt less if she'd hit him. Bobby was abandoning Skandar. Just like his mum had on the Mainland.

Just like she had when she'd galloped away on her wild unicorn into the Wilderness.

'You think I wanted this?' Skandar's voice was hoarse with emotion. 'Okay, so I happened to be brought here by my aunt so I could be the only wielder of my element. Big deal! If literally *any* other spirit wielder had been free last year, I wouldn't have had to step up.'

'But you did. And then you were chosen by Shekoni Saddles. And now you've been invited to this bird society too.'

'*Peregrine* Society,' Mitchell corrected her.

'Shut UP, Mitchell!' Bobby shouted, almost in tears.

'Is this really about some stupid society? If it means you'll stay friends with me then I won't go again,' Skandar said desperately. He was angry, but he didn't want to lose Bobby. Nothing was worth that.

'Haven't you been listening at all?' Bobby practically screamed at him. 'It's not about some society, it's about all the stuff that's just going to happen to you because you're the only spirit wielder. Because your mum's the Weaver. Because you're on this noble quest to get your element back into the Eyrie! It's about not wanting to live in your shadow!'

'None of that is my fault!'

'Unlike Mitchell, I actually *want* to become Commodore one day. But I'm a Mainlander. I need stuff like a Shekoni saddle and an elite flying squad membership to make that happen. Instead all I end up doing is getting tangled up in *your* problems and getting distracted, and then *you're* the one who gets invited to the special societies. That can't keep happening! I have to focus on my future, not help you be a hero.'

Mitchell tried to intervene. 'Roberta, you're in our quartet.

How do you propose to avoid Skandar for the next four years?'

'I'm not going to leave the quartet or anything,' Bobby mumbled, and Skandar felt relief flood through him. 'But I think I need . . .' She hesitated. 'I think I need to branch out.'

'What are you?' Mitchell snapped. 'A tree?'

Bobby hesitated again. 'I need to make different friends – to spend time with people who don't have to worry about musical prophecies, who don't drag their friends on quests every five minutes!'

'That's not fair!' Skandar protested.

'Life's not fair –' Bobby pointed at the metal feather attached to Skandar's T-shirt – 'obviously.'

CHAPTER SEVEN

MENDER

The Peregrine Society meeting, falling out with Bobby, and Dad's letter about Kenna's unhappiness almost made Skandar forget he was starting spirit training with Agatha. Almost. Scoundrel seemed very confused the next day when Skandar appeared by the Eyrie's elemental walls to collect him for the training session.

It was late afternoon, and the younger unicorns usually spent this time of day on their own – play-fighting or hunting while their riders studied above in the treehouse libraries. It was different for the older riders. Some were attending theory classes given by former Commodores and council members, to prepare them for taking part in running the Island one day. Others were still down on the training grounds with their unicorns, where Chaos riders occasionally taught specialist elemental masterclasses.

'C'mon, Scoundrel!' Skandar called towards the group of unicorns dotted around the hill.

Scoundrel looked up, his black horn glistening in the sunshine and then . . . went back to eating some kind of fluffy woodland creature. A squirrel?

'Don't make me come down there,' Skandar threatened.

Scoundrel turned right round so he was facing away from his rider. Smoke started rising off his back as if to say, *Not now, I'm busy.*

Skandar started down the hill, avoiding the elemental debris from a unicorn fight going on over his head. 'Oi, Scoundrel! Spirit training, remember?'

As the coloured shapes resolved themselves into unicorns Skandar recognised, he felt a little spark of hope in his heart. Scoundrel was eating with Red and Falcon; Blade stood a little way off, watching the other three intensely. If Falcon was still hanging out with the other quartet unicorns, then maybe that meant Bobby would change her mind.

Unfortunately, Scoundrel did not want to leave his friends *at all.* He was so annoyed that, as they passed the earth wall, he incinerated a whole line of parsnips and potatoes; it smelled a bit like a roast dinner.

Half an hour later, Agatha was waiting for them at the Nestling plateau entrance. This would be their first spirit training session and Skandar had absolutely no idea what to expect. He should be excited to train in his own element – that was what he'd bargained for with Commodore McGrath, after all. But he didn't trust Agatha and he was still angry with her for sending him to the Weaver without any warning about her true identity. Not to mention he found his aunt kind of intimidating. Mix all that in with the horror that she'd killed all the spirit unicorns on the Island when she'd been the Executioner, and he couldn't exactly say he was looking forward to training with her.

Like the other Eyrie instructors, Agatha now wore a cloak in the colour of her element – bright white – though Skandar noticed the bottom was already covered with a layer of mud. She didn't say a word until Scoundrel was in the centre of the earth training ground.

Agatha fixed Skandar with her brown-eyed glare. 'Before we begin, you need to understand how this is going to go. I don't want to talk about Erika. I don't want to explain my actions as Executioner. I won't be accompanying you as a wacky, slightly haphazard aunt on any whimsical adventures. I have no idea *how* to be your aunt, so I think it's best if we just forget about all that. I am mostly bad-tempered, and spending the last fifteen years under constant watch hasn't exactly made my disposition any sunnier.'

Skandar swallowed, tugging at his green jacket sleeve.

'I am only interested in one thing: bringing spirit wielders back to the Island. My job is to get you through the joust at the end of this year – and then through every year until you're a Predator. That was the deal you made, wasn't it?'

'That's right,' Skandar said more strongly. 'That's what I want too.'

'You faced the Weaver as a Hatchling and triumphed.' Agatha began to pace back and forth in front of Scoundrel.

Skandar was surprised by the sudden change in topic. 'Yes, but—'

'That was pure luck.'

Skandar started nervously threading his fingers through Scoundrel's mane. 'Yeah, it was only because my friends—'

Agatha interrupted him again, and it was the first time any warmth had entered her voice. 'But facing the Weaver did show courage. A great spirit wielder needs courage above all things. Do you know why?'

Skandar thought it was safest to shake his head.

'Because a spirit wielder must not shy away from the knowledge that spirit *is* the death element. The power, the vitality, the *life* of a bonded unicorn –' Agatha ran her hand down Scoundrel's white blaze – 'can be snuffed out like a candle, should *you* wish it.'

A wave of revulsion washed over Skandar. How was he ever going to forget that Agatha had been the Executioner if she talked like this?

She continued. 'As spirit wielders, we are closer to the abyss – the negative space, the silent darkness – than other riders. It takes courage to keep choosing to turn away from it. It is exhausting having to make that choice every single day, as we are pulled towards the dark. But choosing good is the battle of a spirit wielder's life and it is a battle that many – like my sister, like me – have not won. When it comes to the end, you may not be able to fight it either. But if you do, there will be no Triumph Tree to show for it. There will be only the knowledge that you fought the darkness and won.'

Skandar swallowed and thought about how – just for a moment – he'd been tempted to join the Weaver last year. About how more recently his anger at his mum had consumed him.

'But enough of that now.' Agatha pulled on both sides of her messy bun to tighten it. 'Let me see you mould that spirit dagger again.'

Scoundrel's Luck screeched as white light filled Skandar's palm. The dagger took form more quickly this time, as though the magic remembered what he'd done before. It gleamed in the air in front of Skandar's eyes, so bright he couldn't look at it directly. He tried to close his hand round the hilt, but somehow his fist kept closing on thin air.

Agatha let out a low chuckle.

Skandar looked up, frustrated. 'Why can't I feel it? In my other elemental classes I've been able to hold weapons of flame, or ice, or—'

'That's your first mistake,' Agatha said. 'Spirit isn't like the others. Weapons made of fire or water are physically there. Spirit is operating on absence – negative space, remember? It exists on a different plane altogether.'

'So that dagger isn't real?' Skandar asked, pointing at it suspended in the air in front of him. 'How come I can see it, then? If it doesn't exist?' This was already infuriating.

'It does exist,' Agatha countered. 'In your mind. In all our minds.'

'How am I supposed to joust with a weapon that isn't there? With a weapon I can't actually touch?' he asked desperately.

'You *can* touch it, and if you throw that dagger – and believe in its existence with enough force – it will knock a rider from their unicorn as effectively as any other elemental weapon. It's like that moment when you're not quite asleep, and you suddenly feel like you've fallen from a great height. Nothing touched you, but you still felt the impact.'

Skandar blinked.

'It's hard to get your head round, I know. But you have to train yourself to feel where the dagger *should* be. Try closing your eyes.'

Skandar's mind was reeling. This was all way too confusing. But he did as Agatha asked. He summoned the dagger again and this time the white blade was longer, the hilt more ornate. Satisfied, Skandar took a breath and felt for the handle. Just air. He tried again – his hand went all the way through it and the weapon blinked out.

'Argh!' Skandar cried in frustration.

'You haven't closed your eyes,' Agatha chided.

Skandar shut them, irritated. And at last, after several agonising moments, he managed to take hold of the glowing dagger's hilt.

'That's it!' Agatha actually sounded pleased. 'Now try throwing it!'

Skandar opened his eyes, bent back his elbow and then . . . lost his grip on the dagger completely. It disappeared in the blink of an eye.

Agatha coached Skandar until he was able to summon and throw the dagger a few metres. While he was sweating with the effort, Agatha explained more about jousting with the spirit element.

'As you know, once the second whistle is blown you only have the chance to pick one element and one weapon to use. But one of the benefits of spirit is that its weapons are a little more . . . flexible than that. Because the weapons hover between the real and the imaginary, your attack can be intentionally confusing.'

Skandar waited, not quite understanding.

'For example, you could throw a dagger from one direction and make it appear from another. It takes a lot of concentration, but I've seen it done.'

'And it isn't against the rules?' Skandar checked. He was suddenly full of excitement about the spirit element.

Agatha laughed. 'This is the Eyrie, Skandar. Haven't you

realised they're not big on rules when it comes to anything competitive?'

Skandar was about to throw another dagger when a dapple-grey unicorn crashed through the Nestling plateau gate.

Skandar froze, heart hammering. The wild unicorn's eyes glowed like hot coals, its bones creaking and scraping as it moved. There was blood smeared around its bared teeth from a fresh kill. It let out an anguished bellow.

Scoundrel reared up, screeching back.

The wild unicorn was angry. Angry with Skandar.

Scoundrel roared a column of fire, then blasted lightning from his horn, attempting to protect his rider. But the wild unicorn kept advancing, dodging the attacks.

'Throw the dagger, Skandar!' Agatha shouted, fear entering her voice as the wild unicorn pointed its horn right at them and thundered forward, bones screaming.

Skandar didn't need asking twice. He flung the dagger, and as the dapple-grey beast saw the glowing weapon flying towards her, she took off clumsily into the sky, flapping her tattered wings.

'That was the same wild unicorn as . . .' Agatha trailed off as her eyes followed the unicorn's progress round the side of the Eyrie's hill.

'That's the third time I've seen her,' Skandar said, panting. 'But she's never hurt me – hurt us.' Scoundrel's Luck was still growling deeply.

There was something in Agatha's eyes he hadn't seen before. Curiosity, maybe? A little fear; or was it . . . hunger?

'Walk with me, will you?' Agatha asked suddenly, and Skandar dismounted, leading Scoundrel beside them.

Skandar hadn't walked the path up to the Eyrie for a long time, not since before Scoundrel had learned to fly. The sun had sunk completely now, and the lanterns marking the way were the only light as Agatha spoke, her cheekbones shining white through her skin. 'You won't know this yet, but not all wielders of the same element have the same abilities.'

'You mean, some are better at attacking? Or defending?'

Agatha was already shaking her head. 'Not quite. What I mean is that some fire wielders, for example, can do things others can't. They have special gifts. They aren't generally useful in battle, but they can be helpful in other ways.'

'Like what?' Skandar asked eagerly. He couldn't help wondering what Mitchell's gift might be.

'Oh, I don't know,' Agatha said, clearly annoyed to be side-tracked. 'Some fire wielders develop an extremely strong sense of smell, so they can detect smoke from miles away. Very useful for firefighting. Some water wielders can hold their breath under water for hours, like whales.'

'So it's like having a superpower?'

Agatha looked confused. Skandar guessed that the Island hadn't ever needed the concept of superheroes, since it was full of warrior unicorn riders. 'Never mind.'

Agatha continued as though Skandar hadn't spoken. 'Throughout Island history, a small number of spirit wielders have had the ability to bond wild unicorns to their destined riders.'

'To their destined . . .' Skandar was trying to understand. 'So if a thirteen-year-old missed out on trying the Hatchery door and their unicorn hatched wild . . .'

'These gifted spirit wielders and their unicorns could dream together to identify those who should have been destined for one another. Then, using the spirit element, they'd be able to unite them – bond them together,' Agatha finished for him.

Skandar stopped dead. All he could think was *Kenna. Kenna. Kenna.* Scoundrel screeched in protest, impatient for his bloody dinner.

'Skandar?' Agatha touched his elbow, clearly concerned. 'Did you hear me?'

'Even if the rider is over thirteen?' he demanded suddenly, unable to feel his toes. 'Even if the wild unicorn is already wild?'

'Exactly.' Agatha looked slightly alarmed at Skandar's extreme reaction. 'And I've been thinking about that wild unicorn and the fact she seems to be drawn to you, especially when you summon spirit magic. It was a sign, in the old days, that you might have that rare ability. That you might be a Mender.'

Skandar recoiled. 'Mender' sounded a lot like 'Weaver'.

Agatha noticed. '*Not* like the Weaver, making bonds where none should be. Being a Mender is about perfecting a bond that's still waiting to be made. Righting a wrong.'

'Like what I did with Aspen and New-Age Frost last year? Healing the fractures the Weaver had made?'

'No, there doesn't have to be an existing bond for a Mender to make one. Just the potential. If a Mender bonds a wild unicorn to its original destined rider, it will *become* bonded. I've seen it – the horn changes from transparent to coloured, wings fill out, wounds heal – just like that.' Her voice was full of awe.

Skandar's whole body flooded with adrenaline. Questions exploded from his mouth. 'How can I tell which wild unicorn belongs to a rider? How do I bond them? And what about my sister, Kenna? Do you know if she was supposed to be a spirit wielder? Could I bond *her*?'

Skandar had been meaning to ask Agatha about the wild unicorn killings and the Weaver, but suddenly none of that mattered. The shining possibility of Kenna coming to the Island, after all, of her becoming a rider – of Skandar being the one to make her happy again – was more important than any of that. Kenna having a unicorn would fix everything.

Agatha looked more troubled than ever as they stopped under the colourful leaves of the Eyrie's entrance tree. 'These gifts take a while to manifest, and I'm not even certain you *are* a Mender. You've only just started using the spirit element properly. You and Scoundrel aren't at all ready to start dreaming together yet.'

But Skandar was hardly listening. 'So me and Scoundrel have to dream at the same time? How does that work? And in those dreams would *I* see Kenna and *Scoundrel* see the unicorn or would it be both together?' He stopped abruptly. 'Wait – what do you mean we're not ready? I have dreams all the time!'

Agatha looked like she regretted starting the entire conversation. 'Mender dreams are dangerous, Skandar. You can really hurt yourselves.'

An awful thought occurred to Skandar. 'The Weaver's killing the wild unicorns! What if Kenna's—'

'There are hundreds of wild unicorns – you're getting ahead of yourself. It's something to *consider* in the future. We're concentrating on weapons this year. And that's the end of it.' Her voice was so severe that Skandar didn't dare say anything else out loud, though his mind filled with more questions, more possibilities. *Kenna on the Island. Kenna with her unicorn.*

Agatha gestured for Skandar to open the Eyrie's entrance.

Skandar stared at the wide tree trunk. He'd never done this.

All last year he'd made sure to follow another rider through, too afraid of revealing his true elemental allegiance.

Agatha gave him a sideways look and a toothy grin. 'Go on. It's – as the young people say – pretty wild.'

Mind still swirling with thoughts of Kenna, Skandar placed his palm on the rough trunk. Under his hand, the indentations in the bark began to glow, joining up to form a round web of blinding white light. There were a hundred tiny cracks glowing brighter and brighter, and – instead of the door swinging back in a whirl of water, or a flurry of sand – the imperfections winked out like stars darkened by morning. The hole they left was just big enough for a unicorn to pass through.

Skandar felt like crying. How many riders had trained in the Eyrie and never seen this? How could something so beautiful be evil? Angrily, he thought of all the spirit wielders who had been barred from the Hatchery completely. He thought of Kenna. He was going to find out if she had really been destined for a unicorn. He was going to make things better for her, like she had done for him so many times.

Agatha was still grinning as the trunk reformed behind them. 'I might be a grumpy old nag, but it doesn't half cheer me up to see a rider-in-training light up the Eyrie's entrance again. The spirit magic used the imperfections in the bark, did you see? The negative space – the void between – can be beautiful as well as dangerous.'

'Agatha . . . ' Skandar started.

If she wouldn't answer any more questions about Menders, there was something that had been bothering him, a worry he hadn't fully shared with his quartet. He was too afraid of their answers.

'Instructor Everhart,' she corrected him.

'Sorry, yes. Can I ask – you know that verse in the truesong? The one—'

'*Yet another force grows on this Island: True successor of spirit's dark friend. And the storm it will bring when it rises, Will see all we know brought to an end,*' Agatha recited. 'That one?'

Skandar gulped. He didn't think it was a good sign that she'd learned it off by heart. 'You don't think it's actually about me, do you? That verse? Because I'm not doing anything! I'm just trying to mind my own spirit-wielder business. I don't want storms; I want the opposite of storms!'

'Oh, Skandar.' Agatha shook her head. 'Do *try* not to be so self-centred.'

It wasn't really an answer.

Agatha grasped the ladder of the nearest trunk and called over her shoulder. 'Training session over. Oh, and, Skandar?'

'Yes?'

'Don't tell anyone you could be a Mender. And don't try to find out anything more about it. I know what your quartet are like – you broke into a prison last year.'

'You were *in* that prison last year,' Skandar shot back.

But Agatha had already gone.

Of course, the moment Skandar entered the treehouse he was determined to tell the others everything. Mitchell was reading by the fire, his red-painted wall glowing behind him, and Flo was struggling out of her boots after her latest Silver Circle meeting. Bobby wasn't there – the only sign of her was a half-eaten jam, Marmite and cheese sandwich on the counter. *Probably branching out with her new friends*, Skandar thought bitterly.

'So you're supposed to find Kenna's unicorn in a dream?' Flo asked, after Skandar had recounted his conversation with Agatha.

'I don't know,' Skandar said, frustrated. 'I mean, I dream about Kenna a lot and I've dreamed about that dapple-grey unicorn before too. But Agatha said it has to be me *and* Scoundrel dreaming together? How does that work?'

'You think that dapple grey might be Kenna's?' Mitchell clarified, only half listening while searching an Island dictionary for the word *Mender*. Of course, it wasn't there.

Skandar shrugged, although his body was pumping with adrenaline. 'That wild unicorn keeps finding me, doesn't she? And she . . . she feels sort of familiar.'

'It might just be because you've seen her three times,' Flo said gently.

But Skandar didn't want to hear their doubts. He wanted the dapple grey to belong to Kenna. His mind wandered to his rucksack upstairs and the money he'd already saved. The dream of Kenna and Dad on the Island didn't seem so far away suddenly. It seemed . . . possible.

'All I know is that Kenna isn't okay on the Mainland. She still wants to be a rider; she always did. I told you she isn't even writing to me any more because she can't bear it – that's how sad she is!' Guilt flooded Skandar's chest as he spoke. It was *his* fault. He'd left her behind. He should have told her . . .

'Lots of people aren't destined for unicorns,' Mitchell said matter-of-factly. 'They get over it.'

'But what if it's worse if you were supposed to have one? If Kenna's a spirit wielder she would have automatically failed the Hatchery exam. It can run in families, can't it? Look at Erika and Agatha – two spirit wielder sisters. And then me. Surely Kenna should have been a rider too? And what if I can fix her? Mend her bond?'

'Have you forgotten that the Island is exploding?' Mitchell said, crossing his arms. 'The other day you were all *Mitchell, the bard is right, the Weaver's destroying the Island, we have to do something.'*

'Obviously I still care about that, but this is Kenna we're talking about! I need to know if she's a spirit wielder. I have to help her!' Skandar's adrenaline-filled brain was coming up with reason after reason for focusing all their attention on his sister. 'What if the Weaver kills her wild unicorn before I even know for sure which one it is? I need to protect it.'

'You don't even know you're definitely a Mender, Skar,' Flo warned.

Mitchell shut the dictionary. 'I suppose there must be records of the lost spirit wielders. A place they write down the names of thirteen-year-olds who automatically fail the Hatchery exam?'

'There are records,' Flo said, not quite meeting Skandar's eye.

'Where?' Skandar asked urgently.

Flo looked a little ill. 'The Silver Stronghold. You know, where I have my Silver Circle meetings.'

Skandar couldn't believe their luck. 'Can you look at the records? Could you look for Kenna's name?'

'I can't, Skar. Only sentinels and fully trained silvers are allowed to access them. As a visitor, I'm not even allowed *into* that library. Plus, I have to be escorted at all times when I'm at the Stronghold.'

'Couldn't you ask a sentinel to look?' he pleaded.

'Dorian would definitely find out! He knows I'm in your quartet; he's already asked me about you! Imagine what he'd do if he thought I was trying to get information about *spirit wielders* for you!'

Skandar ignored the panic in Flo's voice. He *had* to know if Kenna was destined for a unicorn. Random snippets from Dad's letter popped into his mind: *she was quite affected by her trip to the Island; she misses you a lot; help her forget about unicorns.* 'But what about if—'

'NO!' Flo shouted and fled from the treehouse.

Mitchell stared after her. 'That's the first time I've heard her shout since we faced the Weaver.'

Skandar was already at the door. Flo hadn't gone far; she was sitting cross-legged on the platform outside, tears rolling down her dark brown cheeks.

Skandar sat next to her, unsure of what to say or do. If he'd upset Kenna he would have hugged her. But Flo wasn't his sister, and somehow that made a difference.

'Skar, I need to tell you something,' she managed to whisper. 'And it's not good.'

Skandar's stomach lurched. 'What is it?' The words were loud, bouncing off the armoured trunks nearby.

She took a deep breath, still looking out through the trees, towards Fourpoint twinkling round the bottom of the Eyrie's hill. 'It's about my Silver Circle meeting earlier.'

Skandar sat up straighter so he could see Flo's expression in the lantern light. 'What about it?'

Her eyes were urgent. 'Please, Skar. I don't want this to change anything, okay? I don't want you to think I agree with them. I don't want it to mean we're on different sides.'

Skandar laughed nervously. 'We'll never be on different sides – you've been on my side since I arrived! You saved our lives last year, when you and Blade got between Scoundrel and the Weaver! Just tell me what happened.'

Flo squeezed her eyes shut and took a breath. 'When I arrived at the Silver Stronghold today, the Silver Circle members were all touching fists in a big circle – they really like circles.'

Skandar nodded.

'They explained that it was time to officially initiate me as a member – now I'm a Nestling. They were very excited; there hasn't been a new silver for six years.'

'What did you have to do?' Skandar's mouth was dry.

Flo swallowed. 'Every member of the Silver Circle has to swear an oath when they join.' Flo's voice shook as she repeated the words. '*I swear, by the power of all four elements and the might of my silver unicorn, that I will hereafter defend this Island from the assaults of the spirit wielders.*'

'Well, that's very specific,' Skandar murmured.

'I did it, Skar. I swore the oath!'

Flo wouldn't look at him, but Skandar crawled round so he was sitting opposite her. 'Listen to me, Flo. Listen.' He put a hand on her shoulder. 'I know you didn't mean it. I know you're not like them. I understand why you swore the oath. How could you not? The most important thing is that you didn't want to.'

'Of course I didn't!' Flo cried. 'But I'm worried what they're going to ask of me, Skar. What if I haven't got a choice but to be on their side? And their side is always going to be the opposite of yours, isn't it? I don't want that. I want to choose you.'

'Well, there's your answer,' Skandar half joked, feeling his cheeks redden.

'It's not as simple as that,' Flo said sadly. 'Did you know there was a war, Skar? A long time ago, between the spirit wielders and the silvers. Two brothers on opposite sides – one a spirit wielder, one a silver. A whole war! They almost wiped each other out. It isn't just you the Circle hates – when they see you, they think of that war, of the riders your ancestors killed; they think of what you stand for. They don't care that you're Skandar. They just care that you're a spirit wielder.'

'But why was there a war?' asked Skandar, who'd never been able to understand why people couldn't work things out without needing to hurt each other.

'Each brother wanted to run the Island.' Flo shrugged. 'It was about power. Isn't it always?'

Skandar stared out over the Eyrie, the lanterns blinking along the bridges, the soft murmur of rider chatter floating from treehouses. He couldn't imagine riders turning against each other so violently. And he certainly couldn't imagine fighting Flo. In his desperation to find out the truth for Kenna, Skandar had forgotten what would happen if Flo defied the Silver Circle. She'd be locked up in the Stronghold to train until Blade was fully grown, with only silvers and sentinels for company.

'I *am* going to help you with your sister,' Flo said into the darkness.

'No.' Skandar was startled. 'You can't risk the Circle taking you out of the Eyrie. You don't have to. I'm sure there's another—'

'We're going to check those records.' A determined look had entered Flo's eyes, not unlike the one on Sara Shekoni's face when she'd talked about standing up to Dorian. 'You have to know if Kenna was destined to be a rider. I've seen how upset you've been since she stopped writing to you. I can't imagine how awful I'd feel if Ebb stopped talking to me. I know Bobby's sort of taking a break from things right now –' Flo looked awkward – 'but I'm sure Mitchell will help us plan something – something that doesn't involve *you*, a spirit wielder, going into the Stronghold.'

'Yeah, that probably wouldn't be a good idea.' Skandar laughed. 'But, Flo, thank you – about Kenna. I might not even be a Mender, but if I am it will change everything.'

Flo nodded fiercely, but then her face was clouded by a sad, thoughtful expression. 'I don't think Blade would mind at all if we were locked up in the Stronghold, you know.'

'What do you mean?'

There was a high-pitched scream and they both jumped. An owl? A fox?

Flo shivered. 'I'm starting to experience Blade's emotions in the bond, like you do with Scoundrel, and I can tell he's happiest around the other silvers. Like he belongs.'

'He belongs with Scoundrel, Red and Falcon,' Skandar said stubbornly, trying not to think about Bobby's branching out.

'Have you noticed that when he's with the other quartet unicorns he's always on the edge of the group? It isn't that he doesn't *want* to join in; he just doesn't know how.' Flo shrugged. 'At the Stronghold he's different. He has fun— What was that?'

A lantern had smashed on the ground far below them. The hanging lights were sometimes dislodged in high winds, but there wasn't even a breeze tonight. Skandar looked over his shoulder and noticed a bridge swinging wildly from side to side. Flo was staring at it too. Another hollow scream echoed through the night.

'Probably people messing around,' Skandar said, half to reassure himself. But his mind unhelpfully recalled Rickesh's theory about the First Rider returning as a havoc-wreaking phantom and a shiver went down his neck. Suddenly the shadows on the tree trunks nearby seemed bigger, the shapes cast by surrounding treehouses more sinister. A creature snarled, invisible among the roots below. A branch snapped.

Flo looked over her shoulder for the fourth time. 'Let's go inside. Mitchell will—'

But Skandar never got to hear what Flo was about to say, because something slammed into his shoulder, almost pushing him right off the metal platform. Skandar tried to see what the thing was and realised—

'Gabriel!' Flo squeaked. 'What are you *doing*?'

Gabriel looked down at her, his stone curls perfectly still. There was something seriously wrong. Gabriel's eyes were unfocused; they kept rolling back in his head. And he was making growling sounds that didn't sound human at all, more like a—

'GABRIEL! STOP!' Skandar shouted, as the boy grabbed Flo round the neck and dragged her to the edge of the platform. 'Hey!' Skandar tried to pull Gabriel back, but that only made the earth wielder strike out at him too with an impossibly quick kick. Skandar fell on to his front, his head and shoulders hanging over the twenty-metre drop below. Flo started screaming as Gabriel lashed out at her. He snarled, pushing her right back on to the chain-link barrier that was the only thing between her and the forest floor.

Skandar scrambled up towards Gabriel, opened his mouth to call for help, then—

WHAM!

The side of Skandar's head exploded in a world of pain, and everything went black.

KENNA

THE SILVERS ON
THE SEA

Kenna was cocooned by the sounds of the sea. The dip of the oars as Dad rowed out from the shore, the splash of the waves breaking. The boat was called *Eurydice*, and it was a garish yellow, meant for hire by holidaymakers. Kenna prayed Dad would get away with borrowing it. She wouldn't be around to help him any more. After tonight she wouldn't be in Margate at all. Or at least that was what she hoped.

She'd hardly slept for many nights thinking of this one. Would President Manning come? Would he really take her to the Island? Or had she been the biggest fool? Doubt weighed her down so much she thought she might sink the boat with it. It had grown heavier in her heart as the months had gone by, as she'd waited, as she'd pretended she was like every other person at school. And as she'd watched Dad reply to Skandar's letters instead of her and thought of him in the flat all by himself, the guilt had gnawed away at her too.

Dad stopped rowing as they passed the furthest buoy. The

anchor's chain rattled against the boat as he manoeuvred it over the side. *Splash*. Down it went into the depths. Kenna realised she was humming, like she always did when she was nervous. Dad joined her on the wooden plank across the middle of the boat. He took her hand. It wasn't until his fingers curled round hers that she realised she was shaking.

'You don't have to go,' Dad said quietly. 'You can change your mind.'

'I'm not changing my mind.' Kenna's teeth chattered from the November cold – and from the fear. Fear that he wouldn't come for her. Fear that she would be stuck here without Skandar, without a unicorn—

'Kenna! Look!' Dad's voice was urgent, his gloved hand pointing at the sky ahead of them.

At first they looked like shooting stars. Only when they were closer did they take shape: two silver-winged silhouettes reflected in the water. The third unicorn behind them was darker, an iron grey, like a comet that had lost its shine. The unicorns hovered above the sea, the strength of their wingbeats disturbing the surface, horns facing the boat. Kenna stumbled off her seat, dropping Dad's hand to stand at the prow, unable to hide the wonder on her face.

'We don't have long.' President Manning's voice, sharp and nasal, carried to Kenna on the wind. He rode the larger of the two silver unicorns.

'This is insanity, Father, please. You don't know for sure he's a Mender. And does she even know what you're expecting of her? She's only fifteen. They're children. We don't need a spirit wielder. There's still time to stop this.' Kenna's focus snapped to the person speaking. He was a few years older than her and, even as she marvelled at the unicorns, Kenna noticed the sparking mutation on his cheeks and how it made his handsome face even more striking.

'Rex, enough. They'll hear you,' President Manning snapped, pointing at the boat. 'You didn't have to come.' The president's silver unicorn snarled along with him.

'You weren't even *supposed* to be coming,' the third man said more quietly. Kenna tried not to gasp at his mutation – his eyes were aflame; like two tiny fires.

The boat rocked as Dad came to stand with Kenna at the prow, putting a hand on her shoulder protectively. Kenna heard his breathing hitch as he looked at the unicorns – creatures he'd loved for so long – up close. Then he cleared his throat.

'Excuse me, but if my daughter was destined for a unicorn and you've made a mistake, I think it's about time you took her to the Island where she belongs, don't you?'

Kenna's heart exploded with gratitude. He hadn't always been the perfect dad, but he loved her. He loved her so much that he wanted her to be happy – even if it meant letting her go.

The three riders surveyed Robert Smith.

'I'll take her on my unicorn,' the flaming-eyed man offered, his voice strained.

'I will take her,' President Manning announced pompously. 'You and Rex will protect us.'

'No, I insist,' the flame-eyed man pushed. 'This was my idea. If it goes wrong—'

But Dorian Manning ignored him and urged his silver unicorn closer, its shining hooves skimming the water. Dad helped Kenna on to the edge of the prow, steadying her from behind.

'Good luck, sweetheart,' he whispered into her neck. 'If only your mum could see you now.'

That was all the encouragement Kenna needed to grasp Dorian Manning's hands and let herself be lifted up behind him on to the unicorn's back. She held on to his waist tightly. Kenna had ridden Scoundrel before, but he wasn't fully grown. She could feel this unicorn's muscles under her jeans, the wings beating so powerfully they felt like a weapon.

Then Dorian was turning the silver unicorn away from the boat. The other two unicorns followed, the sea churning as it was disturbed by their great wingbeats. Kenna's stomach lurched at the movement and she panicked, trying to get a last look back at Dad in the boat. He was waving, and laughing, and crying all at the same time. As Kenna lifted a hand to wave back, she thought he suddenly looked very small in the middle of the inky-black sea.

They flew in silence for a while but Kenna was pumped full of adrenaline and excitement, mixed with a little bit of terror. She was flying over the sea. She was going to find her destined unicorn! And she had so many questions it was impossible to bear.

The youngest man, Rex, was flying to her right and she called to him over the wind. 'Are you an air wielder? Your cheeks!'

He looked shocked that she was talking to him but recovered quickly. 'That's right!' he shouted, as the whoosh of his unicorn's silver wings threatened to swallow his words. 'My father is too.' He took a hand off one rein to gesture towards Dorian Manning.

'Elemental allegiances tend to run in families,' President Manning said without turning round. 'Like you and your brother.'

'What do you mean?' Kenna asked loudly, as a strong gust battered them sideways.

President Manning glanced over his shoulder, a glint in his eye. 'Skandar's a spirit wielder too,' he said. 'Didn't he tell you?'

CHAPTER EIGHT

CHAPTERS OF CHAOS

Skandar was lucky. Gabriel's blow had only left him with a mild headache, rather than any permanent damage. Flo had bruises on her neck and painful whiplash, but – despite being very shaken up – she had also returned to training the following week. Gabriel had come back to himself with no idea of what he'd done, only moments after Mitchell had run out on to the platform.

Skandar and Flo had tried to explain to the instructors what had happened, but it was difficult to describe, especially since Gabriel had been very distressed.

'But do you remember anything? Anything at all?' Instructor Webb had asked him.

Gabriel had looked terrified. 'All I remember is that . . . that I wanted—'

'Wanted what?' Instructor O'Sullivan had asked sharply, whirlpool eyes swirling.

'B-b-blood. I wanted blood.' Then he'd burst into tears.

Skandar had not missed the look on the instructors' faces at Gabriel's words, nor their eyes flicking towards him as they'd reassured the Nestlings that they would investigate.

Bobby had burst back into the treehouse after hearing the news from Mariam. For a moment, Skandar had seen the worry on her face, the feathers sticking up on her arms and thought that the other nightmare – the one where Bobby wasn't his friend any more – was over. But she'd started to climb the spiralling rungs of the treehouse trunk as soon as she'd satisfied herself they were safe.

'Bobby, wait!' Skandar had called after her. 'Don't you want to hear what happened?'

'No!' she'd shouted down. 'I'm not getting tangled in another Skandar Smith mystery. I have to concentrate on my training. This is exactly what I was talking about!'

'Bobby!' Flo had called. 'I was attacked too! It wasn't Skar's fault we were in the wrong place at the wrong time.'

'It never is!' Bobby had roared, and slammed her bedroom door.

Gabriel was absolutely devastated and tried to apologise every time he saw Skandar and Flo. The day before the Fire Festival, he even rode Queen's Price over to them while they were supposed to be summoning flaming spears. The point of the spear wasn't too hard to mould – like a dagger it was small and light – but the long shaft was trickier. Fire was the most volatile element, and some riders were finding it almost impossible to keep the fire magic under control – the spears were either losing their shape or fizzling out completely. Skandar felt unnerved as he raised his own spear, the roaring and crackling of the fire magic loud beside his ear. Though at least the magic kept his hands warm.

'I really am sorry,' Gabriel said for the hundredth time. 'I wish I knew how it happened.'

'So do I,' Mitchell muttered, as Red bent her neck and belched some ash at the pointy end of his flaming weapon, making it splutter out. 'What happened to Gabriel – I'm sure it has to be something to do with the elemental disruption. It can't be a coincidence because—'

'You don't believe in coincidences,' Skandar finished for him. Now Mitchell had accepted that the elemental disruption was happening, he had also grudgingly had to accept that the truesong had predicted it. This seemed to have sent him into a kind of frenzy, and he had been visiting Jamie more and more often to grill him about bards, songs and Gabriel's attack. But Skandar thought Mitchell obsessing over the mystery might have had more to do with him receiving yet another stern letter from his father.

Ira had only written a few lines: first about 'not getting involved with the spirit wielder' and then listing ten different kinds of weapon Mitchell should be summoning by now if he was ever going to become Commodore. Mitchell had been putting in extra hours of training alone ever since. 'At least my father's paying attention to me and Red now,' he'd said to Skandar when he'd returned late from the training ground one night. 'At least he has a dream for me. I would have killed for this last year.'

'Honestly, Gabriel, it really isn't your fault,' Skandar grunted, trying to make Gabriel go away so he could concentrate on steadying his spear over his shoulder.

'But I *feel* like it is. If there's anything I can do, anything at all.'

'Why did an earth wielder have to get possessed?' Skandar heard Bobby say to her new friend, Ajay. 'He's so *earnest*, it's exhausting. If it'd been an air wielder they'd have totally moved on by now.'

Skandar felt a spike of jealousy. Bobby used to say things like that to him. But unfortunately Gabriel's attack wasn't exactly helping show her that Skandar could keep a low profile. He was getting more attention than ever. It didn't matter that he had been one of the *victims* – people thought he was somehow behind Gabriel's possession. These theories weren't particularly helped by Gabriel repeating to anyone who'd listen what he'd told the instructors – that he'd felt a strange kind of bloodlust that night, like a wild unicorn had possessed him. Rumours about the Weaver were rife. And, of course, the other popular rumour was that, as a spirit wielder, Skandar somehow had the power to get wild unicorns to possess riders. This had now spread so effectively that Hatchlings ran away from him screaming. At this point the only thing keeping Skandar from really losing his temper was the thought of escaping to a Peregrine Society meeting the following evening.

'THROW!' Instructor Anderson shouted.

Eighteen blazing spears flew above the scorched earth of the fire training ground. Most dropped only a few metres away, though Blade roared a rather alarming column of flame after Flo's. But Bobby's spear soared almost all the way to the red pavilion on the opposite side.

'How exactly did you get it to do that?' Mitchell called over to her.

Bobby shrugged. 'I gave it wings.' Sure enough, as the spear fizzled to nothing in the grass, Skandar caught sight of the fletching at the end of the shaft – three fiery feathers, just like the end of an arrow.

Bobby's new group of friends all congratulated her. He knew Mariam because she was a Mainlander, but the other two were the fire wielder called Ajay and an earth wielder called Charlie. They were the three left from Lawrence's quartet – he was an air wielder who'd been made a nomad last year. Skandar could hardly bear to listen to their admiring comments. Was Bobby trying to *join* their quartet or something? Take Lawrence's place?

Instructor Anderson gave Bobby and Falcon's Wrath a round of applause, his laugh booming across the field. 'Now that's the kind of creative design that can win you a joust.'

Skandar watched Bobby bow sarcastically. Falcon fluttered her perfectly curled eyelashes.

'I miss her.' Flo sighed, watching too. 'It's not the same.'

'Three people don't make a quartet,' Mitchell said bluntly.

'She made her decision.' Skandar's voice was harsh.

Scoundrel shrieked, feeling his rider's annoyance jarring in the bond.

'I know you're angry with her, but think about it from Bobby's point of view,' Flo said. 'She's used to being the best. She's used to being the centre of attention and being in charge.'

'She *is* the best! She won the Training Trial! And she's *always* in charge!' Skandar said loudly. 'I didn't ask to be the only spirit wielder in training.'

'You did actually,' Flo said gently. 'And that was completely the right decision, but Bobby struggles in your shadow. Just give her some time.'

Skandar changed the subject. 'Have you heard anything from the Silver Circle?' He was desperate to find out if Kenna's name was in the spirit wielder records. Ever since Flo had agreed to help, they'd been planning exactly how to get into the Silver

Stronghold. Now the only missing piece was the date of Flo's next meeting.

'I got a letter this morning.'

They didn't have to keep their voices down – the other Nestlings were, as usual, keeping their distance from Skandar and Scoundrel.

Flo took a deep breath. 'There's some kind of big event at the Stronghold at the end of November and the whole Silver Circle has to attend.'

'Well, that's perfect,' Mitchell said, satisfied. 'Jamie's all healed up now, so that'll give him plenty of time to make my disguise and I should be able to hide in the sentinels' library and look at the records. Then Flo will come to get me when the event is over, and we'll leave together. Easy.'

'I feel really bad asking you both to do this,' Skandar said for the thousandth time.

Flo tried to reassure him. 'We *want* to do it.'

'Wild unicorns are turning up dead practically every week now,' Mitchell said seriously. 'What if Kenna's unicorn is next? We have to find out if she was destined to be a rider and then—'

'Find out for sure who's killing the wild unicorns,' Skandar finished for him.

'And why,' Mitchell added.

Skandar swallowed. 'And stop them.' *Stop her*, he couldn't help thinking.

Flo sighed. 'I really thought our second year at the Eyrie might be a bit more ordinary.'

'Yes,' Mitchell said, his eyes rather manic behind his glasses. 'I was also hoping for less mortal peril.'

The next day, with the beginning of November, the Fire Festival arrived. Skandar wasn't going. Given that the Grins didn't believe in elemental separation, they weren't the biggest fans of the festivals, so Rickesh had scheduled a meeting for the same evening. Although Skandar suspected Rickesh had also done it partly for the spirit wielder's benefit.

At their last session, once they'd stopped practising hair-raising dives, Skandar had confided in the rest of the Grins that the stares and whispers around him were getting worse. Wild unicorn bodies were still turning up, and the *Hatchery Herald* now had a dedicated section called *The Island's Revenge*. So far it had reported whole forests igniting in the fire zone, floods in the water zone and tornadoes wreaking havoc across the air zone. Fourpoint, the Eyrie and the Hatchery remained untouched so far – but then, of course, there was what had happened to Gabriel . . .

'Anyone gives you trouble, I'll bash their faces in!' Patrick had announced.

'You're always so violent,' Prim had scolded Patrick, looking up from her insulin pump. She'd told Skandar recently that she had type one diabetes, shortly before nicking one of Scoundrel's Jelly Babies to correct her low blood sugar.

'You're always so un*subtle*,' Fen had told Patrick. 'I'd just push them off one of the swinging bridges. Silent. Deadly. Effective.' She cracked her icy knuckles.

Skandar had been genuinely touched, if not slightly disturbed. 'Thanks a lot. But I'm not sure you murdering my enemies is going to help my reputation.'

'We look after our own, Skandar.' Rickesh had winked at him. 'But, seriously, I'm just looking at the timing for the next meeting . . . it'll be the evening of the Fire Festival.'

'Oh, really?' Adela had moaned. 'I was sort of planning on going with my girlfriend.'

Prim had ignored this. 'Good idea, Ricki. Why go if we're not doing a display?' She shrugged, flicking a glance at Skandar.

'When are we doing a display?' Skandar had asked nervously.

'The Chaos Cup, but don't worry – you won't be doing it. We let the Nestlings off,' Rickesh had explained. 'The displays are sort of in exchange for the instructors not closing down the society for being too dangerous. We do the display, all the important people on the Island are impressed with our skills and the Eyrie leaves us alone.'

So Skandar didn't head off to the Fire Festival that evening with the other Eyrie riders, as they changed their jackets from green to red to match the colour of the new elemental season. Bobby left first to meet up with Mariam, Ajay and Charlie, then Mitchell and Flo went off together, saying they were going to drop in on Jamie to see how he was doing with Mitchell's disguise for the Stronghold. That made Skandar think of Kenna, so he decided to attempt a letter to Dad. He'd sketched Scoundrel mid-flight earlier that day so he thought Dad might like to have it. He settled down on a beanbag inside the treehouse for the harder task – the words of the letter.

Dear Dad,

Thanks for writing to me. I hope you're okay and that work is going well. Can you tell Kenna that I'm thinking about her and I miss her and I'm trying to make things better? That's all I can say for now, but

I promise I'll write with more soon – and when you both come to visit at the end of the year I'll tell you everything. Love you, Skar x

Half an hour later, the rest of the Peregrine Society greeted Skandar and Scoundrel with waves and smiles – except Amber, of course, who barely acknowledged his presence at their weekly meetings.

'Any trouble?' Patrick raised an eyebrow mischievously.

'Not tonight.' Skandar grinned and gave him a high five. Skandar did that kind of thing with the Grins. He felt like a completely different person up here: confident and self-assured – but it was more than that. He fitted in here. He was just like everyone else. They loved flying – so did he. They were interested in wingbeats per minute and top speeds – so was he. He supposed back on the Mainland it might have been what people felt when they belonged to a football team or a book club – though, of course, this one had daredevil stunts and deadly unicorns.

Today they were trying some trick riding. Rickesh flew Tidal Warrior about two hundred metres away from the Sunset Platform. Warrior flapped her wings in mid-air as Rickesh summoned his allied element to create a ring of frothing water. Pairs of Grins sped towards the ring at unbelievable speeds, racing to be the first through. The *whoosh* of their wings was so strong it vibrated the air around the platform, even rustling the leaves on the trees below. Each rider was expected to perform a daredevil stunt as they went through the ring – the more outrageous the better. Rickesh had told a story about a previous

Chaos Cup winner who was famous for using these kinds of stunts in sky battles, although Skandar suspected the Grins mostly did them because they were fun – and pretty dangerous.

So far the best three had been Adela, who had gone through backwards in her saddle, her smoking hair coiling round her as she'd waved back at the platform; Fen, who had lain sideways across Eternal Hoarfrost's saddle, her legs and arms as straight as an arrow; and Marcus, who had loosened Sandstorm's Orbit's girth and let the saddle slip all the way under her belly – with Marcus still in it – so he went through the ring upside down.

Scoundrel was watching the unicorn pairs eagerly, his eyes flicking between black and red as he followed their progress. Skandar knew the unicorn liked being a member of the society just as much as he did.

Then, as the youngest, Skandar and Amber were called together. 'See if either of you can top Marcus's stunt!' Rickesh called.

Skandar pulled on Scoundrel's reins to stop him from taking off immediately. Amber was having similar trouble with Whirlwind Thief, though not enough to stop her sneering at Skandar.

'You know the only reason you have a Shekoni saddle is because Flo's in your quartet, right?'

Skandar grimaced. 'Oh, get over it, Amber. The Saddle Ceremony was months ago.'

Scoundrel snapped at Thief, saliva flying everywhere. Clearly their newly formed friendship didn't stretch to letting the other unicorn win.

Amber tried another tactic. 'I noticed Bruna isn't hanging out with you any more. I bet she's fuming you got into the Peregrine

Society instead of her. She's right for once – it's a disgrace.'

'I was thinking the same thing about you,' Skandar shot back, as Rickesh shouted, 'Nestlings, GO!'

Skandar wasn't ready, but Scoundrel was. Skandar lurched forward in the saddle, desperately plunging his hands into Scoundrel's mane and gritting his teeth against the icy wind. He crouched low as Amber did the same, her chestnut-coloured hair flowing out behind her. All Skandar could think was: *I have to be faster. I have to win this. I have to.*

Scoundrel had never flown so fast in his life; his wings beat so quickly that the black feathers blurred. Skandar could feel Scoundrel's muscles pumping under his legs and could almost taste the unicorn's desperation to win in the bond. Rickesh's water ring was metres away now, and Skandar knew he couldn't wait any longer to do the trick he'd been planning. Carefully he brought one foot up on to the saddle, then the other. He crouched, gripping the front pommel then, letting go of the reins completely, he slowly stood up. He braced his knees, lifting one arm out to the side, then the other.

'YES!' he shouted, and Scoundrel screeched with excitement, the Grins cheering from the platform behind. He'd done it. He was standing upright on the saddle, Scoundrel's wings beating either side of him. Adrenaline pulsed through him; he'd never felt so alive. The ring of water was right ahead. Just a few metres to go and then—

It wasn't.

Rickesh and Tidal Warrior blocked the way, rearing up in the air, shards of ice shooting from the rider's palm straight at the racing Nestlings. Scoundrel reacted at lightning speed, diving down below Warrior's enormous hooves. Skandar was thrown –

luckily – back down into the saddle. But as he ducked a water blast from Warrior's left foot, Skandar saw Rickesh's face and his blood turned cold. Rickesh's eyes were rolling back in his head. He looked like Gabriel had. He looked possessed.

BASH!

Whirlwind Thief hadn't been quick enough to change course and slammed into Tidal Warrior's left shoulder. The noise of the two muscular beasts colliding echoed off the green canopy of the Eyrie below. Warrior closed her gnashing jaws round Thief's neck, who screeched and blasted the bigger unicorn with elements, but Rickesh and his unicorn kept attacking. In the melee Amber was thrown sideways – out of her Nimroe saddle altogether.

Then she was falling. Whirlwind Thief was desperately trying to fly after her rider, screaming and roaring after her, but unable to escape Warrior's jaws. Unicorns know that their most important job of all is to never, ever let their riders fall. Yet Amber Fairfax was falling . . . falling.

The other Grins were panicking as Amber plummeted towards the Eyrie's canopy, screaming; Fen and Adela mounted their unicorns but Skandar knew they'd be too late. Scoundrel knew too; Skandar could sense it in the bond.

Without hesitation, they dived after Amber's falling silhouette – dropping so fast that Skandar's ears were ringing. He thought his head might explode. And then, by some miracle, they were below Amber. Scoundrel stretched out his black neck so she collided with it, sliding backwards against Skandar's chest.

Amber lost consciousness immediately. She'd be very bruised from the impact, but she was alive.

They flew Amber more slowly back up to the Sunset Platform,

Scoundrel puffing with the effort of the dive and his double load. In stunned silence Fen and Adela reached out to lift the unconscious Amber down from Scoundrel's back. Thief trotted across the platform to her rider, and Scoundrel shrieked anxiously in the chestnut unicorn's direction.

Skandar spoke first. 'Where's Rickesh?'

Adela pointed. Rickesh was resting against Warrior's side, the wave of his hair flat as Marcus and Patrick tied his hands behind his back.

Prim was apologising. 'Look, I know you're squadron leader, but we can't take any chances. I'm next in command, and this is what I'm deciding to do. Just until we're sure—'

'You don't need to do that!' Skandar rushed over to them. 'I know what happened.'

'Skandar, I don't know if it's— If I'm safe,' Rickesh groaned.

Skandar could see a burn up Rickesh's bare brown arm from the battle with Thief. All the brightness and humour had gone from his eyes. Now there was only fear.

'This happened the other day. My friend and I were attacked by Gabriel, an earth wielder Nestling. He said he felt like he had wanted blood, like a wild unicorn was controlling him.'

Rickesh swallowed. 'It wasn't a wild unicorn possessing me. It was Tidal Warrior. She was in my head, sending those – those *feelings* into the bond. I know it was her.'

Skandar tried not to look too shocked. 'You're saying your own unicorn possessed you?'

'That's what it felt like.'

'Gabriel's fine now,' Skandar said, trying to reassure him. 'But my friend Mitchell thinks this possession thing is linked to the elemental disturbances.'

'You think this happened to me because of the wild unicorns being killed?'

'Possibly. It's only a theory,' Skandar said, sounding like Mitchell.

Rickesh collapsed back on to his unicorn's flank. 'This can't be happening. The Eyrie can't have riders being possessed in mid-air! And what about silvers? The strength of their magic combined with – with . . .' He trailed off. 'And we've got one in the Eyrie, right – Florence Shekoni? Riders are going to die. Lots of people are going to die. That was scary, Skandar. I had no control. I wanted to kill Amber, Thief, you, Scoundrel. Everyone.'

Skandar didn't know what to say.

'Someone really needs to stop this wild unicorn killer,' Rickesh muttered. 'Else the Grins? We're out of here.'

Skandar was about to ask what he meant, but Prim bustled him out of the way so she could assess the burn on the squadron leader's arm.

As he was preparing to mount Scoundrel to leave, Amber sidled up to Skandar and whispered in his ear.

'Don't you think it's *super* weird how both times a rider has been possessed, you've been there?'

'I guess I'm just unlucky,' Skandar said, although he couldn't help remembering what Bobby had said: *'I need to make different friends, to spend time with people who don't have to worry about musical prophecies, who don't drag their friends on quests every five minutes!'* And now someone around him had been possessed. Again.

Amber sniggered and climbed on to Thief's back.

Skandar's temper flared. This wasn't his fault! How could someone go from unconscious to unbearable so fast? 'You know, I thought you were coming over here to thank me for saving your life. But no, you're just accusing me of something I didn't do. Like always.'

'I'm sorry, but last year I accused you of exactly what you *were* doing. I can hardly be blamed for being *right*!' Amber looked furious. 'And you want me to thank *you*? You got my dad thrown in jail! Because of you, everyone knows he's a spirit wielder! Because of you, my mum is angry *all* the time now.'

Skandar suddenly understood. 'That's why I haven't seen you hanging around with your quartet, isn't it? They've ditched you because of your dad.'

'They haven't ditched me,' she said fiercely, but her voice wobbled. 'I'm warning you, Skandar Smith, if you possess anyone else—'

'I'm not doing it!'

'If you're there when any other rider comes over all murderous, then I'll have no choice but to report you to the Silver Circle.'

'Is that a threat?' Skandar growled.

'Of course,' Amber said sweetly, as Whirlwind Thief took off from the Sunset Platform and flew them away.

The day before Flo and Mitchell were planning to infiltrate the Silver Stronghold, Mitchell and Skandar rode to Fourpoint together to collect the disguise from Jamie. Best friends Scoundrel and Red walked side by side down Fourpoint's main shopping street. Skandar still couldn't get used to Red being so well behaved and clean – it had been ages since she'd burped ash or ignited a fart or even had a flaming hair out of place. Skandar knew Red must have somehow understood that Mitchell was desperate to please his father, but he couldn't help thinking the blood-red unicorn looked a little sadder nowadays. As though reading his rider's thoughts, Scoundrel snorted a few ice crystals sideways at Red. Usually she would have melted them as quick as a spark, eager for a game. But this time she just let them dissolve on her gleaming red coat. Skandar felt Scoundrel's disappointment twang in the bond, and knew that he missed the old Red too.

'Oooh, Chapters of Chaos!' said Mitchell, slowing Red down outside the bookshop.

Skandar sighed. 'Aren't we supposed to be meeting Jamie?'

'We've got time. And I ordered a special book on jousting from Craig – it's new. Thought it might impress my father if I learned some of the new weapon formations in it.'

Skandar knew there was no keeping Mitchell from a bookshop – especially one where he was on first-name terms with the owner – so they dismounted, tying the unicorns to some low-hanging branches outside. Skandar gave Scoundrel one of his few remaining Jelly Babies to say sorry, and the unicorn nuzzled his hand to say it was all right.

A little bell rang over the door as they entered. Another customer was in animated conversation with Craig the bookseller, so Mitchell started pointing out books he'd already read and giving Skandar short – sometimes rather cutting – reviews: 'Honestly, this one had fewer facts in it than a truesong' or 'I would have been better off consulting one of your Chaos Cards!'

'Ah, now this one was good,' Mitchell said, sliding a book called *Beyond the Library* off the shelf. 'It did get me into a bit of trouble when I was younger, though.'

'How can a book get you in trouble?' Skandar asked curiously.

In answer, Mitchell slid his finger down the contents page and pointed to a chapter called 'The Secret Swappers'. 'When I was about ten, my grandmother – my father's mother – got very ill. My father became obsessed with making her better; he was convinced that he should be able to find some way to use his water magic to heal her.'

Mitchell sighed and continued. 'I was desperate to help my father. I thought if I was the one to help him then it would make everything better: my grandmother, my father's opinion of me, the relationship between my parents which had become . . . frosty by that point. So I began researching and I found out about the Secret Swappers.' Mitchell shivered despite the warmth of the shop. 'They trade in secrets. They have knowledge the libraries don't. If you give them a good enough secret, they'll give you the information you seek in return. A secret for a secret.'

'So did you visit them?' Skandar asked impatiently. Mitchell's stories were always *very* detailed.

'Almost.' Mitchell looked a little fearful. 'I had my foot on the ladder, ready to climb to their treehouse, when my father caught me, put me over his shoulder and carried me all the way home, scolding me the entire time.'

'Why? Why was he telling you off? You were only trying to help!' Skandar said, indignant.

'I hadn't finished the chapter,' Mitchell said, sliding *Beyond the Library* back on the shelf. 'I hadn't read the warning. The Secret Swappers aren't nice people, Skandar. If you give them a secret that's false, well . . .'

'Well, what?'

'They kill you.'

Skandar was so shocked, he couldn't think of a thing to say.

With a tinkling of the bell, the other customer left. Craig greeted Mitchell like an old friend, while Skandar tried not to think about exactly *how* these secret swapper people would kill you and attempted to blend into the bookshelves. His last shopping experience hadn't exactly gone well.

But to Skandar's surprise, Craig greeted him warmly too, saying he'd heard all about him and Scoundrel from Mitchell. 'I think your order came in yesterday, Mitchell. Come up to my treehouse. I've got something I'd like to show Skandar too.' Craig flipped the sign on the door from OPEN to CLOSED. Skandar couldn't understand how they were going to get up to Craig's treehouse from here; there didn't appear to be any rungs on the central trunk: it was covered in books.

'Craig?' Mitchell said, looking equally disorientated. 'Where's your ladder?'

The bookshop owner laughed, the bun of hair on top of his head wobbling precariously. When he smiled he looked much younger, perhaps only a few years older than Skandar.

'Ah yes. You'll like this. My late father built it. He was determined to have as many books in the shop as possible.' Craig removed *A Tantalising Treatise on Tree Trunks* from the shelf, reached into the gap the book had left and pulled a hidden lever. With a whoosh, some of the bookshelves slid further out from the trunk to form a spiral staircase that snaked up into the treehouse above.

Mitchell stared at the trunk, his mouth in a perfect 'O'. As they climbed after Craig, he asked Skandar. 'Do you think we could build one of these in our treehouse?'

'What for?'

'More books!' Mitchell insisted.

'I'm not sure Bobby would . . .' Skandar started, but sadness ate the rest of his words. He knew all kinds of hilarious things Bobby would say about Mitchell trying to bring yet more books into the treehouse, but he wouldn't hear them. Now she'd tell someone else.

As they reached the top of the spiral staircase they entered another room with even more books than the shop. Craig set Mitchell rummaging through his latest deliveries, and then motioned to Skandar to follow him to a desk in the corner. It looked old, but well cared for, with a green leather top and gold swirls at the corners.

'As soon as Mitchell told me about you, all I could think about was how hard it must be to train in the spirit element with no books!' Skandar watched curiously as Craig took a key from round his neck and opened a drawer in the desk. 'But then it got me thinking. The books might be gone, but the knowledge isn't.'

Skandar was startled. Did Craig want him to write down what he was learning with Agatha? 'I don't know much yet! I've only just started proper—'

'No, no, you misunderstand me,' Craig said, taking a pile of handwritten notes out of the desk drawer. 'You had the spirit wielders freed last year. They hold the knowledge that was in many of those books – *up here.*' He tapped his head. 'Finding them hasn't been easy – most of the spirit wielders are in hiding because they still fear the Silver Circle. But word is spreading that I'm friendly, and I've been talking to them: noting down what they remember, collecting their stories.'

'That's – that's brilliant!' Skandar exclaimed, unable to believe that this Islander actually wanted to help spirit wielders. 'Can – can I read some?'

Craig passed the papers over to Skandar. 'It's all in note form at the moment; you probably won't be able to understand much. But I'm going to make it into a proper book once I have more.'

Craig went over to help Mitchell while Skandar tried to decipher the bookseller's tiny handwriting. Much of it was very difficult to understand but, as he rifled through, a word caught his eye.

Mender.

'Craig?' Skandar called urgently. 'Could you read something out for me?'

The bookseller rushed over, and Skandar handed him the page. 'Oh yes.' Craig nodded. 'I got this from one of the older spirit wielders. He's been a great help.'

Clearing his throat, Craig began to read his notes aloud:

'Mender: a spirit wielder who possesses the ability to bond a rider to their destined unicorn, even after the unicorn has hatched wild. Menders rely on dreams that they share with their unicorn, in order to identify wild unicorns and riders that should have bonded. In these dreams the rider's dream presence will be pulled towards the lost rider, and the unicorn's presence towards the lost unicorn. Through the bond, the rider and unicorn trade places. This is the most dangerous point, for if a rider's dream presence becomes trapped in the wild unicorn, it often results in death.'

'Death?' Mitchell croaked, causing Skandar to jump; he hadn't realised Mitchell had crossed the room to join them.

'Do you want to hear more?' Craig asked.

Skandar nodded vigorously.

'An anchor is recommended – a person or thing that will bring the rider back to themselves in the event of distress. While more experienced Menders can use their dream presence to wander freely and find lost

riders, younger Menders often benefit from focusing on one particular individual. As a general rule, the younger the lost rider, the easier the mending process will be. The wilder a unicorn becomes, the more energy it will take to complete the imperfect bond.'

'Interesting, isn't it?' Craig said.

'Very,' Skandar replied, his mind whirring.

'Can you believe Craig is going around collecting spirit wielder knowledge?' Mitchell said ten minutes later as they continued on to Jamie's forge. 'A rebel *and* a bookseller – he'll be unstoppable.'

But Skandar couldn't stop thinking about Craig's notes. *The younger the lost rider, the easier the mending process.* Thank goodness Mitchell and Flo were going to the Silver Stronghold tomorrow. Once he knew for sure about Kenna, then he could start on the dreams. How hard could it be? And while he got really good at dreaming, they could focus on stopping the wild unicorn killings so that the elemental disruption would end, and Kenna's unicorn would be protected, and the Island would be safe enough for his sister to come—

'Skandar,' Mitchell said, interrupting his thoughts, as they dismounted by the forge. 'You won't try any of those dreams before you talk to Agatha, will you? Death, Craig said. Death!'

'Of course not,' Skandar said, although he didn't mean it.

The forge Jamie belonged to had a sloping metal roof, supported at the corners by four large tree trunks. Even from outside, Skandar could feel the heat billowing from the fires and hear hammers banging. Occasionally there would be a flash of metal and then a hissing sound as it was cooled in a great circular tub.

Jamie's mismatched green and brown eyes snagged on them.

'You're late,' he scolded Skandar, his tanned brow furrowed.

'Hey! Mitchell's late too!'

'Never mind,' Jamie said, and he pulled a black-clothed object from the big front pocket of his leather apron. He passed it gently to Mitchell who – checking there was nobody watching – gingerly lifted the material aside.

And there it was. Mitchell's genius and, as always, completely reckless plan for getting into the Silver Stronghold unnoticed – a perfect replica of a sentinel mask.

Skandar had given Jamie a detailed sketch of a mask – partly from memory and Flo's descriptions, and partly from skimming through old copies of the *Hatchery Herald* for grainy close-ups of sentinels. Jamie had, reluctantly, agreed that he would forge the mask in secret. Unlike the real sentinel masks, this one wasn't pure silver, but Jamie had managed to find a cheap silvery-grey paint that made it almost indistinguishable from the real thing.

'Jamie, it's incredible!' Skandar whispered.

'I just hope you know what you're doing,' Jamie said ominously, motioning desperately for Mitchell to put the mask into his saddlebag. 'I know some smiths who work at the Stronghold and they say Manning's obsessed with security. Also, aren't they going to notice you're, well, a lot younger than most sentinels?'

'I shouldn't think so,' Mitchell said confidently. 'Two Fledglings joined the Stronghold last year after they were declared nomads. I'm going to use one of their names if I'm asked. I've got it all worked out.'

'Mitchell is scarily relaxed if he has a plan – no matter how dangerous that plan might be,' Skandar murmured to Jamie, who frowned.

Mitchell ignored this. 'Look, Flo is always supposed to call on a sentinel to accompany her in and out of the Stronghold. It'll be completely expected for me – well, sentinel me – to be with her. I'll have my face hidden behind your excellent mask and then when everyone is filing into the arena for the Silver Circle event, I'll check the records. It'll be *much* easier than breaking into the prison last year.'

Jamie didn't look convinced. 'I know you want to help Skandar find out about his sister, but promise me you'll be careful, okay?'

The flames in Mitchell's hair grew brighter. 'I promise, Jamie. You haven't got anything to worry about.'

Feeling guilty to be the cause of all this, Skandar changed the subject. 'Have you heard if Commodore Kazama is searching for the wild unicorn killer? Does she think it's the Weaver?'

'Doesn't everyone?' Jamie ran a hand through his sandy hair. 'Rumour is, Nina's taking the truesong seriously now. I've heard she's even looking into the First Rider's gift, this idea of a helpful weapon. I mean, how can you not? The Island *feels* angry, don't you think?'

'Oh no, oh no, oh no,' Mitchell started muttering. 'Someone hide me, someone hide you, someone—'

But it was too late. Ira Henderson was marching right up to them, and he looked furious.

'What do you think you're doing showing your face in Fourpoint alongside his?' Ira hissed, shoving his chin in Skandar's direction.

'N-n-nothing, Father. I was just—'

'Skandar was visiting me,' Jamie said firmly, stepping towards Ira. 'I'm his blacksmith.'

'It's true,' Skandar said. 'Mitchell never talks to me, even though we share a room. He hates spirit wielders, thinks they're rubbish and evil and . . .'

'I'm in Fourpoint picking up a new book on jousting, Father,' Mitchell said quickly. 'Look, it's new and I thought I could use some of the weapons in the jousting tournament.'

Distracted, Ira Henderson looked down at the book. Skandar and Jamie started to back slowly away into the forge, hoping that Mitchell's dad had believed their garbled story.

'I'm glad to see you've been taking my letters about training seriously,' Ira said, mollified. 'Red Night's Delight looks smart too,' he added approvingly.

'She is. I have. I really have,' Mitchell's voice was dripping with relief.

'I've been invited for lunch at the water yard tomorrow. You will accompany me.'

Skandar and Jamie looked at each other in alarm. Flo needed to be at the Stronghold by twelve.

'Your . . . yard? I . . . tomorrow? What time?' Mitchell asked hoarsely.

'Meet me at home at eleven. There'll be plenty of important people for you to meet, including some of the water council from last year. If you want to become Commodore, Mitchell, you need to make these kinds of connections early. And keep avoiding the spirit wielder.' He glared pointedly towards the forge. 'Don't disappoint me.'

And without waiting for his son to answer, Ira strode off along the street, the water in his plait flashing.

CHAPTER NINE

THE SILVER STRONGHOLD

Skandar knew from the moment Ira asked Mitchell to accompany him to the water yard that the plan for the Silver Stronghold was doomed. Mitchell had changed a lot in the past year – he'd decided spirit wielders weren't all bad for a start – but Skandar knew there was absolutely no chance that Mitchell would refuse his father's invitation.

'I can't let my father down. This is really important to him. I just can't. I'm so sorry, Skandar,' Mitchell was still saying the next morning as he left to meet his dad. 'I'll see you at training this evening.'

And Skandar would never have asked Mitchell not to go with his father to the water yard – the place where the best water wielders trained. He understood how much Mitchell wanted to make his dad proud and how scared he was of him. He knew Mitchell risked his father's anger every day by being friends with a spirit wielder.

So Skandar came up with a new plan. 'Flo, I'm coming with you.'

'You're a spirit wielder, Skar. You can't go to the Silver Stronghold!'

'But think about it – think about it for a minute,' Skandar pleaded. He knew it was risky and probably very stupid, but he'd been mulling it over all night. He was convinced that once he knew Kenna was definitely a lost spirit wielder, the Mender dreams would come to him easily. Craig's notes had said that young Menders had to focus on an individual. Surely knowing the truth about Kenna would help. Surely then he'd be able to tell the difference between an ordinary dream and a magical one?

'If we cover Scoundrel's blaze and I have the mask, what's the difference? They might not even have another big event at the Stronghold this *year*, Flo. And what if the Weaver kills Kenna's wild unicorn before I can protect it . . . before I've learned how to mend their bond?'

'What about Bobby and Falcon?' Flo asked desperately.

'You know she won't agree right now. It's too late. We have to leave in ten minutes. Please, Flo. Please.'

Flo took a deep breath, closed her eyes and said, 'You have to do everything I tell you. *Everything*. And we absolutely have to be back by nightfall – we have a jousting session tonight, remember?'

Skandar rushed at her, crushing her into a hug. 'Thank you!'

'It's not for you,' Flo said in a muffled voice. 'It's for Kenna.'

But an hour later, Skandar was practically in tears. He and Flo were on the edge of Fourpoint, about to enter an avenue of silver birches that led to the Silver Stronghold. Scoundrel's Luck was refusing to have his blaze covered with black hoof polish. He'd even refused to be bribed with a red Jelly Baby, slamming his teeth shut in protest.

'I'm really sorry, boy, okay? There's no other way. Please, can you just keep still?' Skandar looked anxiously at Flo. 'Can't I just leave him here? Go in on foot?'

'The sentinel always rides in with me, Skar.'

'I should have ridden Red,' Skandar puffed, his hands frozen by the November cold as he tried to pull Scoundrel's head down.

'She wouldn't have obeyed you,' Flo said, shivering. 'She probably would have tried to bite your leg off.'

'Scoundrel, pleeeease!' Skandar begged his black unicorn as he snapped at his black-stained fingers. 'It's only for today, I promise. It won't be like last year! I'll rub it straight off once we're out!'

'Skar.' Flo touched his arm, as light as a unicorn feather. 'Hold Blade, okay? Let me try – you're all worked up.'

After a few attempts Flo finally managed to get enough polish on Scoundrel's head to cover up his long white blaze. 'There you go, you silly thing,' Flo said, stroking Scoundrel's sweaty neck.

Skandar wiped furiously at the tears on his cheeks. He hated falling out with Scoundrel. And he also hated seeing his spirit mark hidden like they were pretending to be water-allied again. But it would be worth it if he could find out if Kenna was a spirit wielder. He'd let Kenna down by not telling her the truth before – he could see that now – but he was going to make things right.

Flo looked very anxious. She hated breaking the rules, and smuggling a spirit wielder into the Silver Stronghold was as illegal as you could get. Their ride through Fourpoint hadn't helped either. Overnight there had been more destruction in the zones. Lost and tired Islanders wandered the streets, having fled to the capital. Flo had directed a few families towards her father's workshop, telling them they could get warm and dry there.

As they entered the Stronghold's avenue, Flo took a deep breath and didn't say anything. Then she took another breath. 'Skar?'

'Yeah?'

'I know we talk a lot about the wild unicorns and the elemental disruption, but you don't really talk about *her*, your mum.'

Skandar swallowed. 'You mean the Weaver.'

'She's your mum too, Skar. And I think you might need to talk about that more.'

'What's the point?' Skandar said defensively. 'My mum's alive and she's the villain. There's not much more to say.'

Flo shook her head and Blade snorted beneath her. 'That's not true. She lied to you, to your sister, to your whole family. All those lies – all that hurt – isn't going to just go away. And there's so much you don't know, particularly about why she left you.'

'I know enough,' Skandar said stiffly.

'All I'm saying is if you keep all the stuff about your mum trapped inside your head, your heart, you're never going to be able to trust anyone. If you want to talk, I'm here.'

Skandar thought of Bobby. About the pain of her branching out. Maybe it was better not to trust anyone with his true feelings. But aloud he said, 'Thanks.'

Flo looked ahead suddenly. 'You'd better get that mask on. As soon as we leave the trees, we'll be in full view.' Her gold earth wielder pin shone on her chest as it caught the sunlight beyond the tree line.

Skandar reached into the saddlebag he'd brought and unwrapped the sentinel mask. It glinted as he passed the straps round the back of his head. Just before he pulled it down over his face, he said, 'Thank you for doing this, Flo.'

'Ha! Thank me when we get out alive.'

'I mean it. I know how much you hate stuff like this.'

'I really do.' She smiled at him. 'But something about you makes me feel braver.'

As they emerged from the avenue, Skandar didn't feel very brave at all. The Stronghold rose up in front of them, blotting out the skyline. It reminded Skandar of a circus tent – but without the fun stripes and laughing children. The centre of the Stronghold was a tall silver tower with a spiked top. Sheets of metal flowed out from one side of the tower, creating a canopy with razor-sharp edges supported by great long spikes.

'That's where the Silver Circle event is today,' Flo whispered as they rode closer. 'We train in that arena too, under the roof. It's so shiny you can see your unicorn's reflection.'

But before they could get anywhere near the arena – and the other buildings within the Stronghold – there was a perimeter wall that made very clear that visitors were not welcome. Great silver discs overlapped, reminding Skandar of the Roman shield formations he'd studied in history lessons back on the Mainland. No sentinels stood behind the giant shields – they were embedded in the ground. Solid. Immovable. It looked like a military camp set up for battle. As Scoundrel approached, Skandar noticed that the centre of every circular shield boasted a different elemental symbol: fire, water, air and earth. No spirit symbol in sight, of course.

'What are they expecting? A war?' Skandar murmured, his voice muffled behind his mask.

'Shhh,' Flo said, her brown eyes searching the wall for something.

'But how do we get in? Where's the entrance?'

'Get behind me and follow.' Her voice was suddenly harsher.

'Don't say anything. Not a word.'

Flo and Blade approached the imposing Silver Stronghold, framed through the eyeholes of Skandar's mask. The silver pair looked like they belonged there. Skandar shivered with dread, remembering the oath Flo had sworn to the Silver Circle. What had she said? *Their side is always going to be the opposite of yours.* And he'd never felt it so keenly as she rode confidently towards the silver fortress that a spirit wielder like him should have been running from.

Blade halted in front of one of the shields, silver wings gleaming in the afternoon sun. Skandar noticed that this particular shield had a small grate at its centre rather than an elemental symbol. Flo leaned forward in her Martina saddle and knocked four times on the shield.

The grate slid open with a swish. 'Identify yourself,' came a gruff voice from the other side.

'Florence Shekoni and Silver Blade.' Skandar was surprised by how steady her voice was. 'This sentinel is escorting me to a Silver Circle meeting. Like, um, usual,' she added, her voice quivering over the last two words.

'Stand back!'

Skandar braced himself, not knowing if this was a good or bad sign. The metal grate swished shut again, and suddenly the curved bottom of the giant silver disc was lifting up and outwards to create a hole in the shield wall for Blade and Scoundrel to pass through. Skandar fought hard not to look up at the shield, suspended above their heads like an upside-down drawbridge. He was posing as a sentinel, after all, and this was where the masked guards ate, slept and trained. Sentinels were the only riders without silver unicorns who had permission to enter the

Stronghold. Even the Commodore wasn't allowed inside.

The shield cranked back down to its position in the wall behind them, but there was no sign of the person who had spoken from behind the grate. Skandar felt very exposed; they were surrounded on every side by shining metal tents of varying sizes. They were confusing to look at: too immobile to pass for real tents. They didn't move in the breeze and were pitched on concrete, not grass. The larger ones clearly housed unicorns – some had horns sticking out between silver flaps – but there had to be at least a hundred smaller tents with sentinels entering and exiting. Skandar tried not to look. It was odd being somewhere without treehouses; he supposed the giant shield wall was enough to protect the Stronghold inhabitants from any wild unicorn stampedes.

'So far, too easy,' Flo breathed, the silver in her black Afro flashing in the sun as she looked over her shoulder.

'Okay, how do I get to the records?' Skandar said, starting to sweat behind his mask despite the cold day. He was feeling a lot more nervous now they were actually inside the shining fortress.

Flo pointed ahead at the silver spike that stretched high into the sky. 'The sentinel library's in that tower – on the bottom three levels. Then you'll need to search the shelves for the records.' She dismounted and when she spoke her voice was tight with worry. 'We need to leave the unicorns here. We're not supposed to take them to the Silver Circle event today. I'm guessing there's some kind of display.'

Skandar's stomach swooped. Let Scoundrel out of his sight right in the middle of the Silver Stronghold?

'Flo, I'm really not sure . . .' Skandar clutched Scoundrel's reins tightly. The unicorn squeaked with concern as his rider's anxiety filled the bond – their argument about the blaze completely forgotten.

'Skar.' Flo's voice was firm. 'You have to trust me. I know how things work here. He'll be all right. He just looks like a sentinel's black unicorn. Nobody is going to pay him any attention if he's inside one of these stable tents. In fact, it's better if he's out of sight, don't you think?'

Skandar dismounted reluctantly. He heard Silver Blade shriek a cheerful call of greeting to a silver unicorn in a tent nearby and remembered what Flo had said. Blade felt comfortable here, and so did Flo – even though she would never admit it. They had to trust her; it was the only way they were going to get out of the Silver Stronghold alive. Even so, Skandar could hardly bear the panicked tug on the bond as he turned and walked away from Scoundrel. He forced himself not to look back.

After several minutes of winding through a warren of gleaming tents, Flo turned right at a blacksmith's forge with silver masks stacked outside in neat piles. How many silver sentinels *were* there on the Island? No wonder Dorian Manning had so much power.

'Okay, so this is the south door of the Spear,' she murmured, pointing at an arched metal door in front of them. A few sentinels walked past on their way into the arena.

'The Spear?'

'That's the tower's name,' she explained quickly.

Skandar looked up. Sharp waves of silver metal flowed from the Spear's side like a big-top canvas, creating the arena's roof ahead of them.

'Whatever you do, don't leave the library. All the sentinels should either be in or on their way to the arena by now, so hide in here until the event is over.'

'Florence!' someone called cheerfully.

Skandar didn't have time to move before a young man had put a hand on Flo's shoulder in greeting . . . and blocked the way into the tower.

'Hi, Rex!' Flo smiled, even though she must have been terrified that this Rex person would recognise Skandar.

'Where are you off to?' He glanced at the tower's door in front of them.

'Nowhere,' Flo said, her smile a little wobbly now. 'I wasn't—'

He chuckled. 'Never mind. Come on, we'll be late!' The young man couldn't have been long out of the Eyrie. Five pairs of wings were stacked on the arm of his battered red jacket, showing he'd completed all five years of training. He was taller than Skandar, and much more muscular, with tanned white skin and cheeks that fizzed with silver electricity. Magic sparked just under his cheekbones, lighting up his face even more when he smiled. The mutation made him look almost *more* perfect somehow.

'Who's your friend?' Rex asked. 'Shouldn't he be coming with us to the arena?'

The man's slight frown suddenly reminded Skandar of someone else. He realised Flo had spoken about this rider before. This was Rex Manning – Dorian Manning's son. Fear crept up Skandar's spine.

'Oh, he's nobody,' Flo waved in Skandar's masked face dismissively. 'I'm sure he'll be along in a minute.' She was already turning Rex away.

Skandar stared after them, his dislike of Rex Manning intensifying as he lost sight of Flo. Then he remembered what he was here for.

Kenna.

The south door of the Spear opened easily. Skandar's heart beat faster as he looked around the circular space. As Flo had hoped, the sentinel librarian who was usually stationed inside had already left for the event in the arena, and the whole library floor was deserted. Curved shelves of books lined the walls, and two leather armchairs were positioned right in the centre, a copy of that morning's *Hatchery Herald* – headline **ELEMENTAL DESTRUCTION CONTINUES** – lying abandoned on a coffee table. Skandar couldn't help thinking it was much cosier in here than the rest of the Stronghold.

Skandar had prepared himself for a long search for the records, but he found them almost immediately. They had their very own cabinet, a cabinet with glass windows marked with the sign of the spirit element. It made Skandar both angry and terrified to see the volumes entombed inside, holding the names of the spirit wielders that should have been. It was almost like they were a particularly interesting specimen in a museum, behind glass for all to see – to be studied in years to come – rather than real people who had been cruelly denied their destiny. He felt the hairs stand up on his neck, and he could almost hear his sister's voice as he thought about her. *It's going to be okay, Kenn. I'm going to fix this.* He took a deep breath and tried the cabinet door.

It wasn't locked – though the way Skandar was feeling right now he'd have happily smashed through the glass. Each thin volume was made of the same white leather as *The Book of Spirit*. They were identical, apart from four numbers printed in gold on the spines. Skandar stared at number 2006, and then 2015, and realised they had to be years. The years the thirteen-year-olds were identified as spirit wielders and should have opened the Hatchery door. Of course his name wouldn't be in there – thanks to Agatha he'd never taken the Hatchery exam and never formally been identified. But Kenna had. Kenna's name *could* be here.

Full of excitement, Skandar found the book dated 2021 and opened it. There was a long introduction about the Weaver and a lot of justification about how important it was to rid the Island of the spirit element. Skandar flicked angrily past the process for identifying sprit wielders – the shaking of a hand, the wrongness of the banned element's energy. Then finally he reached an alphabetical list of names. His eyes zoomed down to the two names under 'S', the words blurring as his hand quivered on the book's narrow spine:

Simon Shen

Kenna Smith

Skandar's skin went completely cold, then hot, then cold again. The difference between suspecting and knowing for sure hit him like a hammer. Memories played in his mind as he stared at his sister's name.

Kenna hugging him tightly on the morning of her Hatchery exam, so excited she danced on the balls of her feet.

Kenna coming home after school and taking such great care to pack her bag for the Island.

Kenna asking Skandar whether he thought she'd need both her hoodies, given she'd be getting a rider's jacket.

Kenna sitting behind the front door after midnight had passed – fifteen minutes, twenty minutes, an hour – waiting for the knocks that would never come.

Kenna crying herself to sleep for months because she would never be a unicorn rider.

And a memory he didn't have, but a moment he'd played over and over in his imagination. Kenna in tears, begging Dad to write to Skandar instead of her because she just couldn't hear about unicorns any more.

White-hot fury burst through Skandar's veins. Fury at his mum for giving the Silver Circle an excuse to do this, at Agatha for failing to escape in time to bring Kenna to the Island, at Dorian Manning for doing this to Kenna – to all the lost spirit wielders. At the Island for letting it happen. Because it wasn't just the Silver Circle who'd ousted the spirit wielders – it was everyone else too. And they were still doing it. Nobody really wanted him training at the Eyrie – how could they, when come the summer solstice more names would be carefully written into these books? More misery. More wild unicorns. More stolen lives.

Skandar's hands shook as he returned the 2021 record to the cabinet, and he made a vow to himself. If he was a Mender, if he could dream, he was going to come back for these books one day. He was going to come back, and he was going to bond his sister to her unicorn – and every single one of the other spirit wielders on those lists. And nobody was going to—

'Argh, thank the four elements I'm not the only one!'

A sentinel poked his masked face round the south door and marched straight for Skandar, who took a big side-step away from the cabinet.

'Come on, mate! We've got to get to the arena – it's time, isn't it? Duty calls.'

'Right,' Skandar said gruffly. And then he did the thing Flo had categorically told him not to do. He left the library.

Skandar emerged into a wall of sound. The tower's north door opened right out into the silver arena. Skandar was immediately in the stands, with hundreds of sentinels talking loudly and excitedly – some of them even eating snacks. Scanning the noisy crowd, Skandar noticed unmasked people sitting in a boxed-off area to his right – the Silver Circle. Flo looked completely terrified. Rex Manning sat next her, speaking seriously into her ear. What was going on?

There was a hush as spiked metal gates were winched upwards on opposite sides of the arena, and two unicorns burst on to the sand. The crowd cheered.

One unicorn was a silver giant: her silver horn cut through the air like a knife, flames blasting off her gleaming wings. Her mouth frothed, her eyes bulged and she kicked her hooves up at the stands, clearly wound up by the noise of the crowd. She looked manic. Skandar didn't understand where the bonded unicorn's rider was. *Why were they letting her get so stressed? Why had Dorian dragged the whole Stronghold into the arena to watch* this?

Then Skandar looked, *really* looked, at the other unicorn. At first he thought he was imagining it. A skeletal body; pus oozing from old wounds; bone-splintered knees; murderous, empty eyes. But no. He could smell death. It was definitely a wild unicorn. But why would—

The crowd started to blow whistles and wave brightly coloured flags, shouting and screaming at the unicorns. Metal partitions came up from under the sand, forcing the bonded and wild unicorn nearer to each other, trapping them closer than they would ever have wanted to get. The silver unicorn screeched with rage and the wild unicorn blasted a combination of elements that gave off a horrible putrid stench.

The silver unicorn and the wild unicorn faced each other in the sandy pit, like gladiators ready to fight to the death.

'What the . . . ?' Skandar couldn't process what he was seeing.

'This your first slaying?' the sentinel asked, peering into the eyeholes of Skandar's mask. 'I thought you looked young. Just recruited, is it?'

Skandar managed a nod but he couldn't tear his eyes away from the battling unicorns, reflected over and over on the arena's shining roof.

Slaying. And as both unicorns lowered their horns to attack, Skandar understood.

It wasn't the Weaver killing the wild unicorns.

It was the Silver Circle.

The realisation hit him so hard he stumbled slightly. The sentinel who'd brought him to the arena laughed, the sound half lost in the shouts of the crowd.

The silver unicorn was clearly winning on strength alone as it forced the wild one into a corner. But then the wild unicorn would blast its magic in desperation and the bonded one would be taken by surprise. The wild unicorn, after all, had nothing in the world to lose.

'Looks like this wild one won't last that long,' the library sentinel said to a friend next to him.

'It looks pretty old,' the friend replied. 'Too old to be hers – one from quite a few solstices past, probably. No sense keeping it for the President's big plan. So into the arena it goes. Doesn't stand a chance against Silver Arrow.'

'How – how exactly is, umm, Arrow going to kill the wild unicorn?' Skandar asked, trying to keep his voice level. 'I thought it couldn't be done.'

'Floundering floods! You *are* new, aren't you? When did you arrive? This morning?'

The two sentinels laughed at him, but the friend answered. 'Bonded unicorn horn. Horn has to go right through the wild unicorn's heart. That's the only way to do it, apparently. The Silver Circle's been researching it since practically the beginning of time. And finally one of us sentinels discovered how – in the Wilderness or something. I don't know. Not really my thing. But this – unicorn battles to the death – now this *is* my thing.'

Skandar tried to understand. 'Unicorns don't usually hurt each other, though, unless they're protecting their rider. Why—'

'Ah well,' the sentinel said, wagging a finger at him, 'that's what the whole spectacle's for. The arena, the small space, the crowd. *Trusted* sentinels have been coming to these for months. All of us being here in the arena, pushing them to a frenzy, it drives the bonded ones mad enough that they can't see another way out. They want a kill. They're monsters, after all.'

The unicorns aren't the monsters in this arena, Skandar thought, but he managed to hold his tongue. 'What about the destruction in the zones, because of the unicorn killings? Because of *this*?'

The sentinels seemed completely confused by this question. 'What are you talking about?' the friend spluttered. 'The zone stuff is all down to the spirit element. There's that spirit wielder training in the Eyrie, isn't there? There was a truesong about it and everything – *spirit's dark friend*, remember? Have you been hiding in a cave in the earth zone?'

'It's like I was saying the other day, Ryan.' The library sentinel shook his head. 'Sentinel recruitment has really gone downhill these days. They'll take anyone!'

'Look, you're young,' Ryan said to Skandar, obviously trying to be reassuring. 'It *is* a bit gory, but it's all for a good cause! If the wild unicorns are gone, then the spirit wielder loses his power. The death element is neutralised and the Island goes back to normal. You want that, don't you?'

Skandar forced himself to nod and concentrated instead on the battle. The wild unicorn's bony ribs were heaving with exhaustion, its chestnut mane matted with blood from a wound in its neck. Skandar wanted to make it stop. He was desperate to save the wild unicorn. He couldn't help thinking of all the spirit wielder names in those books. This unicorn should have belonged to one of them. But he was a spirit wielder trapped in an arena full of sentinels. He'd be arrested in seconds.

Skandar looked over at the Silver Circle's box, and even from this distance he could tell Flo was extremely distressed. She was being physically restrained by Rex Manning and another silver rider, as she screamed, 'You're monsters! You can't let Arrow kill it. Don't you realise what you're doing? I quit. I don't want to be part of this any more. I'm breaking the circle. I don't care! Rex, LET GO OF ME!'

The crowd gasped. Skandar ripped his gaze away from Flo and back to the sandy pit. The wild unicorn was backed up against one of the metal partitions, its chest exposed. Arrow lowered her silver horn and pointed it straight at the wild unicorn's immortal heart. Skandar thought he was going to be sick. It felt impossible that a creature that ought to live for ever was about to be killed in front of his eyes. By one of its own. There was a violence to it that he couldn't begin to process.

'NOOOO!' Flo vaulted over the edge of the stands and into the arena. She had no unicorn. She had no armour. It was just her and two very angry unicorns. Arrow stopped short of her killing blow, momentarily distracted by the girl running towards her. The wild unicorn let out a wailing screech.

Almost in slow motion, Skandar realised what Flo was going to do.

'No,' he muttered under his breath. 'No. Don't do it.'

The crowd were shouting at Flo to get out of the arena.

Thank me when we get out alive. That's what she'd said on the way here. But if she tried this, she was never going to survive. It couldn't possibly work. And before he knew what he was doing, Skandar had jumped clean over the edge of the stands and into the pit too.

'Hey! What do you think you're playing at?' the library sentinel shouted after him, but Skandar was already tearing towards the unicorns. Sand flew up behind him as he sprinted, the noise of the furious crowd a blur of sound in his ears. He was almost there—

But he was too late.

Flo had reached the wild unicorn, its skeletal body half collapsed against the metal partition. It bellowed at her, but she didn't stop. The silver unicorn was bending her enormous head again, a hoof sparking as she pawed the sand, readying her killing blow. Flo ignored it. She reached out a shaking hand to the wild unicorn, passed it over a weeping wound, touched the bloody neck, and – as quick as a flash of her silver-shot hair – she vaulted on to its back.

The reaction was immediate. The wild unicorn screeched in alarm. It had never had a rider on its back before and it must have felt strange. Wrong. Injured though it was, the wild unicorn reared up on its back legs, half smashing Flo against the metal partition.

'Whoa!' Flo was saying. 'Whoa, let me *help* you!'

Meanwhile, Skandar couldn't get past the silver unicorn. It was blasting elements all over the place, and up close it looked almost delirious.

Dorian Manning was shouting orders from the Silver Circle's box. Rex Manning looked like he was about to faint. Sentinels were flooding on to the sand, no doubt to arrest the two invaders. Skandar started to panic. If they caught him, they would remove his mask. The silver unicorn roared in fury, fire erupting from her mouth. Skandar only escaped being incinerated because he was standing so close to her, but it was only a matter of time before he was killed by Arrow or captured by the Silver Circle.

Then the wild unicorn galloped straight for Skandar and he had a third thing to panic about. Flo was barely managing to stay on as the unicorn tossed its transparent horn from side to side, kicking out like a bucking bronco trying to unseat her.

'TAKE MY HAND!' Flo yelled, holding hers out to Skandar on the ground as the unicorn swerved towards him.

By some miracle Skandar's pale white hand found Flo's dark brown one and he was yanked upwards against the wild unicorn's side, his stomach sliding over the unicorn's bony back.

Flo let go, clinging on to the wild unicorn's scraggy mane. 'Get your leg over!' she shouted.

Skandar's arms were burning with the effort of holding on to the creature, but somehow he managed to pull himself further over its back and swing one leg round so he was sitting behind Flo. He threw his arms round her waist.

Behind them, the furious Silver Arrow was blasting a column of fire worthy of a dragon at the sentinels attempting to chase after Flo and Skandar. The silvers in the box and the sentinels in the stands were engulfed in thick black smoke, coughing and shouting for help. Chaos reigned. Skandar doubted that Arrow was assisting their getaway on purpose, but right at that moment he was grateful for the silver unicorn's immense power.

'Oh no!' Flo screamed, as they zoomed towards the metal gate at the end of the arena. The wild unicorn wasn't slowing. In fact, it was increasing its speed towards the daylight on the other side. It wanted to get as far away from its silver predator as possible. It wanted to flee all the way back to the Wilderness. It wanted to go home.

So it jumped.

Clean over the gate, then galloped past metal tents, swerving through the maze of silver obstacles. On one turn Skandar almost slipped off its back, which was slicked with sweat and blood.

'We're going to have to throw ourselves off!' Flo yelled.

Skandar thought he'd misheard her. 'I'm sorry, what?'

'Blade and Scoundrel!' She gritted her teeth as they turned sharply by the blacksmith forge. 'They're still in the stables. And we need to get the shield wall open. We need to throw ourselves off if we – and the wild unicorn – stand any chance of escaping.'

Skandar looked down and immediately regretted it. The concrete was passing extremely quickly below them.

'Now!' Flo said, and before Skandar was anywhere near prepared, she let go of the wild unicorn's matted mane, threw herself sideways and landed on the concrete with a sickening thump, rolling over and over. Without Flo to hold on to, Skandar was catapulted sideways. The wild unicorn shrieked at the sudden lightness of its load.

Skandar hit the ground hard, but managed to keep his hands and arms tucked in. Everything hurt. And smelled horrible. He realised he'd landed on a metal grate and the stench of rotting *something* was wafting upwards. He peered through gaps in the metal and saw large dark shapes moving beneath. Wild unicorns?

'Skar, come on!' Flo shouted. She was already limping towards the tent stable, Blade's silver horn visible over the entrance. Skandar struggled to his feet and followed her.

Scoundrel shrieked in greeting as his rider vaulted on to his back.

The wild unicorn had reached the shield wall and was kicking out at it, blasting the metal with mixtures of elements.

'Open the gate!' Flo screamed at someone unseen. 'I'm a silver and this is an order. Open the gate!'

For a moment nothing happened. And then, slowly but surely, the entry shield cranked upwards to create a gap. The wild unicorn careered down the shield line and galloped clean through the gap in the wall. Blade was right on its tail, Scoundrel bringing up the rear. Somewhere under his exhausted relief, Skandar felt deep joy as he watched the wild unicorn gallop towards the Wilderness.

Flo and Skandar didn't talk until they were safely back inside the silver birch avenue.

'That,' Skandar croaked, 'was the absolute maddest thing I've ever seen in my life.'

Flo looked sheepish. 'I couldn't think of another way to save it. Sorry.'

'Don't apologise!' Skandar laughed, a little manically. 'It was brilliant. It was terrifying. It was breath-taking. It was completely reckless. It was perfect. It— Flo, we almost died.'

Flo stared at him. 'Are you all right?'

'No.' Skandar shook his head. 'No, I'm definitely not.'

They grinned at each other shakily, before the smiles dropped from their lips. What on earth had they done?

'You just rode a wild unicorn through the Silver Stronghold,' Skandar said, as it sank in. But then he remembered. 'Flo, I found Kenna's name in the records. She's on the list of spirit wielders banned from the Hatchery door!'

Flo's eyes filled with tears. 'I'm so sorry she never made it to the Island, Skar.' She turned to face him in her silver-edged saddle. 'All I could think when I saw that wild unicorn –' she wiped a tear from her cheek – 'was what if that was Kenna's? What if I was watching Kenna's unicorn die and doing nothing?!' The last two words were a wail.

'That unicorn wasn't Kenna's, though. I told you, I think hers is the dapple-grey one.'

'Skandar! You don't know that for sure!' Flo used his full name in her exasperation. 'And the point is, that could have been Kenna's. Don't you see?' She dropped her voice. 'How could they do this?'

'I don't know.' Skandar still couldn't believe the Weaver wasn't behind it all. He felt suddenly hopeless. They'd saved one wild unicorn today, but what about all the others? The Silver Circle were the most powerful group on the Island, with the most powerful unicorns. They had a whole army of sentinels at their command. A shining silver war camp. How could Skandar possibly stop them? How long before they caught Kenna's unicorn and killed it in that arena?

Flo must have been thinking the same thing. 'As soon as we get back, I'm going to the instructors. Dorian said it'd be Blade's turn when they catch another wild unicorn. They said it was my duty as a member of the Silver Circle. But I'm never going to let them use him like that. I'm never going to their meetings again. Ever!'

'You have to,' Skandar reasoned. 'What about learning to control Blade? Won't the Silver Circle make you leave the Eyrie if you refuse to go? And what about the oath you swore when—'

'I just rescued a wild unicorn! In front of the whole Stronghold! I think it's a little bit late to worry about all that, don't you?' Flo started to run her shaking hands compulsively through Blade's silver mane. When she spoke again all the bravado had disappeared from her voice. 'Skar, I don't know what's going to happen to me. I don't know what I'm going to do!'

Instinctively Skandar reached out a hand towards Flo, not knowing what he could possibly say to his friend who – despite practically having a phobia of getting told off – was probably in the biggest trouble of her life.

As if on cue, there were hoofbeats behind them. Skandar whipped round in his saddle to see a lone silver unicorn streaking along the avenue.

'Let's get out of here!' Skandar cried, but Flo's mouth was set in a determined line.

'It's Rex,' she said, turning Blade to meet the other silver unicorn head on.

'So what?' Skandar urged, but seeing that Flo wasn't going anywhere, he quickly checked the silver mask still covered his face.

Rex slowed his unicorn to a stop in front of Blade. He looked as white as a sheet, the silver electricity in his cheeks sparking wildly. 'I didn't know,' he puffed. 'You have to believe me, Flo. My father hadn't told me either. I think it's awful too. I'm going to talk to him. I'm going to try to stop this.'

'It doesn't change anything,' Flo said. 'I can't be part of

the Silver Circle if it's going to be responsible for murdering unicorns. And the Island, Rex – people have lost their homes. My dad has three families staying in his workshop!'

'I agree it has to stop, but, Flo –' Rex swallowed – 'my father says he's going to take you out of the Eyrie.'

Skandar's stomach clenched in fear.

'I'll tell him it was all a big misunderstanding. That you were upset. That you understand you've done wrong and won't do anything like this again.'

'I'm not upset. I'm furious! And I *would* do it again!'

'But please, Flo. You have to come to the next meeting. I think I can smooth it over if you just agree to do that. I'm his son; he'll listen to me.'

'I'm not coming back, Rex,' Flo said fiercely. 'In the arena, your father told me he wanted Blade to be the next wild unicorn killer. I'll never let that happen.'

'If you don't come back voluntarily, you'll be forced to live in the Stronghold full-time. Don't you understand?'

'Are you threatening me?'

'Of course I'm not! I'm your friend!'

But Flo had clearly had enough. She summoned the earth element to her palm, threw up a sand shield between their unicorns, and galloped Blade away down the avenue. Skandar urged Scoundrel to follow, but he turned once to look over his shoulder.

Rex and his unicorn were still there, watching them go.

CHAPTER TEN

JOUSTING IN THE DARK

Later that evening, Skandar's head was spinning as he flew Scoundrel's Luck down to the Nestling plateau, trying to make sense of everything that had happened that day.

Kenna was a lost spirit wielder. That didn't mean that she *definitely* would have opened the Hatchery door, but given who her mum was, and who Agatha was, and the fact that Skandar had been destined for a unicorn – well, it seemed pretty likely that there would've been a unicorn waiting for her inside. Skandar could hardly control his rage when he thought about the night Kenna should have tried the Hatchery door. But if Skandar was a Mender and able to identify her unicorn from a dream – then he might be able to fix things, to bond them together, after all.

The Weaver wasn't responsible for killing the wild unicorns. At first Skandar was relieved his mum wasn't behind it, but once they'd returned from the Stronghold he felt unsettled. The idea of Erika Everhart killing wild unicorns and causing elemental chaos on the Island had meant he could focus on her being evil, rather than the fact she was his mum. But now what? Where was she? What was she doing? A tiny part of him thought: *What if she's sorry for last year? What if she doesn't want to be the Weaver any more?* It had been easier to squash those feelings when he thought she was the killer.

Mitchell was horrified when Flo and Skandar described the brutal way the immortal creatures were being killed by the Silver Circle – a bonded unicorn's horn running through a wild heart. Bobby had been nowhere to be found, but as Flo and Skandar tried to wash the blood from their wounds as best they could, the three of them agreed to tell the Eyrie instructors that evening. Despite Rex's assurances, Skandar kept expecting Dorian Manning to turn up any minute and drag Flo and Blade back to the Stronghold for ever.

Scoundrel soared down to a landing strip marked out with colourful lanterns, meeting the ground with a clink of his armour. This would be the Nestlings' first mock tournament, where they'd go head-to-head using different elements in the dark. It was all in preparation for the real jousting tournament at the end of the year, when six of them would be declared nomads and leave the Eyrie. According to the instructors, jousting in the dark was a good way for beginners to improve their skills – it was easier to see the glow of the magic. Skandar suspected it had something to do with the instructors' sense of drama too.

Skandar winced as his gashed knees smarted under his armour – his and Flo's injuries were still fresh from the Stronghold getaway. Gritting his teeth against the pain, he looked round for Blade and Red. Unfortunately since Red was on her best behaviour nowadays, there were no fiery farts to help Skandar identify his friends in the dark.

When he eventually found them, Mitchell was already talking strategy. 'Okay, so there are four pistes – these lines of torches – one for each element.' Mitchell pointed. 'There's an instructor on each one, judging the jousts. It shouldn't be too hard to speak to them between the matches.'

'Wish I got a spirit piste,' Skandar muttered. 'I'd win every time.' He saw a swish of a white cloak in the distance and wondered why Agatha had even bothered to come.

'Should we speak to Bobby?' Mitchell asked. 'We could do with her tackling Instructor Saylor. She *is* good at persuading people to listen to her. Mainly because she never lets anyone else talk, but—'

'I don't think we can wait,' Flo interrupted, grimacing as moving her mouth reopened a cut on her cheek. 'We need the instructors' support now if we're going to convince the Commodore that the Silver Circle are behind the killings. And *I'm* going to need their support if Rex can't persuade his father I should stay in the Eyrie.' Her voice was high-pitched with fear. 'We need to be ready if they come for me and Blade. And I don't think Bobby would agree to help us because of the way she's been feeling about –' Flo glanced at Skandar – 'things.'

Skandar's heart clenched, though with sadness or fear he wasn't sure. He knew what Flo meant. Because of the way Bobby was feeling about *him*.

'Okay, okay,' Mitchell said. 'We'll tell them now.'

'I'll talk to Instructor Saylor,' Skandar called to his friends as he and Scoundrel were summoned to joust Meiyi and Rose-Briar's Darling on the air piste. The riders and unicorns would rotate between pistes, all practising with weapons of the four *official* elements. Skandar was surprised Meiyi wasn't refusing to joust the spirit wielder, but perhaps she wanted to beat him.

Once they were in position at the end of the line of torches, Scoundrel's mane burst into flame in three different places as Skandar tried to hold him back. The black unicorn had learned very quickly that jousting meant galloping as fast as he could towards the unicorn at the other end – which for Scoundrel was enormous fun. *He* didn't have to mould a weapon of pure magic. Or worry about one hitting him. All he had to do was go as fast as possible, which was basically his favourite thing. Skandar could almost hear Scoundrel thinking: *But why do we have to wait for a whistle?*

'Whoa boy, steady,' Skandar murmured.

'Riders ready?' Instructor Saylor called. Skandar held up his right palm to signal – his Hatchery wound catching the moonlight – and Meiyi did the same at the opposite end.

Instructor Saylor blew the whistle sharply, the veins of her throat crackling. Scoundrel exploded forward with a half-rear, nearly throwing Skandar out of his saddle. The round shield on his left arm clanked against Jamie's armour. He recovered just in time to hear the second whistle. The signal for weapons.

The Nestlings were nowhere near as quick at summoning weapons as the instructors. Skandar's palm glowed yellow, and he moulded one of his favourites – a sabre of pure lightning that fizzed and crackled. Pleased with how the weapon had turned out, Skandar wrapped his hand round the curved hilt. Meiyi, however, wasn't doing so well. As they galloped closer, Skandar saw the fire wielder struggling to mould an electrical bow in her hands. The air magic at the top and bottom kept escaping, breaking out of its shape.

The tips of the unicorns' horns passed each other: black and grey. Meiyi panicked as Skandar drew back his right arm ready to swipe at her armoured chest, adrenaline blotting out the pain of his injuries from earlier. Abandoning her bow, Meiyi moulded a tiny sparking arrow barely bigger than her hand and threw it. The attack was premature. Skandar had time to knock it away with his round shield and then strike Meiyi's chest at exactly the right moment to knock her clean out of her saddle.

'Skandar and Scoundrel win!' Instructor Saylor chimed, holding up the arm on Skandar's side of the piste to indicate that – since he'd unseated his opponent – he had the victory.

Riderless Briar roared and snapped her teeth at Skandar's knee. Scoundrel reared up and flapped his wings aggressively, snarling and keen to retaliate. Skandar managed to turn Scoundrel away from the angry grey unicorn, dismounted and rushed over to make sure Meiyi was okay. Briar galloped furiously across the plateau, with Instructor Saylor chasing after her on North-Breeze Nightmare.

Meiyi was struggling to get up under the weight of her armour. Not everyone was lucky enough to have Jamie Middleditch as a blacksmith – his armour somehow weighed practically nothing, while still protecting against the hardest of blows.

Skandar stuck out his hand to help Meiyi off the ground.

'Coming to possess me, are you?' Meiyi shouted through her helmet.

'What? No! I'm trying to help you up.'

Alastair and Kobi rushed past the burning torch line. 'Don't touch her, spirit wielder,' Alastair snarled. The earth wielder's mutation somehow made him look even angrier – the skin on one half of his face was stony and cracked like ancient rock.

'Can't move for spirit wielders,' Kobi said. 'We practically have one in our own treehouse.'

'Speaking of . . .' Alastair murmured, lip curling.

It was Amber, climbing down from Thief. 'Meiyi! Are you all right? Let me help you!' She shoved past the boys – who had been far too busy insulting spirit wielders to actually help their friend – and stretched a hand down to Meiyi.

'Oh, great, it's you. No, thanks.' Meiyi rolled over away from Amber, chainmail clanking.

'Did you possess her?' Amber turned to Skandar. 'Why is she still on the ground? I mean it, Skandar, twice might be unlucky, but three times?' She sounded genuinely angry.

'I didn't do anything!' Skandar protested. 'I just beat her in our joust!' He could feel Alastair and Kobi's eyes on him too.

Amber shook her head, the star mutation on her head crackling. 'Did you take out your anger with Bruna on Meiyi? Did you? I've heard spirit wielders have terrible tempers—'

'*You* would know, Amber,' Kobi drawled. 'Why are you even talking to us?'

'We've told you not to be seen with us in public,' Alastair said. 'It's bad enough you're still in our quartet. Bad enough that Whirlwind Thief hangs around with the spirit unicorn. Maybe we should suspect you of possessions too, since you're half spirit wielder?'

Amber opened her mouth, but no words came out.

Meiyi had managed to sit up. 'We're not *friends* any more, Amber. Don't embarrass yourself.'

Amber's shoulders slumped, her chestnut hair falling over her face.

Skandar felt fury reignite in his chest. People like Alastair, Meiyi and Kobi were exactly the kind of Islanders who were responsible for those lists of spirit wielder names. The suspicion. The blame. The fear that meant the Hatchery door remained closed to his elemental family. Somehow Amber going on about him possessing people didn't annoy him as much. He'd seen how her mother treated her last year – how she'd been raised to hate spirit wielders – and guessed how confused she must be about her dad. It wasn't her fault Simon Fairfax had gone bad, just as it wasn't Skandar's fault his mum was the Weaver. What excuse did the other members of the Threat Quartet have except that they wanted to punish Amber? To make her feel small.

'Get out of here,' Skandar growled at the three sniggering Nestlings.

'Or what?' Meiyi giggled, flicking her straight black hair. 'You'll possess us?'

'Get out of here,' Skandar said again. 'This isn't how friendship's supposed to work, you know? You're all supposed to look out for Amber . . . no matter what happens.' And when they didn't move, he placed a hand on Scoundrel's flank and summoned the spirit element into the bond, letting the light grow brighter in his hand.

Kobi looked scared, Alastair looked angry and Meiyi screamed, 'We'll tell! You can't threaten us like that!'

'Leave Amber alone. It's pathetic,' Skandar said, his voice full of disgust.

The three Nestlings stared at the glowing ball of white in Skandar's hand. Then Alastair and Kobi scrambled to help Meiyi struggle to her feet and she clinked off to collect Briar from Instructor Saylor.

The star on Amber's forehead was spitting sparks. 'I don't need you to fight my battles for me, spirit wielder.'

'You're welcome.'

'Just because our unicorns are friends, it doesn't mean we are.'

'I know,' Skandar said with a shrug.

Amber's nose wrinkled, clearly rattled. 'Sticking up for me doesn't mean anything. It doesn't mean I'll stop telling people you're possessing riders and killing the wild unicorns.'

'I know.' Skandar sighed. 'That's not why I did it.'

Amber looked thoroughly confused as she galloped Thief away.

With Instructor Saylor still busy with Briar, Skandar returned to Mitchell and Flo to find them whispering frantically; Mitchell was even throwing his arms around wildly.

'What's wrong?' Skandar asked immediately.

'Dorian Manning has already got to the instructors,' Mitchell said gloomily.

'He told them I had a breakdown at the Stronghold!' Flo cried.

'And that she was hallucinating because of an overload of magic in the bond from Blade,' Mitchell added.

'And they believed that?' Skandar asked, incredulous.

Mitchell put on Instructor O'Sullivan's sharp voice. 'I know that's what Flo *told* you she saw, but silver magic can be very overwhelming. She was most likely confused.'

'Instructor Webb said if I disobey any more of the Silver Circle's orders, Dorian Manning is going to insist I train in the Stronghold. For everyone's protection.' Flo's mouth wobbled.

'I'm going to talk to Agatha,' Skandar said determinedly.

'We can't trust her,' Mitchell protested. 'She doesn't have any power anyway – it's not worth the risk!'

'I won't tell her I was at the Stronghold.' Skandar was already handing Scoundrel's reins to Mitchell. 'But even though she doesn't have much influence, she must know a lot about the Circle, given her, umm—'

'History of being their Executioner?' Flo finished for him.

Skandar found Agatha lurking in a dark corner of the training ground.

'I'd advise against creeping up on me in the shadows.' Agatha turned on the spot.

Skandar still found her brash manner a little unsettling, but he was starting to get used to it. Like she'd said, she'd been forced to kill spirit unicorns and then imprisoned for fifteen years, so you couldn't exactly expect her to be chirpy all the time.

'That was a well-constructed sabre,' she mused. 'Although next time you'd be better off going for your opponent's left-hand side. Since you're right-handed, if you attack from the right you expose your own chest. Attack from the left with the blade across your body and your arm shields you.'

'Right, thanks,' Skandar said hurriedly. 'Ag— Instructor Everhart, I need to tell you something.'

Agatha's sinewy cheeks flashed as she turned towards him.

Skandar told her everything they'd found out at the Stronghold – well, not quite. He left out the part about Kenna and made it sound like Flo had been there alone.

'And also I, umm, *Flo* overheard some sentinels saying that the Silver Circle were targeting the young wild unicorns. But she didn't understand why that was,' Skandar finished breathlessly.

Agatha stayed very still for a moment. 'I thought this might happen. I thought you being here, a free spirit wielder, would make Dorian Manning do something . . .' She searched for the right word.

'Evil?'

'Well, I was going to say "stupid" – but yes. Although it's not just about killing the wild unicorns, don't you see? Dorian Manning obviously thinks you're a Mender.'

Skandar stared at her.

'Commodore McGrath must have told him what you did last year to fix her bond with New-Age Frost. It's been a long time since there's been spirit magic on this Island; it wouldn't be surprising for Dorian Manning to jump to that conclusion.'

Skandar frowned. 'But I don't see how that has anything to do with the Silver Circle killing the wild unicorns.'

Agatha sighed, clearly frustrated by Skandar's slowness. 'What was the first thing you wanted to do when you found out you might be a Mender?'

Skandar swallowed, Kenna's name in the spirit wielder records swimming across his vision. 'I wanted to bond my sister to her destined unicorn.' He suddenly remembered what the brainwashed sentinel had said in the arena: 'If the wild unicorns are gone, then the spirit wielder loses his power.'

'Exactly,' Agatha said. 'But what if you didn't stop with Kenna? What if you decided to right the wrongs that had been done to your fellow spirit wielders? What if you decided to build an army of them? An army with bonds much stronger than the Weaver's. Bonds that should always have been made. True bonds.'

Agatha was right – when he'd seen the spirit wielder names he hadn't just thought of Kenna. He'd felt fury at the whole Island for what they'd done, for what they were doing right now. And it was still there deep within him: the idea of finding and bonding all the lost spirit wielders. Perhaps Dorian Manning *should* be worried about him.

Agatha was still talking. 'And my theory is that's why the Silver Circle are targeting the younger wild unicorns. It makes sense; their destined riders will still be alive. No use wasting energy killing a wild unicorn that's five hundred years old – a Mender wouldn't be able to bond it to anyone anyway. Its rider would be dead.'

'The younger the lost rider, the easier the mending process will be,' Skandar said, accidentally repeating Craig's note on Menders.

'What?' Agatha snapped.

Skandar hesitated. If he was going to ask Agatha more about the dreams, he needed to catch her in a good mood. Which was absolutely not while they were talking about spirit armies. He changed tack. 'But what should we do about the killings? The other instructors don't believe Dorian's behind it. We have to do something! Especially if the Silver Circle are doing this because of me!'

Agatha arched a brown eyebrow. '*We* aren't going to do anything. Nobody is going to believe two spirit wielders over the whole Silver Circle. Especially when they're conveniently blaming the magical destruction on the spirit element, and more specifically on *you*. No. I need to stay out of prison, and *you* need to train in the Eyrie.'

'But—'

'The only way anyone will believe the Silver Circle are doing this is if they see it with their own eyes. And you can't risk being involved in that, can you?'

As Agatha swept off into the night, he had the distinct feeling that although she'd been trying to talk him out of it, her last two words had sounded rather like a challenge. *Can you?*

Skandar arrived back at the fire piste at the exact moment Bobby drew back the fiery string on her perfectly formed flaming bow and launched an arrow right at Romily's armoured chest. He grinned, despite their falling-out, and then immediately felt sad. Bobby was the best. She didn't need a Shekoni saddle or a Peregrine Society invitation to prove that. None of them, not even Flo and Blade, really stood a chance against her magic. Really, they were all in her shadow. He just wished he could make her see that she could be the best *and* still be his friend. He missed her. He missed her teasing and her jokes and her honesty. He missed their talks about life on the Mainland. He missed how she pushed him to be braver. He knew it was selfish, but he wanted her back – like before.

He thought about his mum. Maybe this was what would always happen to him? Maybe that's what being a spirit wielder really meant? People abandoning him. He thought about Erika leaving her young family. About Flo swearing the silver oath. About Kenna refusing to write to him. Even Mitchell had tried to leave him at first.

Back on the piste for the second round, Midnight Star and Falcon's Wrath galloped towards each other. Romily waved her shield wildly to try to deflect Bobby's magic weapon, but it was no use. The arrow hit her hard in the chest again and she only just managed to stay in the saddle.

A few other riders were watching Bobby and Romily now, their own matches finished.

'Two to zero,' Instructor Anderson called, the flames at his ears flicking as he held up an arm on Bobby's side of the piste.

'C'mon, Romily!' Elias and Walker shouted. The trio were very close. Because of the number of unicorns hatched in their year, there'd never been a fourth member to complete their quartet.

'Flo,' Skandar whispered, as Falcon and Star moved back into position to joust the last point. 'You know what Dorian said about using Blade for the next killing. Did he tell you when it might be?'

Flo shook her head, her voice miserable. 'I don't know *when*, but he said I'm supposed to ride Blade with the hunting party – the riders that catch the wild unicorn to be killed. I'll get an hour's warning to fly to the Stronghold and join the hunt.'

'But how do the hunters know where to go?' Skandar asked quietly, as Instructor Anderson blew the first whistle. The muscles in Falcon's hindquarters rippled with power as she launched herself forward.

'The sentinels track a herd, tell us its position and then we're all supposed to catch the targeted wild unicorn together. Dorian told us all about it in the arena. Not that I'm going to help them,' she added fiercely. 'Even if it gets me thrown out of the Eyrie.'

Skandar thought hard. The truesong warned that the unicorn deaths and the elemental unrest were linked, and Skandar was getting more worried by the day that the Island he loved might very well destroy itself. And now Skandar knew for sure that one of the wild unicorns in the Wilderness had been destined for Kenna, there was no way he was going to risk the Silver Circle getting their hands on it. They had to stop the Silver Circle killing the wild unicorns.

'An hour,' Skandar murmured, a plan forming in his mind. 'What if you didn't have to disobey Dorian? What if you could do what the Silver Circle want *and* stop them from killing any more wild unicorns?'

'Skar, what are you—'

Just then screams broke out among the other riders. Skandar looked up sharply towards Bobby and Falcon, but he could barely see them. A tornado flew from her hand, followed by a blast of fire, then she flung sharp rocks towards the watching crowd, followed by a wave of water. Romily was so terrified that she urged Midnight Star away into the night sky. Other riders followed, the dark causing collisions and confusion.

Skandar jumped on to Scoundrel's back. 'Bobby!' he yelled. 'BOBBY!'

'She's possessed! She's not responding to anything. Look at her eyes!' Mitchell shouted, as he and Red galloped over from their own joust.

Elemental debris spiralled in the multiple tornadoes Bobby had summoned. She sat on Falcon's back in the middle of it all, unseeing and uncaring as destruction surrounded them.

Flo shrieked as three lightning bolts exploded from Bobby's palm and struck the ground by Blade's left hoof. The silver unicorn reared up in anger, blasting back a mixture of flint and sand from his hooves.

'We've got to do something!' Skandar cried.

'It'll wear off in a minute,' Mitchell said, though he didn't sound very convinced. 'Isn't that what happened with Gabriel? And Rickesh?'

'But it's Bobby! What if she hurts herself?' Skandar insisted. 'I'm going to get her off Falcon. Then at least she won't be able to summon magic.' A soaring piece of flaming rock flew past his left ear, as if to make the point.

'Skar, you can't go over there. You'll get hurt; Scoundrel will get hurt!' Flo pleaded. She struggled to keep Blade under control; smoke was building up from his back.

Skandar ignored her and galloped Scoundrel straight towards Bobby and into the swirling storm. There was a flash of electricity and Falcon's teeth lit up in the dark, her jaw wide open in a menacing roar. Skandar felt Scoundrel's confusion in the bond. Falcon was his friend. Wasn't she? But Falcon flapped icy winds with her wings and Bobby lifted her palm, glowing red for a fire attack this time, her eyes completely vacant.

But Skandar was ready. He summoned the spirit element to his palm, the cinnamon smell filling his nostrils as he reached out with a ball of white magic and took hold of the yellow cord between Bobby's and Falcon's hearts. Their attack died in the bond. Bobby screamed with wrath, her eyes rolling back in her head like a vengeful zombie. Before she could recover, Skandar rode Scoundrel right up to Falcon, and pulled Bobby sideways out of the saddle.

It was more difficult than Skandar had anticipated, and Scoundrel screeched in alarm as their combined weight pulled his rider off his back too. Skandar and Bobby hit the ground hard in a tangle of limbs, armour and smoke.

Skandar recovered first, ignoring the pain in his already battered body, and turned Bobby over, removing her helmet so he could see her face. She spluttered, then coughed, then opened clear brown eyes.

'Skandar— I— Falcon—' she choked out, sitting up. And then her breathing worsened, becoming a whistle and then wheeze.

'Breathe, Bobby,' Skandar said, gripping her hand through the panic attack. 'It's over now. It's over.'

'I've. Never. Felt. Anything. Like. That . . . The bloodlust . . . the need to kill . . .' Her breathing started to improve. 'Is that really what Falcon's like? Is that what she really wants all the time?'

'I think it's what she'd be like without the bond,' Skandar said quietly. 'If she'd hatched wild.' He thought for a moment of the dapple-grey unicorn. Of Kenna.

Flo had caught a very confused Falcon and led her over.

But as Falcon dipped down her great grey head to check her rider, Bobby jerked away from the unicorn. 'I can't – I can't be near her right now.'

Instructor Saylor galloped over on North-Breeze Nightmare. She looked terrified.

'Bobby was possessed,' Mitchell said quickly. 'Just like Gabriel. Possessed by Falcon through the bond.'

Instructor Saylor's usually sunny face turned grim. She crouched next to Bobby on the ground, murmuring words Skandar couldn't hear. After a moment she rose, her yellow cloak billowing in the night breeze. 'I'll take Bobby back to the Eyrie, get her checked out at the healer treehouse. Can you take Falcon's Wrath with you?'

Flo nodded, clutching the unicorn's leather reins.

'Come on, sweet pea,' Instructor Saylor murmured, as she helped Bobby to her feet.

Skandar, Mitchell and Flo walked back to the Eyrie with the unicorns. It was too difficult to fly; Falcon was making an enormous fuss about being separated from her beloved rider. Skandar couldn't help but notice that Blade was back to his aloof and imperious self; there was no sign of the cheerful greeting he'd given his silver unicorn friend back in the Stronghold.

Which reminded Skandar of his plan. 'I think I know how we

can stop the Silver Circle *and* make sure Flo doesn't get locked in the Stronghold,' Skandar said, his breath swirling in the cold of the night.

'But none of the instructors believed us!' Mitchell protested.

'Instructor Everhart did,' Skandar said determinedly. 'And she gave me an idea.'

'Uh-oh,' Flo breathed, and shut her eyes.

'We need to stop the Silver Circle killing the wild unicorns, right?' Skandar said, as they reached the Eyrie's colourful entrance tree.

'Yes . . .' Mitchell and Flo sounded very wary.

'And if nobody believes what we're saying, then we have to *show* them. Show the Commodore the truth. With you as an insider, Flo, with knowledge of when the hunters are going after another wild unicorn, I'm sure we could somehow get the Circle caught.'

Mitchell narrowed his eyes. 'That all sounds very vague.'

Flo sighed. 'It all sounds very *dangerous*. But we can't let the Silver Circle keep getting away with this. Look what's happening to the zones. Look what just happened to Bobby! What if she'd injured herself – or worse? What if she'd killed someone else? And that's before we even start worrying about the Silver Circle killing Kenna's unicorn.' She took a deep breath. 'Okay, I'm in.'

'I'm obviously in,' Mitchell huffed. 'But it's going to require a far more detailed plan than that, Skandar. Quartet Meetings every night for – for – well, until Blade gets summoned to join the hunt.'

'It definitely needs your blackboard,' Skandar said, a half-smile on his lips.

Mitchell beamed. 'I thought you'd never ask.'

CHAPTER ELEVEN

UNICORN HUNTERS

The Threat Quartet weren't the only riders now convinced Skandar was responsible for the possessions. After what had happened to Bobby, the rest of the Eyrie had put together spirit wielder, wild unicorns and magical possession and – surprise – got Skandar. And it didn't help that most of the Eyrie seemed to know that he and Bobby had been in a fight for weeks. Many Islanders didn't even bother to keep their voices down as they traded theories about how exactly he was using the bond to possess his fellow riders. The other Mainlanders – Sarika, Gabriel, Zac and Mariam – generally stood up for him, but most of the other Nestlings had started avoiding Skandar in the Trough or at training.

'It won't be for ever,' Zac had said, trying to cheer Skandar up after earth training one day – Benji and Cursed Whisper had refused to joust *'the spirit wielder'* again. 'People just like having someone to blame, don't they? Once the killings stop, I'm sure it'll all pass over.'

But it wasn't passing over, and Skandar and his friends were still waiting for their chance to stop the Silver Circle's killings. Flo had been ordered to resume her meetings, with dire warnings about being on her last chance. And, sure enough, Dorian Manning had again insisted she prove her loyalty to the Silver Circle by allowing Blade to be used on the next hunt. Ironically, this was exactly what Flo, Mitchell and Skandar wanted. But November had turned to December, and it still hadn't happened yet.

Meanwhile, more and more of the Islanders in the Eyrie had families who had been displaced by the unpredictable magic raging in the elemental zones. And the destruction was getting more serious by the day. The *Hatchery Herald* was filled with reports of cavernous cracks swallowing fields of crops, of fires refusing to be extinguished by even the strongest of water wielders, of rivers rising in impossibly large waves and washing away treehouses, of winds faster than a hundred kilometres per hour tearing whole forests apart.

And on top of all that, the zones were being plagued by more wild unicorn stampedes than usual. Skandar wondered whether it was the elemental destruction that was unsettling the creatures, or the fact they were being hunted. As a result, the streets of Fourpoint were packed with those whose homes had been destroyed, or who believed the capital was the only safe place left on the Island.

Mitchell had developed a theory about the Island's revenge, having spoken to an older water wielder when he'd had lunch with his father. 'She confirmed what I've thought all along,' Mitchell told them one night as they sat round the blackboard. 'The Island doesn't have *feelings*; it's all about equilibrium, balance. The wild unicorns are embedded deep in the magical fabric of this Island – many have been here for centuries. Longer, even. And they're allied to all five elements. So if you take them out, then it makes sense that the magic of the Island would become unbalanced. It makes sense that our bonds with unicorns – which are actually *made* of elemental magic – would be affected. Destruction in the zones, possession of bonds, it all *looks* an awful lot like the Island is taking revenge, doesn't it? But it isn't, not really.'

Flo sighed. 'It makes sense, Mitchell, but I don't think it's going to matter very much to people getting injured or losing their homes whether it's unbalanced magic or the Island's revenge, do you?'

And that wasn't the only thing Skandar had to worry about. After recovering from being possessed, Bobby had – unfortunately – remembered that Skandar had saved her. They'd got into a huge argument.

'I cannot *believe* you saved me without my permission!' Bobby had shouted at him from her hammock in the healer's treehouse. 'Now I'm the girl Skandar Smith rescued. Great.'

Skandar hadn't been able to stop his temper rising. 'Well, I *am* sorry! Maybe I should have just left you to kill everyone?'

'Maybe you should have!' Bobby shouted back at him.

'Next time I will!'

'Good!'

But Bobby had a bigger problem. She wouldn't get back on Falcon's Wrath. The best rider in their year had completely lost her nerve. Flo and Mitchell had both tried to speak to her on her own, tried to explain how important it was that she train for the jousting tournament that looked a lot closer now December had arrived. But even the threat of being declared a nomad couldn't make Bobby ride Falcon.

On the last day of training before their week off, Mitchell tried to force the issue again. 'Are you going to try riding Falcon during our winter break? It might be good without the pressure of training.'

Skandar watched the conversation from a beanbag under his painted seascape and could see Bobby's eyes were flinty. 'I told you – I'm not riding Falcon at the moment.'

Mitchell looked hurt, but jabbed a finger at the blackboard anyway. 'Roberta, we need you for the plan.' He hadn't said this aloud before, but they all knew it was true. 'Apart from Scoundrel, Falcon is the fastest flier in this quartet. We need you to be on board with the plan *and* riding by the time the Silver Circle summon Flo and Blade. Without you . . .' Mitchell tailed off, as Bobby disappeared up the tree trunk and into her bedroom.

Flo sighed. 'The old Bobby would have been horrified to miss even one training session, but the new one? She doesn't seem to care about anything. Not us. Not even Falcon.'

'It can't be fun having a unicorn in your head like that,' Mitchell murmured. 'Feeling the most bloodthirsty urges of the creature your soul is linked to. It's a reminder of what unicorns actually are. Ferocious. Magical. And deadly.'

'Gabriel and Rickesh are okay now,' Flo pointed out.

'But Gabriel wasn't *riding* Queen's Price when he was possessed. And Rickesh is an adrenaline junkie *and* a Rookie. He's got more experience.'

Skandar looked up from his sketchbook. 'She's not going to listen to us. She doesn't even want to be *near* me.' He went back to his sketches of Scoundrel, dreaming of a dapple-grey unicorn. He hadn't told the others, but he was thinking of sleeping in Scoundrel's stable over the winter break, to see if the Mender dreams would come.

'Well, we can't let her be declared a nomad,' Mitchell said sternly. 'A quartet with three people just doesn't add up. We all have to stay together. This branching-out nonsense needs to stop. I want us all to make it through to Preds, leave the Eyrie without having our pins smashed to pieces, and become Chaos riders. I'm not having Roberta Bruna ruining that for me.'

'But how do we get through to her?' Skandar asked desperately.

Mitchell frowned, and went back to the blackboard. 'I'll think of something.'

The week of the winter solstice arrived. The Hatchlings were still training – and the Fledglings, Rookies and Preds were – well – partying. During the winter break, each den held a dance for its own wielders, but they were each allowed to invite one other person. The Nestlings, however, weren't old enough to go to the den dances and were on rest for a whole week. Skandar was glad to stop jousting practice. He'd been avoiding the spirit element – partly because he was terrified of being possessed while using it, and partly because most of the other riders reacted with fear and anger when they saw the spirit weapons. Many of them refused to joust him altogether, just like they'd dropped out of the race the day of the Saddle Ceremony, especially as Scoundrel wasn't exactly shy about blasting the white element from his wings. But Skandar was trying to forget about it. He had big plans for the break that mainly involved sleeping in

Scoundrel's stable and trying to dream of his sister's unicorn.

Mitchell and Flo had both advised Skandar against trying to have a Mender dream, but Skandar thought the spirit wielder that Craig had spoken to must have been exaggerating. How could Skandar possibly die if his body was safe in Scoundrel's stable?

'Didn't Agatha say it was dangerous too?' Mitchell asked as Skandar left their bedroom with a blanket the first night of the winter break.

'We know the Silver Circle are targeting young wild unicorns!' Skandar argued. 'There's no time to waste. And once I've had the dream, I'm going to ask Agatha to teach me how to actually *do* the mending and then when Kenna comes to the jousting tournament at the end of the year, I'll be ready.'

She'll be able to train in the Eyrie with me – maybe even sleep in our treehouse, Skandar thought to himself. *She'll never have to go back to the Mainland and Dad can live with us on the Island too if I give him the money I've saved.*

The first night in Scoundrel's stable, Skandar was full of hope. He tucked himself right under Scoundrel's downy black wing and laid his head on the unicorn's side and they both fell asleep immediately. But eight hours later Skandar woke in the morning light to Scoundrel chewing on a clump of his hair and straw down one trouser leg. No dream.

By the fourth night, Skandar wished he had training to distract him. All he'd managed to conjure was a terrifying nightmare, in which Rickesh's phantom version of the First Rider had chased him around the colourful burial trees in the graveyard. Was it possible that Skandar wasn't a Mender, after all? He was lonely and miserable. There was no Peregrine Society meeting that week. The nights had become bitterly cold – even snuggled up against Scoundrel in his stable. There was no mention of Kenna in Dad's Christmas card. Skandar missed hearing her voice in the way she wrote her sentences, which words she chose, but she hadn't even signed her name. And as if that wasn't enough, the rest of his quartet kept disappearing for hours at a time.

Of course, Bobby wasn't speaking to him, and that alone made Skandar desperately sad. He hadn't told the others, but he'd taken to sneaking into Falcon's stable and combing her already perfect mane. He felt like it brought him closer to Bobby, perhaps because Falcon was joined to her rider through the bond. Skandar had started to talk to Falcon, ask her questions about Bobby. 'What do you think I can say to her that will get her to change her mind?' Mostly Falcon bit him or gave him an electric shock in response, but somehow even that was comforting.

But it wasn't just Bobby who was making Skandar feel gloomy. Once they'd planned how they were going to get Commodore Kazama to witness the Silver Circle's crimes, Mitchell and Flo kept vanishing as well. Skandar thought Mitchell was probably hanging out with Jamie somewhere – the two had been spending more and more time together, researching truesongs. Or perhaps he was evading Skandar because of Ira, who had started writing to Mitchell to warn him that *if he ever wanted to be taken seriously as Commodore he had to avoid the spirit wielder and keep the Silver Circle on side.*

At the time, Mitchell had moaned in despair – 'My father's acting like I'm going to win the Chaos Cup by the end of the year! I can't even qualify until I'm a Rookie!' But now Skandar wasn't sure whether Mitchell had taken it more to heart.

And Flo? Part of Skandar wondered if she was choosing to

spend time with Bobby away from him. It made him feel jealous and hopeless. Was his whole quartet *branching out* from him just like Bobby had done? Were they fed up of all the trouble he got them into? Maybe they were in the dens with all the other riders of their own element? Maybe they preferred it to hanging out in the treehouse?

One evening – the day of the winter solstice – Skandar was alone in the treehouse once again. Moodily, he threw another log on the stove, letting the book about fire weapons fall off his knees. With nobody to distract him, he felt the doubts descend. He still hadn't managed to have a Mender dream. Their plan to expose the true killers of the wild unicorns seemed hopeless. Rex had apparently managed to smooth things over with the Silver Circle, but what if Dorian had smelled a rat and never called Blade up to kill one of the wild unicorns in the arena? What if the Commodore didn't arrive in the Wilderness in time to see the wild unicorn hunters for herself? What if Kenna's unicorn was killed before they could do anything about it? And he suspected that Agatha had been wrong about him being a Mender. He still hadn't managed to have one of the stupid dreams. He was never going to be able to right the wrong that had been done to Kenna; he was the worst brother in the whole—

'Skandar!' Mitchell's voice broke through his avalanche of gloomy thoughts.

He blinked. Mitchell was standing in front of him, brandishing a piece of black cloth.

'I need to tie this round your head,' he said matter-of-factly, leaning down towards Skandar.

'Oi!' Skandar swiped at his friend's arm. 'What are you doing?'

'Please don't ask me any questions,' Mitchell pleaded. 'I'm

not good at lying and I need not to tell you anything that will accidentally ruin it.'

'Ruin what? Have you decided I'm going to bring about the end of the world again? You're not going to hand me over to your dad, after all, are you?' Skandar joked, hoping to goad Mitchell into telling him what was going on. Though honestly he was mostly pleased Mitchell was here, including him in something.

'Please, Skandar,' Mitchell begged. 'Flo will *kill* me if I tell you anything. And I will if you ask me. I know I will.'

'All right, all right.' Skandar let Mitchell tie the blindfold round his head.

The fire wielder took Skandar's hand and guided him out of the treehouse, along five bridges swinging unsteadily under their feet and then talked him down three ladders. But once they reached the forest floor, Skandar lost track of which direction they were heading in. Mitchell wasn't that good at helping him avoid the roots of the Eyrie's trees underfoot either, and there was a lot of 'oh sorry', 'ouch' and 'that was my foot'.

'Okay,' Mitchell said, as they finally came to a halt. 'I need you to take two steps in front of you, bend down – that's it – and take hold of this.' Skandar sensed Mitchell bending down near him, and then guiding his hands to some kind of metal handle. Skandar pulled at it and realised it was attached to whatever he was standing on.

He felt Mitchell's arm brush against his; he was standing close. 'I need you to follow my instructions very carefully. No spirit wielder improvisation, got it? Hold on tighter than you've ever held on to anything in your life or you *will* die—

'I'm sorry, what?'

Mitchell continued as if Skandar wasn't panicking. 'And I

don't think Flo would be too happy if that happened either. I mean, she only mentioned spoiling the surprise but, yes, killing you would probably do that too, I suppose.'

'What sur-PRIIIIISSSE?' Skandar was halfway through the word when whatever he was standing on plummeted downwards.

After a stomach-lurching few seconds, they came to a juddering halt.

'You can let go now,' Mitchell said rather sheepishly.

'Mitchell,' Skandar said crossly, ripping off his blindfold. It made no difference; it was completely pitch black wherever they were. 'Are you trying to kill—'

'I told them it would be easier to do this in a treehouse, but apparently it *wouldn't have the same emotional impact.*'

'What are you talking—'

'SURPRISE!' The underground space was suddenly ablaze with flaming torches and full of people. Skandar spotted Flo first, then Jamie. On either side of the blacksmith was a tall blonde woman with a violin and a man with a bushy brown beard who looked so like Jamie they had to be his parents! Flo's parents and twin brother were there, as well as Craig the bookseller and most of the Peregrine Society – though not Amber. Rickesh gave Skandar a goofy wave and Prim rolled her eyes. And then the most surprising person of all came into view: Agatha Everhart. She wasn't smiling exactly, but it was close.

'What's all this? Where . . . ?' Skandar had been so shocked by the crowd that he hadn't realised where he was.

It was the spirit den, but it had been completely transformed.

The Weaver's scrawling writing had been washed away so that the black marble shone. Right across the back curve of the wall, the four entwined circles of the spirit element had been painted in gleaming white paint. There was even one of Skandar's sketches of Scoundrel taped underneath it. A few fluffy white beanbags were scattered about, sheepskin rugs padded the floor and new books filled the old shelves. A round marble table adorned the centre of the circular den, with orange Shekoni drinks and food set out for a party. Skandar spotted at least three jars of mayonnaise.

Flo rushed up to him and gave him an enormous hug. 'Do you like it? We thought you might need cheering up. You weren't allowed in the Well and I know you're sad about your sister and the dreams aren't working for you yet and my mum made some white paint and we just wanted . . .' Flo gestured around, a little out of breath.

'We wanted to show you that you've got friends, Skandar. People who think spirit wielders are an okay bunch,' Jamie said, grinning. 'Who think you trying to bring spirit back to the Eyrie is pretty damn brave.'

'Are you glad I didn't tell you why I was abducting you now?' Mitchell's hair flared with his smile.

'You did all this? For me?' Skandar's voice was choked with emotion. 'I thought you lot had gone off me or something.'

'We're sorry,' Flo gushed. 'We had to organise it all! We wanted it to be different from how the Weaver left it. Agatha's the one who's been getting us in and out of the den.'

Agatha inclined her head, looking rather regal in her grubby white cloak.

Two hours later, Skandar was still having one of the best times of his life. He couldn't believe they'd done all this just for him! Rickesh had told everyone how fast Scoundrel was; Agatha had been goaded into telling them stories about the Eyrie in the old days; Jamie's parents had played music so they could all swing each other wildly around the den; and now Skandar, Mitchell and Flo were sitting in a circle eating the last of the hot dogs and mayonnaise. Skandar's cheeks hurt from smiling. The only person missing – the only person who would have made it all perfect – was Bobby Bruna.

'Did Bobby not . . . ?' Skandar asked vaguely.

'She's not feeling well still,' Flo said quickly. 'I'm sure she would have loved to come.'

Mitchell wasn't listening. He was staring over at Jamie and his parents in one corner. They were all laughing at Jamie's mum trying to make him play the violin. It sounded awful.

'I thought we were the same,' Mitchell murmured, rubbing furiously at his eyes under his glasses.

'What do you mean, Mitchell?' Flo asked him gently.

He jumped, remembering they were sitting with him. 'It's just that Jamie's parents don't want him to be a blacksmith, do they?'

'I think they'd rather he was a bard like them,' Skandar agreed.

'Yes, but –' Mitchell struggled to put his feelings into words – 'they're still here, aren't they? They're still supporting him. They're still coming to his spirit wielder friend's underground party. They still smile at him. They still love—' Mitchell broke off, unable to finish his sentence. 'They're still here – even though they don't approve of what he's doing.'

'Mitchell.' Flo leaned forward and took one of his hands in hers. 'Listen to me. Your dad's the one who's in the wrong. You're a wonderful, wonderful person. His prejudices against the spirit element, his need for you to fulfil *his* dream of being Commodore – all that is *his* problem. He should love you as you are – not who he wants you to be.'

Mitchell sniffed and pushed his glasses back up his nose. 'But why doesn't he? I'm his son; shouldn't it come naturally? And I don't think he even *likes* Red. He's always saying she's untidy and unfit to be a Commodore's unicorn. And Red's making this big effort to change herself for him – for me – but I can tell she's unhappy. I wish we were good enough for my father as we are, but I don't think we ever will be.'

'Maybe he doesn't realise how he's making you both feel,' Skandar said softly. 'Maybe you should talk to him; it might change things.' He was trying very hard not to think about his own mother – who hadn't listened when Skandar had tried to change her mind last year.

Mitchell shook his head violently. 'He never used to talk to me about anything and now he's got this Commodore dream for me. He took me to lunch! If I tell him I want to be friends with a spirit wielder, that I prefer it when Red is scruffy and stinky, that I believe in truesongs, that becoming Commodore might not be what I want – he'll go back to ignoring me again. I just know it!'

'How do you know if you haven't tried?' Flo asked, a sad smile on her lips.

Agatha loomed over them. The momentary softness in her expression had disappeared and her eyes were hard again. 'Skandar, we need to get people out of here now. It's late – I'm not sure how pleased Instructor O'Sullivan would be if she knew I'd brought you all down here, not to mention us sneaking the non-riders in. I think it's time we call it a night.'

Skandar scrambled to his feet. 'Sure, of course, er, Instructor Everhart.'

Together, Agatha and Skandar took it in turns to ferry people up to the surface. Skandar brought Flo, Mitchell and Jamie up last and they waved goodbye on the Divide. Flo left to check on Blade, and Mitchell went with Jamie and his parents to let them out of the Eyrie's entrance tree. For a moment Skandar thought he was alone in the clearing, with only the fault lines for company, until a white shape swept out of the shadows.

'You've got good friends,' Agatha said almost reluctantly, as she fell into step beside her nephew.

Skandar smiled. 'I'm lucky.' Though he couldn't help thinking about the Bobby-shaped hole in the evening. She would have teased him so much about the mayonnaise.

'You *are* lucky. They'll help you fight the darkness of the spirit element – if you let them. I didn't have that; neither did your mother. We isolated ourselves; we only had each other. Other elemental influences might have . . . balanced us out a bit.'

An owl hooted into their silence from somewhere in the trees above.

'Ag— Instructor Everhart?'

'Mmm?'

'The other dens all have names. The Furnace, the Well, the Hive, the Mine . . . but what was the spirit den called? Before, I mean.'

'The Sanctuary,' Agatha answered at once, her voice unusually hushed.

As he watched her disappear up the nearest ladder, Skandar thought the name was perfect. Tonight the spirit den had felt safe. Like he belonged there. A true sanctuary for a spirit wielder.

Skandar was almost at the treehouse when a fully armoured Flo came hurtling towards him, chainmail clinking.

'Skar!' She took a couple of deep breaths. 'It's tonight. They're rounding up the next wild unicorn tonight. Blade and I have to meet the hunting party in an hour.' She pointed and, sure enough, Silver Blade was gleaming in the forest below – ready to go.

Skandar stared at Flo. They'd been planning this for weeks, but suddenly it felt terrifying.

'What's going on?' It was Bobby; she'd come along the bridge opposite.

'Blade's hunt is happening tonight,' Flo said, her voice full of fear.

'Tonight?' Bobby blinked. 'So your plan is happening now?'

'Yes,' Skandar said urgently. 'Right now. We haven't got much time.' He took a deep breath, swallowing all his hurt. 'Come with us, Bobby. We need you. If this goes wrong and the Commodore doesn't turn up, then we're going to have to protect the wild unicorns ourselves. Flo's going to be pretending to be *with* the Silver Circle, so she can't help us. And your magic is the best.'

'I can't.' Bobby took a step back. 'I'm not . . . riding Falcon at the moment. And – and I don't want to be your sidekick. I told you. I don't want to get involved!'

'It's not about heroes and sidekicks, Bobby,' Flo said, Bobby eyes shining. 'It's about taking a stand. It's about doing the right thing.'

'I can't,' Bobby said again. 'Falcon, she was in my head. My beautiful Falcon, she was terrible. I . . .'

'We've got to go,' Skandar said desperately. He didn't want to give up on Bobby coming, but they only had an hour for everything to be in place. 'If you change your mind, the plan is on Mitchell's blackboard.'

'I'm sorry,' Bobby choked out, and fled down the nearest ladder to the forest floor. Skandar thought she was probably going to the stables. She'd been spending more and more time there to avoid the treehouse.

'I'll get Mitchell,' Skandar told Flo.

Flo's expression was a mix of determination and panic. Skandar pulled her into a hug. 'We're a silver and a spirit wielder,' he murmured. 'We can do this. We can stop them.'

He felt her nod into his shoulder, and then she climbed down to Blade to ride for the Stronghold.

Skandar stumbled through the door of the treehouse, and found it impossibly calm given what was about to happen. Mitchell had fallen asleep on a beanbag by the stove, a half-open book resting on his chest.

Skandar didn't have time to feel bad for waking him.

'*Whatisit?*' Mitchell asked, but as he looked up into Skandar's face realisation dawned.

'It's happening?' he croaked.

'It's happening,' Skandar confirmed grimly.

'Where's Bobby?' Mitchell asked. 'Is she here?'

'We tried to convince her, but I don't think she's coming. She knows where to find the plan if she changes her mind.'

Mitchell stood up suddenly and rushed over to the stone box they used as a fridge. 'I've got an idea,' he said, and retrieved jam, Marmite, cheese and two slices of bread.

'We don't have time to eat!' Skandar pulled at his hair in frustration. 'We've already lost about ten minutes. You've got to meet Flo outside the Stronghold; you've got to get the message to the Commodore!'

But Mitchell was too busy holding his nose while clumsily spreading Marmite on top of the jam. He added the Cheddar cheese and placed the second slice of bread on top to finish the sandwich. Then he started scribbling a note. 'I'm leaving Bobby this,' he explained to Skandar while writing, 'just in case she comes back here. I want her to know we need her. I think the sandwich will help.'

Skandar read the note over Mitchell's shoulder.

This is an emergency sandwich because this, Roberta, is an emergency. We have to stop the Silver Circle killing another wild unicorn. What happened with you and Falcon was terrible, but you're really strong. The strongest person I know. If we don't stop them, it's going to keep happening. And it's going to keep happening to people who aren't as strong as you. Please, Bobby. Eat the sandwich and help us. M x

Skandar had never heard Mitchell speak to Bobby like that. Sure, this was a note, but they usually communicated in snipes and sarcastic comments.

He wasn't exactly sure how a sandwich was going to help Bobby get back on Falcon's Wrath, but right now anything was worth a try.

Forty-five minutes later, Skandar and Mitchell were hiding with their unicorns in some scrubland near the targeted wild herd. The riders had convinced their unicorns to lie down, and Skandar was now huddled into Scoundrel's side against the perishing December cold of the Wilderness. The herd was a large one – about thirty wild unicorns in various stages of decay. Exposed bones flashed in the moonlight; transparent horns glowed eerily. Noxious smoke swirled around them in clouds when they squabbled and blasted elements, but mostly they were peacefully chomping on the remains of a family of goats.

The plan had gone without a hitch so far. They'd ridden to the avenue of silver birch trees outside the Stronghold, and Flo had managed to slip out to share the location of the herd. Adding the co-ordinates to his pre-written note for the Commodore, Mitchell had flown Red all the way to Fourpoint while Skandar had used his friend's spare compass to scope out a hiding place near the herd. At Council Square Mitchell had pressed the anonymous note into the hands of Nina's personal librarian – a good friend of his mum's. He insisted that the Commodore of Chaos read it immediately, that it was a matter of life and death.

Waiting alone for Mitchell to get to the Wilderness had been one of the longest waits of Skandar's life. Until now. Until they were waiting for the hunters to arrive.

It was the first time Skandar had been back to the desolate plains since he'd faced the Weaver last year, and every shadow seemed to morph into a black shrouded figure. *She isn't the threat*, he told himself. But his mum *was* out here somewhere, even if she wasn't hunting wild unicorns. Skandar shivered. He found it hard to believe that just over an hour ago he'd been eating hot dogs.

'If we've got the timings right,' Mitchell was murmuring to himself, 'Flo and the hunting party should get here –' he squinted at his watch in the darkness – 'any minute. And if the Commodore took the note seriously, then she and the Council should arrive about the same time.'

'If Flo was here, do you know what she'd say?' Skandar whispered.

'What?'

'This is one of the most dangerous things we've ever—'

'Do you hear that?' Mitchell interrupted him.

Hooves thundered across the barren Wilderness. Closer. Closer.

Three silver unicorns led a pack of sentinels, their silver armour flashing in the flaming torchlight. Two of the unicorns were fully grown silvers Skandar didn't recognise. The third was Silver Blade. The sentinels riding behind were loaded up with chains, ready to capture the young wild unicorn and take it back to the gladiatorial arena. To fight to its impossible death.

The hunting party galloped closer to the wild unicorns. They raised their transparent horns in alarm and Skandar twitched, half rising to his feet.

'Skandar. No.' Mitchell forced him back down. 'The Commodore will be here. She'll *be* here.'

Seconds passed like minutes. Skandar's heart raced. The sentinels spread out around the herd, their voices raised as they tried to identify the young unicorn they were going to capture. Their movements were practised, assured – they'd clearly done this many times before.

Still no Commodore.

'Mitchell . . .' Skandar breathed. 'We can't wait—'

'She'll be here,' Mitchell insisted again, his breath visible in the cold of the night.

Magic exploded into the dark sky above the herd. The wild unicorns bellowed and screamed in alarm as the sentinels began to swing their chains. Skandar was up on his knees in the scrubland now. For a moment the smoke cleared.

And he saw her. A wild unicorn he recognised with his whole heart. Her dapple-grey coat shining in the light of the moon.

Skandar couldn't wait for the Commodore any longer.

He was in his saddle within seconds. Scoundrel flapped his wings as he stood up, rider already on his back.

'Skandar! No!' Mitchell cried. 'Wild unicorn injuries never heal! What if—'

'Kenna's unicorn is in that herd!' Skandar shouted as Scoundrel reared, fired up by the determination and fury in the bond.

'You don't know for sure that's Kenna's unicorn!' Mitchell called over the terrible bellowing of the wild unicorns.

But Skandar wasn't taking any chances. He galloped Scoundrel right into the middle of the herd, and shouted at the top of his voice. 'If you want to hurt them, then you're going to have to go through me!'

Skandar was barely aware of Red Night's Delight joining him in the fray. Everything was happening impossibly quickly. The sentinels were shouting at the two young riders to get out of their way. One of the silver unicorns roared a river of flame from his mouth, and Skandar only just raised a water shield in time. A wild unicorn launched itself at a sentinel's throat. Flo called Skandar's name as Blade reared and rocks exploded from his hooves. Mitchell fired an arrow from a flaming bow right at another sentinel. The noise of the elemental magic and the screeching of the wild unicorns was deafening.

Then, quite suddenly, the hunters dropped back and started to take off into the dark sky. One of the older silver riders grabbed Blade's reins and yanked so that Flo was forced to follow.

'Skar! Get out of there! They're going to make it look like—' But her shouts were lost as Blade was pulled alongside the stronger silver unicorn, out of the Wilderness and back towards the Stronghold.

Bones creaked; gunge dripped; growls shook splintered jaws; ghostly horns turned inwards. Thirty pairs of hungry eyes focused on Skandar and Mitchell – trapped in the middle of the herd. The stench of death was unbearable.

'If we attack, they'll blast us to oblivion.' Skandar spoke from the corner of his mouth.

'We're going to die, we're going to die,' Mitchell croaked over and over.

One of the wild unicorns bent its transparent horn, pointing it right at the two boys. It had been dying for a very long time – its skull was almost entirely visible, the skin completely rotted away. It was a living nightmare. Skandar's brain had frozen, and Scoundrel's fear spiralled in the bond with his own. They both knew that if they tried to defend themselves, twenty-nine other blasts would come straight at them.

'Mitchell, take my hand,' Skandar murmured, stretching his arm slowly over Scoundrel's wing.

'Why?' Mitchell whispered, gripping it over Red's feathers. 'Do you have a plan?'

Skandar shook his head. 'No. I'm just scared.'

'Me too.'

Then the sky lit up with air magic.

Lightning bolts, spinning tornadoes, ice-cold winds catching on tendrils of electricity. The wild unicorns all turned their horns up to the sky, assessing the new threat. Skandar did the same.

'Hey, Mitch!' a voice called from above. 'Thanks for the sandwich!'

Bobby had come to save them.

Falcon's Wrath fired two lightning strikes – one from each hoof – right at two wild unicorns. The citrus smell of the air magic mixed with charred rotting flesh and the herd began to panic, seeming to forget about the two riders in their midst.

An electric zap of hope and happiness brought Skandar back to himself. Bobby was here. Bobby was back. She must have followed them. Did that mean . . . ? But there wasn't time. The herd might have broken their circle round Scoundrel and Red, but they were still here – blasting off elements at the sky as Bobby fired arrow after arrow with her lightning bow.

'Now might be a good time for some magic?' Bobby yelled, as two wild unicorns took off after Falcon – their wings tattered but still carrying them into the night sky.

Red – apparently not remembering, in the midst of battle, that she was supposed to be well-mannered nowadays – happily ignited a fart and sent a wild unicorn behind her screeching in the opposite direction. Mitchell was grinning to himself between fireball throws. 'The sandwich worked; she liked the sandwich!'

Skandar summoned the spirit element into the bond, and the white light burst into his hand. He willed it brighter and brighter until its glow blotted out the moon. The wild unicorns started to bellow, and Scoundrel bellowed back – that same noise he'd made when they'd faced the Weaver. Skandar thought about what Agatha had said about the dark. Was Scoundrel fighting it too? Were spirit unicorns closer to wild unicorns than others?

The wild unicorns closest to Skandar skittered back. All of them – except one.

Skandar stared into the grieving eyes of the dapple-grey unicorn. There were fresh wounds on her back, and a new bone stuck out from her ribcage. Immortality was taking its toll on her.

'I'll fix this,' Skandar told the wild unicorn. 'I'll get Kenna here, you'll see.'

She screeched and turned, galloping off into the Wilderness.

Suddenly, Skandar heard shouts. Eight unicorns burst into the Wilderness.

At first Skandar thought it was the Silver Circle's hunters, returning for their wild unicorn prize. It crossed his mind for a moment how he must have looked. A spirit wielder – hand glowing ghostly white – protecting a herd of the most gruesome creatures on earth. But it didn't matter what it looked like, because it was the right thing to do.

Then Skandar's gaze returned to the approaching group of riders and this time he saw them, *really* saw them. Eight palms glowed the yellow of the air element and he realised—

'It's the Commodore. Nina and the Council of Seven!' Mitchell sounded relieved that a rescue party had arrived.

But as Bobby landed Falcon next to them, she voiced exactly what Skandar had been too slow to realise. What Flo had been trying to tell him.

'They're going to think it's *us* killing the wild unicorns!'

KENNA

THE FLAME-EYED MAN

Kenna paced round her circular room in the Silver Stronghold's tower. She'd been on the Island for weeks now, and she was fed up – and scared. She'd spent hours anxiously fiddling with the miniature unicorn she'd brought from her mum's box of old things. Asking for exact details of when Dorian would find her unicorn or where she'd be staying hadn't seemed to matter that much back on the Mainland, but it mattered now her days were spent in a locked room. It mattered now she still had no unicorn. It mattered now she was beginning to feel more like a prisoner than a guest.

Dorian Manning had at least given her a book to read – *The Book of Spirit*. It had a bright white cover, with four interlinked gold circles. It was a little battered, as though someone had dropped it from a great height. She'd read it so many times that she could recite whole sections by heart. It was her only companion apart from the silver-masked sentinels who dropped off food and water for her, morning and night. Every stain, every torn edge, every folded corner greeted her like an old friend as she turned the book's pages. She spent hours squinting at the margins, where previous owners had left comments or tiny drawings. She liked to imagine the riders who might have written the notes. Spirit wielders like her. Like her brother.

Kenna didn't know how to feel about Skandar. She didn't understand why he hadn't told her he was a spirit wielder. Did he know that she was one too? Had he really been keeping this secret from the very beginning, from the night he'd left the Mainland? Kenna had worked out what had happened. She wasn't stupid. She'd read all about spirit wielder mutations, and the marks on that woman's cheeks – the one who had come to fetch Skandar from Flat 207 – now made an awful lot of sense.

Did Skandar have a spirit wielder mutation too? Did Scoundrel's Luck have a white blaze like other spirit unicorns? Kenna felt so hurt every time she thought about meeting the black unicorn last year. Why hadn't Skandar told her the truth then? When they were growing up together, they'd never had secrets.

On her better days Kenna thought Skandar must have had a good reason for keeping his secret. He loved her; she was sure of that. He wouldn't have wanted to hurt her on purpose. In these more positive moments, she liked to imagine telling Skandar she had a unicorn now and they were both spirit wielders. She liked to imagine them training together and writing joint letters to Dad. Sometimes she even pictured them in the Chaos Cup together, riding under the finishing arch neck and neck . . . joint Commodores of Chaos.

But on other days Kenna felt crushed by all the lies he must have told her. She'd try to go to sleep but then she'd think of another lie – about water magic, or his quartet, or Scoundrel's habits. Did his quartet know? Had they all been laughing at Kenna too, while she'd read his letters under the table in Maths or English or Spanish – blinking back tears as the horrible wanting, the terrible jealousy, had eaten up any happy feelings she'd been clinging on to? Had Skandar thought about her having to fill the empty unicorn-less days, the nights poring over drawings from a rider sibling – drawings of what had once been her own dreams?

And the worst thing of all was that Skandar understood the agony of the Island leaving you behind. For a few hours after he'd been banned from the Hatchery exam, he'd felt it. And yet he hadn't even bothered to tell Kenna the truth.

It was evening again. Three sharp knocks.

Usually the sentinel just left the tray outside and disappeared down the staircase before she'd even opened the door. But today was different, and Kenna lived for anything out of the ordinary.

The silver mask glinted in the light from the lantern above her door. Kenna put her hands out for the tray without really looking at him. She'd given up asking to see Dorian Manning. She had the feeling her demands only made him less likely to speak to her.

But as long as Kenna got her unicorn eventually, she didn't care.

The sentinel didn't let go of the tray. She looked up into two flaming eyes.

'It's you,' she said, surprised.

'Hello, Kenna. May I come in?' His voice was kinder than it had been the night she'd left the Mainland. 'I'd like to talk to you.'

'Umm, sure,' Kenna said, moving back so he could get

through the door. The man put the tray down and went to sit on the one and only rickety old chair. Kenna perched on the end of her bed, watching him curiously.

The masked man looked around the tower room, eyes blazing. 'I'm so sorry, Kenna.'

'Why are you sorry?' Kenna asked. 'It's not your fault it's taking so long to—'

'You weren't supposed to even enter the Silver Stronghold. Rex Manning joined us at the last minute. If it had just been me and Dorian I could have managed it, but I couldn't take down two silvers and guarantee your safety.'

'What do you mean *take down*?' Kenna asked warily. She was suddenly conscious of how small the tower room was, of the short distance between his chair and where she was sitting.

He fixed her with his fiery gaze. 'It was never Dorian Manning's idea to bring you here, Kenna. I planted the idea in his head that it would be useful to have a spirit wielder loyal to the Silver Circle. He liked the idea of eliminating any possibility of a spirit wielder army, and then having one left who answered only to him. You. He thinks if he finds you your unicorn, he can blackmail you into doing his bidding. He thinks you're weak because you're a Mainlander, that you'd do anything for a unicorn.'

Kenna's mind was reeling. Army? Blackmail? 'Wh-what does he want me to do?'

'He wants you to use the spirit element to kill Scoundrel's Luck. A unicorn for a unicorn.'

Kenna couldn't speak.

'It doesn't matter,' the man said quickly, seeing the look of horror on her face.

'Of course it matters!' Kenna cried. 'I'm never going to do that. I'd never kill my brother's unicorn!'

'It doesn't matter,' the man said again.

'Why not?'

'Because your mother is coming for you,' he said simply. 'She couldn't get you from the Mainland herself – too many are searching for her – but she's coming for you, I promise.'

Kenna hardly dared breathe. 'But she's dead.'

The man ignored this and moved towards her. Kenna stood up to find that her whole body was shaking.

'She'll get you out before the summer solstice,' the flame-eyed man murmured, and handed her an envelope.

On the front it said: *For my daughter, Kenna Everhart.*

CHAPTER TWELVE

ACCUSED

Skandar, Bobby and Mitchell stood in front of the Commodore of Chaos and the full Council of Seven. Nina Kazama couldn't have looked more different from the excitable Pred Skandar had met on his first day at the Eyrie – when she'd shown the new riders around and handed out sandwiches. She looked powerful, furious and terrifying. She looked like a Commodore.

Back in the Wilderness, the wild unicorn herd had scattered the moment the eight fully grown unicorns had appeared – as though they'd been able to sense the mighty power of the air wielders. Skandar had been pulled roughly from Scoundrel by the Justice Representative and bundled on to the back of a strange unicorn, earth vines winding themselves round his wrists.

Skandar had been afraid to say anything the whole ride to Council Square. He knew how guilty he looked. The Silver Circle were probably laughing themselves hoarse in their Stronghold right now. This was exactly what they'd wanted, after all – for him to be blamed for the very crime they were committing. As the Council, the Commodore and the accused processed into Fourpoint, Skandar wondered whether the Silver Circle had been working up to something like this for months. They'd told the shopkeepers not to serve him, threatened Jamie, spread rumours about him killing the wild unicorns and even tried to prevent his training – working against him at every turn to protect themselves. And now, if the Commodore believed he was as guilty as the Circle had made him seem, he wasn't just going to be thrown out of the Eyrie – he could very well end up in prison.

Skandar had felt his separation from Scoundrel like a knife in his chest as the black unicorn had been led away to the Council's stables. Would he see him again? Would he ever be allowed to ride him, to fly him? Or would he end up like Agatha? Under guard, Arctic Swansong imprisoned to ensure she could never use the spirit element.

He'd felt no better as they'd been marched through Council Square. The treehouse complex was the most impressive he'd seen outside the Eyrie. They'd walked up a long wide ramp leading to a sturdy metal walkway. The four enormous treehouses on each edge of the square had spiked metal bars protecting their entrances. Giant elemental shields adorned each corner – water, earth, fire and air. Skandar had felt more illegal than ever as he was shoved – along with Mitchell and Bobby – through a door and into the most imposing room he'd ever seen.

Each Council member sat on a throne shaped like a tornado – with wide swirls of metal at the top, bending to a narrow point where the rider placed their feet. The thrones were on a high platform lining one wall – stretching to either side of the Nestlings. The room must have been designed especially for an air council, for the final throne – at floor level, flanked by the others – belonged to the Commodore herself. Her throne was much larger, the vast metal back designed to mimic a jagged lightning bolt. After a horribly long silence, Commodore Kazama spoke.

'What I'm struggling to understand, is why you were in the Wilderness tonight at all. If you weren't killing the wild unicorns, spirit wielder, then what *were* you doing?'

Skandar swallowed, his neck prickling with nerves at her calling him *spirit wielder* instead of his name.

'It can all be explained, Commodore,' Mitchell said, his voice high-pitched. 'We were trying to show you that the Silver Circle were responsible for the killings.' He sounded brave and terrified at the same time. '*I* wrote that note, the anonymous one that explained where to find the wild unicorn herd. It's my handwriting; I can prove it right now, if you need me to?' Mitchell drew feebly in the air with his fingers.

Skandar couldn't believe Mitchell was owning up to this; his dad was going to *kill* him.

'Why would you want to get yourselves caught?' the Justice Representative asked, electricity dancing in his eyes as he blinked.

Bobby tried this time. 'No, no. We weren't trying to get *ourselves* caught. There was a hunting party from the Silver Circle in the Wilderness tonight. They left when they heard you coming. We were trying to get you to see—'

A slow clapping echoed around the Council chamber. Skandar spun round to see Dorian Manning marching into the room, closely followed by all the instructors from the Eyrie.

'These Nestlings really do have wild imaginations,' Dorian Manning simpered to Nina Kazama as he made a shallow bow towards her throne. 'But I don't think you need to bother yourself with the fire wielder or the air wielder, Commodore. This was all down to the spirit wielder. I'm sure of it.'

Instructor O'Sullivan thundered up to Nina's throne – pushing right past Dorian – closely followed by Agatha, blue and white cloaks swirling behind them.

'Persephone, now don't be upset.' Dorian turned to face the water instructor, the tip of his silver tongue just visible as he licked his lips. 'I know you *like* the boy. But I will oversee his and the spirit unicorn's imprisonment at my Stronghold.'

'Upset? Upset?' Instructor O'Sullivan's whirlpool eyes swirled in anger. 'I'm not upset, Dorian. I. Am. Livid.' She turned to Nina. 'These Nestlings should have been brought straight to me. The Eyrie is responsible for them, not the—'

'That's hardly the point here,' Dorian interrupted, and Skandar thought the spiky-haired water instructor would have lashed out and hit him if she hadn't been under the eyes of the entire Council of Seven. 'The point is, we now know *who* is killing the wild unicorns.'

'YES!' Skandar shouted loudly, unable to contain himself any longer. 'YOU! I've seen your gladiator arena. I've seen it all! I know what you're doing.' At Skandar's accusation there were gasps from the Council of Seven; even Nina looked between Dorian and Skandar in shock.

'Is there any truth to this, Dorian?' an elderly member of the Council asked, her glasses slipping all the way down the end of her nose.

'How could there be?' Dorian Manning scoffed. 'In what world would we allow a spirit wielder to set foot in the Silver Stronghold?' He waved a thin hand dismissively in Skandar's direction. 'Delusional.'

Bobby took a step towards him. 'Now look here, Dogbreathy Muppet—'

Despite the dire situation, Skandar's mouth twitched. He was extremely glad Bobby was with them.

'Enough.' Nina Kazama rose from her throne – and though she spoke quietly everyone obeyed. 'I have a question, President Manning.'

'Of course, Commodore.' Dorian bowed again, more deeply this time.

'If Skandar Smith really is killing the wild unicorns, how is he doing it?'

'Exactly.' Instructor O'Sullivan sniffed. 'He's only in his second year of training. Apart from the fact wild unicorns are supposed to be *invincible*, he'd be lucky to battle one and survive. I should know. I've had this wound for over a decade.' She touched the angry unhealed welt on her neck.

'He managed it last year!' Dorian crowed. 'Who knows what tricks the Weaver taught him!'

'Agatha Everhart.' Nina ignored Dorian. 'You have been teaching Skandar for a few months now. Is he capable of this?'

Agatha took one step towards the throne, and Skandar could sense the revulsion of the Council. He thought it was more than her being a spirit wielder. She had killed countless unicorns. In their eyes she would always be the Executioner.

'Commodore, spirit wielders can kill bonded unicorns because of their affinity with the bond itself.' Agatha spoke calmly and precisely despite the Council's whispering. She sounded respectful – something Skandar had never heard in her voice before. 'But wild unicorns have no bond, so spirit magic cannot kill them. There is no reason to suspect a spirit wielder of these crimes more than a rider of any other element. And Skandar has a good heart. He wouldn't do this.'

Nina nodded to her.

'You can't trust *her*!' Dorian Manning spluttered. 'She's the Weaver's sister, for pity's sake! She and Skandar are probably in cahoots! Skandar was there! In the Wilderness!' Spittle flew from his mouth.

Nina sat back down on her lightning-bolt throne. 'I have made my decision.'

'With all due respect, Commodore,' Instructor O'Sullivan started, 'Skandar is a rider training at the Eyrie. His behaviour comes under *our* jurisdiction.'

'Please, Instructor—' Nina stopped herself, looking her age for the first time. After all, Instructor O'Sullivan had been her teacher less than a year ago. Then the Commodore remembered herself, her power. 'I have made my decision.'

Skandar held his breath.

'I have no evidence of a wild unicorn killing. I still do not fully understand who was in the Wilderness tonight and why, but without *evidence* I can only assume that Skandar and his friends were simply in the wrong place at the wrong time.'

Skandar felt his shoulders relax just a fraction. He saw Mitchell close his eyes in relief beside him.

'However –' Nina fixed Skandar with a hard stare – 'I am only giving you one more chance, Skandar Smith. Your agreement with Commodore McGrath was clear. You may stay training in the Eyrie for as long as you pass the challenges required of all riders and you do no harm. Tonight was a close call, do you understand me?'

'I understand,' Skandar said quickly.

'President Manning, I have to take into account that your judgement is clouded on this matter. Your hounding of the boy so far has been . . . unprofessional at best. It is not Skandar's fault that Rebecca—'

'How dare you speak her name!' Dorian Manning had turned even paler, his green eyes bulging. 'You are a Mainlander – you were a child living far from here when it happened.'

Skandar glanced at Mitchell and Bobby who looked equally confused.

'You cannot possibly understand the nefarious nature of spirit wielders.'

'Dorian . . .' Nina warned.

'You would truly allow the spirit wielder to continue his training after *this*? Clearly you haven't the first idea of the danger you're putting us all in. For the sake of the Island I hope you lose the next Chaos Cup.' Dorian Manning spat the last two words, and marched from the room.

'I'll be stationing my own guards in the Wilderness from now on,' Nina called after him. 'We can't afford any more wild unicorn deaths.'

Nina continued as though Dorian hadn't just insulted her and stormed out. 'Since you're all here in the middle of the night –' her gaze rested on each instructor in turn – 'I have something urgent I need to discuss with you. Nestlings, you may wait with your unicorns until the instructors are ready to escort you back to the Eyrie.'

'Umm . . . are you going to tell my father about this?' Mitchell asked tentatively.

'I think this should stay a confidential matter, don't you?' Nina winked and looked for a moment like her old self.

Mitchell sagged with relief. Getting arrested by the current Commodore probably didn't chime with Ira's grand plans for his son.

Once they reached the door of the Council chamber, Skandar was already thinking about being reunited with Scoundrel. But, just as the door was about to close, Bobby shoved the toe of her black boot into the gap, so it was open just a crack.

'Don't you want to find out the *urgent* thing Nina wants to discuss with the instructors?' she whispered, putting her ear in the gap between the metal door and its frame. Skandar was *so* pleased she was here.

Skandar and Mitchell quickly copied Bobby, and the voices echoed from the chamber as clear as a bell.

'. . . researchers have found that the imbalances are getting exponentially worse the longer time goes on.'

'But what are you saying?' It was Instructor Webb's voice.

'Every time a wild unicorn is killed, it causes an elemental disturbance. But then the disturbances continue, expanding like ripples, and they get worse until—'

'Until what?' Instructor Saylor asked, her voice soft.

'Until we find the Weaver! Stop the killing – it's the obvious answer!' Instructor Webb barked.

'I agree that needs to happen, Bernard. I don't know how much to believe of what those Nestlings said tonight . . . but now my own guards are in the Wilderness I'm hoping that will protect the wild unicorns. It won't solve the problem, though. Even if no other wild unicorns are killed, the damage to the Island is done. And it will only get worse.'

'Practically speaking, what does that mean? More fires, more floods . . . ?' Instructor Anderson asked.

'More possessions,' Instructor O'Sullivan added ominously.

Nina's breath was so deep that it carried around the whole chamber. 'Practically speaking, my researchers tell me we have to find an answer before the Island's magic reaches its peak at the summer solstice. Or this Island is going to become uninhabitable. It's going to self-destruct entirely.'

There was a long beat of silence.

Nina continued. 'I'm in emergency meetings about possible new locations, but –' she paused – 'it's highly likely that if we must leave, riders will have to split up by elemental allegiances.'

'No,' Instructor O'Sullivan said flatly. 'That goes against everything the First Rider built. Everything we believe in.'

'There are too many unicorns, Persephone. The Mainland might welcome the non-riders, but the unicorns? That's prohibited by the Treaty. That's a hard no. Of course, as Dorian reminded me, it's entirely possible I won't win the Chaos Cup this year and so this decision will be in somebody else's hands by the solstice. But I have to lay the groundwork *now*.'

'Are we even going to be able to *have* a Chaos Cup?' Instructor O'Sullivan demanded.

'I refuse to be the first Commodore in history to cancel it,' Nina said fiercely.

'What about the bard's truesong?' Agatha spoke up. 'What about this gift left by the First Rider?'

Nina sighed. 'I've had teams searching everywhere for it, but we've had no luck. Given that we don't even know what it actually is – it feels like a distraction at this point. A dream.'

'Everything else in that truesong has been accurate so far,' Agatha insisted.

'I know,' Nina said, 'but we have to make plans for if we

can't find it. Or if we *do* find it, and it doesn't do what the bard promised. Remember the song only talks of one immortal death, not *multiple* deaths.'

'The Eyrie will help in any way it can,' Instructor O'Sullivan announced forcefully. 'But splitting up our riders? Leaving the Island? That has to be a last resort.'

'I promise you it is,' Nina said seriously, 'but the way the situation is evolving right now . . . as Commodore I have to plan for the worst.'

It was past midnight by the time Mitchell, Bobby and Skandar were putting their anxious unicorns to bed. None of them had said much on their flight back to the Eyrie with the instructors, horrified by what they'd overheard.

Mitchell left the stables quickly to send an urgent letter to Jamie. Bobby and Skandar made their way out of the east door of the wall together and Skandar suddenly felt shy. He'd assumed Bobby turning up to save them in the Wilderness meant she wanted to be friends again, but what if he was wrong? He wasn't sure if he could take it.

'Bobby?' he murmured, as they passed by sleepy treehouses on the way to their own.

She stopped and turned to face him, mid-bridge.

'Why did you come to save us tonight?'

She put a hand on one hip. 'Because that plan had more chance of backfiring than Red on roller skates.'

'Really, though?'

Bobby looked out over the Eyrie's network of treehouses, lamps burning softly in the dark. 'I guess I had a kind of epiphany after you and Flo tried to convince me to come to the Wilderness. I was hiding in the stables, watching you get Scoundrel ready, thinking how terrified you looked. I thought to myself, he doesn't look much like a hero. And that's when I realised it isn't because you're Skandar Smith – spirit wielder, Weaver's son, Executioner's nephew – that you always end up saving the day. It's because you actually give a damn about doing the right thing. And I don't think there are many people that do.'

Skandar dared to hope.

'I realised that sometimes there are more important things than trying to be the fastest or the strongest or the most successful. That I don't have to *be* in your shadow; none of us do. We can all be heroes if we're brave enough. We just have to try our best. And tonight it was my turn.'

'Riding Falcon must have been really hard.'

'It was.' Bobby looked right at him. 'But, like I said, I'm a hero – so it had to be done.' She grinned. 'Also, a sandwich always helps.'

'They *are* for emergencies,' Skandar said.

Bobby laughed loudly, and he thought it was one of the best sounds he'd ever heard.

'Come on, spirit boy,' Bobby said, punching him on the arm. 'Time to break the news to Flo that the Island's a ticking time bomb.'

Flo was not calm when they arrived. She and Blade had been escorted back to the Eyrie by three sentinels and she'd been stuck in the treehouse for hours with no idea what had happened to her friends.

Once Flo had wiped away her tears of relief, they settled on beanbags by the stove, warming their hands. Despite his joy that he and Bobby were friends again, Skandar could barely look at his quartet as Mitchell told Flo what they'd heard. That the chaos would only get worse; that the Island might self-destruct on the summer solstice; that the riders might have to go their separate ways – split by elemental allegiance.

Skandar gulped back tears as he imagined having to say goodbye to his friends without knowing whether he would ever see them again. Bobby not talking to him for a couple of months had been awful. But all of them? And would he have to go with the water wielders, who'd voted against allowing him in their den? He'd never belong with them, not like he belonged with his quartet.

'But it sounds like Nina doesn't trust the Silver Circle if she's stationed her personal guards in the Wilderness? That's a good thing, right? There won't be any more deaths. Kenna's unicorn will be safe for now.' Mitchell glanced at Skandar.

'You heard Nina – she said the damage to the Island is unfixable. Even with no more deaths, the elements are going to *stay* out of balance. They're going to get *more* messed up,' Bobby said, and then more loudly, 'I hate that there's nothing we can do!'

'Yes, there is,' Skandar said, determined. The Island was his home. He wasn't going to let the Silver Circle take that away from him. 'We do what the truesong says. We find the First Rider's gift.'

'Nina's been looking for his tomb for months,' Bobby countered. 'It's not like we're just miraculously going to find it!'

Skandar got to his feet. 'Nina isn't *us*, though.'

'No.' Mitchell raised his eyebrows. 'She's the Commodore of Chaos, so she has access to about a million more books, riders, research—'

'No, listen,' Skandar interrupted. 'Okay, so Nina is the Commodore. So what? Last year we did the impossible! We stopped the Weaver's plan *and* we saved New-Age Frost. And, no, we don't have fancy people to help us, but you know who we do have?'

Nobody said anything.

Skandar pointed at each of them in turn. 'We have Mitchell Henderson, who is better than any library, who comes up with the most bonkers-but-genius plans ever seen on the Island. We have Bobby Bruna, who won the Training Trial last year and is the most ambitious rider out there, with unbelievably strong magic. And we have Florence Shekoni, who has the might of a silver behind her, and is the bravest rider I know. I mean, she just went undercover with the Silver Circle! Come on! If anyone can find this bone weapon, we can!'

'And we've got Skandar Smith,' Mitchell said, a wide grin now plastered across his face. 'The only rider actually able to wield the spirit element on this whole Island.'

'Who is so open-minded that he never judges anyone, letting them be their best selves,' Bobby added quietly.

Flo smiled. 'And is so kind that last year he revealed his true element to Aspen McGrath, because he couldn't bear to see others in pain.'

It was a few moments before Skandar could find his voice again.

'All the people looking for the First Rider's tomb, they're not like us. I think we can do this. We *have* to do this.' Skandar's heart sank a little as he said it, knowing that they would have to find the weapon before he could concentrate on Kenna again. But if there wasn't an island for Kenna to come to, he'd never be able to unite her with her destined unicorn.

'All right, all right,' Bobby said, shifting on her beanbag. 'But where do we start?'

'We need a plan,' Mitchell said, sounding excited.

There was silence as they all tried to come up with something. And then an idea – a dangerous idea – dropped into Skandar's mind. 'How about the Secret Swappers?' he suggested.

'Oh, Skar, you can't be serious.' Flo's voice had a thousand warnings in it. Mitchell looked a bit ill.

'If we want to find the First Rider's tomb, then we have to do things differently,' Skandar insisted.

'Oi!' Bobby said. 'Mainlander here. Can you explain, please?'

'Oh, sorry.' Mitchell looked flustered. 'There's this treehouse—'

'Old, creepy, falling-down treehouse,' Flo interrupted, full of doom.

'It's definitely not a *cosy* location,' Mitchell accepted.

'Not helping.'

'Mitchell told me about them months ago,' Skandar explained to Bobby. 'These people called the Secret Swappers. They collect secrets. I bet they've got loads about the First Rider!'

'What's the catch?' Bobby asked, looking between Flo's anxious face and Mitchell's frown.

'They won't tell you anything, unless you give them a secret of your own,' Flo answered.

'And whatever secret you tell them has to be a good one. And it has to be true, otherwise they sort of get very angry,' Mitchell continued.

'What do you mean they *sort of get very angry*?' Bobby asked suspiciously.

'They try to kill you,' Skandar said bluntly. 'Apparently.'

'What?!'

Flo made an *I told you so* face.

But Mitchell rallied. 'Look, I don't like it either, but I suppose all we have to do is tell the truth! That's not hard, is it?'

'No, it's not. It's easy,' Skandar said, trying to sound as blasé as possible.

Flo groaned. 'We'll have to be really, *really* careful.'

'Like more careful than when we got arrested for killing the wild unicorns, then?' Bobby joked.

Flo gave her a stony look.

'So when shall we go to see them? Now?' Skandar half got up from his beanbag.

'We can't be seen going to that treehouse,' Flo said immediately. 'Eyrie riders aren't allowed to visit the Swappers.'

'What about at the Water Festival?' Skandar suggested. 'It's only a few weeks away. And it'll be crowded – nobody would notice us.'

Mitchell nodded. 'It'll be difficult to get the Secret Swappers to trade a secret about the First Rider. We'll have to give them something really good.'

'I don't think we have to worry too much about that,' Skandar murmured.

Because he had a secret only five other people in the whole world knew. And if it saved the Island, it was worth trading with the Secret Swappers.

Wasn't it?

CHAPTER THIRTEEN

THE WATER FESTIVAL

The quartet had to wait until the beginning of February for the Water Festival and their visit to the Secret Swappers, but the time flew by. Jousting training for the Nestlings had become more intense than ever. The only time Skandar felt at all relaxed was when he was flying drills with the Grins. Amber did try to annoy him at the meetings – loudly telling anyone who would listen to watch out for Skandar possessing them in the air – and eventually Rickesh forbade her from mentioning the elemental disturbances altogether, saying they all needed to concentrate.

Rickesh and the other Rookies were taking their preparations for the Chaos Cup display very seriously, hoping to be noticed by famous riders who might ask them to train at their yards once they left the Eyrie. Amber and Skandar weren't experienced enough yet to be taking part, but they'd still been made to learn all the moves. One of Skandar and Scoundrel's favourites was an arrow roll – when Scoundrel shot like a bullet through the air, folded his wings, and then rolled over and over as they sped forward through the sky.

But no matter how much he tried to distract himself with the Grins, Skandar couldn't ignore that the Nestling jousting tournament was getting closer.

'Where do you think you're ranking at the moment?' Skandar asked Mitchell anxiously one day, as they combed the elemental debris out of their unicorns' manes after earth training. Skandar had been in a particularly ferocious joust against Bobby; she'd slammed him from Scoundrel's back with a rock-hard mace that had sand pouring from its spikes. The tiny grains were trapped all along Scoundrel's black mane.

In answer, Mitchell produced a very creased notebook from the pocket of his red jacket and started thumbing through the pages.

Skandar frowned. 'Umm . . . What's that?'

'I've been keeping a tally of joust results from every training session.'

Skandar's jaw dropped.

'What?' Mitchell said, offended. 'I hate to remind you, Skandar, but the bottom six riders get declared nomads after the tournament, remember?'

'I think it's useful to know how we're all doing,' Flo said, joining them. 'Who's the best?'

Mitchell looked like he didn't want to answer.

'It's me, isn't it?' Bobby danced over from Falcon's stable, trying to peer at the calculations.

Mitchell sighed. 'Yes, it is you, Roberta. Although obviously you missed quite a few sessions so—'

'Knew it,' Bobby punched the air. 'How did the grass taste today, Skandar, eh?' she teased.

'Very funny,' Skandar growled, but he was secretly pleased Bobby was poking fun at him again.

'So where are the rest of us?' Flo asked, looking a little worried now. She still didn't have full control of her weapons due to the unpredictable surges in Blade's power.

Mitchell's face was very close to the page. 'Based on how many matches we've won and lost, Red and I are in eighteenth place. Flo and Blade in tenth. And Skandar and Scoundrel . . . in thirtieth. There are thirty-seven Nestlings, so if we perform the way we have during training, we'll all be safe!' Mitchell shut the notebook, satisfied.

But Skandar felt deflated. Thirtieth? That was far too close to the danger zone. Based on his ability, it didn't feel fair. His spirit training with Agatha had been going from strength to strength. He could summon spirit swords, lances and even a bow and arrow. That was particularly tricky – notching a not-quite-real arrow to a not-quite-there bowstring. Agatha had even started teaching him how to create the illusion of a weapon coming at his opponent from one side, while actually attacking from the other. He'd only managed the illusion with a tiny dagger – and he'd had no real opponent – but if he mastered it before the Nestling tournament? He might even stand a chance against Bobby.

Unfortunately, he wasn't getting any real-life practice. There were many more fire, water, earth and air training sessions than he had spirit ones. And since their plan had backfired with the Silver Circle, Commodore Kazama's warning had been ringing in Skandar's ears: *I am only giving you one more chance, Skandar.*

As a result, he hadn't dared to summon his allied element with anyone other than Agatha. What if he used a spirit weapon to win a joust and something bad happened? What if he got possessed through the bond – like Gabriel, like Rickesh, like Bobby? The more he learned about the spirit element, the more Skandar understood its risks, its unknowns, its darkness. He was learning to love it, but he didn't trust it yet. So he didn't use it in jousts, not even when they were allowed to use any element they pleased. As Nina had said, the night in the Wilderness had been a *close call* – and he knew for sure that he wouldn't be so lucky if anything else went wrong.

When the day of the Water Festival arrived, it felt good to change into their blue jackets and leave the Eyrie. As Scoundrel, Falcon, Blade and Red landed in Element Square, Skandar felt excitement replace his worries – for a moment at least. Although the quartet were using the festival to visit the Secret Swappers, Bobby had insisted they have an hour or so to enjoy themselves first. Fourpoint was busier than Skandar had ever seen it. Islanders who lived in the zones often celebrated elsewhere, but with all the elemental disruption they had swelled Fourpoint's numbers considerably. Many treehouses were already full of extra guests, and it was clear from the makeshift beds under trees that space in Fourpoint was running out, even if kindness wasn't. But the wall of noise as they wound through the streets seemed to indicate that – just for tonight – many wanted to forget about their troubles and have a good time.

Within seconds of entering Element Square, Skandar was soaked to the skin. The quartet had accidentally ridden into the middle of a battlefield, as Eyrie riders joined full-grown Chaos riders in a water fight – firing every kind of water attack they could think of, the bright blue magic of their palms lighting up the square. Laughing as Scoundrel shook water from his wings like a giant wet dog, Skandar rode him towards a line of eight enormous unicorn ice sculptures.

'Hey! Why does he look so familiar?' Bobby pointed to the nearest rider as Falcon tried to dry herself with a blast of fire. The icy rider had his fingers extended, a frozen jet of water shooting from his palm, a fierce expression on his face. His unicorn was baring its teeth.

'He *does* look familiar,' Flo agreed, riding Silver Blade round the base of the statue to take a better look.

'It's – it's my father,' Mitchell croaked, staring up at the ice rider, as Red tried to back away from the unicorn sculpture. 'They must be honouring the water council from last year. I really hope Nina kept her word about not telling him about that note . . . Look, there's Aspen McGrath as well, the taller one at the front.'

Skandar's heart jolted in his chest as he looked at New-Age Frost. Memories of the Weaver galloping the former Commodore's unicorn towards him in the Wilderness came flooding back.

He felt suddenly as though he would always be that terrified boy, waiting for his mother to take away the thing he loved the most. In fact, clutching Scoundrel's reins, he realised he *was* still waiting. He didn't believe he'd defeated her for good. She could be in this crowd, hiding in the shadows – watching him, biding her time. And a small part of him was still five and asking Kenna why other children at school had a mum and they didn't – a part of him that *wanted* to see Erika again. The Water Festival felt very loud and bright, the jackets and lanterns blurring together in a cerulean swirl.

'Skar? Are you coming?' Flo asked. 'We're going to get food.'

But Skandar was only vaguely aware of her words. He was frozen by New-Age Frost's icy eyes.

'You two go ahead.' Bobby's voice was firm. 'We'll catch you up.'

Skandar was dimly aware of Bobby riding Falcon next to Scoundrel.

'Personally I've always thought New-Age Frost was a bit of an ugly mule.'

Skandar choked out a laugh. 'He was my favourite for years back on the Mainland. I had a poster of him on my bedroom wall. I used to stare at it all the time – it really annoyed my sister.'

'I bet.' Bobby grinned. 'Who did Kenna like?'

'Mountain's Fear – Ema Templeton,' Skandar answered automatically, trying not to think about how many months it had been since Kenna had written to him.

'Air wielder. Good choice,' Bobby said approvingly. 'I think I'd like Kenna.'

'I think you would,' Skandar agreed. 'Probably more than you like me.'

'Almost certainly.' Bobby cocked her head to the side, and looked him right in the eye. 'Are you okay now?'

Skandar nodded. He was. Bobby had reminded him of something. He wasn't as vulnerable to the Weaver as he imagined. He wasn't alone. He didn't have to do this by himself.

'Do you want to go on the ice slide?' Bobby asked, pointing at a tall gleaming structure on the far corner of Element Square. People were climbing icy rungs to the top platform and then sliding down on mats, screaming all the way until they were thrown through the air to plop in a steaming hot-tub. Unicorns watched riders intently as they flew through the air, clearly unsure whether to rescue them or not.

'I don't really want to leave Scoundrel,' Skandar said. 'Maybe we could get one of those icicles from the fountain, though, the colourful ones?' A sign nearby read IKE'S IMAGINATIVE ICES – MORE FLAVOURS THAN YOU CAN COUNT.

'Sure,' Bobby said. 'Skandar?'

'Yeah?'

'I don't want the Island to self-destruct. And I *absolutely* don't want to be stuck with just air wielders – with Amber! – for ever. We've got to find this weapon.'

'We'll find it,' Skandar said with more confidence than he felt.

'Talking of Amber,' Bobby said, changing the subject at lightning speed as usual, 'have you noticed that her unicorn, Whirlwind Thief, has started hanging out with our lot around the Eyrie's hill?'

Skandar shrugged. 'I've seen them together a bit.'

Bobby scowled. 'I don't like it. It makes me think Amber's up to something.'

But Skandar thought Bobby's problem with Amber and Thief was that they'd beaten her and Falcon in a fire joust earlier that week.

He hung back and watched Bobby break off blue icicles the length of her arm. The stall owner had taken one look at Skandar queuing up and waved him away, fear in his eyes. Luckily Bobby hadn't noticed, otherwise Skandar thought Ike might have ended up with one of his own ices in quite an 'imaginative' place.

They slurped on their icicles while listening to a bard singing nearby.

'Jamie told Mitchell that his mum sang her truesong when she was still a teenager. Apparently everyone was really impressed,' Skandar said, as the singer started a tune about the triumphs of a water-allied Commodore he'd never heard of.

'What was it about?' Bobby asked curiously.

'A fish shortage the following summer. It came true.'

Bobby sniggered. 'Oh wow. The *glamour.*'

After that, they joined Mitchell as he led Red along a line of blue festival stalls. Bobby eyed the unicorn, looking mischievous. 'Red is positively *gleaming* today. Prettier than a parched penguin.'

'Er . . . thank you,' Mitchell said suspiciously, while Skandar giggled at the made-up saying. They didn't have penguins on the Island, so Skandar was pretty sure Mitchell didn't have the first clue what one looked like.

'Storm incoming!' Bobby yelled. Then Falcon let out a roar like thunder, electricity exploded around Falcon's wings, and she fired a tiny thunderbolt from every single one of her grey feather tips . . . right at Red.

The result was that all the hair on Red Night's Delight stood up on end, including her mane and tail. She looked halfway between a fuzzy soft toy and a science experiment gone wrong. Scoundrel hissed at his friend in rhythm – which Skandar was convinced meant he found the whole thing funny. Red ignored him, and kept turning her head to look up at Mitchell as though saying, *Fix this!*

'Forking thunderstorms! What did you just *do*?' Mitchell cried in anguish.

Bobby was ecstatic. 'Good girl, Falcon! Just like we practised! I've – been – wanting – to – try – that – for – ages,' she managed to say between howls of laughter.

'Now look here—' Mitchell said, sounding very like his father.

Skandar left them to it and wandered towards the stalls, thinking that this argument might go on for a while. He kept his distance from the sellers in case they recognised him. The stalls reminded him of beach huts on the Mainland, though they were selling an array of water-themed food, souvenirs and clothing. Skandar shut out the stares coming his way and admired the wooden waves which arched over the stall openings, shielding customers from the spray from the wings of unicorns in the water fight. He stared longingly at WATER WHISPERERS that sold surf and paddleboards. He and Kenna had *always* wanted a surfboard, but they'd never been able to afford one. Bobby and Mitchell had to drag him away towards WATER TO WEAR, a stall that glittered with sapphire jewellery and flowing cerulean scarves.

They found Flo queueing up for fish kebabs at FRED'S FROTHING FISH STICKS.

'Do you want some too?' she called over. Skandar nodded enthusiastically, glad that she'd offered and that he wouldn't have to approach the stall himself. The smoking grill smelled incredible.

Once she reached the front of the line, Flo had trouble holding Blade back from the sizzling sticks that frothed up with butter.

A dashing young man melted out of the crowd, his unicorn gleaming. 'Let me take him.'

'Oh.' Flo looked flustered. 'Thanks.' The two silver unicorns looked magnificent next to each other. Skandar couldn't help but notice how relaxed Blade looked in the other silver unicorn's company. It made him feel irritated.

'Look who's here,' Skandar muttered.

'Who's that?' Bobby and Mitchell asked at the same time.

'Rex Manning,' Skandar replied through gritted teeth, as he

watched Flo and Rex talking. 'I met him at the Stronghold when I was pretending to be a sentinel.'

'President Manning's son?' Mitchell asked, frowning.

'Why is Flo being so friendly? I thought she hated the Silver Circle. Didn't she quit?' Bobby asked.

'She can't quit, remember?' Mitchell corrected her, while trying to pat down Red's electrified mane again.

'Rex is different, apparently,' Skandar said. 'Flo said he talked Dorian out of making her train in the Stronghold full-time after she saved the wild unicorn. And he's been trying to stop the wild unicorn killings.'

'Oh yeah, right.' Bobby rolled her eyes. 'If he'd actually wanted to stop his dad, he could have gone to the Council!'

'Fathers can be complicated,' Mitchell said quietly, glancing back at the ice sculptures.

'Well, I don't trust him,' Skandar announced flatly, as Rex passed Blade's reins back to Flo and caught up with his friends. Seeing Rex reminded Skandar of something Dorian Manning had said to Nina – something about a woman, Rebecca? Nina had said his judgement was clouded; Skandar hadn't understood it at all.

'How's your sparkly friend?' Bobby asked Flo sarcastically, as she handed them each a sizzling fish stick.

'Rex was trying to convince me go to the next Silver Circle meeting. Apparently Dorian's stopped killing the wild unicorns because he's too afraid of Nina catching him. But I said I wouldn't,' Flo added quickly. 'Rex is going to cover for me, say I'm ill. I don't trust Dorian.'

'Since when did you become such a daredevil, Flo?' Bobby asked, half smiling. 'While I was branching out, you broke into the Stronghold, rode a wild unicorn like a bucking bronco and then went undercover in a hunting party. Now you're risking being locked in the Stronghold for not going to your meetings! I mean, what happened to the girl who got worried when we broke into a nice, friendly prison last year?'

'You didn't see those poor unicorns in the arena, Bobby. It was cruel, evil. I can't ever be part of that.'

'Roberta –' Mitchell cleared his throat – 'please stop using that "branching-out" expression. It doesn't make sense.'

'Branching out,' Bobby said, and stuck out her tongue. 'What are you going to do? Get Red to fart on me?'

'She doesn't do that any more,' Mitchell protested.

Skandar couldn't help but smile at Mitchell and Bobby's bickering. Things in the quartet were definitely getting back to normal. Even if nothing else was.

'You won't be smiling in a minute,' Mitchell muttered ominously. 'It's Secret Swapper time.'

CHAPTER FOURTEEN

THE SECRET SWAPPERS

The Secret Swappers occupied a treehouse on one of the shabbiest streets in the capital. As the quartet rode to the end of the row of dark trees, they found themselves squeezing their unicorns past groups of friends; parents and children; old men huddled with their own unicorns.

None of the faces they passed looked excited about the festival; they looked tired and lost. Not everyone *could* enjoy the festival – of course they couldn't. These people had lost their homes, their livelihoods, their normality. Killing the wild unicorns had caused elemental disruption, and everyone was paying the price. Anger surged in Skandar's chest as he thought about the selfishness, the cruelty – all because Dorian Manning had wanted to ensure there were no spirit wielders left, to ensure Skandar couldn't create an army to threaten the Silver Circle's power. But as Skandar looked into the faces of those displaced by the magical devastation, the thought of building an army was more attractive than ever.

Unlike most of the other treehouses in Fourpoint, there was no sign of anybody bedding down beneath the Secret Swappers' tree. The quartet dismounted and left their unicorns under the low-hanging branches. A single ladder clattered against the tree's trunk. The wooden treehouse above was rotting at its corners; its roof sagged in the middle.

Mitchell was just taking a brave step towards the ladder when the door of the treehouse above was thrown open with a bang.

'Please! Please just tell me one more word! It'll solve everything,' a young man cried.

A gruff voice came from inside the treehouse. 'Your secret was five words, so the secret you get back is five words. Rules are rules!'

'I'm begging you!'

'Get lost,' the gruff man growled, then slammed the door shut.

The younger man sobbed as he climbed down the ladder. When he saw the four Nestlings staring he shouted, 'Don't bother! It's never a fair swap!'

Skandar couldn't help wondering what the young man had wanted to know so badly.

'Should we make our secrets really long if they're dealing in the number of words?' Bobby whispered to Flo.

Flo shook her head quickly. 'They'll just cross out the unnecessary ones. There's no point. And we don't want to annoy them, remember?'

'Do you think that charming chappie at the door is the one who comes after you if you swap them a lie?' Bobby asked Mitchell.

'C'mon,' Mitchell said briskly, ignoring the question.

At the top of the ladder, Bobby knocked on the door, grimacing as she rubbed grime from her knuckles.

'I'm coming, I'm coming.' The gruff man opened the door again. He was younger than Skandar had expected from his voice, maybe fifty, with a scraggy beard and black beady eyes. There was a fairly fresh-looking scar above his eyebrow.

'It's Eyrie babies, Moira!' he shouted over his shoulder. 'Waste of time?'

A woman's voice echoed back. 'Send them packing, Raf. They've only been riders five minutes; don't know enough yet to interest us.'

The man went to shut the door without a word to any of them, but Skandar quickly stepped forward. His right sleeve was pulled up, and he lifted his arm level with Raf's chin. The spirit mutation glowed in the lamplight. Raf stared down at the white translucent skin, as Skandar opened and closed his fist so the man could see the muscles and tendons working alongside the stillness of the bones.

Raf licked his chapped lips.

'I need some information,' Skandar said forcefully. 'I've got a secret to swap.'

'You'd better come in then, spirit wielder,' Raf rasped, and the quartet followed him into the dimly lit treehouse.

The inside was just as horrible as the outside. It smelled damp and musty, of rotting wood and ancient paper. Everywhere Skandar looked, he saw towers of shallow wooden drawers. Some were short and stacked on top of each other precariously; others reached all the way to the sagging ceiling. Every tiny drawer had one thing in common: a silver handle with a paper tag. Bobby lifted up a tiny tag as she passed one, squinting—

'Best put that down, girly.' An elderly woman, who must have been Moira, was sitting on top of one of the smaller higgledy-piggledy towers. She looked all wrong sitting on something so unstable; halfway between a rebellious schoolgirl and a scolding grandma.

Bobby dropped the label, but Moira's gaze now rested on Raf.

'I thought I told you to send the Eyrie chicks away.' Moira's voice had a warning in it that Raf had clearly learned to identify. He rushed over to her tower and grinned toothily up at her.

'One of them's that spirit wielder – the one training in the Eyrie. *This* one.' Raf reached back and roughly pulled Skandar forward, his blue sleeve still pushed up over his elbow.

Moira's face changed immediately, and she jumped down from her perch as though she was thirty years younger. Flo was so shocked she accidentally bumped into a tower of drawers, and Mitchell had to help her steady it as they wobbled ominously.

'We want to know about the First Rider and the queen of the wild unicorns,' Skandar blundered.

Mitchell took over. '*Specifically* we want to know about the weapon the First Rider made from the Queen's bones, and where to find it. Do you have any secrets that will help us?'

Moira turned her bright blue gaze on Mitchell. 'You aren't the first to come here seeking secrets about the First Rider. But we have, so far, been unable to share what we have. Nobody gave us a secret juicy enough for the swap.' She smacked her lips. Skandar couldn't help thinking about what happened if you gave the Swappers a false secret: *They kill you*. He wasn't sure if it was an empty threat or a real possibility, but he certainly wasn't willing to risk it.

Flo looked confused. 'But if you could help the Commodore

find this weapon, surely you would? It could save the Island!'

Moira sniggered. 'I think you're getting us mixed up with other people, silver girl.'

'What other people?'

'Good people. We don't give away our secrets. We only swap them. That's our trade. If we helped every poor soul who came in here wanting information, where would that get us?'

'Has Nina Kazama been here already?' Mitchell asked slowly.

'Can't disclose the identities of our clients,' Raf said, licking his lips again.

'They know what we need,' Bobby said, clearly impatient. 'Let's do this.'

To give themselves the best chance of having a secret accepted, each member of the quartet had decided to share one. After all, they didn't know what information the Swappers already had – and the more words they swapped, the better. They'd agreed not to reveal their secrets to each other, so it felt awkward scrawling the words down on the ratty slips of paper Raf had given them.

Moira whipped away each of their paper slips as soon as they'd finished. Her grey skirts swirled and her long white hair swung as she paced between the mismatched towers of drawers to read them. Skandar got the feeling she was enjoying this moment, gobbling up their closely guarded secrets like a hungry gull.

Almost immediately she tutted and pressed Bobby's secret back into her hand. 'This is of no interest to me. Mundane Mainland matters aren't traded here.'

Bobby scowled and crushed the paper in her fist.

To Mitchell she said, 'We have this already.'

'Impossible!'

Moira ignored him. She read Flo's next, and her blue eyes widened just a fraction.

'You've surprised me with this one, silver girl.' The old woman tilted her head in Flo's direction. 'I'll accept it, earning you an eight-word secret about the First Rider.'

'Wait a moment,' Mitchell said. 'What about Skandar's? If you accept his too, can't we have a longer one?'

'That's not how it works, son of Ira.' Moira shrugged. 'A secret for a secret.'

'But how much do you have on the First Rider? How do we know—'

'Do you want it or not?' Moira had her back half turned, but Skandar could just about see as she lovingly opened a tiny drawer and removed a curled piece of paper. She handed it to Flo, who unfurled it with a look of excitement and dread. Moira, meanwhile, wrote out a tag for the secret Flo had swapped, and placed the secret delicately inside the drawer.

'*Take the gift from tomb to elemental crossing,*' Flo read.

'That's not a secret!' Bobby cried. 'That's a riddle! What does it mean?'

Skandar thought it sounded like a line from a bard's song.

Moira's laugh was sharp. 'I don't write the secrets, and it's not my job to interpret them. Many have been passed down from my mother, and her mother before that. And when I die, my daughter will guard them.' She gestured into the corner, and for the first time Skandar noticed a young woman nestled in a pile of rags, fast asleep.

'But that secret *is* about the First Rider's gift? About how to save the Island?' Mitchell checked.

Moira sniffed. 'That's what my label said.'

She looked down to read Skandar's secret.

Skandar had been expecting the Secret Swapper to react with fear and revulsion, perhaps even demand he leave the treehouse. It wasn't every day you find out the Weaver has a son, and he's training in the Eyrie – and he's standing right in front of you. But instead her face was transformed with delight as she read and reread his words.

'That's some secret you carry, spirit wielder,' Moira murmured. 'Twelve words.'

Skandar was starting to feel very sick, like this had been an enormous mistake. What would happen to him if the Island found out he was the Weaver's son? Would Scoundrel be locked up like Arctic Swansong? He swallowed hard, half wishing he could snatch the piece of paper back. 'So, um, will that secret stay here, then? Unless . . .'

'Unless someone comes seeking it – and brings a secret worthy of the swap,' Moira answered, all business again.

'Right,' Skandar croaked. He didn't trust Moira one bit. Everything she said sounded like it had a double meaning, and it was making his head hurt.

Moira started to search the towers, picking up labels, tutting and then dropping them again. 'I know it's here somewhere,' she muttered. After what seemed like an age, she returned from the far end of the treehouse, carrying a piece of paper in her hand ever so carefully – like it was an injured bird. She handed it to Skandar. 'The longest secret I have about the First Rider's gift is eleven words. You gave me twelve, I know, but –' she shrugged – 'nothing much I can do about that.'

'Hey!' Bobby said indignantly.

Moira's blue eyes flashed dangerously. 'It's all I've got. Take it or leave it.'

Skandar stretched out his hand for the curled, yellowing slip of paper and read: 'The First Rider carved a staff from the Last Queen's bones.'

'What's a staff?' Flo asked immediately.

'It's sort of a long stick with a round top,' Skandar answered, thinking of books he'd read about wizards on the Mainland.

'A *staff*?' Bobby scoffed. 'How are we going to save the Island with that? It doesn't even have a pointy end!'

Moira attempted to wave them from the room, but Mitchell refused to budge. 'There was nothing in those secrets about the exact location of the bone staff.' He gritted his teeth. 'It's no use telling us what the weapon is if we can't find it!'

But Moira was having none of it. 'Now, now, chicks. We've shared, we've swapped, and now you need to GET OUT OF MY HOUSE!'

'We didn't want to stay anyway – it smells!' Bobby shouted back.

'Don't forget,' Raf growled, 'if either of those secrets turns out to be a lie – we're coming for you.' And he ran his hand across his throat.

The quartet were the last through the Eyrie's entrance later that evening. Skandar could sense Scoundrel's irritability at being left for so long outside the Secret Swapper's treehouse. Plus, the unicorn was hungry. Back at his stable, Skandar tried to cheer him up with a Jelly Baby, but, as he retrieved the squashed bag from his blue jacket pocket and turned it upside down, nothing came out but a shower of white sugar.

Scoundrel snatched the empty bag angrily out of Skandar's hand with his teeth – and incinerated it with a fire blast. Dad wasn't as good at remembering to send Jelly Babies as Kenna had been.

'I'm sorry, okay?' Skandar tried to pat the unicorn's neck, but Scoundrel electrocuted his hand. 'Ouch! We're going to see the Grins later, remember? For a party!'

Scoundrel's annoyance was still vibrating in the bond as Skandar left the stables.

Within seconds of entering their treehouse, Mitchell had retrieved his favourite object.

'Right!' He tapped his white chalk loudly against the blackboard. 'Quartet Meeting number—'

Bobby sighed loudly. 'I really missed this.' Skandar couldn't tell if she was joking.

'Oh, never mind the number, then,' Mitchell said, pushing his glasses up his nose. 'Read me those secrets again.'

Flo went first: 'Take the gift from tomb to elemental crossing.'

Then Skandar: 'The First Rider carved a staff from the Last Queen's bones.'

'It's just mysterious nonsense!' Bobby said moodily. 'Apart from the fact the First Rider made a bone *staff*. Which is the lamest weapon imaginable.'

'You're wrong about Flo's clue,' Mitchell said. 'I'm not sure Moira knew how valuable that secret was. It tells us exactly where to take the gift.'

'Where? What's an elemental crossing?' Bobby demanded.

'Ohhh,' Flo breathed. 'The Divide.'

'Where the fault lines meet!' Skandar said excitedly.

Mitchell wrote 'the Divide' on the blackboard. 'And we

already know from Nina that we have to take it there by the summer solstice.'

'Oh!' Skandar jumped, suddenly realising something else. 'And Rickesh was right.'

'Who?' Bobby asked.

'Rickesh, squadron leader of the Grins. When he told me the story about the First Rider, he mentioned his tomb. And now we know for sure that the bone staff is actually *in* the First Rider's tomb.'

'We still don't know where the tomb *is*, though,' Flo said.

'We've practically cracked it,' Bobby crowed sarcastically.

'It's more than we had this morning,' Flo retorted, her voice even.

KABOOM!

The whole treehouse shook. The quartet jumped to their feet, too nervous to go outside. Flo was the first to climb to the window of their treehouse.

'Can you see anything?' Skandar asked desperately.

'Leaping landslides,' Flo breathed, one hand going to her mouth.

'What is it?' Bobby asked crossly. 'We can't see!'

'There's a massive electrical storm over the Silver Stronghold,' Flo said, her voice hollow. 'I think that noise was a lightning bolt hitting the Spear.'

'The tower? The tall tower where the library is?' Skandar asked, trying to understand.

'Yes,' Flo confirmed. 'Although it's not a tower any more. It's cracked in two.'

The aftermath of the Spear's collapse was still sending smoke into the sky over the Silver Stronghold hours after Skandar had flown Scoundrel to join the Grins. The evening had been filled with water-balloon fights – Rickesh had stolen them from the festival – and way too much cake that Adela had 'borrowed' from her mother's stall. The sugar rush had resulted in frozen-handed Fen daring Prim to knock on Instructor O'Sullivan's door at eleven p.m., which she'd immediately done without getting caught. Prim had then dared Fen to steal one of the masks from the first sentinel she could find. That hadn't gone quite so well, and it was only Fen's speedy getaway that had stopped her getting in serious trouble.

At one point, Marcus and Patrick had attempted to sing the truesong from the Saddle Ceremony to Skandar, very loudly and off key, but Rickesh had eventually yelled at them to shut up. Skandar had brought his Chaos Cards along, and – as the only Mainlander – taught everyone else a game he'd seen other children playing at school where you battled with your cards. Of course, he'd never been popular enough on the Mainland to join in. He'd only had Kenna to play with. Even Amber had wanted to play – mainly, Skandar suspected, because she wanted to beat him.

At two a.m. Rickesh had fetched blankets so that they could sleep up on the Sunset Platform. Within half an hour seven members of the Peregrine Society were fast asleep against their unicorns' sides and looking completely unlike an elite flying squad. The eighth member, however, couldn't sleep – despite being cuddled up under his unicorn's black wing.

Guilt rolled uncomfortably in Skandar's stomach. Just like his quartet, the Grins were beginning to feel like family, but they couldn't replace Dad, couldn't replace . . . Kenna. He missed his sister so much it hurt. All he wanted was for her to have a unicorn and the life she'd been destined for. For them to live on the Island together. No doubt she'd be a Peregrine too. But if his quartet didn't find the bone staff soon, there would be no Island for Kenna to come to – even if Skandar turned out to be a Mender, after all. Had the Secret Swappers given them enough information? Skandar murmured their clues to himself: *staff, elemental crossing, Last Queen's bones* until his eyelids became heavy. The swapped secrets began to mix in his tired mind with the tune of the truesong – *only one hope, from tomb, carved, true successor, staff* – and finally Skandar fell into a fitful sleep and began to dream.

He had been running for hours. His legs hurt and there was a bloody gash on his calf. How had he got it? Wait. Something was wrong.

These weren't his legs.

He began to panic. He raised his hand to his head – his hair was too long. And these weren't his hands either! He wasn't himself. He needed to see. Who was he? A tug on his heart. The bond. Scoundrel. In his mind, in his heart, he was still Skandar. But whose body was this? Whose shoes was he running in? Who am I?

And suddenly he was out of the unfamiliar body, floating, taking one of the stranger's hands to anchor himself. Not a stranger – his sister. Happiness exploded in his chest at seeing her again after so long. 'Kenna!' he shouted in welcome, but she didn't react, didn't even glance his way. She looked so tired and scared. But there was something else in her face that he hadn't seen in years. Hope.

They ran hand in hand. He watched her like a hawk as she searched desperately for something, someone. 'Where are we?' he tried to ask her, but she still couldn't hear him, couldn't even see him. It was barren here, desolate. The trees were colourless, decaying. It didn't look like Margate, or anywhere he'd ever been on the Mainland. He looked down at the cracks in the battle-scarred plain. Was this the Wilderness? Was Kenna . . . here?

A sharp tug on the bond snatched Skandar's attention. He looked down at his chest, almost instinctively, and for the first time ever he saw his own bond. White. Shining. Stretching out into the Wilderness, lighting it up for miles.

Scoundrel? *he thought, touching the shining cord.*

And then he was rushing along it, the Wilderness blurring on either side of him, leaving Kenna far behind. Some deep-rooted instinct told him not to turn back. Not now. Not if he wanted to find . . .

The wild unicorn was silhouetted in front of the moon, its coat dapple grey. As Skandar's dream presence collided with hers, he knew they'd met before. This unicorn had found him time and time again.

Where is she? Where is she? Where is she? *The question was not words exactly but the very meaning of the unicorn's existence. Skandar tried to distance himself from the creature's body, like he had Kenna's, but he was trapped.*

Suddenly he was drowning in the wild unicorn's sadness, in her loss, in her loneliness – in the endless sense of missing someone. Of hatching alone, of waiting all those months as a foal in the Wilderness, of watching over the barren ground just in case. Just in case one day her destined rider would come.

Kenna's coming, *Skandar thought back desperately.* She'll be here. *But the more he tried to separate his own thoughts from the wild unicorn's, the more tangled they became, and he couldn't remember if he had two legs or four, whether he had wings or arms, whether he was lost or found . . . And there was so much pain. Pain everywhere.*

'Skandar! Wake up! Are you okay?'

Someone was shaking him. Skandar opened his eyes, saw Rickesh's concerned face and was sick right on to the platform.

His head hurt so much; he felt like someone had wrenched it open.

Scoundrel nudged him insistently with the side of his head, sweating and frothing at the mouth. He sniffed Skandar's hair with his soft nose, and then puffed smoke at him.

Skandar coughed. Satisfied, the black unicorn got to his feet and stood protectively over him.

'What *was* that?' Patrick looked worried. 'You were making all these weird noises. You sounded like . . . like a wild unicorn.'

'Some dream, spirit wielder,' Amber said shrewdly, and as the fog in Skandar's brain started to clear, he wondered whether her dad had ever told her about Menders.

'Are you okay?' Rickesh asked again.

Skandar sat up slowly, disorientated yet certain of one thing: that had been no ordinary dream. He and Scoundrel had been in it *together*. Their dream-selves had swapped places, just like Craig the bookseller had described. And Skandar was pretty sure your dreams didn't usually try to kill you either. Could this mean Skandar was a Mender, after all? Skandar felt real hope. If it'd been a Mender dream, then the dapple-grey unicorn *had* been meant for his sister.

As the Grins dispersed in the early-morning light, Skandar tried to shake off the feeling that Kenna was really here on the Island. Of course she wasn't. The dream had just been showing him what destiny *should* have given Kenna. The shining possibility of Kenna and her unicorn together at last.

But if Skandar was a Mender, he could make that dream more than a possibility.

He could bring it to life.

THE EYE OF THE STORM

Lightning has a smell. Kenna hadn't realised that before the storm to end all storms. When it hit, she was rereading Erika Everhart's letter – the letter that finally told her the truth – trying not to worry about how time was slipping towards the summer solstice. Trying not to think about all the secrets Skandar had kept from her and how the last one had broken her heart. But she couldn't help but wonder what he would do when he found out she was on the Island.

It didn't matter. He'd lied about everything. She owed him nothing. But there was a twinge of longing that gripped her chest. A memory of Skandar's seventh birthday played out in her mind. She let herself see him – wide-eyed and gappy-toothed – hugging her over and over because she'd managed to bake him a cake in the shape of a unicorn. It had taken her weeks to save the money for the cake mould and days of secret midnight baking to perfect the wings. Once Skandar had blown out the candles, Dad had clumsily cut his son the first piece. Kenna remembered seeing Skandar wipe away a flurry of tears. He hadn't wanted the cake sliced. He'd wanted the unicorn to last for ever.

CRACK!

At first Kenna couldn't work out why she was smelling sparks, chlorine and fresh air. She looked up to see a sliver of night sky through the top of the tower. Then the roof started to shear and split until stars filled her vision. The whole tower creaked and crunched, and Kenna glanced down at the floor of her prison – at a crack running right through the middle.

Terror caught up with shock as the jagged lines in the roof and floor grew wider, the tower groaning. Her head swam as one side of the room started to break away from the other. Kenna spotted the tower's spiral staircase through the chasm in the floor, and in that moment she also glimpsed freedom. Amid the noise of the crumbling tower, as pieces of metal sparked and scraped and debris fell from the ceiling, she knew what she had to do. She wasn't going to wait for the summer solstice to be rescued. She didn't like to rely on other people – she was going to rescue herself.

She shoved *The Book of Spirit* under her arm, sat on the edge of the hole, and jumped down to the quivering staircase. A sharp piece of metal sliced into her calf, but she gritted her teeth against the pain. Just as she landed, a lightning bolt struck the stone floor of her room, right where she'd been standing.

The tower started to cleave in two, the noise almost unbearable, and the staircase shuddered and twisted. Kenna concentrated on her feet, trying to ignore the distant shouts and the carnage around her. She was not going to die. Not before she had a unicorn. Not when she was so close.

And then she emerged into more chaos – silver-masked

guards pointing at the tower, unicorns screeching, riders screaming – but Kenna kept moving until she found herself by a wall made of shields. Or at least that was what they must have been before. Many were bent or missing altogether, the storm's destructive power too great for them to withstand.

Kenna stepped through one of the gaping holes – unwavering and unnoticed – and escaped Dorian Manning's clutches much sooner than she could have hoped.

At first it was wonderful being outside after spending so long trapped in the tower. She ran, trying to get as far away from the Stronghold as possible, but it soon grew dark. Kenna was hungry, cold, scared – and completely lost. She could barely see her hand in front of her face; the ground was uneven under her black school pumps. Maybe she should have stayed in the Stronghold and waited like she'd been told? Maybe she'd ruined everything?

An ear-splitting screech came out of nowhere, and Kenna dropped to the ground instinctively. Wild unicorns. The small cut on her calf suddenly seemed horribly significant. Could they smell her blood? Kenna started to shake as hooves thundered towards her. She covered her ears and braced for impact.

It never came. Instead, there was a loud snorting from above her head. Then a shriek. Kenna opened one eye, and in the light of the moon she saw a dapple-grey unicorn shining above her, its transparent horn blocking the sky like it had snagged on a star. Kenna swallowed a scream as the wild unicorn nudged her shoulder with its nose, the smell of rotting flesh overpowering. But then it ruffled its wings and trotted ahead of her. When Kenna didn't follow, it looked back.

She was very confused. Why wasn't it eating her? Weren't wild unicorns supposed to be deadly?

'Are you trying to make me follow you?' Kenna whispered, and the unicorn screeched, rearing at the moon.

So the disappointed girl from the Mainland followed the lonely unicorn from the Wilderness. On and on they went, until they reached a small barren hill with skeletal trees perched on its brow. Lights hung from the bony branches, and voices spoke in low tones.

Kenna turned to the unicorn in amazement. 'You brought me to other people! You knew I was in trouble and—'

She stopped. Could this be her destined unicorn? Kenna reached out to touch the unicorn's dappled neck, ignoring its bloody wounds and scabbing skin. After all these months of looking, what Dorian really should have done was ask for her help.

But before Kenna's fingers could make contact with the matted coat, another unicorn emerged from the trees – a rider silhouetted on its back. This unicorn was wild too, its horn ghostly in the moonlight. As the figure rode into the light, Kenna could see that the rider was cloaked in black, a white stripe painted from the crown of their head to the tip of their chin. The rider's face contorted with rage at seeing the dapple-grey unicorn, and, palm glowing white, let a ball of pure power fly right at its rotting flank.

'No!' Kenna shouted. 'You don't understand. I think that's my destined—'

'That unicorn isn't your destined anything,' the rider snapped, throwing another ball of light.

Before Kenna could say more – before she could shout that the wild unicorn had found her, that it had saved her – it screeched, stretched its tattered grey wings, and galloped off into the dark. Kenna collapsed to her knees, tears already falling, mouth open in a silent scream of longing for the creature she had only just met but felt she had known for ever.

Then one word changed everything.

'Daughter.'

The rider dismounted from the wild unicorn's back. 'You're early.'

Kenna's mother pulled her up off the ground into a tight hug, and suddenly nothing else seemed to matter.

CHAPTER FIFTEEN

THE TOURNAMENT

Mitchell, Bobby and Flo had been both horrified and fascinated by Skandar's Mender dream. Skandar had played down the pain and what might have happened if Rickesh hadn't been there to wake him. He focused instead on telling them about the dapple-grey unicorn. They agreed that Kenna couldn't possibly be *on* the Island, but that he needed to talk to her after the jousting tournament in a couple of months' time and be completely honest. Then they could all try to find the wild unicorn together – if there was still an island left by then.

The next few months were gruelling for the quartet. By day they were practising for the Nestling joust, desperate to craft the most effective weapons, improve their reaction times and ensure their unicorns were at their very fittest. For Flo, the Spear's collapse meant that Circle meetings had been cancelled until further notice and without the help of her fellow silvers she had to work extra hard to control Blade's power. In March, the quartet didn't even attend the Chaos Cup Qualifiers, and Skandar was so busy focusing on his own training that he completely forgot about turning fifteen until a birthday card from Dad turned up two weeks later.

But training was only the half of it. Though the wild unicorn killings had stopped, the elemental destruction continued day and night. In the evenings, the quartet could be found at Mitchell's blackboard – or behind great stacks of books in the four elemental libraries of the Eyrie, searching for clues about the First Rider's burial place. Skandar tried to concentrate on the dusty volumes, but his mind often wandered. He kept sketching Dad and Kenna on scrap paper, imagining breaking the news to his sister about her true destiny . . . and about Erika Everhart. He didn't attempt any more Mender dreams. He didn't want to take the risk without further training, not when Kenna was coming to the Island so soon. He knew already which unicorn he'd be searching for when she arrived.

But by the Air Festival in May, despite their desperate efforts, the quartet were still no closer to finding the First Rider's tomb. And as if that wasn't stressful enough, Skandar and Agatha were having the same argument they'd been having for weeks. The disagreement was part of the reason he hadn't told Agatha about the Mender dream. That, and the fact he was afraid she'd be so angry she wouldn't help him bond Kenna to her unicorn after the tournament. He was also scared that Agatha would fixate on the problem that even if the mending worked, Kenna would be an illegal spirit wielder. If he was *really* honest, Skandar thought Agatha might make him wait to unite Kenna with her unicorn – and he didn't want to.

'Skandar, I'm deadly serious. If you don't use the spirit element, there is a huge risk you're not going to make it through the tournament,' Agatha said, stomping back from setting up a target across the field.

'And I'm telling you that it's riskier for me to *use* the spirit element. What if I get possessed and kill a unicorn? Or have you forgotten it's the death element? They'll lock me up for good. It's not worth it; I'm not ranked that low!' Skandar summoned a spirit bow, feeling for where it ought to be – trusting that it existed, even though its shining brilliance came from a different plane altogether.

'But how precise is the Henderson boy being? Is he accounting for nerves? Distraction by the crowd? What if you're consistently against the strongest riders? Me training you all these months hasn't been for my own entertainment, you know.'

Skandar carefully felt for the string of the bow with three fingers, moulding a ghostly white arrow with his other hand. He snatched it out of the air. 'I don't know, okay? But what I'm sure of is that if I give Dorian Manning any excuse, he's going to have me out of the Eyrie. You heard what Commodore Kazama said.'

'She also stood up to Manning. She's on your side.'

Skandar frowned. 'She said I was on my last chance. And Dorian *hates* me. It's personal somehow – Nina said something about him having clouded judgement. Who was that woman he mentioned – Rebecca?'

Agatha looked suddenly distressed. She turned away from him as she answered, her voice clipped. 'Rebecca was a fire wielder. She was also Dorian's wife.'

'Was?'

'Her unicorn, Cloud Blazer, was one of the Fallen Twenty-Four, and Rebecca . . . She didn't cope well with the loss. Couldn't eat, couldn't sleep. She was dead within a year.' The spirit instructor's white cloak flapped in the wind.

Skandar's stomach squirmed. His mum was responsible for Cloud Blazer's death – for Rebecca's. No wonder Dorian hated spirit wielders.

Agatha turned to face him, clearly back in instructor mode. 'Fire the arrow!'

Skandar shot the spirit arrow and hit the target positioned fifty metres away.

Agatha rubbed her mutated cheeks compulsively, a habit Skandar had noticed when his aunt got particularly frustrated with him. 'See!' she shouted, pointing at the target. 'You're actually quite good with spirit weapons. It comes naturally to you – unlike a lot of other things. Like self-preservation, for example.'

Skandar rolled his eyes, something he'd picked up from Bobby.

'You've even mastered illusion with some of the more basic weapon shapes. You could win the whole tournament if you just used—'

'I don't need to win the whole tournament,' Skandar said reasonably. 'I just have to finish above the bottom six. That's all.'

Agatha stroked Scoundrel's blaze as if to calm herself. 'Look, I understand your point, I do, but I need you to promise me. If you come up against someone really good in the knockout round – someone you *know* is going to beat you – *please* use the spirit element.'

Skandar swallowed.

'They can't throw you out just for using it,' Agatha added. 'That's not what you agreed with McGrath last year. Is it?'

Skandar shrugged.

'Is. It?' she said more forcefully. 'And if you come last, then you'll be thrown out of the Eyrie anyway!'

Skandar finally gave in. 'Okay. I promise. If I know I'm going to lose, I'll use it.' He paused, and then decided to ask the thing that had been occupying his mind since the Water Festival. 'Agatha?'

'Do you mean "Instructor Everhart"?'

'Yes, er, sorry. I was wondering about if the Island becomes uninhabitable after the summer solstice. What do you think the Weaver will do?'

Agatha froze, and Skandar could tell that she hadn't thought about this before.

'I was just worrying about the Mainland,' Skandar added quickly. Although that wasn't strictly true.

Agatha's eyes were distant. 'No doubt Erika will survive the chaos – perhaps even use it to her advantage. It would take more than the Island's destruction to get the better of her.'

Skandar wasn't exactly sure of the emotion in Agatha's voice, but it sounded a lot like . . . pride.

That evening, Skandar returned to the treehouse to find Jamie and Mitchell reading a book together about truesongs. The fire wielder really had had a change of heart about them. Skandar thought Jamie must really like Mitchell to put up with all the bard talk; he wondered whether he should try to gently remind Mitchell that the blacksmith had been trying to *avoid* his parents' career for his whole life. Although everyone was talking about truesongs now. The news that the Island wouldn't heal without the First Rider's fabled gift seemed to have trickled up to the Eyrie, and every conversation Skandar heard – on swinging bridges, in the Trough, around the stables – was about where the First Rider might have hidden it. At least it seemed to have deflected some of the attention away from him.

Skandar settled down on the blue beanbag. 'Any luck?'

Jamie sighed. 'Nope. One of my mum's friends – this really old bard – he sang his truesong last night and everyone was so excited, thinking it might have more information about how to fix the Island.'

'And?'

'We couldn't make sense of it, to be honest.' Jamie shrugged. 'It was about shattering spears and family ties . . . or was it shattering ties and family fears?'

'If it was shattering spears, it could have been talking about what happened at the Silver Stronghold,' Mitchell mused, nose still in *Truesong Tragedies*.

'Honestly, it was way too cryptic to be useful,' Jamie said, shifting away from Mitchell on the beanbag slightly so he could look at Skandar.

'How's your armour holding up? I'm going to make Scoundrel a new breastplate before the tournament. I know it's only a few weeks away, but I've been experimenting with this new technique to make it less brittle on the corners . . .' And Jamie was off, his passion for his craft shining as brightly as Blade's armour. Even Mitchell looked up from the book he was reading to listen – which was practically unheard of.

Later, Skandar decided to go down to the post tree to put another letter in his capsule to send to Dad. He'd sent three since his Mender dream, and all he'd had back was the late birthday card. Skandar was desperate to make sure Dad and Kenna were both coming to the jousting tournament. He was scared about how they'd react to him telling them everything – not leaving anything out, not even the Weaver – but he knew it was the right thing to do.

It was dark by the post trees, and Skandar had to unhook a nearby lantern to locate his capsule. He twisted off the lid, went to put his latest letter inside, but found that there wasn't enough space. Confused, he shook out the capsule, and a bunch of letters fell out. He squinted at them in the dark and realised they were *his* letters. The ones he'd been sending to Dad! No wonder he hadn't had a reply. As he looked closer at the envelopes, Skandar saw they all had red stamps across the address that read:

DENIED BY RIDER LIAISON OFFICE: RETURN TO SENDER

The letters had never even left the Island.

In almost no time at all, the day of the Nestling joust arrived. The weeks leading up to the tournament had been a flurry of excitement, on Bobby's part – and nerves for the rest of them. It hadn't helped when Charlie, whom Bobby had hung around with earlier in the year, was declared a nomad two days before the tournament. He'd been performing badly in jousts for months, and the instructors clearly didn't think it was worth him competing. Skandar hadn't gone to watch when Albert had been declared a nomad the previous year; he hadn't been able to bear it. But this time he'd gone down to the Nomad Tree with the other Nestlings to say goodbye to Charlie and Hinterland Magma, to see his earth pin broken – one piece hammered into the bark, the others given to Mariam and Ajay, now the only two members of the quartet.

Two days later, Scoundrel's Luck joined thirty-five other

armoured unicorns in the Chaos Compound – an enclosure tucked behind the main arena in Fourpoint. Riders led their unicorns in tight circles, armour flashed in the May sunshine, elements fizzed off flanks, manes and tails. For the next few hours, this would be the Nestlings' base. The place where they would wait nervously for their next joust. Even from here, Skandar could hear the arena beginning to fill up with spectators – their footsteps echoing in the stands as they found their seats.

He imagined Dad and Kenna arriving. The Rider Liaison Office hadn't yet responded to his questions about his letters to Dad being returned, but they *had* confirmed that the Smith household in Margate had received an official invitation to the Nestling joust. After he'd found that out, Skandar had relaxed a bit. What did letters matter now the day had come when he would actually be able to speak to his dad and sister? Nerves snatched at the end of his every breath. And not just about the tournament. He was going to tell his family the truth at last.

Jamie arrived with some of the older blacksmiths and started checking Scoundrel's armour. He looked as anxious as Skandar felt. If Skandar was declared a nomad, Jamie was out of a job.

Saddlers buzzed around their riders too, though Flo's dad had already checked Scoundrel's saddle up at the Eyrie. Olu had tried to calm Skandar down by telling him everyone at Shekoni Saddles would be cheering him on from the stands. It hadn't helped.

'Goodness, there are sentinels everywhere,' Flo said. Her and Blade's shining armour made it difficult to look at them directly.

Red joined them too, although Mitchell didn't look up as he spoke. He was checking his notebook. 'Nina must be worried about the solstice approaching. I mean, the Commodore has stopped the Mainlanders coming. That's pretty drastic.'

'WHAT?' Skandar stared at Mitchell. 'What do you mean the Mainlanders aren't coming?'

He finally looked up, mortified. 'Flaming fireballs! I thought you knew!'

Flo closed her eyes briefly and took a deep breath. 'Skar, two of the Mirror Cliffs collapsed last night. According to Dad, Nina was already considering stopping Mainlander families visiting this year for safety reasons, and that made up her mind.'

'But . . . she can't. I need to see my— That's not . . .' Skandar bit his lip, but a hot tear escaped down his cheek. He needed Kenna on the Island. He was a Mender, but he couldn't do anything if she wasn't here. His disappointment was so strong he could hardly stay upright in his saddle.

'I'm sure Nina will organise another visit, Skar.' Flo's voice was full of concern.

Mitchell nodded. 'Definitely.'

But Skandar couldn't help thinking: *Only if there's an island left to visit.*

There was a flurry of movement over by a wooden noticeboard that had been hammered into the ground. Skandar saw Bobby and Falcon barging their way towards it.

'Group stages are up!' Jamie sprinted away, fighting through the crowd of riders, trying to see who Skandar was drawn against in the group stage. Their rankings in the first round would determine who they jousted in the knockouts. The best-ranked riders would joust the worst ranked – it was the fairest way to do it so that the good riders weren't drawn against each other and knocked out prematurely.

Jamie was frowning as he jogged back to Scoundrel. 'I'm not going to lie, Skandar – it's a tough group. Amber and Whirlwind

Thief are in there, and Farooq and Toxic Thyme, as well as Niamh and Snow Swimmer.'

The crowd started to clap. Skandar guessed the four referees must have taken their places by the jousting pistes. The rest of the quartet moved towards the compound exit. Scoundrel screeched after them, but Jamie held him back.

'You have to use the spirit element.'

'Jamie! Not you as well. You know it's too dangerous.'

Jamie shook his head. 'It's who you are, Skandar. It's who Scoundrel is. The Silver Circle are controlling you with fear, but you have to stand up to them. You have to be brave.'

'I can't lose him.' Skandar twisted his hands in Scoundrel's mane, as though that would keep them together. 'I'd rather be declared a nomad than lose him.'

'You can't become a nomad either, Skandar,' Jamie said seriously. 'You need to stay at the Eyrie – to train, to learn.'

'What for?' Skandar said incredulously. 'So I can win the Chaos Cup?'

'Who cares about that?' Jamie said, frustrated. 'It's about getting spirit wielders into the Hatchery again, isn't it? It's about fixing this Island – and I'm not talking about the bone staff. I'm talking about it being rotten at its core. I'm talking about generations of unicorns being born wild because of prejudice against spirit wielders. Stopping that – it's on you, Skandar. I'm sorry but it is.'

'I-I—' Skandar stuttered. He'd never heard Jamie speak like this before.

'Be brave for the lost spirit wielders, Skandar. For your sister, for all the Mainlanders and Islanders who've missed out since. You're the only one fighting for them. But if you let

Dorian Manning win, if you let the Silver Circle scare you into submission—'

'Last call for Group Three!' Instructor O'Sullivan's voice echoed over the tannoy.

Skandar gathered up his reins. 'I've got to get out there.'

'Do the right thing!' Jamie called after him.

But Skandar wasn't exactly sure what that was any more.

Thirty minutes later, things were not going well. Skandar's supporters from Shekoni Saddles had winced as Amber knocked him clean out of the saddle with a terrifying electrified mace; Mariam and Old Starlight had obliterated him when his fiery broadsword had lost its shape completely, flaring off sideways and petering out; his friends from the Peregrine Society had covered their eyes as Marissa and Demonic Nymph had swiped him off Scoundrel with an enormous ice spear – and that had just been three jousts. In all he'd lost eight in a row. Eight out of eight. It was his worst performance to date. He didn't know if it was the crowd or the sentinels patrolling or how upset he was that Kenna and Dad weren't here, but he'd come bottom of his group. His Shekoni saddle had meant he hadn't fallen off *every* time, but his was still the very worst performance of all the Nestlings. As he left the arena, Skandar caught a glimpse of Agatha in the stands, head in her hands.

Before the real knockout rounds began, the bottom two riders from each group had to face a qualifying joust to get into the final thirty-two. Skandar just about scraped through against Mateo, but only because Hell's Diamond reared and threw him off as soon as the first whistle sounded. But Skandar was still so low on points that if he lost the next joust, he'd be knocked out of the tournament and declared a nomad. He wasn't even sure the spirit element could save him.

Skandar, Mitchell and Flo were waiting to find out who they were jousting in the first full round of the knockouts when a voice cracked like a whip through the hubbub of the Chaos Compound.

'I will not have my son disgrace himself by associating with a spirit wielder!'

Before Skandar knew what was happening, Ira Henderson had appeared by Red's horned head and caught hold of Mitchell's reins. The strand of flowing water in his braid flashed blue as he tried to yank Red away from Scoundrel.

'Oi!' Skandar shouted, as Flo cried, 'Mr Henderson!'

But Mitchell dismounted immediately and grabbed Red back from his father.

'Don't touch her.' Mitchell's voice was shaking but his words were clear. 'And that *spirit wielder* happens to be my best friend.'

'I come here to congratulate you on your performance in the first round, and now you disappoint me like this? You're not the son I thought you were,' Ira replied. His voice was serene and emotionless. 'You'll never become Commodore.'

But for once Mitchell was undeterred. 'You're right. I'm not. I'm not the son you thought you had, or the one you desperately want me to be. I'm someone completely different. Someone who doesn't want to dedicate their whole life to becoming Commodore. Someone who is starting to realise that they like the less predictable, beautiful kinds of magic. Not just the battling kind.'

'If you're talking about truesongs, then—' Ira started.

But Mitchell cut him off.

'If you ever stopped telling me who I am or what I should be doing, you might find out that I am *actually* quite excellent. *We* are excellent.' He glanced at Red. 'And what I've been doing with *the spirit wielder* this whole year is trying to find a way to save the precious Island you want me to be Commodore of one day. So maybe –' Mitchell's voice rose higher – 'maybe the real problem here is *you*.'

Ira didn't reply. But just as he turned on his heel to march away, Red let out a fart – the longest and loudest Skandar had ever heard – lit a hoof, looked right into Ira's face and kicked back. The fart ignited, bigger and brighter than ever before. Flo and Skandar cheered very loudly. Ira Henderson gagged, looked furious and then stormed out of the enclosure. Mitchell shook like a leaf as he watched him go.

'Wow, that was incredible,' Flo breathed. 'I think Bobby would call that—'

'Badass,' she and Skandar said together.

Mitchell smiled weakly. Red shrieked, then burped ash all over herself in celebration. Scoundrel shrieked back happily.

'Results are up! Results are up!' someone yelled, interrupting the moment.

Skandar didn't have the heart to jump off Scoundrel and check the board like everyone else. He let Mitchell break the news.

'Skandar.' His eyes were wide. 'You've been drawn against—'

'Me,' Bobby said, riding over. She still had her helmet on so Skandar couldn't really see her expression.

'You have to throw your match with Skandar,' Mitchell said.

'Mitchell, you can't ask her to do that! It's not fair,' Flo said.

'Yes, I can. I've checked the scores. If Skandar loses, he's out of the Eyrie, but Bobby only lost one joust in the group stage. If she gets knocked out of the tournament now, she's ranked so high that she won't be declared a nomad. Only six people

– 292 –

are, remember? And four have been eliminated already, so it's only the two lowest ranked who'll be declared nomads if they're knocked out this round. Roberta, you need—'

'Mitchell, stop. All of you leave me alone, okay? I need to concentrate. I should have got a clean sweep in my group.' Bobby's voice was choked, and Skandar wondered whether she had her helmet on because she didn't want them to see her face.

'Bobby, are you . . . ?' Skandar tried to reach out a hand, but Falcon moved sideways and all he got was a brush of chainmail.

Flo, Mitchell and Skandar watched Bobby ride towards the other side of the enclosure. Red squeaked out a half-hearted fart, but – perhaps sensing the sudden seriousness of the situation – didn't reach back to light it. Jamie stroked the red unicorn's nose, giving Skandar a significant look.

'The spirit element,' he hissed. And Skandar's stomach turned over.

Bobby and Skandar were first to joust. The noise of the crowd – booing and whispering – was overwhelming as Scoundrel walked out into the sunlight, his spirit wielder blaze gleaming on his forehead.

Falcon's Wrath was rearing at the opposite end of the line of stakes, her slate-grey wings flickering with electricity. Skandar couldn't help but notice how perfect the unicorn looked – not a hair or a feather out of place. Falcon was at her most beautiful. And that meant she and Bobby were at their best. Flo's words echoed in his mind: *if you keep all the stuff about your mum trapped inside your head, your heart – you're never going to be able to trust anyone.* After everything that had happened this year, could Skandar *really* trust Bobby to lose on purpose? She was born to win. It would go against her very core.

Skandar waited for Instructor Saylor's whistle. Scoundrel was pawing at the sand with his hoof, impatient to gallop.

First whistle. *Be brave for the lost spirit wielders.*

Scoundrel exploded forward, black muscles rippling – legs so powerful that it almost felt like they were flying. The black unicorn's whole life had been a battle so far, and he wasn't about to give up now.

Second whistle.

Skandar wasn't giving up either. He wasn't giving up on finding the bone staff, he wasn't giving up on the lost spirit wielders, he wasn't giving up on Kenna, and he was never giving up on this Island.

He made his move in a split second. A shining white bow formed in his right hand and the spirit magic shimmered around it. Skandar lifted it, moulding three spirit arrows at once. He notched the first on the bow, letting go of Scoundrel's reins, trusting his Shekoni saddle would keep him in place. Skandar ignored the shouts from the stands as the crowd saw the fifth element in a joust for the first time in almost two decades.

The only sign that Bobby was surprised was a slight tightening of her grip on her fizzling broadsword.

Skandar loosed his first arrow right at her armoured chest. Then the second at her right shoulder. Then the third at her shoulder again.

As the grey and black unicorns thundered towards each other, Skandar finished his attack with a secret weapon. He concentrated hard on the third arrow and told himself it wasn't really there at all. It wasn't heading for Bobby's shoulder; it was heading for her chest. And as Bobby swung back her sword, he prayed the illusion had worked.

Bobby deflected the first arrow with her shield easily, swiped the second arrow away with her sword hilt. But the third – yes! She tried to swat it away from her shoulder with her armoured elbow, but there was only empty air. Falcon stumbled. The third and final arrow flew right at Bobby's chest, and she rocked backwards with the force of it. Scoundrel galloped past Falcon – snorting sparks – as Bobby's broadsword missed Skandar completely.

Instructor Saylor held out an arm towards Skandar and Scoundrel. 'One point to zero.'

The crowd wasn't sure whether to cheer or boo, but then an explosion of whistling and clapping came from the left stand. Skandar grinned as he saw a big orange SHEKONI sign and Flo's dad, mum and twin brother all cheering him on.

At the other end of the jousting piste, Bobby had taken off her helmet and seemed to be mouthing something at him. She made a cutting gesture across her throat, and Skandar bristled. He knew Bobby was competitive, he understood why she wasn't going to throw the match, but she didn't have to be so aggressive about it.

Skandar turned Scoundrel in a tight circle at the end of the piste, trying to calm him before the riders went again. The unicorn's ribs were moving quickly under Skandar's armoured legs, the fast bursts along the jousting piste exhausting and exhilarating him in equal measure.

Instructor Saylor shouted for them to get ready. Skandar pointed Scoundrel's shining black horn right at Falcon's grey one. Inside his helmet, the noise of the crowd was dulled. It was just him and Scoundrel. He took deep breaths. In. Out. In. Out. He was going to get the point. He was going to win this. As a spirit wielder.

First whistle. Scoundrel thundered forward.

Second whistle. Skandar summoned a sword this time, a

sabre moulded from pure spirit magic. It was faultless – the best weapon he'd ever made. And then – as he saw Bobby riding towards him, her favourite lightning bow in hand – something changed. Everything changed.

Skandar wanted to kill Bobby. He was going to do it now. And once the sword had run her through, she was going to bleed on to the sand, and he would be there. And he would taste it . . . He was so *hungry*. And blood was *energy*. Blood was *life*. Blood was all he wanted.

For a moment – only a moment – something cleared in Skandar's brain. He saw himself, almost from above. Scoundrel was rearing in the middle of the arena, his black hooves pouring out pure white light. Skandar's sabre had split into a hundred shining white daggers, and they soared in every direction. Bobby and Falcon had summoned a thick shield of glass, and Instructor Saylor was running towards them, trying to shelter behind it. But she wasn't fast enough. A spirit dagger flew towards Saylor's back, then another, then another.

And Skandar was so lost in rage – in his determination for death – that he wasn't sure if he would ever find himself again.

Bloodlust reigned in Skandar's heart, as Scoundrel's Luck galloped full tilt at Falcon's Wrath.

Skandar regained consciousness to the muffled sound of arguing.

'You can't just leave him tied up in there!' Flo.

'It was my fault. I convinced him to use the spirit element!' Jamie.

'He's in our quartet. He should be in our treehouse.' Mitchell.

'He's dangerous! It's for your own—' Dorian Manning.

'He was *possessed*. He didn't mean to go on a spirit frenzy. It's just what happens when a rider's possessed through the bond. It's been happening for months, but nobody would listen to us.' Mitchell again.

A spirit frenzy? Skandar tried to rub his eyes, but one of his wrists was cuffed. He pulled on it. A chain rattled against an unfamiliar treehouse's wall.

'The tournament shouldn't have even gone ahead.' He recognised Instructor O'Sullivan's voice outside the door. 'It was foolish of us not to take the possessions more seriously.'

'How's Instructor Saylor?' Flo asked tentatively.

'She's alive –' Instructor O'Sullivan sighed – 'but badly injured.'

Skandar froze. An image was coming back to him. An image of spirit daggers flying at Instructor Saylor. He'd wanted blood. He'd wanted to kill. And Bobby. He hadn't heard her voice outside. Oh no. Had he . . . ?

'Bobby!' he yelled. 'Is Bobby okay? Please just tell me – is she alive? Please.' Tears of distress ran down Skandar's cheeks. 'Please, somebody! Please, you have to tell me!' He pulled on his chains, rattling them loudly to try to get their attention.

'Calm down, spirit boy.'

Skandar's heart practically stopped. Something moved in the darkness and then—

'Bobby! I'm so— Are you okay?'

'Oh, stop, will you!' Bobby hissed. 'I've been in here for hours. If you keep shouting your mouth off like that, you're going to get me rumbled.'

'Why are you in here?' Skandar asked, distracted from his thousand other burning questions. 'I thought you wouldn't want to be anywhere near me!'

'Skandar –' Bobby's voice was much softer than usual – 'I

understand what it feels like to be possessed by the bond. I've been there, remember? I know you didn't mean to hurt Instructor Saylor. Man, though – that spirit magic was wild. I've never seen anything like it.'

'Is Saylor really badly hurt?' He bit his lip to try to stop his whole face from quivering.

'The healers say she'll recover, but yeah.' Bobby nodded. 'She's not in a good way.'

Skandar thought he was going to vomit. 'Scoundrel? Where's Scoundrel? Has Dorian—'

'He's fine,' Bobby said firmly. 'He's in the stables. Under guard. Dastardly Mango was ready to have you carted off to the prison straight from the arena. I don't think Amber helped your case either – I saw her talking to him down on the sand – but Instructor O'Sullivan managed to get you both back here.'

'Under guard?' Skandar croaked.

'Two sentinels,' Bobby whispered.

'WHERE IS SKANDAR? Take me to him NOW!' The voice was so loud that Bobby ducked.

Agatha crashed through the treehouse door, ignoring Dorian Manning's squawks and Instructor O'Sullivan's warnings. Her skeletal cheeks flashed as the door closed behind her, wild eyes eventually coming to rest on Skandar's face. She threw herself to her knees and enclosed him in a suffocating hug. Something about it felt so familiar to Skandar, so comforting, that he relaxed into it as though they'd done this a thousand times before.

'I'm so sorry,' Agatha breathed. 'It's all my fault. I told you to use the spirit element if you thought you were going to lose. You warned me, but I didn't listen.'

'Can I just point out,' Bobby said, 'that I was going to lose the match. I was going to *throw* myself off Falcon. That's what I was trying to tell you, Skandar.' Her half-smile disappeared. 'I can't believe you thought I'd rather win than keep you in the Eyrie.'

'I wasn't thinking straight,' Skandar said, feeling even worse. 'To be honest, I was always going to use the spirit element. It's *my* element. It's nobody's fault. And it isn't *my* fault that I got possessed either. Dorian is just using it as an excuse to come after me.'

'That's the spirit,' Agatha nodded at him, sounding a little more like herself. 'I mean, poor choice of words, but you get the point.'

After a lot of wrangling, Agatha managed to prise the key to Skandar's shackles out of Dorian Manning's clutches and free him. By the time Skandar emerged from the treehouse, the president had gone.

Mitchell, Jamie and Flo all ran at him and hugged him close.

Instructor O'Sullivan cleared her throat. 'Skandar, this is extremely serious. I need you to listen to me.'

Agatha put a protective hand on Skandar's shoulder.

'The incident at the tournament is being investigated by the Commodore of Chaos.'

'He shouldn't be treated differently from any other rider who has been possessed,' Agatha said forcefully.

'I agree,' Instructor O'Sullivan said, 'but an entire arena just watched the one and only spirit wielder in the Eyrie try to kill an instructor and attack a member of his own quartet. Let's not forget that the whole Island is currently obsessed with a truesong that contains a verse predicting the *true successor of spirit's dark friend*. We have to tread carefully.'

Skandar couldn't feel his toes. 'What does that mean?'

Instructor O'Sullivan took a deep breath, whirlpool eyes swirling. 'It means, Skandar, that until the Commodore's investigation is concluded, you are forbidden from riding Scoundrel. You are forbidden even from touching him. Do you understand?'

Agatha opened her mouth to argue, but Instructor O'Sullivan held up a hand. 'Agatha, please. You're both on extremely thin ice. We have to be seen to be taking every possible precaution. If Skandar has no physical contact with Scoundrel, then there's no chance of him using the spirit element – even if he's possessed again.'

'He's just a child, Persephone,' Agatha said, her voice raw. 'It's cruel.'

'It's this or he's declared a nomad immediately. Skandar, you're extremely lucky you're a Shekoni Saddles rider. Olu Shekoni fought hard against your immediate arrest – he has so much influence across the Island, I think that's what convinced President Manning to let us keep you and Scoundrel in the Eyrie for now. Though if you *are* declared a nomad, you would be without the Eyrie's protection, and I've no doubt that Manning would have you and Scoundrel imprisoned in the Stronghold for good.'

Agatha was silent.

'The tournament has been postponed until further notice. Once the Island is restored to full health then you'll have every chance of competing to get into Fledgling year again.'

'But what if the investigation says I was responsible?' Skandar asked desperately. 'What if they don't clear my name? What about Scoundrel?'

'We'll cross that cable bridge when we come to it,' Instructor O'Sullivan said.

But she didn't meet Skandar's eye.

CHAPTER SIXTEEN

A TALE OF TWO SISTERS

Nina Kazama refused to be the first Commodore in history to cancel the Chaos Cup. And so, the day before the summer solstice – despite the devastation in all four elemental zones and the looming destruction of the Island itself – the *Hatchery Herald* published a whole issue dedicated to the riders and unicorns who would be competing later that day. Skandar had already decided he wouldn't go.

'I don't understand how Nina can allow the race to go ahead,' Flo said.

Mitchell leaned closer to the newspaper. 'She's justifying it by saying the possessions only affect developing riders – like those training at the Eyrie. According to her researchers, the bond is still unstable for younger riders – which makes us more vulnerable to attack. To be fair, all the evidence does point that way.'

'Which is why we're not allowed to ride our unicorns to watch the Chaos Cup,' Bobby said moodily. 'It's going to take *ages* to walk to the arena.'

'I'm tempted not to go at all.' Flo cast a side glance at Skandar, who had smothered his sausages in mayonnaise but still hadn't eaten a bite. She elbowed Mitchell.

'What? Oh yes. Me too! The summer solstice is tomorrow! And we're no further forward with the First Rider's tomb.'

'You don't have to stay because of me.' Skandar sighed, finally looking up from his plate. 'And let's be honest, we've been through every book, talked through every possibility. A few hours watching the Chaos Cup is hardly going to make a difference now.'

'Jamie's coming with us,' Mitchell said tentatively. 'Why don't you come too?'

Skandar shook his head roughly. 'I'm not leaving Scoundrel.'

'But—' Flo tried.

'I need to be near him,' Skandar snapped. 'E-even if I can't touch him. Anyway, I still don't have a white jacket and I'm done with pretending to be a water wielder.'

So, as his friends decorated their faces with their favourite competitors' names, and put on jackets in their own elemental colours, Skandar headed to Scoundrel's stable alone.

It had been like this since the jousting tournament. He felt flat, completely empty of emotion. Nothing made him angry or upset: not the whispering behind his back, nor thoughts of Kenna and her wild unicorn. For the first time in his life he found it impossible to sketch anything. Nothing made him happy or excited; he had to actually remind himself to smile if someone told a joke or tried to be kind to him. The Chaos Cup would have put pressure on him to be enthusiastic, and he wasn't sure how long he could keep up the pretence or bear the fearful stares that followed him everywhere. It was better to be here, sitting outside Scoundrel's stable – better than all that effort.

Of course, Skandar wasn't alone with Scoundrel. He was never allowed to be alone with him any more. Two sentinels stood to attention at the black unicorn's stable door – silver masks flashing, swords shining in their scabbards. At first he'd accepted Instructor O'Sullivan's decision, but after a day or two he'd started dreaming about Scoundrel – about riding him, about stroking his soft neck or simply touching his warm nose. He'd come down late one night to beg the sentinels to let him past, just for a moment – just for *one* moment of contact. But they wouldn't let him through.

Skandar was so distraught the first night they hadn't let him pass that he'd shouted and cried himself hoarse back at the treehouse. The rest of his quartet had tried to comfort him, but they didn't understand. They *couldn't* understand. And all he'd succeeded in doing was scaring them. Since then he'd pushed all his emotions deep inside himself, like he used to when he was being tormented at school and he didn't want Dad to know or Kenna to worry. That way his friends wouldn't know how much he was suffering. Although Scoundrel's Luck always did – the occasional pulses of reassurance he sent through the bond were the only thing keeping Skandar sane. *I'm here. You're okay. We still have each other.*

So day after day, night after night, Skandar sat outside Scoundrel's stable. The sentinels were silent, but occasionally – and very surprisingly – Skandar had Silver Blade for company. The silver unicorn often chose to return to the stables during the day, away from the other playing unicorns and the sunshine, and stand by Scoundrel's stable. Skandar had never seen him like this. Blade looked between Skandar and Scoundrel with his dark stormy eyes as though trying to understand their distress, and made deep rumbling sounds of comfort.

But on the day of the Chaos Cup, Skandar's miserable vigil

was disturbed by someone else entirely.

'What in the name of all five elements are you doing?'

Skandar looked up into Agatha's concerned face and sighed. He hadn't seen his aunt since the night of the tournament and their hug.

'Get up!' Agatha hissed at him. Instead of waiting for him to do as she'd asked, she pulled him roughly to his feet. No hug this time, then.

'Ouch! What are you doing?' Skandar complained. 'I'm fine here. Just leave me alone.'

Agatha ignored him, steering him forcefully by his elbow.

Skandar managed to shake off her hand once they were out in the Eyrie's forest. 'I don't want to be away from Scoundrel! Surely you of all people can understand that?'

'It isn't healthy to sit in the dark all day,' Agatha snapped.

'What? So you suddenly decide you want to be my aunt now?'

Skandar wasn't sure why he'd said it, but he felt guilty enough that when Agatha motioned for him to follow her up the ladders to her treehouse, he obeyed.

Skandar was shocked to find that Agatha's treehouse was the same one Joby had lived in the previous year. Inside, though, the décor couldn't have been more different. There were no fluffy rugs, no colourful cushions, no squashy beanbags.

'Sit down,' Agatha ordered gruffly.

Skandar looked around. The ill-omened treehouse was almost empty apart from two ornate iron chairs by the wood-burning stove, a sheepskin rug and, for some odd reason, an iron rocking horse – no, rocking *unicorn* – by the only window. Skandar stared at the toy's sharp horn and settled on one of the chairs – made slightly more comfortable by a fluffy white blanket draped over its seat.

'Tea.' Agatha handed him a steaming mug without waiting to hear if he wanted it or not.

Skandar took a sip into the awkward silence. 'What is this?' he asked, momentarily distracted from his sombre mood. 'It actually tastes . . . good.' He'd never really liked tea; he and Kenna had a theory it was a joke played by adults, who just tipped away the disgusting brown water when children weren't looking. But this? This tea was delicious!

'It's from the fire zone,' Agatha explained. 'It's got a smoky flavour, sort of like fire magic, don't you think? Only tea I can stand.' Agatha tucked a greying strand of hair behind her ear. It reminded him so much of Kenna that his heart ached for his sister. It still hadn't sunk in that she hadn't come to the tournament. He'd even stopped checking his capsule in the post tree. He loved Dad, but he couldn't face being disappointed that the letters that came with the Jelly Babies were from him and not Kenna. On top of Scoundrel being locked up – and on top of the very real possibility that the entire Island would implode, scattering his quartet for ever – it was too much.

'How are you?' Agatha's question was stilted.

'How do you think?' Skandar shot back, then sighed. 'Look, I'm sorry, okay? I just . . . Not even being able to touch Scoundrel's Luck. It's—'

'I understand.' Agatha nodded, then took another sip of tea.

'How do you do it?' Skandar whispered. 'How can you bear to be away from Arctic Swansong all the time?'

'Honestly?' Agatha said. 'When the sentinels caught me on Fisherman's Beach – after I brought you last year – I was ready to die when they took him from me again. I almost welcomed it.

But then this scrawny, scrappy little spirit wielder came to visit me in prison.' She winked at him.

'There was such passion in your eyes, such a need to understand yourself and do the right thing. To fight the darkness. I thought – I thought there might be hope for spirit wielders. You were willing to do anything to save the Mainland. However idiotic.' She raised a wiry eyebrow. 'You didn't even really care about keeping yourself safe. Your determination – it reminded me so much of my sister.'

Skandar was shocked; Agatha had never been so nice to him. 'My mum?'

'Your mother. My sister. Commodore Everhart. The Weaver. She's had so many names, but once – to me – she was just Erika. My talented, beautiful older sister. I don't know how she was when you saw her, Skandar, but—'

'She wasn't exactly friendly,' Skandar said, trying to force down the memory.

'She wasn't always like that.' Agatha sighed sadly. 'And much of what she's become is my fault.'

Skandar didn't dare speak. He felt like he was back on the Mainland, listening to Dad talk about Rosemary Smith, desperate for scraps of information about the mum he'd never known. Skandar had thought that wanting might have gone away after he'd found out she was the Weaver. But even though it made him feel ashamed, if anything the desire for information had become stronger. He didn't know why Agatha had finally decided to talk to him about his mum today. Perhaps she was trying to distract him from Scoundrel's anguish vibrating in the bond? If so, it was working.

'Erika and I were very close growing up. Like you and Kenna, Erika is only a year older than me – that meant we were friends as well as siblings. But Erika was always very much the older sister, charged to take care of me. And that responsibility weighed heavily on her young shoulders. My parents used to tell the story of the night I was born. At three in the morning I'd finally quietened to sleep, but they couldn't find Erika anywhere. They searched and searched until they found her sitting by my crib, eyes wide open and a sharp stick in her hand. She wasn't even old enough to talk – she could only just walk – but instinctively she wanted to protect me.

'Then, when I was nine, something happened that had a deep and lasting impact on Erika. My parents were busy – they were always busy – so she was supposed to be looking after me at the beach. Some of Erika's friends were building sand unicorns nearby, and she told me to stay where I was so she could say hello. Annoyed at being left – I had a temper, even then – I decided to go rock climbing – something she'd forbidden me from doing. I still remember the anger pulsing through me as I reached for the next foothold, handhold, foothold, until I was impossibly high. And then I fell. I didn't wake up for three weeks.

'Erika tortured herself during that time. I always suspected that she'd made promises to some unseen power that if I woke up, she'd never leave my side again. Because that's how she acted once I got better. I couldn't move for Erika, every which way I turned. And I loved her for it. I loved that we were inseparable. Then the time came for her to try the Hatchery door.'

Skandar let out a breath of understanding.

'You see the problem?' Agatha nodded. 'Erika knew that if she became a rider, but I didn't open the door the following year, then we'd be separated our whole lives. She wanted us to train in the Eyrie together. She needed us to be on the same path, so she could keep it safe for me.'

Skandar couldn't help but think of what he and Kenna had always said growing up. How they'd planned to go to the Island, one year apart. Kenna first, then him. He understood that longing. That love.

'So we came up with a plan.' Agatha sighed. 'We searched my father's personal library – he was a spirit wielder too – for anything that might help me get a unicorn if I couldn't open the door. After hours and hours, we eventually found an ancient tale about a spirit wielder who had been able to *forge* a bond between a person and an unhatched unicorn. A person that unicorn *wasn't* destined for. We got carried away with the idea of it. We assumed we'd be allied to spirit, like so many members of our family. We ignored all the dire warnings about the risks of such a bond – the horror of joining two souls never meant for each other. It was too close to the summer solstice to really think about the rights and wrongs.

'So, at sunrise on the summer solstice, Erika Everhart opened the door, and hatched Blood-Moon's Equinox. But she left her newborn unicorn – just for a moment – and returned to the inner chamber. The eggs for the next year's hatching had already been moved into place, and she took one. The rest of that day is a blur. I waited anxiously at the back of the Hatchery until the walls rose up to let the new riders out. I ran up and down, trying to find her hatching cell. And there she was with Blood-Moon, beaming. And in the cell behind her – as we'd planned – was the egg. My back-up plan.

'I took the egg – the elemental blasts of the newly hatched unicorns exploding all around me, masking the crime. I ran and I hid the egg until later that night. Then Erika took it back from me to hide in the Wilderness until the following year.' Agatha must have seen the horrified look on Skandar's face, and she rushed on. 'You see, it was always the plan that we'd get the egg back to the Hatchery if I opened the door. Erika *promised* me she'd return it – she swore she'd find a way – as soon as she saw me go through the Hatchery door the next year.'

'And you did open the door. You hatched Arctic Swansong, didn't you?' Skandar pushed, impatient for the rest of the story.

'I did. But unfortunately Erika didn't keep her promise.'

'She didn't return the egg to the Hatchery?' Skandar breathed.

'No. She told me she did. For years she insisted that she'd taken the egg back. But she lied to me – her first lie.'

Skandar's heart was hammering. 'What did she do with the egg?'

'She did what Erika Everhart always does. The most impossible thing. She forged herself a bond. Something you have to understand about your mother, Skandar, is that she is brilliant – a genius – and she was even then at fourteen. All her Hatchling year she'd read about how to create a forged bond in preparation for joining me to the unhatched unicorn. She'd read about the power it would bring. In our first training session I told you how spirit wielders must strive to resist the pull of the darkness. She never could. Erika won her Training Trial at the end of her Hatchling year, but that wasn't enough. By the time I arrived at the Eyrie she had two bonds: one true bond to Blood-Moon's Equinox and a forged bond to that poor wild unicorn.'

'But you must have noticed a wild unicorn hanging around her!'

'She sent the wild unicorn away. It lived alone in the Wilderness. I know I should have realised something was wrong. As her sister, I should have . . . There were signs. The forged bond is full of darkness. It doesn't work like a normal bond – there's no reciprocity, no change in a unicorn's nature. They stay wild, full of vengeance. Erika became impossibly powerful without explanation. But though she became more volatile, many of the other risks of a forged bond never materialised. I believe it is because the true and forged bonds balanced each other out. She was on track to become Commodore for the third time in a row.'

'And then Blood-Moon's Equinox died,' Skandar said, realisation hitting him hard.

'And then Blood-Moon's Equinox died,' Agatha repeated darkly. 'The wild unicorn took hold of my sister completely. Those years of abandonment had made the creature furious.'

'The Fallen Twenty-Four,' Skandar realised.

'It isn't an excuse,' Agatha said sharply. 'You must not excuse her actions. Because of her, because of me, there was a rider who opened a door during my hatching ceremony and never found their unicorn waiting inside. Because of both of us, twenty-four unicorns died – and countless others since. Her actions cannot be excused, but they can be understood – somewhat. And she did try to run from the forged bond when—'

'When she came to the Mainland,' Skandar finished for her. 'And met Dad.'

'Exactly. For a while I thought it had worked. I justified becoming the Executioner so I could stay alive, support Erika's new life – her attempt to change. I was worried what would happen if the Silver Circle killed me and she found out – how vengeful she might become. I believed I needed to stay alive to protect her – but also to protect everyone else from her; do you understand?' Agatha's voice was suddenly desperate.

Skandar wasn't sure he *could* entirely understand. Agatha

and Erika's relationship was even more complicated than he'd imagined. Two sisters bound together by love and secrets. He couldn't help thinking of the Secret Swappers – did they know any of this? He shivered.

'I thought distance from the wild unicorn could loosen the hold of the forged bond. I really believed that, but when it came down to it . . . Erika couldn't resist.'

'She still has the forged bond,' Skandar said, putting it all together. The bond he'd seen between the Weaver and the wild unicorn had been different – it hadn't been able to settle on a particular colour, like it was spinning out of control. 'I saw it last year, in the Wilderness.'

'That wild unicorn will outlive her. That's what a forged bond does. It takes away your humanity little by little. Until there's nothing left. Humans cannot die for ever the way wild unicorns do.' Agatha's voice was hollow. Instinctively Skandar reached out and held his aunt's hand. They sat like that for a while, the realisation of what was awaiting Erika Everhart – her sister, his mother – hanging between them like unspoken heartbreak.

Skandar withdrew his hand first. 'Why are you telling me this now?'

'I didn't like you sitting in the dark like that. It reminded me of Erika when she lost Blood-Moon. That hopeless look in her eyes. I need you to fight the pull of the dark, Skandar. I need you to fight harder than she did, do you understand?'

'What if they never let me near Scoundrel again?' Skandar voiced the fear that had haunted him every second since the jousting tournament.

'You still have to fight on.'

'How?'

'You'll find a way.'

'I'm a Mender,' Skandar blurted. He didn't feel like he could hide it from her when she'd been so honest with him.

'How do you know?' Agatha asked, her voice dangerous.

'I – I had a dream. About my sister and her wild unicorn.'

'I told you it was too dangerous—'

'Argh!' Skandar stood up, his brain ready to explode with all the new information about his mother and this new kind of dangerous bond. He kicked the iron chair leg. 'None of it matters if we don't find the First Rider's gift before the summer solstice, before the magic gets completely out of control! Who cares if I'm a Mender if the Island isn't going to exist any more?' All his fears were spilling out. 'They're going to separate riders by element. Am I supposed to go with the water wielders? Or will it be a family reunion? Me, you, the Weaver and her furious wild unicorn?'

'Don't be ridiculous—'

Skandar was pacing now. 'If only I could find the bone staff, that would fix everything. The Island would be saved; the Commodore would let Scoundrel go. It would prove I had nothing to do with the wild unicorn deaths, the possessions, the Island's revenge. It would mean we could all stay together.' The faces of his quartet flashed in his mind. Bobby. Flo. Mitchell. And Kenna. Kenna would have an island to come to.

Agatha shifted in her chair to look at him. 'A bone staff?'

'Yes,' Skandar said impatiently. 'The First Rider killed the Wild Unicorn Queen and carved a staff from her bones. And it's in his tomb, so we need—'

Agatha looked confused. 'That's not how the spirit wielders told it.'

Skandar stopped pacing. 'What do you mean?'

'When my father told the story of the First Rider and the Wild Unicorn Queen, they were never enemies. They were allies. The way the spirit wielders told it, the First Rider and the queen of the wild unicorns founded the Eyrie together.'

'But how can they be allies if he made a weapon from her bones?'

Agatha shrugged. 'I don't know. I've never even heard of any bone staff. That's just the story I heard. Maybe it's only a tale for children of spirit wielders.'

'Or maybe not.' Skandar had his hand on the door. 'Agatha—'

'Instructor Everhart.'

'*Really?* After all this? You're still insisting on me calling you that?'

'Fine. You may call me *Aunt* Everhart in private,' she said begrudgingly. 'Where exactly are you going? Not back to Scoundrel's stable again?'

'The Chaos Cup. I need to tell my friends about this. If the First Rider and Wild Unicorn Queen were allies, then that gives us another clue about the tomb. It means they might be buried *together*.'

Skandar's lungs were on fire as he hurtled through Fourpoint. He sped past locked saddlers' workshops, deserted treehouses and abandoned smiths' forges. When Skandar made his way through a tunnel and into the stands, an enormous roar of sound met his ears. Thousands of Islanders were on their feet, waving flags and cheering at the big screens set out in the arena. There were sentinels everywhere – and Skandar wasn't surprised. Nina Kazama might have wanted to go ahead with the Chaos Cup, but she knew it was a risk.

Skandar looked away from the silver masks and scanned the

crowd for his quartet and Jamie. He knew they had tickets for the East Stand, and he pushed past riders clad in elemental colours and food sellers with boxes of tacos and popcorn to reach them.

'Skar!' Flo cried. Her smile was so wide, he felt himself grinning back without trying.

Mitchell squeezed Skandar's shoulder in welcome; Jamie slapped him on the back. Bobby gave him a distracted wave, not taking her eyes from the screen.

The race was in its final stages. There was no way his friends would listen to his theory about the Wild Unicorn Queen until it was over.

The noise of the crowd crescendoed as the Chaos unicorns came into view. All the spectators turned their faces to the sky as the most powerful unicorns in the world soared above their heads. The commentary was blaring from huge loudspeakers, the words echoing around the arena. 'I'm getting reports that this year's Wildcard – Leo Crawford – has just had to land and is *out*. So it's Nina Kazama on Lightning's Mistake, followed by Alodie Birch on River-Reed Prince out in front.'

'She's in the lead, she's in the lead!' Flo jumped up and down, supporting the Shekoni Saddles rider.

'But here comes Ema Templeton, gaining on the two leaders. Look at Mountain's Fear coming up on the inside!' the commentator shouted.

Skandar felt his throat tighten as he watched Mountain's Fear catch up with Lightning's Mistake and engage her in battle. Kenna and Dad would surely be watching the Chaos Cup together back in Margate. He wondered if Mountain's Fear was still Kenna's favourite.

'Look at that huge wave!' Bobby shouted, hitting Skandar

on the shoulder and pointing at the sky. Nina and Lightning combined the air and water elements – spinning the wave into a whirlpool – knocking Alodie and River-Reed Prince off course before they were able to defend themselves.

'I can't believe she's kept up her speed,' the commentator was saying. 'She's only a few wingbeats behind Mountain's Fear.' Skandar *could* believe it, though; Nina Kazama had been a member of the Peregrine Society too. And even though she was heading the investigation against him, he couldn't help cheering her on. She'd protected him and Scoundrel from the Silver Circle so far, hadn't she?

The commentator's voice broke through his thoughts. 'Ema's not giving in without a fight. Losing time in that sky battle might have cost Nina the Chaos Cup.'

'Oh, shut up!' Flo screeched, stamping her feet. 'Come on, Nina! Win it again!'

The camera zoomed in as Nina leaned right down against Lightning's neck, urging her on. Watching her gain back the distance, Skandar chanted along with the crowd. Nina was a Mainlander just like him: she'd been to an ordinary school and grown up in a Mainland home. Then she'd been called to this strange island, to race the most powerful creatures on earth. Could she really win the Chaos Cup for the second time? Skandar's mum was the only rider who had ever done that. And now Skandar knew her journey to Commodore had drawn on the magic of two unicorns instead of one.

'Ohhh!' a cry went up from the commentator. 'Exquisite fire magic, but Federico Jones's flaming lances haven't slowed them.' The commentator was almost shouting now.

Sure enough, as they dived towards the arena's sand, Nina

and Ema were not at all fazed by the fire weapons that had narrowly missed their unicorns' flanks.

'That's slowed Federico Jones, though. He's falling back. This is a two-rider race now. Lightning's Mistake looks like she's got a lot of energy left. Neither of these air wielders are trying any magic – it's all about speed; it's all about getting across that finishing line first.'

'Nina's going to do it!' Bobby shouted.

'And they're coming in to land now. One thing's for sure, it's going to be another win for the air element, but who will it be? They must land and pass under the arch to finish. They *will* be disqualified if they don't touch down in time.'

There was a dramatic pause in the commentary. Skandar didn't dare breathe.

'And they're both down.' The commentator's voice was breathless with excitement. 'They're neck and neck!'

Even from this height in the stands, Skandar could see KAZAMA painted in yellow across Nina's armoured back, TEMPLETON in the same colour across Ema's, as they raced towards the finish.

'Are we going to see this Mainlander make history again? Could it be a second Chaos Cup win for Commodore Kazama?'

The two unicorns – Mountain's Fear, grey with a bone-white mane and tail, and Lightning's Mistake, ochre brown – raced towards the finish. Nina raised her palm, so quickly Skandar almost missed it, and threw a single lightning dagger sideways at Mountain's Fear. Ema's unicorn was distracted – just for a moment, but it was enough.

'What an assured display of her allied element; a weapon moulded at such speed! It's going to be the decider! Nina Kazama is going to do it again. She's going to get there first!'

An almighty cheer went up from the crowd. Skandar was shouting at the top of his voice along with everyone else in the stands. He craned his neck to read the confirmed result on the screen. He wanted to get lost in it for a moment. What if this was the last ever Chaos Cup? What if the riders and unicorns had to leave the Island and scatter for ever? He wanted to enjoy it – just in case. Just in case they couldn't save their home.

'And it's Nina Kazama and Lightning's Mistake! Nina Kazama is the winner of the Chaos Cup for the second time. Commodore of Chaos, Nina Kazama – air wielder and Mainlander – wins the Cup for the second year in a row.' Nina disappeared through a gap in the arena wall to the Chaos Compound – Ema right on her tail, the other competitors trailing behind.

'I can't believe it! I can't believe it!' Flo was saying over and over again.

'Yes!' Bobby punched the air. 'An air wielder wins again! Although –' Bobby's face fell, as yellow fireworks exploded above their heads and the Peregrine Society started their flying display – 'now I'm going to have to win the Chaos Cup *three* times. Such a lot of effort!'

As the commentators repeated the result, Skandar became aware of Mitchell turning his shoulder protectively. Mitchell's body language made the rest of his quartet look away from the images of Nina throwing her arms round Lightning playing over and over on the arena's screen.

Something was wrong with Jamie.

The blacksmith's mismatched eyes were glowing like hot coals, there was billowing white steam coming from his ears, and his wavy hair was blowing in a breeze nobody else could feel.

Then he started to sing.

CHAPTER SEVENTEEN

A NEW SONG

'Is it the Island magic? Is he being possessed?' Skandar shouted over the crowd. Jamie seemed to be in a kind of trance.

'No!' Mitchell said, placing Jamie's limp arm round his shoulder and starting to move him along the row. 'It must be his truesong. We have to get him to a place where we can hear it. NOW!'

'But Jamie's not a bard. How—'

'He's a bard by birth,' Mitchell grunted. 'I suppose that's enough.'

Other spectators shifted and grumbled; a few even pointed at Skandar – 'Hey, isn't that the spirit wielder?' – as they manoeuvred themselves out of the stands.

'. . . *where ancient mirrors lament sinking ships,*' Jamie sang, as they exited the arena.

'The Shekoni Saddles tent!' Flo pointed to a small orange marquee not too far away as the quartet spilled out of the arena.

'How long is it going to last?' Bobby asked, as Flo unzipped the flap of the Shekoni Saddles' temporary workshop for the Cup.

'It depends,' Mitchell said, unhooking Jamie's arm from round his neck and helping the blacksmith sit on the floor. 'He might sing the whole thing on repeat for the next hour, or he might never sing it again.' Mitchell grabbed a notebook out of his jacket and started scribbling.

Skandar stared at the blacksmith – the blacksmith who'd never wanted to be a bard – as he fizzed with elemental magic and continued his song:

> 'Where spirit's swansong was snuffed to silence,
>   All five must follow his first and last steps,
> The last must fight on but mean no violence,
>   And pay the Queen their last respects.'

Jamie was silent, then keeled over sideways.

'Is it me? Or did that make even less sense than the last truesong we heard?' Bobby asked, the feathers on her wrists all standing up.

'Hang on, hang on,' Mitchell was still scribbling. Skandar bent down to try to rouse Jamie, but he was fast asleep.

'If that was the end, I think we missed a lot of his truesong,' Flo said sadly.

'At least we heard some of it,' Mitchell countered. 'And I think it might be useful.'

'Useful for *what*?' Bobby protested.

'Mitchell's right,' Skandar said quickly. 'The song mentioned the Queen, which must mean the queen of the wild unicorns. That's the whole reason I came to find you. Agatha told me that –

according to old spirit wielder stories – the First Rider and the Wild Unicorn Queen might have been allies, not enemies.'

'Personally I'm not sure I'd carve a weapon out of my friend's bones,' Bobby scoffed. 'Maybe yours, Mitch, if you were being particularly annoying.'

'Bobby!' Flo gasped.

'But if they were allies,' Skandar insisted, 'they might be buried together. Don't you think?'

'The First Rider can't have been allied to a wild unicorn!' Mitchell spluttered. 'That's ridiculous—'

Skandar raised his eyebrows. 'Do you know anything about the First Rider's unicorn? Do you even know its name?'

Jamie groaned, and Mitchell bent down to look into his face, avoiding the question.

'What happened?' the blacksmith croaked.

'You sang your truesong,' Mitchell explained gently.

Bobby sank into a deep bow. 'All hail the blacksmith bard.'

'You're kidding?' Jamie closed his eyes, as if in considerable pain. 'My parents are never going to shut up about this!'

Skandar's quartet waved goodbye to Jamie at his forge. Mitchell insisted on watching until the exhausted blacksmith was up the ladder and safely inside before they began the long walk back.

'All I'm saying,' Skandar puffed as they finally reached the top of the Eyrie's hill, 'is that if the First Rider is buried with a unicorn then—'

'There would be a tree . . .' Flo trailed off in thought.

'*Where a unicorn rests, a tree grows,*' Skandar said, smiling at her. 'You told me that in the graveyard last year.'

'But what about a *wild* unicorn? Is it the same?' Bobby asked.

Mitchell crossed his arms. 'If it is, it's not like we would miss a wild unicorn tree. They're allied to all five elements. Imagine the leaves, they'd look—'

'Like that?' Bobby had a hand on one hip and was pointing up at the Eyrie's entrance tree.

Skandar, Bobby and Flo stared up at the leaves in amazement. Skandar had always loved the entrance tree's chorus of colours, but he hadn't really *seen* it until now. The leaves so obviously matched those he'd seen last year at the graveyard – the yellow leaves even crackled to an unseen breeze.

Mitchell looked delighted. 'The entrance to the tomb must be here!'

'Oh yeah!' Bobby punched the air. 'Isn't it annoying how I always save the day?' She winked at Skandar, but he was looking up at the gathering dark.

'We need to be quick. It's getting late and the summer solstice is tomorrow, and I don't exactly trust the Island not to self-destruct early.'

'Skandar, shut up for a minute!' Bobby scolded him as she placed her hand on the trunk and opened its door in a sizzle of electricity. 'We're talking about finding an ancient tomb here. Even *I* need to concentrate.'

The quartet searched on both sides of the trunk, passing through its entrance over and over in flashes and swirls of their various elements. But as the sun started to sink, and more riders returned from the Chaos Cup, singing and laughing as they walked through the trunk, it soon became clear that the entrance to the First Rider's tomb was somewhere else – even if he and the Wild Unicorn Queen *were* buried together under the tree.

'I say we take a break, and have another look at Jamie's

truesong,' Mitchell said, getting to his feet after fruitlessly pulling on a tree root.

Skandar was about to say that they should keep trying, perhaps even climb the tree, when he heard screaming.

'I'm not imagining that, am I?' Bobby asked, as they hurried further into the Eyrie.

Skandar looked up and saw riders sprinting along the swinging bridges.

Kobi came careering through the trees towards Skandar's quartet, his dark brown face stricken. When he saw them standing there together, he yelled, 'Are you ordinary?'

Skandar thought this was a very odd thing to shout – though, to be fair, none of his quartet could exactly be described as ordinary.

'Are you possessed?' Kobi shouted again.

'Oh,' Skandar said, slowly catching up, 'no, we're – we're fine. What's going on? Did someone attack you?'

The noise Kobi made in response was halfway between a laugh and a sob. 'Did *someone* attack me? Try half the Eyrie!'

'Half the Eyrie is possessed?' Flo asked, horrified. There was a long, chilling scream from above. Instinctively the quartet huddled closer together.

Kobi nodded, his frosted eyelashes fluttering wildly. It was strange seeing the water wielder like this – vulnerable, frightened. Usually he was the one picking on others with Meiyi and Alastair. 'Some of the possessed riders have their unicorns. They're the most dangerous.' Kobi started to climb a nearby ladder. 'Get inside! It's not safe out here!'

'What about our own unicorns?' Skandar asked, thinking about Scoundrel being guarded by the sentinels. He felt the unicorn's absence with a jolt, the bond searing with sadness. Perhaps he could get Scoundrel now, with everyone distracted, perhaps—

'The instructors are guarding the stables. There's nothing you can do. GET INSIDE!'

Once he'd disappeared, there was an almighty blast of fire overhead, and Skandar saw Instructor Anderson and Desert Firebird facing down Sarika and Equator's Conundrum. It was clear, even from below, that Anderson was trying to force Conundrum to the ground rather than actually knock the black unicorn out of the sky, but Sarika was firing attack after attack from her palm at Firebird – her fingernails flaring, seemingly intent on reducing her instructor to cinders. Burning leaves and blackened twigs rained down on the quartet.

'Come on!' Skandar shouted, pointing in the direction of their treehouse.

The quartet rushed up the ladders, and along the familiar bridges – dodging other riders fleeing their possessed friends, elemental magic exploding through the armoured trees. Faces blurred past Skandar as he ran; there was no time to check if their eyes were clear or . . . something else.

Finally, they were safely inside. And once they'd heaved the bookcase up against the treehouse door, the quartet collapsed on to colourful beanbags. All except for Bobby – who was, of course, starting to make herself an emergency sandwich. Skandar found the sharp Marmite smell mixed with the sweetness of the jam strangely comforting. He really must be losing it.

Mitchell dragged his blackboard into view.

'*Now*, Mitchell? Really?' Flo said.

'We can't exactly go outside to enjoy the balmy summer evening,' he snapped.

'I always knew I'd find myself in a zombie apocalypse one day,' Bobby said thoughtfully.

'What's a zombie?' Flo asked, distracted.

Bobby started to explain through a mouthful of sandwich, but Mitchell cut her off. 'Enough, Roberta! Don't you see? The magic is completely unbalanced now. Half the Eyrie's possessed. It won't be long before Nina starts trying to evacuate us.'

'Can you write up the bits of Jamie's truesong we heard?' Skandar asked, pointing at the blackboard. 'If we assume the tomb is underneath the Eyrie's tree, then all we need is the entrance, right?'

Mitchell read out the words as the chalk scraped on the board. First, the fragment they'd heard on their way to the workshop:

'. . . *where ancient mirrors lament sinking ships.*'

And then the end of the song:

'*Where spirit's swansong was snuffed to silence,*
All five must follow his first and last steps,
The last must fight on but mean no violence,
And pay the Queen their last respects.'

Bobby groaned. 'Have I mentioned before how much I *hate* riddles?!'

Flo ignored her. 'A swansong is a final act before death.'

'How can a swansong be snuffed to silence, though?' Mitchell mused.

They went around and around. Earthquakes rumbled beneath the Eyrie. Impossibly high winds tore through its trees, battering the sides of the treehouse like furious fists. Scoundrel's emotions were totally muddled – one minute the bond was filled with fear, then excitement, then fear again. Skandar watched midnight come and go, bringing with it the solstice. He tried not to think about the five sharp knocks on Mainlander doors, the small crowd of rider hopefuls waiting on the chalk unicorn at Uffington before climbing into helicopters to take them to the Hatchery. Would there still *be* a Hatchery door to try at sunrise?

Some time before morning, the quartet fell asleep right on their beanbags.

Knock. Knock. Knock.

Skandar jerked awake. The others slept soundly. Scared it might be a possessed rider, Skandar climbed the tree trunk to peer down at the platform through the round window.

It was Rickesh. He didn't look possessed – just very, very worried.

Trying not to wake the rest of his quartet, Skandar shifted the bookcase just enough to squeeze out of the treehouse door.

'Rickesh?' Skandar blinked in the bright mid-morning light. 'Are you okay?' There were cuts up the squadron leader's arms.

'The Grins are leaving, Skandar. Are you coming with us?' His voice was flatter than usual, more serious.

Skandar frowned. 'What do you mean "leaving"? Where are you going?'

Rickesh put a hand on Skandar's shoulder. 'Do you know what peregrine means?'

'It's a type of fast bird, you told us—'

But Rickesh was already shaking his head. 'No, no. The name. *Peregrine* means wanderer. Listen, this Island isn't going to be inhabitable after sunset. I'm not exactly keen on our society being separated by element, being forced to go somewhere our unicorns might not even be able to fly freely.'

'I can't leave—' Skandar started, but the squadron leader interrupted.

'Don't worry. The Grins have Scoundrel's Luck. Amber Fairfax grabbed him when his guards were distracted by the mass possession last night.'

All the breath left Skandar's lungs. 'Where? Where is he? *Amber* got him?'

'Sunset Platform.'

Rickesh turned to go, and Skandar didn't think twice about following him.

The climb to the top of the Eyrie had never taken so long. Lots of ladders had broken rungs, and whole platforms had collapsed in the chaos the night before. Even the prospect of being reunited with Scoundrel couldn't distract Skandar from the view out over the Island. Parts of Fourpoint had completely disappeared; many of its colourful treehouses had been reduced to piles of wood and rubble. The stands of the arena had partially collapsed and the great arch of the finish had toppled. Skandar's heart ached with sadness for the place he loved most in the world.

The Sunset Platform was a hive of activity. Prim was giving orders; Patrick was loading up his unicorn with saddlebags full of supplies; Fen was turning Hoarfrost in a circle, trying to calm him. Marcus was having an intense conversation with Adela.

Then Skandar spotted Amber and Whirlwind Thief in the furthest corner. A black unicorn stood patiently beside them.

Scoundrel's Luck.

The bond exploded with a happiness so pure it made Skandar want to jump in the air. Scoundrel shrieked with joy – wings glowing white, galloping towards his rider across the metal platform – and then Skandar was running and running and throwing his arms round Scoundrel's ebony neck. The smell of his unicorn was of home; of friendship; of twin souls. Their emotions were completely in sync as whole waves of relief and excitement and love rolled through the bond, almost knocking Skandar over with their intensity.

'Hello, my boy.' Skandar didn't even try to stop his sobs. 'Hello, my beautiful boy.' Skandar wound his hands into the unicorn's black mane and rested his forehead against his soft black coat. Scoundrel turned his head and nuzzled Skandar's neck, blowing on it with his hot breath. They could have stayed like that for ever.

After a while, Amber edged tentatively across the platform towards them. Skandar tried to rub the tears from his eyes, though he suspected his whole face was red.

'Thank you.' He could hardly get the words out, his voice choked up from crying. 'Really.'

'It's nothing.' Amber shrugged, the electric star on her forehead crackling.

'Umm, I'm not saying I'm ungrateful,' Skandar said, slowly getting hold of his emotions, 'but why did you? All year you've been telling people I'm responsible for the possessions. Bobby even said you talked to President Manning down in the arena, after I—'

'Bobby Bruna should keep out of other people's business.' Amber rubbed her upturned nose, sounding a little more like herself. 'I was trying to tell the president that it *wasn't* your fault, actually. That you'd been possessed. He didn't listen to me though, obviously, since my dad's a spirit wielder.'

'Sounds familiar,' Skandar muttered.

'But we're even now. You saved my life at that Peregrine Society meeting and stuck up for me against my quartet. And I reunited you with Scoundrel, and Scoundrel with you – so that counts for two. Now we can go back to loathing each other. I'm *super* looking forward to it.'

Skandar laughed, and Amber flicked her chestnut hair and went back to Thief.

Rickesh and Prim came to check on him. A ghost of a smile passed over Prim's lips as she saw the rider and unicorn reunited, but then she was all business. 'You're coming with us, then? We're planning on leaving before sunset, just ahead of Nina's evacuation, so—'

Skandar was already shaking his head. 'I can't tell you how grateful I am that you've kept Scoundrel safe up here, but I'm not coming with you. This Island is my home.'

Rickesh sighed. 'It's home for all of us, Skandar, but it's not going to last much longer. We'll make a new home, and perhaps we won't even have elemental allegiances. The First Rider didn't, when he washed up here.'

Skandar stared at Rickesh. The story the Rookie had told him all those months ago came flooding back.

'The First Rider was a fisherman – not much older than a Hatchling – when he washed up at the foot of the Mirror Cliffs.'

Prim and Rickesh noticed the look on Skandar's face. 'What?'

Skandar scrambled up on to Scoundrel's back. It had felt so incredible to be able to hold Scoundrel close, but this? Riding again felt perfect. Just for a moment everything was right with the world: the destruction of the Island was muted, the Grins were blurred out and it was only them – Skandar and Scoundrel – united at last in a bubble of blissful happiness.

Then reality came crashing back down. Skandar backed Scoundrel up, ready for take-off.

'Where are you going?' Prim demanded.

Scoundrel extended his great black wings as Skandar replied. 'I'm not giving up on the Island just yet. And neither should you. Don't leave until sunset, okay?'

'Why?' Rickesh called after him.

'Promise me!' Skandar shouted, and Scoundrel's Luck took off from the Eyrie's highest platform. The pair plummeted through the air until they could swerve and land by his treehouse.

Skandar didn't even bother to dismount. 'Bobby! Mitchell! Flo! Get out here!'

Bobby emerged first, and the look on her face when she saw Skandar astride Scoundrel was comical. 'How did you get him back?' she asked suspiciously. 'Wasn't one unicorn thief enough for your family?'

'Very funny,' Skandar said. 'It doesn't matter. Listen, I think I've worked it out.'

'Worked what out?' Flo yawned, pushing the door of the treehouse open. Then she saw Scoundrel on the platform and squealed with excitement.

Mitchell was still putting his glasses on as he walked out.

'I think I know where the entrance to the tomb is!'

'How? What? Where? . . . Is that Scoundrel?' Mitchell blinked.

'The Fisherman's Beach! That's where the First Rider washed up. He was a fisherman, remember? *Ancient mirrors lament sinking ships*? Agatha told me when she brought me to the Island that sailors found it almost impossible to land safely on that beach –

beneath the Mirror Cliffs! See? And *'his first and last steps'* – his first steps would have been on that beach and perhaps—'

'His last ones were too – on his way to the tomb?' Bobby was practically bouncing up and down, keen for action.

'What about *spirit's swansong* being silenced?' Flo asked.

Skandar took a deep breath. 'Okay, so this is going to sound a bit self-centred, but I think that part of the truesong might be about me.'

Bobby sighed dramatically but gestured for Skandar to carry on.

'I think it's talking about how Arctic Swansong flew me to the Island. But also I kind of stopped the death of the spirit element on the Island, didn't I? *Snuffed to silence*. By coming here, by making that deal with Aspen McGrath last year?'

'And Agatha and Swansong dropped you off at Fisherman's Beach?' Mitchell asked, trying to catch up for once.

'Yes! Below the Hatchery! We have to go. Now!'

The Eyrie was in chaos as the instructors rushed about, preparing for the impending evacuation amidst the damage from the previous night's possessions. Within minutes the quartet were armoured up and Scoundrel, Falcon, Blade and Red were soaring away from the Eyrie's hill, heading straight for the Mirror Cliffs in the distance.

As the four unicorns fell into their usual flying formation, Blade suddenly began to screech and roar. The sound was so loud it made Skandar's ears ring.

'What's wrong with him?' Mitchell asked Flo in alarm, his helmet askew.

But despite everything, Flo was laughing. 'He's happy! He was so worried when Scoundrel and Skandar were kept apart, but now he's so happy that we're all together again! I think he finally understands that he's a part of this quartet too. That it wouldn't be the same without him. That he belongs!'

Bobby couldn't help grinning either. 'Trust Blade,' she called over the sound of their unicorns' wingbeats. 'Trust Silver Blade to finally start enjoying himself while the world is ending.'

And those words brought them all back to the moment. The disaster that was unfurling beneath them. It was true. It did look like the world was ending. The magical devastation that Skandar could see over Scoundrel's wings was terrifying: at least a quarter of Fourpoint was on fire, and the air was filled with the constant rumble of landslides and earthquakes. Skandar didn't blame Commodore Kazama for trying to keep her people safe.

As the four unicorns flew over the Hatchery, Skandar saw the chunk missing from the clifftop where two of the Mirror Cliffs had collapsed. Then before he knew it, they'd reached the edge of the Island, and the quartet swooped down towards Fisherman's Beach.

Scoundrel landed a little way from Red, Blade and Falcon, and Skandar allowed himself ten seconds to panic. The sun was already high in the sky. How many hours of the solstice did they have left before sunset? They were really far from the Eyrie's tree; was this really where the tomb's entrance was? How long would it take them to find the tomb, let alone the bone staff? And what if they couldn't *win the fight* for it like the bard's truesong had said?

'You genius! You absolute genius!'

Skandar was brought back from his panicking by Bobby's voice. Surely she wasn't talking to . . . She couldn't be talking to *Mitchell* in such a complimentary way?

'I have my moments,' Mitchell said, struggling to keep the grin off his face. 'Although it was obvious as soon as I landed. This part of the Mirror Cliff doesn't reflect me properly: I'm too wide and bendy, and Red looks like she's shrunk. The reflective panel must have been bent out of shape when the other cliffs fell.'

'You're sure this is it?' Flo asked as Skandar rushed over to see what all the fuss was about.

'If we smash through that part of the mirror, I bet you there isn't just cliff behind it. Trust me on this, it looks different from the rest.'

Immediately Flo's Hatchery wound glowed green, and she crafted a javelin out of the earth magic – its point a sharp flint. Before anyone could even react, she threw it right at the Mirror Cliff.

The glass exploded, sharp shards flying and coming to land on the pebbled beach, reflecting the blue sky above in fragments.

'Floundering floods, Flo! Some warning would have been nice!' Mitchell cried, brushing pieces of glass out of Red's mane. 'What has got into you?'

Bobby was staring at Flo, a look of respectful awe on her face.

Flo shrugged. 'I'm an earth wielder – sometimes I'm sensible, sometimes I like to throw rocks at things.'

Skandar drew his gaze back to the cliff. Instead of his and Scoundrel's reflection, now all he could see was a gloomy tunnel, just wide enough for a unicorn to pass through.

They had found the path to the First Rider's tomb.

THE SUMMER SOLSTICE

The morning of the summer solstice arrived at long last, and – of all the people in the world she could have thought about – Kenna thought about Dad. She thought about what he might be doing today. She thought about him making his way down Margate High Street to buy a paper. She thought about him putting too much sugar in his coffee and stirring it in as he read the latest article breaking down the results of the Chaos Cup. She thought about how he'd insisted on rowing her out to meet the unicorns on the sea. How proud he'd been of her. Kenna swallowed. Would Dad still be proud of her after sunset?

Since finding Erika Everhart in the Wilderness, Kenna had asked her mum many times whether she could write to Dad and tell him the good news, that his beloved 'Rosemary' was still alive. But Erika had told Kenna to wait. It wasn't time yet.

One thing was for sure, though – Kenna knew Dad would never have approved of her riding on the back of her mum's wild unicorn. Robert Smith had always drilled the distinction into his children. Bonded and wild. Bonded you could control. The wild ones would eat you. Bonded you could race. The wild ones would kill you.

But as Erika Everhart's wild unicorn streaked across the Wilderness, Kenna's hands safely fixed round her mum's waist, she forgot all about her dad's fears. The solstice had arrived. They were riding towards her future at last. The one she'd come here for.

Erika slowed her wild unicorn to a walk across a grassy clifftop and Kenna looked up at the Hatchery for the first time. She didn't feel excitement or wonder, like she'd expected. Instead, she felt a profound sadness – an eternal, immoveable disappointment. Her mum was right: she would never belong on this Island; she would never be like the rest of them. And she would hate them for it.

She was overcome with misery and rage. She wished she could howl at the sky for ever. She wished she could take hold of the sinking sun and squeeze until it burst into a thousand splintered pieces.

Then – as though the Island understood the turmoil deep within her bones – the clifftop trembled violently, there was a deafening crash of thunder and a lightning bolt reached down with a searing elemental fist and struck the Hatchery.

A crack opened in the side of the grassy mound, the earth a gaping maw. Kenna clung to her mum's black shroud as the wild unicorn reared, delighting in the destruction.

Erika laughed high and shrill. 'Well, that makes things *much* easier.'

All the hairs stood up on Kenna's arms as her mum began to sing:

'Yet another force grows on this Island:
True successor of spirit's dark friend.
And the storm it will bring when it rises,
Will see all we know brought to an end.'

'I've never been a great believer in truesongs,' Erika said to Kenna, as they moved towards the open wound in the Hatchery's side, 'but I have to admit I do like that verse.'

And then there was no more time for hesitation or sorrow. No space for worries about what Dad would say, or Skandar, or even the younger Kenna – the one who'd dreamed of opening a door to a new life.

There was only this. The choice she was making, the future she was choosing.

CHAPTER EIGHTEEN

ONE SHORT

The unicorns did not like it in the tunnel. Scoundrel kept trying to turn round, scraping Skandar's knees against the rocky interior. It smelled salty and damp and very old. The opening they'd come through lit the way for now, but the tunnel was becoming darker with every step. Scoundrel's unease made Skandar wonder if his unicorn knew something he didn't about what lay ahead.

'So . . . do we think it's a metaphorical fight?' Flo asked, her voice echoing.

'Yeah,' Skandar said, trying to reassure himself more than anything. 'I mean, the First Rider died thousands of years ago, right?' He tried not to think about Rickesh's vengeful phantom theory.

As usual, Mitchell was more worried about what would happen next – *after* they'd retrieved the bone staff. He was muttering about taking the staff back to the fault lines, planning the quickest routes back to the Eyrie.

Bobby, meanwhile, had produced a sandwich from inside her armour.

'How can you eat at a time like this?' Flo asked her. 'We could be attacked at any moment!'

'I thought you said the fight was metaphoric—'

The whole cliff trembled, sending chunks of rock crashing from the tunnel roof. Bobby dusted debris off her crust and fed it to Falcon.

Time was running out. Skandar patted Scoundrel on the neck and tried to encourage him forward. The black unicorn planted his hooves, refusing to move.

'Come on, boy! I know you don't like it in here; I don't either.'

'What's that?' Mitchell's voice was sharp and serious. The tone sent a shiver down Skandar's spine. He looked up.

A flaming unicorn blocked the path in front of them. Though at a second glance Skandar wasn't sure exactly *what* it was. The crackling creature was made entirely of fire. There was no skin or mane or hoof. Just roaring orange flames.

'Do we think it's here to help us or kill us?' Bobby whispered.

As if in answer, the flames of the unicorn's body started to grow in height and width – until it lost its shape completely, and the tunnel ahead was ablaze with a scorching inferno. The heat seared Skandar's skin; Scoundrel shrieked in alarm.

'Back up! Back up!' Flo coughed as her silver unicorn took a few steps back from the fire.

'I think that's definitely the way,' Skandar said, once they were a safe distance from the raging flames.

'You think?' Bobby said sarcastically. 'Lucky we've got the sharpest lemon in the tree with us.'

'You've done that one before,' Skandar shot back. He was

rattled. He'd never seen elemental magic rage on its own like that. It made him wonder if someone was there, beyond the flames, controlling it.

'Do you think that's the Wild Unicorn Queen?' Flo asked, her voice awed.

'I think it's some *form* of the Wild Unicorn Queen,' Mitchell said. 'The tomb must be further ahead. There's no way we're under the Eyrie yet. I think we have to get through the flames.'

'Wait a minute!' Bobby said. 'You're my quartet and I love you and everything, but I'm not literally walking through fire for you.'

'You won't have to.' Mitchell gritted his teeth. 'I'm the fire wielder. I'm the only person who's going anywhere near that.'

'No, Mitchell!' Flo cried. 'It's too dangerous. Can't we all try to put it out with water attacks?'

'The magic's too strong; I can feel it. And I don't think that's how this path is supposed to work. I'll be okay,' he told her. 'I've been reading all about truesongs and bards – basically everything my dad doesn't believe in. The magic in this tunnel – it's *old*. It's the kind of magic bards sing about.'

'Oh, sorry.' Bobby rolled her eyes. 'I didn't realise you'd been reading about flaming demon unicorns this whole time. If *only* we'd known!'

'No, Roberta,' Mitchell said, patiently for once, 'but we've been moulding weapons from magic all year, and I think that's what I can do here. If Red Night's Delight and I work *with* the fire magic – try to mould it – then maybe we can hold it back for you all to get through.'

'Mitchell,' Skandar started. 'I'm not sure—'

'I'm right,' he interrupted. 'Let me try it, okay?'

ONE SHORT

Mitchell rode Red towards the roaring inferno blocking the tunnel. Skandar wished Ira Henderson could see his son right at that moment: how brave he was, how selfless. He wished Mitchell's dad could see that being Commodore wasn't all his son was worth.

Mitchell's palm glowed bright red as he threw his own magic into the blaze ahead. He began to move his palm this way and that, shaping his own flames into a circular firestorm. Red – her mane tangled, her coat back to its scruffy self – reared up at the fire, her hooves adding to the inferno, helping her rider. Skandar couldn't see his friend's face, but he could see his limbs shaking with the effort of controlling the magic – even his fingers looked tired.

Then Mitchell rasped over his shoulder. 'Go on three! Okay?'

'Go where?' Bobby cried.

But Mitchell had already turned back to the flames in front of him, and with his right palm he punched forward.

'One!' he shouted.

He punched again.

'Two!'

He punched a third time.

'Three!'

A ring opened in the raging firestorm. A gap just big enough for a unicorn to jump through.

'Go!' Mitchell bellowed.

Falcon went first. Despite her previous complaints, Bobby was calm as she jumped through the inferno and landed neatly on the other side. Bobby's smoke-blackened figure was just visible through the fire, waving cheerfully as if this was just a nice day out. Flo and Blade went next and cleared the obstacle too.

'What are *you* going to do?' Skandar called to Mitchell. Flames licked dangerously at the hole in the firestorm.

'I'll stay here. Hold this off. For the way back!' Mitchell called, his voice strained with exhaustion.

'Are you sure?'

'GO!' Mitchell cried. So Skandar pointed Scoundrel right towards the blaze and jumped him right through the middle. The hole closed behind Scoundrel's tail.

'Do you think that's it? No more crazy fire?' Skandar wondered, looking over his shoulder to try to get a glimpse of Mitchell. Scoundrel shrieked for Red too, and his distress echoed around the tunnel.

Bobby coughed up some ash. 'Only one way to find out,' she spluttered, and Falcon led the way deeper into the tunnel.

Flo followed on Blade, but kept looking over her shoulder. 'I wish we didn't have to leave Mitchell.'

'I know,' Skandar murmured. 'I don't like it either.'

'Hey, you two!' Bobby called from in front of them. 'Guess who's up next?'

Skandar only caught sight of the air unicorn for a heartbeat. The shape was much harder to make out than the flaming creature that had come before it – its outline sparked with electricity, while the rest of its body was pure tornado, sucking in the rock of the tunnel around it.

'Here we go,' Bobby said, her brown fringe lifting in the wind. The creature was blown apart by the force of its own storm, countless small tornadoes spinning off around the small space. And as if that wasn't hard enough to get past, every other second there was an explosion of forked lightning, illuminating the tunnel.

'Do you think we can try to gallop through it?' Skandar asked Bobby. 'Avoid the lightning?'

'No way.' She shook her head. 'The tornadoes would slow us down, then we'd get fried by a strike. Just let me think.'

Skandar and Flo waited as Bobby counted under her breath. Skandar couldn't help worrying about how long they were taking. He didn't want them to be stuck in this tunnel if the Island started to self-destruct.

'Okay, listen up,' Bobby called, interrupting Skandar's spiral of fear. 'I'm going to follow Mitchell's example and summon my own tornadoes. If I time it right, I think I can use my magic to interrupt the flow of the air ahead of us – make the tornadoes bounce off each other.' She grinned at Skandar. 'Like one of those old arcade games.'

'What about the lightning strikes?' Flo said, jumping as another one hit the tunnel floor like a gunshot.

'They have a pattern,' Bobby replied. 'If you go when I tell you, then you'll get through to the other side of the storm completely non-frazzled.'

'Bobby . . .' Flo looked terrified.

'Trust me, Florence. I'm the best rider in the year, remember?'

'And the humblest,' Skandar said, trying to lighten the mood. It wasn't exactly easy, given they were in a tunnel that was trying to kill them.

Falcon and Bobby faced the electrical storm, Bobby's palm glowing bright yellow. One, two, three tornadoes flew from her hand – but they didn't spin about at random like the rest of the air magic ahead of them. Bobby was in complete control, the tiniest flick of her wrist sending them the way she commanded. When they grew too large or too small, she reshaped the air like clay on a wheel. Skandar wasn't sure he'd ever appreciated just how beautiful the air element was before.

'There are going to be three more flashes of lightning,' Bobby shouted, without taking her eyes off her tornadoes, as they bounced the tunnel's magic further and further to the sides, creating a safe passage through the storm. 'There'll be none of Mitchell Henderson's trademark counting. When I say go, you go.'

'Got it!' Skandar shouted back, the wind roaring in his ears. Flo nodded, determined.

Flash. Bang!

Flash. Bang!

Flash. Bang!

'GO!' Bobby yelled.

Silver Blade and Scoundrel's Luck exploded past Falcon's Wrath, bolting down the windless path Bobby had moulded through the magic.

Flash. BANG! All the hairs stood up on the back of Skandar's neck as a lightning strike hit right behind him. Flo half turned in her saddle.

'Don't look back!' Skandar shouted to her. 'Keep going!'

Flash. BANG! The second lightning strike. Flo screamed, urging Blade faster. It wasn't only Bobby who had learned the pattern. They needed to beat the third strike on the far edge of the storm.

Flash. BANG!

Skandar and Flo were completely out of breath as they watched the third fork of lightning hit. Bobby whooped from the other side of the electrical storm, giving them a thumbs up.

'Do you think there'll be elemental unicorns for all four of us?' Flo asked, watching Bobby manage her tornadoes.

'It's possible,' Skandar said. A line from Jamie's truesong echoed in his head: *All five must follow his first and last steps . . .*

Five. It made sense. Down here on the path to the First Rider's tomb, the magic felt old, like it belonged to a time before. Before there was prejudice against the spirit element. Which meant if there *were* five unicorns, they were one rider short. They were missing a water wielder.

Skandar didn't have the heart to mention the problem to Flo. Not yet.

With half their quartet stuck behind them, Skandar and Flo carried on in the eerie calm. The distant blaze of fire and the flashes of electricity lit up the darkness of the tunnel from behind them. 'Do you know what I wish sometimes?' Flo said. It was just wide enough for the spirit and silver unicorns to walk shoulder to shoulder, though occasionally their armour clashed, echoing loudly along the tunnel.

'What?'

'I wish we could both be ordinary. Sometimes I shut my eyes, and I imagine us differently. I watch myself hatch my egg, and my unicorn is born chestnut, not silver. Then I watch you walk the fault lines, and Scoundrel's blaze is just a mark – and you're truly a water wielder.'

'But then we wouldn't be *us*, Flo.'

Skandar thought about Bobby suddenly, and the extraordinary magic she'd just performed. He thought about Mitchell's bravery – how he'd been the first to face the tunnel's challenge. He thought about Flo throwing herself into the Stronghold arena and on to a wild unicorn's back. He thought about how Amber had risked everything rescuing Scoundrel's Luck for him. 'And I think the truth is,' he continued, 'I think the truth is that nobody in the whole world is ordinary. It's like a spirit weapon. You can imagine ordinary, but it doesn't quite exist. Not really. So I think we're better off trying to be as extraordinary as possible.'

'Well, it all sounds really easy when you put it like that –' Flo sighed, keeping her eyes on the tunnel ahead – 'but it isn't. It's hard, Skar.'

'I tell you what,' Skandar said, trying to cheer her up. 'Once we've fought through the rest of this tunnel, won the bone staff and saved the Island, we can do something ordinary.'

Flo laughed. 'Like what?'

'Oh, I don't know, something boring.' It was wonderful – just for a moment – to have this silly conversation in the middle of an ancient tunnel. Perhaps he was just delirious with terror.

Flo was really laughing now. 'You can't actually think of anything, can you?'

Skandar was laughing too. 'Of course I can. Just – just give me a minute to—'

'Skar!' Flo's laughter snuffed out.

This elemental unicorn wasn't at all what Skandar had expected. He'd been thinking it might be made of sharp rocks, or maybe soil, but the strange creature was shaped completely out of sand – like a really impressive sandcastle.

'Let's just try to get past it,' Flo said. Though as soon as Blade had taken one more step, the sand unicorn collapsed to the tunnel floor. Suddenly, yellow grains were cascading from every surface of the tunnel like a fountain.

Too late, Skandar realised what was happening. 'It's filling up! It's going to block the way!' he shouted. The wall of sand ahead was already up to the height of Blade's chest. It was like they were stuck inside a giant hourglass. The sand was scalding hot – as if it had been baking on beaches for a thousand years. Within seconds it had completely filled the tunnel ahead.

But Flo had a look of determination on her face. Her palm was glowing green already. Missiles of sharp rock exploded against the sand wall, the earth wielder flinging her arm backwards and forward over and over. Blade soon got the idea and started shooting tiny rocks from his own horn. Slowly but surely, Flo was creating an opening.

She gritted her teeth. 'Okay, Skar. I'm almost through. Once I've got a gap to work with, I'm going to create my own tunnel of sand to keep the hole open wide enough for you and Scoundrel to get through. Just like digging at the beach.' She gulped. 'I hope.'

'But that sand,' Skandar shouted over the constant fizz of hot sand spilling from all sides of the tunnel. 'It's going to be so heavy.'

'Bobby might be the best rider, Skar, but I ride a silver unicorn. Blade and I are strong. We can handle this.'

Flo sent another rock blast at the sand tunnel, and it exploded all the way to the opposite end. A chink of light appeared.

'What if I can't do this on my own?' Skandar said suddenly. 'I'm not a water wielder. What if I can't get to the bone staff, what if—'

'You can do anything,' Flo said. 'You're Skandar Smith.' She said it with such conviction that – at least for now – Skandar believed her.

Flo's arms shook with the effort of holding back the sand as her own earth magic swirled and expanded. An image jumped into Skandar's head of him and Kenna on Margate beach. They'd been building a sandcastle fort for hours, and Kenna had suddenly realised that the sea was going to come in and wash it away. At top speed she'd started to pile up heaps of sand, desperately trying to build a wall against a tide that was always going to come in. For a moment, the memory was so real that Skandar could have sworn he heard his sister's laugh as the sea rushed over her toes.

'Skar, it's time!' Flo shouted.

Skandar shook himself out of his childhood, the ghost of his sister's laugh still echoing around the tunnel. He had to focus. His friends were counting on him.

Scoundrel did *not* want to go into the sand tunnel. It was so hot that Skandar decided to douse them both in a spurt of water from his palm as they entered it. Scoundrel shrieked with the fear Skandar was feeling. Would the tunnel hold? He tried not to let himself imagine the tonnes of sand above collapsing on top of them both.

They made their way slowly. The gap was too narrow to risk moving any faster than a walk.

'Skar!' Flo shouted, her voice shaking. 'Skar, I don't know how much longer I can hold it!'

'We're almost there!' Skandar shouted back without turning round. 'A few more metres.'

Flo screamed and Skandar made the mistake of looking back over his shoulder.

The tunnel of sand was collapsing behind him. He could no longer see Flo, trapped on the other side, but the cascade of hot grains was moments from sweeping him and Scoundrel into its boiling depths.

'Scoundrel, go!'

The black unicorn didn't need telling twice. Burning sand was already falling on to his hindquarters and tucked wings, as they threw all caution to the wind and galloped towards the opening.

They made it. Just. Scoundrel's back hoof was caught by the swirling sand, but he dislodged it just in time for the hole to close.

'Skar! Are you okay?' Flo's voice was muffled.

Skandar sighed with relief. She was all right. Or at least as all right as was to be expected.

'I'm fine!' he called back. 'I made it!'

'I *really* don't like this place.'

'Me neither!' Skandar half laughed. 'I'm carrying on, Flo. Okay? I'll be back before you know it.'

'I'll try to clear the way somehow,' Flo said. 'So we can get home.'

Home, Skandar thought. He just hoped their home was still out there.

Skandar had hardly shaken all the sand out of his hair before a water unicorn shimmered, bright blue, up ahead. The elemental creature looked unreal – like a mirage, almost transparent against the rock of the tunnel. Skandar blinked and the unicorn crashed to the floor. It splashed against the sides of the tunnel, and then – as if caught in a terrible storm – it writhed upwards, fighting an unseen force as it morphed into a giant tidal wave right before Skandar's eyes.

Skandar wished, not for the first time in his life, that he really *was* a water wielder. If only they'd thought to bring Kobi with them, or Rickesh – he'd seen the Rookie only that morning. The elemental obstacles had been brutal so far, and Skandar didn't have any clue how—

The wave was cresting at one side of the tunnel, white spray hissing on its brow. And what do waves do after they crest?

They crash. And this particular one was going to crash right where Scoundrel was standing.

Skandar summoned the water element to his palm without the first clue how he was going to stop them being washed back into the wall of sand. The smell of the element – of salt and mint and wet hair – stuck in the back of his panicked throat.

'Come on, Skandar, think,' he told himself. 'What can you do? What are you good at?'

Scoundrel – obviously thinking this was no time for his rider to be having a conversation with himself – pointed his horn up at the rapidly approaching water, flapping his wings in alarm.

Wings. Skandar's hand went to the metal peregrine feather under his armour.

Fight – or flight. In this situation, he definitely had a better chance at *flight*. He was a member of the Peregrine Society, the Eyrie's elite flying squad. Suddenly he had a plan.

The wave crested and its peak started to descend towards them – and just as Skandar had hoped – the water curled over as it fell, creating a hollow tunnel of clear, water-free air. The place gifted surfers dreamed of riding their boards.

Skandar had never had a surfboard, but he did have a unicorn. And they were going to fly right through the middle of the wave.

A jolt of understanding went through the bond. Scoundrel had seen the opportunity to escape the water and his black-feathered wings snapped out. One, two, three beats and Scoundrel had taken off practically from a standing start; he was heading right for the curl in the wave, the water frothing and spraying at them from all angles.

Once they were level with the hole, Skandar decided to

summon water and spirit side by side into the bond. If they were going to fly through the churning water, they might as well be at one with it.

Scoundrel pumped his wings back, and then—

WHOOSH.

The black unicorn shot, like a bullet, under the curl of the wave. They were cocooned by water on every side. Slowly but surely, Scoundrel's mane, then his whole neck, then his whole chest, his head, his legs, his hooves, his hindquarters and finally his tail turned to water, so he matched the shimmering water unicorn responsible for the obstacle.

The water was rolling and roaring around them, as though it was angry they'd outsmarted it. As his knee skimmed the edges of the curling wave, Skandar could hardly tell which water belonged to the tidal wave and which made up his unicorn. He could feel the doubts starting to creep into his mind as the wave surrounded them completely – *I don't know if we can do this, boy* – but Scoundrel poured reassurance into the bond and took the lead. Scoundrel flipped them sideways – one wing brushing the crest of the wave, the other pointing downwards, manoeuvring them through the water – and Skandar barely noticed as his helmet flew off his head, the hungry water claiming it like a prize.

Another pump of Scoundrel's wings. And—

'Woohoo!' Skandar cried. They were out. They were soaked to the skin, but they were out. The feeling reminded him of walking the fault lines exactly two years ago.

They landed and Scoundrel's usual black colour slowly returned, like ink spreading through a pool of water. He flapped his wings.

'Oi!' Skandar laughed as the black unicorn shook water all

over his already sodden clothes. Then he looked ahead of him for the first time. He'd reached the end of the tunnel. A great round door, almost identical to the one at the Hatchery, loomed in front of him.

Skandar dismounted. He knew what he needed to do.

With Scoundrel's reins in his left hand, he stretched out his right palm and rested his Hatchery wound against the round granite door. For a moment, the only sound was his own heavy breathing – perfectly in time with Scoundrel's.

Then the door of the tomb creaked open.

CHAPTER NINETEEN

THE PHANTOM RIDER

Skandar led Scoundrel through the round doorway, his heart beating wildly in his chest. The tomb was a vast oval, with an earthy floor that smelled very similar to the fresh pine of the Eyrie. Coloured rocks on the ground were arranged to depict the five elemental symbols. Roots poked down through the muddy ceiling: an upside-down forest of withered limbs, twisting and intertwining – not unlike the stalactites of the Hatchery's inner chamber. Skandar swallowed. The vastness of the root system confirmed what he'd guessed hours ago: the tomb was under the Eyrie's great entrance tree, with its coloured elemental leaves, and so it must belong to both of them – the First Rider and the Wild Unicorn Queen.

It was odd – as Skandar and Scoundrel explored the oval space, they could find no grave to speak of, and certainly no bone staff. The only thing that really stuck out was in the centre of the room. A mound of soil: fresher, darker than the rest of the earthy floor. It was deadly quiet in here – too quiet – a kind of silence Skandar had never heard before. It seemed to press against his ears. He wished the others were with him; Mitchell would have started studying the elemental stones, Flo would have said something reassuring and Bobby would have made a sarcastic comment about coming all the way here for nothing.

Skandar stepped closer to the pile of earth. Scoundrel dug his hooves in and tossed his horn away from the heap of soil. The jolt knocked Skandar sideways slightly, and his stumble dislodged a white stone from the interlocking circles of the spirit symbol underfoot.

Three things happened at once.

Scoundrel shrieked in alarm, the sound echoing around the oval tomb.

The roots above Skandar's head started to writhe, like the arms of rattling skeletons.

And a dazzling white unicorn and rider exploded from the mound of soil, blocking the tomb's exit.

Skandar leaped on to Scoundrel's back instinctively. They were stronger together. Always.

Skandar tried to squash his terror and braced himself to look at the white unicorn and rider again. They glimmered in and out of focus, their bodies fluid and features blurred. Were they ghosts? Were they magic? Were they real at all?

Then the phantom rider spoke – and the whole thing felt very real indeed.

'You seek my bone staff, spirit wielder.' White light flowed out of his mouth like spectral words, but his voice was strong. Human.

Skandar's own voice shook as he answered. 'Yes, I need it. We need it. Wild unicorns have been killed, and the magic – it's destroying the Island.'

The First Rider's unicorn reared up on her back legs and let out a terrible, mournful cry. A wild unicorn's cry. Though her body was shining white, her horn was unmistakably transparent.

'You're the Wild Unicorn Queen,' Skandar breathed as her hooves came back down.

'The *last* queen of the wild unicorns,' the First Rider confirmed. 'She is angry that her herd has been harmed. The riders were supposed to LEAVE THEM IN PEACE!' The First Rider's shining face contorted in fury, and the last four words were so loud that Skandar had to cover his ears. He could feel Scoundrel vibrating with fear underneath him as the First Rider's bellow echoed round the tomb.

'I'm sorry,' Skandar rushed on. He was terrified and desperate. He thought of his friends fighting the elemental magic back in the tunnel. He thought of the Grins up on the Sunset Platform getting ready to leave. He thought of the newest Hatchlings, who might never set foot in the Eyrie. He thought of Kenna stuck on the Mainland, her destined unicorn in the Wilderness here on the Island – wild for ever. They were all counting on him. He took a deep breath, swallowing down his fear.

'I'm sorry for what's happened, but I need to stop the magical destruction. Otherwise there won't be an Island left – the Queen's whole herd will be homeless. I'm running out of time. I need the bone staff – *the Island* needs it. Please, can you give it to me?'

The First Rider's laugh was horribly hollow, the white light jolting with each sound he made. 'You must win the bone staff, Skandar Smith. I will not give it freely.'

'Why not?' Skandar demanded, forgetting how afraid he was for a moment. 'Didn't you hear me? The Island is going to be destroyed. There's no time for games!'

'You must win the bone staff,' the First Rider said again, as though Skandar hadn't spoken.

'How do I win it, then?' Skandar pleaded, the First Rider leaving him no choice but to play along.

The glowing rider inclined his head, businesslike all of a sudden. 'A spirit joust. Best of three rounds.'

'You want . . . you want to joust?'

The First Rider was already waving Skandar to the back of the oval. 'The Island can only be saved by one worthy of the staff's power. If there is no such rider, the end of the Island has truly come. Therefore if you win, I shall give you the bone staff.'

'What about my friends? Will you stop the magic in the tunnel? Those unicorns out there? They're all you, aren't they?' Skandar turned to the Wild Unicorn Queen.

The First Rider answered for her. 'If you win, you and your friends will be free to leave.'

Skandar swallowed. 'What if *you* win?'

'The Island will be destroyed. Your friends will remain in the tunnel, fighting. And you and Scoundrel's Luck will remain with me.'

'For how long?' Skandar asked, fearful of the answer.

'A little longer than for ever.'

'What if I refuse to joust?' Skandar asked, knowing that this wasn't really an option. He needed to save his Island, his home, his friends. He wasn't going to abandon them. But his fear made him ask if there was a way out.

'Refusing will have the same consequences as losing,' the First Rider clarified.

And so there was no way out, even if Skandar had wanted one.

The Wild Unicorn Queen was already pawing her shining hooves at the ground, ready to attack. Skandar clutched Scoundrel's reins, fear clawing at his chest. How could he possibly win against the First Rider – the rider who'd founded the Eyrie? And a Wild Unicorn Queen? Again, he wished Bobby, Flo and Mitchell were with him. He didn't want to do this alone. He didn't even have a shield.

Despite what the First Rider had said, Skandar *did* think about trying to flee from the tomb with Scoundrel. Of course he did. But only for a second. The Island was his home, and maybe one day it could be Kenna's too. The idea of the unicorns having to leave this magical place, riders split up by element, quartets splintered. He'd never see his friends again. And Skandar wasn't going to let that happen without an almighty fight.

So as the ghostly white shapes of the entombed rider and unicorn flowed towards him, what could Skandar do but face them?

Scoundrel roared, trying to give Skandar courage, and galloped towards his adversaries. The oval was a lot shorter than an ordinary jousting piste, and Skandar had less than two seconds to mould a spirit weapon. A sabre – one of his favourites – took shape in his right hand, but the First Rider had already thrown three white axes, and they were spinning through the air. Skandar lost control of the shining sword in his own hand, but Scoundrel managed to avoid two axes by swerving wildly across the tomb's chamber, narrowly missing the mound of soil. The third axe brushed Skandar's shoulder and he cried out, pain searing through him.

'One to zero,' the First Rider said from his position at the other end of the tomb, sounding almost bored.

Skandar barely had time to recover before the Wild Unicorn Queen came for him and Scoundrel again, and this time he made an even bigger mistake.

He moulded a bow, thinking multiple arrows would give him more of a chance to hit the First Rider. But the First Rider had the fastest reflexes Skandar had ever seen. It was as though he knew where the arrows were going to come from before Skandar had even loosed them from his bowstring. Before Skandar could slow Scoundrel down – before he could even think about defending himself – a spear was leaving the First Rider's hand and heading right for his chest.

All Skandar could do was try to stay on Scoundrel's back. If he fell, he would lose. The Island would be gone. His friends would endlessly wrestle their allied elements in the tunnel, and he and Scoundrel would join the First Rider and the Wild Unicorn Queen down here . . . for ever.

The spear smashed into Skandar's chest, Jamie's trusty armour crushing inwards, leaving him winded. Skandar rocked backwards in his saddle – but Scoundrel, understanding, threw his own weight forward to counterbalance the spear's impact.

'Thanks, boy,' Skandar wheezed, struggling to breathe through his dented armour.

'Two to zero.' The First Rider's voice reverberated around the tomb. The only way Skandar and Scoundrel could win now was if the First Rider ended up on the ground. Skandar was drenched in sweat – his hair sticking to his forehead – and the bond was so frazzled with his and Scoundrel's fear that he could barely think straight.

Before the queen of the wild unicorns could come at them for the last time, Skandar unstrapped his dented breastplate. He couldn't breathe with it on, and it was impossible to move freely enough to throw any kind of weapon. The black armour landed on the earth with a thump, leaving his chest completely exposed.

'You're putting up a good fight,' the First Rider called, 'but the bone staff won't be leaving this tomb with you if you cannot win it.'

Fight.

The last must fight on but mean no violence.

The line from Jamie's truesong blazed across Skandar's mind. Of course! The whole time he'd been trying to attack a wild unicorn, which was exactly what the Silver Circle had done to get the Island into this mess. If Skandar's theory was right, he might just win – but if he was wrong? The First Rider would almost certainly kill him.

The two unicorns reared at either end of the tomb: one black as the night sky; one a ghostly, shining white. Skandar's injured shoulder was throbbing, his chest bruised, his limbs exhausted. But his head was clear.

The unicorns exploded towards each other.

Five strides apart.

Four strides apart. A shimmering spiked mace appeared in the First Rider's hand.

Three strides apart. Skandar took his right palm off Scoundrel's reins; it glowed white.

Two strides apart. The First Rider swung back his weapon, ready to land his final winning blow on Skandar's unarmoured chest.

One stride apart. Skandar made his move.

His palm cut quickly through the air. Up and down in front of the Wild Unicorn Queen's swirling white eyes. The spirit magic poured through the bond, lighting up the dim tomb with Skandar's shield. He'd never summoned one before, but the shining barrier reminded him of what happened when a spirit wielder opened the door to the Eyrie. A thousand imperfect stars knitting together to make a beautiful impenetrable web.

The Wild Unicorn Queen skidded to a halt just before the magical barrier, but the First Rider wasn't ready for it. The sudden change in speed threw him forward over the Queen's head. His strange flowing body spiralled through the air and hit the spirit shield. As he landed in a swirling heap by Scoundrel's right hoof, the mace flew from his hand and dissolved into thin air.

Skandar dropped his palm, and the shield blinked out.

The tomb was deathly silent – until, very slowly, the First Rider rose from the earthy floor and stood by the Queen's shoulder.

'I cannot say I expected that,' the First Rider said. And even though Skandar couldn't quite focus on his shimmering face, he could sense that there was a smile hidden there. 'Certainly it falls outside the jousting etiquette I invented.'

Skandar waited, his chest painful with every anguished breath.

'But you are a worthy winner, all the same.' The First Rider inclined his head. 'You have a good heart, Skandar Smith.'

'Thank you,' Skandar breathed. He cast a worried glance towards the door, thinking of his friends back in the tunnel.

'Your companions are perfectly fine,' the First Rider said, following his gaze. 'The moment you were victorious in the joust, the Queen ceased her elemental magic. They are rushing along the tunnel to find you, as we speak.'

'What was the point of all that?' Skandar asked, unable to stop himself. 'If all I needed to do was joust you to win the bone staff, what was the point of all the other elemental stuff in the tunnel?'

The First Rider paused, and Skandar had the sense that the rider was weighing him up.

'Do you know how I came to be on this Island, Skandar Smith?'

'Yes,' he answered. 'You were a fisherman. You washed up on the beach, where the entrance to the tunnel is.'

'That is right. I was younger than you at the time. I was very weak as I lay in the surf of the waves. I thought death was coming for me, and then *she* came.' The First Rider laid his hand on the Wild Unicorn Queen's neck, and a contented growl came from deep within her belly.

'She wasn't a queen then. She was a wild white foal, only a few months old. Her coat was a little dirty, as I remember it.' There was warmth in the First Rider's voice. 'She found me there on the beach, and I was filled with wonder. Where I came from, unicorns were mythical beasts. They did not appear to dying young fishermen on far-flung beaches.

'She saved me. She gave me strength to go on. I barely noticed her bloodthirsty nature; the way her very essence was death itself; how her skin rotted with every passing hour. We do not notice the imperfections in those we love. Although I saw her tear eagles from the sky and take down fully grown bears to spill open their guts, I knew deep down she would never do that to me. I'm sure you understand that feeling.' The First Rider gestured to Scoundrel's Luck, whose eyes were fixed curiously on the queen of the wild unicorns. Skandar nodded.

'We grew strong together. She taught me about the Island; she let me ride on her back. I taught her to fight, showed her human ways the wild unicorns had never known. One day, when I was almost a fully grown man, she pierced my palm with her horn. I didn't understand it. The pain was terrible, burning, excruciating. I didn't understand until the magic came. She had chosen to share her gifts with me. I had always been destined for her, long before I'd been washed up on this Island. She had called me across the waves.'

The Island is calling you, Skandar Smith. Agatha's words that early summer solstice morning suddenly had a weight to them – a rightness, a history. Skandar had barely understood until this moment.

'Which element were you allied to?' Skandar asked curiously.

'That is not a question I know how to answer,' the First Rider said, and continued with his story. 'She became Queen, but she was different to the others. I was always with her; I could share her magic in a way that made us unstoppable. She understood that our partnership made her stronger, not weaker. She had something the wild unicorns had never known – friendship. And she wanted that for her kind, so she showed me the chasm where the unicorn eggs appeared on the Island. We built a mound of earth to protect it. We watched the eggs hatch wild each year, their immortality stretching before them. And we wondered. We wondered whether we could change things, whether we could make more partnerships like ours.

'So we left the Island. We searched the world for those people who went about their lives with an incomplete bond – colours that flashed about them while they slept, while they worked – and we told them about the Island. About the unicorns. Some of them joined us. The Queen taught me how to bond the unicorns with the humans they had called – how to mend the links between their souls. Their immortal lives compressed so they could feel true joy, true meaning. Unlike the Wild Unicorn Queen, their horns filled with colour. We no longer called them wild. Then children were born on the Island, and the Hatchery door determined which of them would be called inside. We found that if they bonded with their unicorn as it hatched, they could live and learn together. They could grow up in true partnership, just as I and a wild white foal had done years before.

'We built the Eyrie to train them and we watched the bonded unicorns gain in strength; we invented the Chaos Cup to keep them focused. But in their strength we saw a danger. That one day they could turn on the wild unicorns, the ones who had never found a rider to grow up with. For if the wild unicorns were killed, we knew that the Island would retaliate. The wild unicorns were here before us all – don't forget. They are woven deep within the elemental fabric of this place. And for as long as there is death they will remain.

'So, when I was old and wizened and ready – finally – for the death that had almost claimed me as a young fisherman, the Queen and I decided to protect the Island from itself. We knew our successors would make mistakes – we all make mistakes, we all lose our way sometimes. So we made an object that would allow the Island to find its way back from the brink.'

'The bone staff,' Skandar murmured.

'The Queen sacrificed herself – gave her immortal life to me – knowing that the staff I carved would hold the power of all five elements in harmony, just as we had throughout our lives.'

Skandar couldn't help asking the thing he'd been wondering since he'd seen the First Rider emerge from the mound of earth.

'But are you dead or still alive or . . . ?'

'That's a rather personal matter,' the First Rider said.

Skandar didn't have a response to that, so he changed tack.

'I still don't understand why there were elemental protections around the tomb, though?'

'The bone staff is about harmony, Skandar. Harmony between wild unicorns and bonded. Harmony between the elements. No spirit wielder could have made it to this tomb if they were acting alone. You and your friends worked together to get here. The Queen and I knew that as long as there were riders of each element capable of working together, there was hope for the Island. It only takes a few good riders to change things – but you know that already.'

At that moment the roof of the tomb shook so violently that clumps of earth rained down on Skandar and Scoundrel.

'I have talked for too long. There is not much time left.'

Skandar watched as the First Rider walked over to the earthy mound in the tomb's centre and – like the goriest lucky dip – plunged his shining white arm into the soil, pulling out a long white staff.

Silently, reverently, the First Rider passed it from his own spectral hands to Skandar's solid, dirty ones. The staff had no joins that Skandar could see; tiny elemental symbols were the only imperfections carved into the cold bone. Fire at the very bottom, then air, then earth, then water and then, finally, the spirit symbol was carved into the round orb at the top.

'I hope nobody will ever need it again,' Skandar said rather fiercely.

The First Rider shook his head. 'It will always be needed, Skandar. In a hundred years, in a thousand. Mistakes are inevitable; all that we can hope for is that each time we make one, we become a little kinder. So don't forget to return it here. Once your task is complete.'

The First Rider mounted the Wild Unicorn Queen once more, and raised a hand in farewell. Their bodies flickered like faulty bulbs.

'The one you love the most will betray you, Skandar Smith. Be wary. When it matters the most, they will turn against you.'

'What?' Skandar cried, taken aback. 'Who do you mean?'

He thought of his quartet first. Of Bobby's face, of Flo's, of Mitchell's. Then of his family: Kenna, Dad, Agatha.

But, like two reigning stars, the outline of the First Rider astride his beloved Queen grew brighter and brighter – until Skandar blinked. And they were gone.

The door of the tomb opened. Scoundrel shrieked in welcome as Silver Blade, Falcon's Wrath and Red Night's Delight jumped through the gap, their riders ready for a battle.

Bobby was the first to notice the bone staff in Skandar's hand. 'You've already got it? What a let-down! Did you even have to do anything, or was it just lying about here while we all held off angry elemental unicorns?'

Skandar didn't want to talk about it yet. He collapsed to the earthy ground. The pure horror of the alternative, of if he'd lost, hit him all at once.

Suddenly, arms were round him, pulling him closer. The arms of a quartet.

'You're okay, you're okay,' Flo kept saying.

'We're here, spirit boy,' Bobby croaked.

Mitchell clutched Skandar's arm, silent but smiling.

For a moment Skandar relaxed, then his memories came flooding back in a tidal wave of panic. 'We have to get to the Eyrie!'

They left the tomb. Without the Wild Unicorn Queen's magic,

they rode a lot more quickly down the tunnel this time – but it still seemed to take far too long.

'What time do you think it is up there?' Flo worried.

Skandar's stomach clenched. 'I don't know. I think the First Rider would have told me if we wouldn't make it for sunset. I don't think he wanted the Island to be destroyed.'

'Are you saying you actually met—'

But Flo's question was lost to Bobby and Mitchell's cheers as they finally emerged from the tunnel's mouth and hooves crashed on to the stones of Fisherman's Beach.

One, two, three, four unicorns took off into the sky, their majestic wings reflected in the Mirror Cliffs until they were soaring over the clifftop belonging to the Hatchery.

A sharp cry of pain echoed below. 'Did you hear that?' Skandar asked, looking down at the Hatchery's green mound between Scoundrel's wingbeats.

He stared.

There was a hole in the side of the Hatchery, like a wild unicorn's immortal wound. The sight of it made Skandar want to cry.

'We can't worry about that right now,' Mitchell shouted over the wind, Red flying by Scoundrel's left shoulder. *'From tomb to elemental crossing,* remember?'

So Skandar turned Scoundrel's Luck away from the Hatchery and gripped the bone staff in his left hand.

Ahead he saw the outlines of seven unicorns flying out from the Eyrie. The Peregrine Society were leaving, their winged shadows lengthening in the last light of the solstice.

Please, he begged someone, anyone – maybe even the First Rider. *Please let this work.*

THE CRY IN THE DARK

Empty egg stands stood like soldiers along the Hatchery's inner chamber. Kenna tried not to imagine Skandar in here, his hand atop a unicorn egg, Scoundrel's horn piercing his palm. The way it was supposed to be.

Instead, Kenna looked down at the cart full of unhatched eggs the Weaver had wrestled from the sentinels before they'd been able to transport it to the Wilderness. During the fight, Kenna had hidden in one of the barred hatching cells in the dark – her only company a rickety iron chair. The shouts had turned her stomach. She was doing the right thing. This was what she wanted. Wasn't it?

But the doubts had disappeared when Erika had fetched her from the cell, eyes alight with wild excitement.

Now Kenna stretched out her hand, stroking the white shells of the eggs in turn. Eggs that hadn't found their destined riders this summer solstice, eggs that would hatch wild and alone. Kenna tried not to think about the dapple-grey unicorn that had rescued her in the Wilderness. That unicorn was the past, her mum had said. That unicorn was not enough.

Erika stood with her wild unicorn a little distance away from the cart, listening out for more sentinels. She sang the same spine-tingling verse under her breath – half lullaby, half threat:

> *'Yet another force grows on this Island:*
> *True successor of spirit's dark friend.*
> *And the storm it will bring when it rises,*
> *Will see all we know brought to an end.'*

Kenna placed her hand on an egg. There was no pain in her palm to tell her it was the right one. No destiny. That was how Erika Everhart wanted it. She wanted Kenna to choose, not *be* chosen. She wanted Kenna to be extraordinary, like her. She wanted them to be unstoppable.

So, with her mum's help, Kenna lifted her chosen egg out of the cart. Kenna cradled it in her arms lovingly.

'Come.' Erika helped Kenna kneel on the cold rock of the Hatchery floor, the fire pit smouldering behind her. The Weaver pointed to the egg in her daughter's arms.

'Destiny does not control Kenna Everhart any longer.'

There was an almighty thunderclap over the Hatchery. Kenna looked up in fear.

'Do not worry,' her mum reassured her. 'No matter what, the wild unicorns will remain; they always do.'

The Weaver's wild unicorn kneeled on its bone-splintered knees, allowing her to sit atop its rotting back. Kenna balanced the unicorn egg in her lap. One of her hands supported the egg's side; the other was placed on the very top, just like Dorian

Manning must have once instructed Skandar to do. Kenna's movements were assured, practised, inevitable.

The white light of the spirit element erupted into the Weaver's palm. Coils of spirit magic encircled Kenna and the egg, brown hair whipping her face in a furious breeze.

The Weaver sat serenely on her wild unicorn's back, magic pouring from her wrinkled palm. Behind the white stripe, her eyes were all concentration.

Kenna closed her own eyes.

The coils of spirit magic spun faster and faster, spiralling green, then red, then blue, then yellow – never still, never settling.

There was a blinding flash of pure white light.

A loud crack.

A scream.

CHAPTER TWENTY

THE REUNION

'Where is everyone?' Flo breathed as the quartet burst through the Eyrie's entrance. There was a haunted silence to the place – as though even the birds had left. At least four of the tallest trees had been uprooted; multiple treehouses had fallen and lay in sad heaps on the forest floor. Even a part of the water wall had collapsed, its seaweed trailing on the ground.

'It doesn't matter!' Skandar said, glancing up at the sinking sun. 'We'll worry about that afterwards.' He clutched the bone staff, focusing on the weight of the orb in his hand. *It only takes a few good riders to change things*, the First Rider had told him. Skandar hoped they weren't too late.

The quartet rushed into the clearing. It should have been filled with the Eyrie's residents watching the new Hatchlings walk the fault lines, but instead the Divide was empty – no golden ring or elemental instructors in sight.

Mitchell was already planning. 'The fault lines cross right at the centre of the Divide, so if we plunge the staff into the ground there it'll tap into the zones, into the magical fabric of the Island. Wild unicorns hold all five elements in balance; the bone must be like a sort of lightning rod, a reset button—' He sighed. 'Why am I pretending I know what I'm talking about? It's just a theory!'

But Skandar knew Mitchell was right. It made perfect sense to him the way the First Rider had explained it. The bone staff represented a wild unicorn's sacrifice – a Queen's sacrifice for an island she loved. Riders had been burying their bonded unicorns in the Island's elemental ground for centuries. Returning the Queen's bones to its earth seemed like the easiest way to send a signal: *We made a mistake, but we can do better.*

Skandar hurled himself from Scoundrel's back, bone staff in hand. His finger scuffed the spirit symbol carved into the round bone of the orb.

'I think we all need to hold it when we put it in the ground!' he called to Flo, Bobby and Mitchell. They dismounted and sprinted over.

He showed his quartet the elemental marks twisting up and around the length of the staff.

'So, we each hold on to our own part of the staff?' Mitchell checked. He sounded dubious.

'We had to work together to get into the First Rider's tomb, didn't we?' Skandar said, trying to convince them. 'It makes sense we have to work together to do this too, don't you think? The staff's all about harmony between the elements. Between the bonded and wild unicorns.'

'How do you *know* all this stuff?' Bobby asked. 'It's like you've become some kind of bone oracle!'

'The First Rider told me – or his phantom – or whatever he was.'

'Okay, we're going to need to talk about *that* later,' Bobby choked out. 'Also, we've got another problem.'

'What?'

'We don't have a water wielder. And the Eyrie is completely abandoned.'

Skandar's heart sank as he realised that she was right. They'd managed to find a way round that particular problem down in the tunnel, but Skandar could never be a true water wielder.

'The riders can't have all left the Island yet,' Mitchell said reasonably. 'Let's just fly down to Fourpoint—'

'We don't have time!' Flo wailed.

'What choice do we have?' Mitchell snapped back at her.

'Let's try the staff,' Skandar said. 'It might just need to be in contact with the ground.'

The quartet positioned themselves on the Divide in a circle, each with a right hand on their own elemental symbol along the bone staff.

'On one,' Skandar breathed. 'Five. Four. Three. Two. ONE!'

They plunged the staff into the earth and . . . nothing happened. They waited. And waited. They tried different combinations of their hands. They tried each of them alone. But the earthquakes continued to rumble, the lightning striking overhead, the red glow of fire in the distance.

'ARGH!' Skandar shouted in frustration. 'We're going to have to find someone. We're going to have to risk it!'

'Wait,' Flo said. 'Wait, someone's coming!' She was looking through the Eyrie's armoured trees, past the fallen treehouses and into the dark of the forest.

'You're joking,' Bobby said, following her gaze.

'Odds they're a water wielder are one in four, I suppose,'

Mitchell said sceptically, squinting into the shadows.

'It might be one of the instructors!' Flo said excitedly. 'Coming to check the Eyrie! It might even be Instructor O'Sullivan!'

But Skandar had stopped listening to his friends. Because the person he could see was not the water wielder they so desperately needed, or one of the Eyrie instructors – or even an Islander at all.

It was Kenna.

Like a rebel queen, Kenna walked through the armoured trees of the Eyrie as the vengeful earth toppled them on either side of her. She stood on the edge of the clearing, looking out over the fault lines; wild joy transformed her face. She suddenly seemed a lot older than her sixteen years. And though she was shrouded with debris and covered in cuts, she was smiling down at something at hip height.

A unicorn.

A wild unicorn.

A wild unicorn *foal*.

Skandar did not understand. He could not understand. He did not *want* to understand. Even as he took in the transparent horn, the raw red eyes, the half-rotten hooves, the wrinkled, ageing skin. The creature's immortal lifespan had already taken its toll in the minutes since it'd been hatched. And that felt terribly wrong in a creature that had only just seen the world for the first time. At the sight, all four bonded unicorns began to bellow. Red was trying to flee to the stables; Blade was rearing up on his back legs; Falcon was frothing at the mouth; sweat was pouring from Scoundrel's neck.

Then, shakily, almost instinctively, Skandar put a palm on Scoundrel's shoulder and summoned his element to see if it was there – the connection only visible to a spirit wielder.

No. This can't be happening. A wave of sickness swept over him as a cord between Kenna and the wild unicorn's hearts became visible – though it flickered uncontrollably, unable to settle on a colour, spinning with all five elements. Just like the Weaver's own. And Skandar realised the truesong verse hadn't been about him at all.

A forged bond would make Kenna the Weaver's true successor.

No. No. No. No. No.

Even as his quartet were reacting in shock, in revulsion to the wild unicorn inside the Eyrie, Skandar was moving towards his sister as if in a nightmare. Kenna in the Eyrie. It was something he'd dreamed about so many times – but not like this. Never like this.

'Who did it?' Skandar croaked, looking at last into his sister's face.

'Oh, I think you might have heard of her,' Kenna said, venom in her voice. There was something missing from Kenna's eyes when she looked at Skandar. Something he couldn't quite identify. Something that had certainly been there before, without him ever knowing it.

He remembered the question he'd asked her before he'd tried to take his Hatchery exam: *You won't hate me if I become a rider?* And his blood went cold.

'The Weaver did this to you?' Skandar asked, but it wasn't really a question. Fury was boiling in his veins like lava. The Weaver had *hurt* Kenna. Nobody hurt his sister. Nobody. How dare Erika? How dare she do this? How *could* she do this to her own child? Scoundrel shrieked in confusion at the sudden explosion of anger in the bond. Skandar managed to choke out three more words. 'She . . . Why? How?'

'Our *mum* gave me what I wanted, what I *needed*.' Kenna took a deep breath and spoke slowly, deliberately. 'Our mum, who is alive and who YOU KEPT FROM ME!' Skandar's rage was eclipsed as Kenna's scream of betrayal rang out across the clearing. 'How could you lie to me like that, Skar? I'm your SISTER! She's *my* mum too! How could you?'

Tears were already rolling down Skandar's cheeks. And they were tears of shame, not anger. All his excuses for not telling his sister seemed so pathetic now. He tried anyway. 'I didn't want to make things worse for you. The Weaver, she – she's not a good person. And I— Last year she had a whole army, Kenn. She was going to attack the Mainland. I didn't know what to tell you!'

'The truth, little brother,' Kenna said, her voice shaking with rage, 'would have been good.'

'I'm sorry.' Skandar was sobbing. 'I'm so sorry, Kenn!'

'It's not enough,' Kenna said very quietly. And then louder: 'It's not enough! You *knew* I was destined for a unicorn. You knew all of it! That I was supposed to pass the exam, that I might be a spirit wielder. But you kept that all for yourself while I was stuck back on the Mainland. Did you really think I was ever going to be okay with that? And still you let me fly Scoundrel last year. You let me feel all that *power*. And you knew!'

'I didn't know for sure! But I know now. You're one of the lost spirit wielders. Your name is on the list of Mainlanders who automatically failed the Hatchery exam. I've seen your destined unicorn, Kenn. It's dapple grey and it's been following me – and I think I can bond you to her. If I'm a Mender, if you just let me try . . . I think I can fix—'

'I already have a bond,' Kenna said softly. She gestured down at the wild unicorn, true delight in her smile.

'*We do not notice the imperfections in those we love,*' the First Rider had said.

But all Skandar could think about was how it had felt that moment in the arena, being possessed by the darker side of Scoundrel. The part of his unicorn that was still wild. The part that wanted death, destruction and *blood* more than anything else. The part of him that a true bond balanced out. The part of him a forged bond could never tame.

Flashes of the dapple-grey unicorn kept galloping across his mind, and sobs choked him all over again. This was wrong. It was all so wrong. He didn't know how to make this better; he didn't know what to do. One moment he wanted to hunt down the Weaver and make her pay for what she'd done. Another moment all he wanted in the world was for his sister to look at him like she used to.

'Kenn, please believe me that I'm so sorry. I was going to tell you when you came to the tournament, but then the Island . . . Are you—' Skandar didn't know how to finish the question. He didn't know what he was checking for. Are you bloodthirsty? Are you evil? Are you full of darkness? Are you going to try to kill me? Scoundrel? He tried again. 'Are you . . . okay?'

Kenna shook her head violently, her bottom lip wobbling.

Something in Skandar broke.

'She left me,' Kenna whispered. Her brown eyes were heavy with unfallen tears, though she still wouldn't quite meet his gaze.

Skandar didn't know what to feel. There was so much he didn't understand. How had Kenna even got here? He didn't know whether to blame her for the forged bond or blame himself. How was she supposed to know any different? Was it any wonder Kenna had been taken in by the Weaver? If he'd been in her position, what would he have done? He couldn't be sure. He'd gone with Agatha, after all, not knowing who she was. Gone with her without a second thought because she said she could get him to the Hatchery. And wasn't that exactly what Kenna had done? It wasn't a case of being good or evil, was it? Wasn't it all about the options they'd had in front of them?

Kenna spoke again. 'Mum just . . . left me. It was her plan to bring me here, but now she's g-gone.' The last word was more of a sob.

'Of course she did,' Skandar said bitterly. 'That's what Erika Everhart does.' He would never forgive the Weaver. He would never forgive the Weaver for any of this.

Finally, Kenna looked right at Skandar. 'There's so much I don't understand. All I wanted was a unicorn.'

And that was the moment. That was the moment Skandar's love for Kenna won over everything else. How could she understand what she'd done? Of course she couldn't. Like so many others, all she'd wanted was a unicorn.

So Skandar took a step towards Kenna and opened his arms, his heart. 'It's okay,' he said. The wild unicorn foal growled at him.

They both looked down at it. Skandar tried not to recoil.

'It's not okay.' Kenna started to cry and everything came out at once. 'I just wanted a unicorn so badly. This man called Dorian Manning came to the flat, Skar. He came and he told me he'd get me one. He was catching wild unicorns and keeping them under the Stronghold for me.'

Skandar suddenly remembered what one of the sentinels in the arena had said: '*Too old to be hers.*'

'He thought *I* would bond you, didn't he?' Months ago Agatha had guessed Dorian believed Skandar was a Mender. And here was the proof.

'I don't know, but he didn't tell me I'd have to kill Scoundrel in exchange.'

'He wanted you to do *what*?' When Skandar had seen the gladiator arena in the Stronghold, he thought he'd seen the very worst of Dorian Manning's nature. Apparently not.

'But I didn't know, Skar!' Kenna rushed on. 'And then Mum told me yesterday she was the one responsible for the Silver Circle discovering how to kill the wild unicorns – they didn't realise, but it was *her* plan. Why would she want that? Why would she want to destroy the Island? And I left Dad all alone, and I-I told him to write all your letters because I didn't want to lie to you. I bet he forgot Scoundrel's Jelly Babies loads of times, even though I tried to remind him.'

Skandar burst into tears. It was her. He hadn't recognised the Kenna he'd first seen in the clearing, but this – this was definitely his sister. The one that worried about their dad and about sending Jelly Babies to Scoundrel. He pulled her into a tight hug.

'I'm so sorry, Kenn,' he sobbed into her hair. 'I'm so sorry. I should have told you about Erika. I should have told you about the spirit element. I should have warned you. This is all my fault.'

'I forgive you,' Kenna said, her voice muffled. And even though Skandar couldn't see her face when she said it, he wanted so badly to believe her. 'And I have a unicorn now. I know she's not exactly . . . conventional.'

Skandar swallowed down his own horror at the foal. 'How do you feel? Do you feel . . . any need for blood or, um, a need to kill anything?'

Kenna actually laughed then. 'What? No! I feel fine, Skar. I actually feel pretty great. Although my hand really hurts!' She held it up for him to see.

And there it was. The round puncture the wild unicorn's horn had made when it pierced Kenna's palm, with a red line snaking up each of her fingers. A fresh Hatchery wound.

'I can't believe it,' Skandar breathed. 'You're a rider, Kenna. Look, it's just like mine.'

Skandar held his right palm up to his sister. And Kenna held her own up to her brother. They interlinked their fingers. Both riders at last.

A black unicorn and a wild unicorn shrieked beside them, and Skandar had a sudden understanding that their new lives on the Island weren't going to be anything like they'd imagined all those years ago. He was beginning to learn that life never really turned out how you expected it to. But as Skandar looked at their entwined hands and thought about his friends' determined faces as they'd burst into that tomb to save him, he was pretty sure that the one thing you *could* count on was love.

'I hate to interrupt the family reunion.' The rest of the quartet had come to join them. 'But there's kind of an Island apocalypse going on and we still haven't found a water wielder.' Bobby inclined her head. 'Hello, Kenna, nice to meet you. Wild unicorn? That's different.'

Mitchell and Flo were staring at the wild unicorn – varying levels of revulsion on their faces. When they saw Skandar looking, they hastily tried to rearrange their expressions.

'Maybe I can help?' Kenna asked abruptly, dropping Skandar's hand. 'I mean, is there anything I can do maybe?'

Mitchell looked at her impatiently. 'But you're a spirit wielder. It said so in the Stronghold records. We need a water wielder.'

'She's only trying to be nice, Mitchell. Don't be rude,' Flo said quietly, though her eyes were still flicking between Kenna and the wild unicorn foal.

'Wait – Kenna might be on to something,' Skandar said, his head buzzing.

'Mm-hmm. Wild unicorns are allied to all five elements,' Bobby said in a singsong voice. 'Wasn't that exactly how we worked out where the tomb even was?'

Skandar thought about Kenna's forged bond – how it wouldn't settle on any one colour – and remembered his conversation with the First Rider:

'Which element were you allied to?'

'That is not a question I know how to answer.'

So perhaps Kenna had been destined to be a spirit wielder once, but now things were different for her. Perhaps she was allied to all five – just like her unicorn.

'I think Kenna should hold the bone staff with us,' Skandar said, determined. 'Come on.'

Glancing back at her newly hatched unicorn, Kenna followed the quartet to the Divide. 'What should I do?'

Skandar pointed to the water symbol carved into the bone staff. 'See there? Can you grab hold of it? We're going to put it into the ground all together.'

'Is being a rider always this *epic*?' Kenna asked in awe.

'Skandar, the sun!' Mitchell pointed. Skandar's heart lurched. The day was almost over.

Skandar, Bobby, Flo, Mitchell and Kenna positioned themselves on the Divide in a circle, each with their right hand on an elemental symbol.

'On one,' Skandar breathed for the second time. 'Five. Four. Three. Two. ONE!'

Five elemental hands gripped the bone staff, and together they plunged the First Rider's gift into the earth of the Divide.

Skandar closed his eyes as he did it, thinking about all the love he had for the Island. He didn't think of grand or impressive things. They weren't what really mattered. He remembered the moment his and Scoundrel's eyes had met in the Hatchery. Falcon and Scoundrel racing on their first day of Nestling year. Snow frosting the Eyrie's trees. The surprise party in the Sanctuary. Mitchell at his blackboard, his face lighting up as he thought of a new way to solve a mystery. The smell of Bobby's sandwiches. Scoundrel's call as they'd been reunited on the Sunset Platform. Sitting next to Flo on Wildflower Hill – surrounded by the smell of beauty and the feeling of family.

For five whole seconds Skandar kept his eyes shut.

Then he felt something. A pulse of energy was coming out of the orb he was grasping, into his fingers, up his arms, right into his heart from the staff itself. His spirit mutation tingled.

Skandar's eyes flew open. The others still had their hands fixed firmly round the bones, but they too were staring at the ground underneath their feet. The Divide glowed deep red, then yellow, then green, then blue. Within seconds the colours left the circle and rushed like spilt ink into the four fault lines of the clearing, illuminating the armoured trunks around them with their elemental light.

'It's working!' Flo cried. 'It's working!'

Then the top of the bone staff glowed bright white under Skandar's hand and flooded into the earth of the Divide below it. Another pulse from the orb sent out shockwaves of blinding light down all the fault lines – mixing with the colours of fire, air, earth and water – and onwards, onwards into the four elemental zones. The whole Island was bathed in white, just for a moment – like the birth of an elemental star. The wonder of it filled Skandar's lungs until he felt like he could burst with happiness, with pride, with belonging.

This was his Island. And his element was helping to heal it.

As the solstice sun finally sank into the sea, the white light of the bone staff darkened. Skandar noticed a stillness in the air, in his bond with Scoundrel – in his very soul – that had been missing before. The awe on his friends' faces told him they could feel it too, their unicorns shrieking in celebration. The elements were at peace once again.

Then the whole bone staff started to quiver violently.

'What's happening?' Bobby gritted her teeth, trying to keep hold of the shaking staff.

'Is this supposed to happen?' Mitchell asked.

'I don't know!' Skandar said. And then suddenly the rounded orb had come off in his hand, and the other elemental pieces came apart. The bone staff was breaking, breaking . . .

Broken.

They stared at the five pieces of bone staff laying on the Divide. All Skandar could think was that the First Rider had said to return it. He'd said the Island might need it again, and now it was broken. Was it his fault?

'Umm, Skandar,' Mitchell muttered, looking over his shoulder – away from the bones.

Mitchell wasn't often speechless, so Skandar looked over his own shoulder too.

Dorian Manning and his unicorn were galloping at breakneck speed through the Eyrie's trees – closely followed by Rex on his own silver unicorn and six silver-masked sentinels. Behind them was Commodore Kazama and the full Council of Seven.

'WE MUST KILL THEM BOTH! KILL THEM ALL!' Dorian Manning was frothing at the mouth, his eyes wild and unfocused as he burst into the clearing.

'Well, that's disappointing,' Bobby said, and they sprinted to mount their unicorns. 'I was hoping Daftest Moocow had already left the Island.'

'Daftest who?' Kenna asked.

'I'll explain later,' Skandar said, and vaulted on to Scoundrel's back, realising with a stab of panic that in their hurry they'd forgotten to pick up the pieces of the bone staff.

But it was too late. He couldn't worry about that now. 'Kenn, take your unicorn to the Divide. We'll protect you both.' Kenna's eyes were wide with fear, but Skandar knew she had a lot more to be afraid of than Dorian Manning. The Commodore wasn't exactly going to be pleased to see Kenna bonded to a wild unicorn – just like the Weaver.

The quartet positioned Scoundrel, Blade, Red and Falcon around the Divide. Four unicorn horns faced outwards at Dorian Manning and the other incoming unicorns. Four palms glowed the colours of their riders' allied elements.

Dorian's palm glowed red and a fireball flew at the four friends.

In a flash, all four palms glowed blue and four water shields blocked the president's attack. His fire fizzled out. They were lucky his emotions were so out of control – four Nestlings wouldn't usually be able to fight off a fully grown silver.

'That girl broke into the Hatchery with the Weaver. They attacked me and my sentinels. She's bonded to a WILD UNICORN!' Dorian screamed, intent on attack.

'He *really* doesn't like you, Kenna,' Bobby observed, as she blocked a water blast with her air shield.

'My wife is dead because of you!' he screamed, silver tongue flashing. 'SPIRIT WIELDERS KILL EVERYONE! THE DEATH ELEMENT MUST BE STOPPED!'

Flo and Bobby's joint lightning shield deflected a sandy onslaught of arrows.

'Honestly, I could do this all day,' Bobby said happily.

'Dad! Stop!' Rex Manning had reached his father and was trying to get his attention. 'You have to stop this! Can't you see Skandar and his friends just saved the Island? Dad, they didn't kill the Fallen Twenty-Four; they didn't kill Mum.' Rex stopped talking – his usually serene face lined with a frown, electricity crackling in his cheeks.

'ARGHHHH!' Dorian Manning started to mould another weapon, but he was interrupted by four unicorns landing between Skandar's quartet and the silvers. Instructor O'Sullivan, Instructor Webb, Instructor Anderson and even a slightly shaky Instructor Saylor had arrived.

'How *dare* you attack my Nestlings?' Instructor O'Sullivan's eyes were swirling so fast, they were a blur. 'How *dare* you attack riders inside the Eyrie? It is FORBIDDEN.' With the last word, she drew back her palm and punched it forward. The water jet left her hand with such speed and force that it smashed Dorian Manning clean out of his saddle. He turned over on the ground, coughing and spluttering.

'What is happening here? We're supposed to be evacuating, and then I get an emergency message from the Silver Circle about—'

Nina's mouth fell open as Skandar and Scoundrel moved towards her and Lightning's Mistake, revealing the white bones of the staff behind them.

'Is that the First Rider's gift?' she said, her voice hushed. 'I *thought* something had changed – the elements were quiet when we rode through Fourpoint. Was it you? Did you find it? Did it really work?' With each question the excitement in Nina's voice grew, so that by the last she sounded just like the enthusiastic Pred who had showed Skandar around the Eyrie his first day on the Island.

Skandar smiled at her and croaked, 'It's over.'

A huge grin spread across Commodore Kazama's face.

'Never mind that!' Dorian spluttered from the ground. 'She's bonded to that wild unicorn –' he pointed at Kenna – 'Skandar's sister.'

Rex Manning pushed his unicorn closer to Nina. 'Commodore Kazama.' His voice was so full of sorrow and regret that Skandar thought he might burst into tears. He pushed his perfectly wavy hair out of his eyes. 'Please don't listen to my father. It was the Silver Circle that killed the wild unicorns. My father, he – I couldn't stop him. He was worried that Skandar was going to bond the lost spirit wielders back to their destined unicorns. And then he brought that poor girl to the Island – he wanted a spirit wielder of his own. He was going to ask her to kill Scoundrel's Luck after Skandar had bonded her to her own unicorn.'

'Can spirit wielders do that? Can you?' Nina asked Skandar quickly.

'Maybe. Probably. I don't know for sure,' he answered

hesitantly. 'I've not done any actual mending yet or anything,' he added, hoping this wasn't going to get him and Kenna in even more trouble.

Rex was still talking. 'I tried to make Dad listen, but he didn't heed the warnings of the truesong – and by the time he realised the consequences, it was far too late.' Rex hung his head, his silver unicorn still and quiet.

'So you see,' Mitchell piped up, 'we were telling the truth all those months ago, back in the Council chamber.'

'Take Manning away,' Nina said, her voice the most dangerous Skandar had ever heard it. Four sentinels dismounted and wrestled Dorian's arms behind him.

'You can't do this! You have no authority! There must be a head of the Silver Circle!' he cried. Instructor O'Sullivan's whirlpool eyes followed Dorian's every step to make sure he really did leave the Eyrie's precincts.

Agatha suddenly burst through the trees. She'd clearly run a great distance – her white cloak was torn to shreds and sweat poured down her crinkled forehead.

'What's happening? I got the message that—'

Instructor O'Sullivan shushed her.

'And what are we going to do with you?' Nina asked, her eyes falling on the wild foal.

Kenna had inched forward to join Skandar, her honey-coloured wild unicorn following behind her. Skandar saw the instructors and the whole Council of Seven recoil.

Agatha looked like she'd seen a ghost. Her face turned deathly pale. 'No,' she rasped. 'No, not again.'

'Who did this?' Nina demanded of Kenna. Skandar could sense that the Commodore was trying to keep the fear out of her voice. After all, the only other rider they'd seen bonded to a wild unicorn was the Weaver.

Skandar answered for his sister, who was a combination of starstruck and terrified at meeting the two-time winner of the Chaos Cup. He put the pieces together as he spoke. 'The Weaver did it. She must have forged a bond with a unicorn egg down in the Hatchery – Kenna's wild unicorn has to be from one of the eggs left unhatched after the ceremony this year. And well . . . Kenna, show them your palm.'

Kenna held up her right hand. And there it was – her Hatchery wound, still dripping with blood. Skandar couldn't help thinking it should have healed by now.

Two members of the Council of Seven screamed in terror; others yelled in rage.

'Oh, for goodness' sake,' Bobby said impatiently from Falcon's back, the grey unicorn standing between Red and Blade a small distance away from the Divide. But Skandar understood the Councillors' reactions. A bond with a wild unicorn went against everything the Island believed in. Kenna was exactly what they'd been taught to fear.

'I didn't mean for any of this to happen,' Kenna wailed, hearing their reactions. 'Dorian Manning turned up at my door on the Mainland and said he could find my destined unicorn. And then the Weaver promised me things.' Skandar prayed that she wasn't going to tell them the Weaver was their mum. 'She promised me *this* but I—' Kenna broke off and took a deep breath. 'Can I stay here?'

One of the Council members cleared his throat uncomfortably, his voice full of warning. 'Commodore, if the Mainland finds out about this – if the Mainland finds out that a child was taken outside the summer solstice . . .'

'I'm aware, Oliver,' she waved a hand at him dismissively.

'I won't tell anyone on the Mainland about it, if that's what you're worried about,' Kenna rushed on. 'I just want to train in the Eyrie. Like my brother.'

'So that part was true?' Nina turned to Skandar. 'She's your sister?'

'Yes.' Skandar nodded. 'So it makes sense that Dorian would try to mess with Kenna. He was trying to use her, force her to wield the spirit element for him. Against me! Please, can't she stay here? Like every other rider?'

'But she isn't *like* every other rider, is she?' hissed another of the Council members with long dark curly hair that sparked wildly at the ends. 'You can't allow a wild unicorn into the Eyrie, for lightning's sake!'

Instructor O'Sullivan joined the conversation by riding right into it, Celestial Seabird snarling at the unicorns around her. 'I don't mean to be rude.' Her face was taut. 'But the Eyrie's role on the Island, as it has been since it was founded by the very rider that gifted us that staff –' she pointed to the Divide – 'is to train riders who hatch unicorns. Young riders who bear the Hatchery wound and who are blessed with a unicorn's magic.'

Skandar felt a rush of affection for the water instructor.

'We will train her for the same reason we train all other riders. To tame the chaos, to command the elements, to deepen the bond. And hope that it makes us all – unicorn *and* human – a little less monstrous. It isn't her fault that she has fallen victim to the Weaver, like so many before her.'

Nina closed her eyes for a moment, readying herself. 'No, Persephone.'

Kenna cried out and Skandar's heart dropped through the floor. Bobby said, 'Are you serious?' Mitchell and Flo were silent.

Instructor O'Sullivan tried to argue. 'But suspicion of the spirit element, and in particular this boy, is what caused the wild unicorn killings in the first place. Perhaps it's time we gave the spirit element more of a chance.'

Nina shook her head. 'Kenna is not a spirit wielder. Her bond is a perversion. She is not like other riders. Her presence on the Island will cause panic and fear, especially after the year we've had. I cannot make this decision now. I cannot make it alone.'

'But you're not saying no?' Skandar asked breathlessly.

'I'm not saying yes either,' Nina said sternly. 'I have a responsibility to this Island as Commodore, and I must be sure to make the right decision. For everyone. Kenna and her wild unicorn will stay at the Eyrie – *under careful watch* – until a decision has been reached.'

Nina's attention suddenly moved from Skandar. She looked hard at Rex, who flinched from his unicorn's back, cheeks flashing. Then for some reason she looked at Instructor Saylor on North-Breeze Nightmare. 'Skye, will you be retiring from the Eyrie as planned?' Nina's voice was gentle.

The air instructor smiled sadly. 'Yes, I think so. After my injuries, I'm afraid I wouldn't do the air training at the Eyrie much justice.'

'I'm so sorry, Instructor Saylor,' Skandar blurted. 'I didn't—'

She turned her gaze on him, tendrils of electricity sparking up her neck. 'It is *not* your fault, Skandar. No apology is necessary, especially after all the good you've done since.'

'I wonder . . .' Nina said, looking between Rex Manning and Instructor Saylor.

Instructor O'Sullivan somehow managed to look excited and sly at the same time. 'A little more unity between the Eyrie and the Silver Circle wouldn't hurt, would it?'

'My thoughts exactly,' Nina said.

Skandar had no idea what was going on.

'He's very young,' Instructor O'Sullivan muttered.

Nina shrugged. 'So am I. Rex, how about it?' she asked abruptly. 'Do you think you can manage to be the air instructor at the Eyrie *and* the head of the Silver Circle?'

Rex's mouth fell open in shock; Skandar thought it was probably the least perfect he'd ever looked. 'Are – are you serious?'

'Very.' Nina grinned. 'I think you might be exactly what the Silver Circle needs.'

Rex bowed his head. 'It would – it would be an honour, Commodore.'

Flo looked delighted, as did the other instructors, but Skandar couldn't help feeling that Nina and Instructor O'Sullivan had only been so keen to offer Rex both jobs so they could keep a close eye on the new head of the Silver Circle.

As the Council of Seven turned to leave the Eyrie, Commodore Kazama motioned to Skandar to come closer. 'I'm sorry I can't say yes to Kenna's training right now,' she whispered, 'but I promise you I'll do my absolute best to persuade them she means no harm.'

'Thank you,' Skandar breathed.

Nina nodded and rode away.

Instructor O'Sullivan let out a long, slow breath. 'Skandar,' she said, a glint in her swirling blue eyes. 'Are there any other Island-changing shocks you'd like to get out of the way? You know, just while we're at it?'

Skandar could feel Agatha's eyes on him, but he tried not to meet her gaze. He didn't think it would help Kenna's case if they were to reveal that they were the children of the Weaver herself. So he shook his head and hoped nobody visited the Secret Swappers trying to prove any different.

'Persephone,' Instructor Anderson said, the fire flickering around his ears with sudden urgency, 'the evacuation; we should probably—'

'Goodness!' Instructor O'Sullivan cried. 'Yes! They still think we're leaving!'

'Let us break the exceedingly wonderful news,' Instructor Webb said, wiping a tear from his eye.

'You too, Instructor Manning. Let's go,' Instructor O'Sullivan called to Rex, who was saying something to Flo.

'It's going to take me a while to get used to hearing Instructor *Manning* without cringing,' Skandar said, as they started to make their way to the stables together.

Blade fell into step with Scoundrel, Flo looking over her shoulder to make sure the others were out of earshot. 'Thank goodness Kenna turned up when she did. Although I feel so sorry for her. I bet the Weaver tricked her into the forged bond. Into all of it.'

Skandar nodded vigorously, feeling a fierce stab of affection for Flo. Kenna wasn't in *league* with the Weaver. It was like the First Rider had said – everyone makes mistakes sometimes. And now Kenna was here, Skandar was going to do everything he could to help her – wild unicorn or not.

Flo suddenly yawned, clapping a hand over her mouth. 'Sleep. I need to sleep for a hundred years.'

Bobby sniggered. 'Someone already tried that. It didn't go so well. Everything got really overgrown and then some random guy decided to wake the poor girl up with a kiss. Without asking, I might add. Disgraceful.'

Kenna burst out laughing, and Skandar realised that it had been a really, *really* long time since he'd heard that noise. It was pure magic.

'Told you me and your sister would get on.' Bobby winked at Skandar. 'Forged bond or not. And don't worry,' Bobby added to Kenna, 'Commodore Kazama's a good one – a Mainlander like us. I'm sure she'll get you cleared to train.'

'So what's the plan now?' Mitchell asked impatiently, looking around the abandoned Eyrie, as though someone was going to jump out and start doling out instructions. Following Mitchell's gaze, Skandar looked up and saw seven familiar unicorns returning to the Sunset Platform. The Peregrine Society had flown home.

Skandar grinned at Flo. 'The plan? I think we should do something completely and absolutely . . . *ordinary.*'

CHAPTER TWENTY-ONE

THE BEGINNING

A few weeks later, Skandar Smith walked with Agatha Everhart between rows of newly grown saplings. Skandar's hand was curled round a watering can; Agatha's was curled in a fist. Ahead of them – each clutching a watering can of their own – were Bobby Bruna, Mitchell Henderson and Flo Shekoni. Kenna Smith was not helping with the task, too keen on asking question after question of the new Fledglings.

The jousting tournament had been fought again, without any possessions this time, and the quartet had – mostly – done better than Mitchell's predictions. All of them except Bobby, who had lost to Amber Fairfax in the final. They were absolutely *not* talking about it. Although Skandar was less bothered by Amber's victory than he would have been a few months ago – after all, she had reunited him with Scoundrel. And due to the tournament being fought *after* the summer solstice – when the Nestlings had technically already become Fledglings – the instructors had decided that this year they would not declare nomads of the bottom six.

The new Hatchlings – who'd bonded with their unicorns as the Island was self-destructing around them – had finally got to walk the fault lines and discover their allied elements. Skandar could hardly believe how close they had come to never being able to enter the Eyrie.

Jamie Middleditch had recovered from singing his truesong. He hadn't even been that excited to hear that it had helped the quartet find the bone staff. 'That's great and everything,' he'd moaned, 'but my parents won't stop going on and on about how young I am to have already sung my truesong. They're so *proud* of me!'

'Surely that's nice, though?' Flo had ventured, trying to be positive.

Jamie had looked glum. 'I just wish they could be this proud of me for being a blacksmith. For making armour that survived an attack by the first-ever unicorn rider!'

'Just about,' Bobby had muttered.

Jamie hadn't heard her. 'That's way better than singing some stupid song.'

'Well, I'm proud of you,' Mitchell had said, his blush matching the fire in his hair. 'And I'm quite clever, so that's got to count for something.'

Mitchell was proud of something else too. After finding out his son had helped win the bone staff, Ira Henderson had come up to the Eyrie himself to congratulate Mitchell and Red. Mitchell said it was a little awkward, but perhaps it was the beginning of his dad finally accepting that he couldn't control who Mitchell's friends were or who he was going to become.

Although the bone staff had brought the elements back into

balance, it hadn't magically fixed all the damage that had been done over the course of the year. Everywhere you went, from Fourpoint to the Eyrie and out to the zones, Islanders were helping to rebuild what had been destroyed. It didn't matter whether you were a new Hatchling or a blacksmith or the Commodore of Chaos – you helped. There was a lot of work to be done, but Skandar thought there was something beautiful about the whole Island coming together to help each other. Despite that, the broken pieces of the bone staff still played on his mind. He'd thought he might at least return them to the First Rider's tomb, but – when he'd gone back to fetch them the evening after the solstice – the pieces had disappeared.

Skandar and Agatha continued to walk as he sorted through everything that had happened. He bent down to water one of the trees and felt a little stab of pride. A few days after the summer solstice, the wild unicorns the Silver Circle had been keeping for Kenna had been freed from their prison under the Stronghold. But Skandar had written to Commodore Kazama about the ones that had been killed. He'd suggested that their bodies should be recovered – that they should be buried just like bonded unicorns. Only once before, in the Island's long and bloody history, had a rider ever thought to bury a wild unicorn. But Nina had agreed with Skandar – it was the very least the fallen immortals deserved.

And so here they were, walking round the outer edge of the Eyrie's walls, where the wild unicorns had finally been laid to rest.

'They'll be beautiful when the leaves come through,' Agatha said, though there was something in her voice that told Skandar this wasn't what she really wanted to talk about.

'You're worried about Kenna,' he said.

'Of course I'm worried about her!' Agatha snapped and then dropped her voice. 'Look at what the forged bond did to Erika, and that was diluted for years by her true bond to Blood-Moon's Equinox.'

'Maybe that was the problem, though.' Skandar shrugged. 'Maybe Kenna will be different.' He couldn't pretend he hadn't thought about it, worried about it, had nightmares where a dapple-grey wild unicorn screeched her agony into the Wilderness. He'd tossed and turned, wondering whether a forged bond could be safely undone somehow. But Kenna seemed fine. Completely herself. No bloodlust in sight. And she loved her wild unicorn so much that Skandar wasn't sure – even if it were possible – whether she'd ever forgive him if he parted them. So it seemed all they were waiting for now was the Commodore to approve her training at the Eyrie.

'Wild unicorns aren't like bonded ones, Skandar. I know your friends are pretending for Kenna's sake that it's no different, but that unicorn didn't give anything up for Kenna.'

'What do you mean?'

Agatha rubbed at her mutated cheeks, frustrated. 'When you bonded with Scoundrel's Luck, he gave up his immortality to live his life alongside yours. But that wild unicorn will live for ever, even after Kenna dies. Ultimately, a forged bond means that a rider is exposed to a unicorn's primal nature. It only takes; it doesn't give. Think about how you felt being possessed by Scoundrel's bloodthirsty nature for only a few minutes. Skandar, the warnings Erika and I read about all those years ago . . .'

'Kenna's allied to all five elements!' Skandar protested. 'Surely that means the wild unicorn has given her something?'

'Think about that for a minute. Five allegiances pulling

you different ways. Five mutations possibly. Five ways for the unicorn's power to take over—'

True successor of spirit's dark friend.

'The First Rider was bonded to a wild unicorn, and *he* was good!' Skandar insisted. 'He built the Hatchery, founded the Eyrie – discovered the bond in the first place. Kenna could be like him.' Skandar pushed aside the First Rider's warning, the words that had been going around and around in his head since he'd heard them down in the tomb:

The one you love the most will betray you, Skandar Smith. Be wary. When it matters the most, they will turn against you.

Agatha was already shaking her head. 'Skandar, if what the First Rider told you is true, then his *wasn't* a forged bond. The queen of the wild unicorns shared the privilege of her magic with him after years of friendship and love. It was a bond rooted in grace. But a forged bond is fundamentally rooted in greed: in taking something that never belonged to you.' Agatha sighed. 'And what was Kenna doing with Erika all that time? Kenna said she escaped from the Silver Stronghold when the Spear fell – that was weeks ago! Erika constructs this elaborate plan to bring Kenna to the Island, to bond her to a wild unicorn, and just *leaves* her? That isn't like Erika at all. Do you truly believe Kenna has *really* forgiven you after everything you kept from her? You said she was angry when she arrived in the Eyrie and—'

'She wasn't herself,' Skandar said stubbornly, and stopped by another sapling to look into his aunt's face. 'I would know if she wasn't okay. She's my sister.'

'And Erika is mine.' Agatha put a heavy hand on Skandar's shoulder. 'Be careful, be watchful – that's all I'm asking.'

Yet as he watched Kenna laughing with his three best friends in the world, Skandar couldn't take Agatha's warning seriously – not really. This was Kenna. Kenna who had rocked him to sleep. Kenna who had wiped away his tears. Kenna who had believed he could become a rider before he'd ever believed in himself. She had the kindest heart he'd ever known. And not even a wild unicorn bond was going to change that. If anyone was going to fight the darkness and win, it was Kenna.

Skandar looked more closely at the sapling by his knee and blinked. On one of the fragile new branches a leaf had sprouted – white as snow. White as the spirit element.

It felt hopeful somehow. It felt like the beginning of something.

EPILOGUE

*T*wo unicorns crossed a battle-scarred plain on a moonless night. *The first unicorn galloped across the Wilderness, urged on by a maskless rider. The second unicorn walked in time with its rider's rotting heart. It was a slow beat, a steady beat, the rhythm of a heart accustomed to chaos.*

The maskless rider reached the meeting point first, the flames in his eyes the only light in the endless darkness. He watched the Weaver approach; the thump, thump *of her unicorn's decaying hooves beat on the dust like a funeral drum.*

The rider's eyes flickered with fear as the Weaver's immortal creature circled him. He was always afraid of her. And it made him feel alive.

The Weaver sensed that she instilled terror in him. She would always be feared. And it made her feel nothing.

'I don't understand what it was all for. We lost Kenna to the Eyrie.' The words tumbled out of his mouth, fluttering like a dying bird's wings.

The white paint on the Weaver's lips cracked as she smiled.

'Kenna Everhart is exactly where she needs to be.'

ACKNOWLEDGEMENTS

First I want to thank *you*, reader, for believing in these bloodthirsty unicorns so much that you have followed Skandar and Scoundrel's Luck all the way to the end of their second adventure. It is impossible to express how much it means to me that you have chosen to spend your time reading this book, over anything else you could have been doing! Knowing you are on this journey with me feels something like how I imagine the unicorn–rider bond – pulsing reassuringly around my heart.

Writing a second book in a series is very different from writing the first. And I owe so much gratitude to those who have supported me, both during the whirlwind of excitement that came with the publication of *Skandar and the Unicorn Thief* and during the process of bringing *Skandar and the Phantom Rider* from first draft to bookshelf.

Just as family and friendship are important to Skandar, they are very important to me. So thank you to my wonderful family, whose slightly shy 'Annie' suddenly became 'that unicorn woman'. To my mum, Helen, who is always ready with an encouraging word or a hilarious story to cheer me up when things get stressful.

To my brother Hugo for so often staying up stupidly late on the other side of the world so we can talk life, unicorns and everything. To my brother Alex and my almost-sister-in-law Hannah for your big-hearted enthusiasm for this series – I'm pretty sure most of Kent has heard of Skandar, thanks to you!

Thank you to Sharon, Sean and Ollie for being such enthusiastic cheerleaders of these stories – your support means so much. To all my friends, thank you for being there when I need you – whether by squeezing in a quick mid-tour lunch or spending a weekend away playing silly games in the garden – and for understanding that I love you even when my schedule has made it difficult to be together. And in particular, thank you to Ruth, Aisling and Claire – my fellow writers who read this second story before the rest. Your kind words of excitement and encouragement came exactly when I needed them.

To my agent, Sam Copeland, for all your advice and guidance – and of course your invaluable sense of humour as I navigated my way through this second book – thank you. And thank you to my film agent, Michelle Kroes, and the team at Sony for helping to bring these unicorns closer to the big screen!

Just as Skandar finds his second family at the Eyrie, the incredible team at Simon & Schuster has become a second family to me. Bringing *Skandar and the Phantom Rider* to readers has been a real team effort, and I am grateful to everyone who has been part of that.

To Rachel Denwood – your ambition for this series is just as big as your enormously warm heart. To Ian Chapman and Jonathan Karp for your confidence in me as a writer and your passionate support of this series. To my UK and US editors Ali Dougal, Kendra Levin, Deeba Zargarpur, Lowri Ribbons, and Katie Lawrence – if I thanked you in every language it would be nowhere near enough. Your insight, dedication and passion for Skandar is truly humbling and I couldn't be more grateful that together we have

ACKNOWLEDGEMENTS

made this sequel shine just as much as its beautiful blue cover.

To Laura Hough, Dani Wilson and the whole sales team at S&S across the world who have worked tirelessly to put Skandar literally everywhere you could think of to buy a book. To Sarah Macmillan, Ian Lamb and Eve Wersocki Morris and the rest of the marketing and publicity teams both in the UK and in the US for finding and organising such brilliant opportunities to spread the word about bloodthirsty unicorns. To Sophie Storr, production whizz, and to the design team at Simon & Schuster, as well as Sorrel Packham, and Two Dots Illustration Studio for bringing a scene from *Skandar and the Phantom Rider* to life for this truly exceptional cover. To Maud Sepult, Theo Steen, Amy Fletcher and the international and foreign rights teams for helping these unicorns fly across the globe. And to all my editors, translators, copyeditors, proofreaders and publishers all over the world – thank you for continuing to believe in these stories and me.

Just as Skandar has found more friends along his way, so has this series. To Florentyna – I am so grateful to you for championing Skandar and helping these unicorns soar. To the incredible booksellers I have met since the publication of *Skandar and the Unicorn Thief* – among them Cat, Robbie, Rach, Amanda, Rhiannon, Craig and so many more (I'll go over my word count if I list you all here!) – and to so many others I am yet to meet, I am so humbled by your support for Skandar and your commitment to getting books into the hands of readers. To all the librarians, teachers and book bloggers who have recommended Skandar to those in their schools, classes and communities – thank you. It's truly magical, and I'm so grateful.

And last of all, to my husband, Joseph, who is always so happy when he's standing back and watching me and Skandar soar. But this book – like the last – would not exist without him and his unshakeable belief, unwavering support and unswerving love for me.